BEYOND THE YELLOW DOORS

JULIANA ANDREW

BLUEPRINT PRESS
INTERNATIONALE

Beyond the Yellow Doors
Copyright © 2023 by Juliana Andrew

All rights reserved. No part of this publication may be reproduced, distributed, or transmitted in any form or by any means, including photocopying, recording, or other electronic or mechanical methods, without the prior written permission of the author, except in the case of brief quotations embodied in critical reviews and certain other non-commercial uses permitted by copyright law.

ISBN
978-1-959365-86-0 (Paperback)
978-1-959365-87-7 (eBook)

BEYOND THE YELLOW DOORS

Juliana Andrew

Also by Juliana Andrew
Vienna
The Curse of the Infinity Bracelets
Seventh Crossing
The Ladies of Avanloch
The Arcadia Project

In Memory of Roy
My Husband, My Love, My Soulmate
Always and Forever

Book cover design by

PARAMITA BHATTACHARJEE
Creative Pharamita

Special thanks to Lorraine Dick

Beyond the Yellow Doors

Chapter 1

Thunderstruck

The unrelenting drumming of the rain on the windows was beginning to irritate my usual calm disposition. Why was I still here anyway? It was three forty five on a Friday afternoon before the Labor Day weekend. I buzzed Shannon, my girl Friday, and told her to grab her hat and coat because we were done for the day. I donned my raincoat and collected a few current files to peruse over the weekend if I had the time, or the inclination to do so. I took the oversized black umbrella down from the coatrack and proceeded into the front office to pick up my secretary and walk her to her car. She was still sitting at her computer typing.

"Whatever you are doing, put it away until Tuesday. There is nothing that requires immediate attention."

She hemmed and hawed until I went over and closed out the report that she had been working on. "Who's the boss here anyhow? It's the last few days before your kids head back to school, so go spend some quality time with them and Mel."

She asked me what I was going to do besides work on my boat, and was Irene going up to the cabin with me. I laughed and asked her what she thought. She said she guessed yes to the boat thing, and no to Irene joining me. She asked me if I had anything work-wise planned for her husband. I told her that it was a work-free weekend. I locked the door and set the alarm. My office was situated above a pawn shop that was almost always open so I never thought too much about break-ins. We huddled under the umbrella as we made a rush to the parking lot that we shared with the pawn shop. I told Shannon to have a good weekend.

"See you on Tuesday, nine o'clock sharp, and not one minute earlier." I ordered as I closed the car door. She smiled and waved as she drove off.

I stopped at the liquor store and picked up a couple bottles of wine as I usually did before heading up country. I was planning on having my neighbors, Ruth and Harvey over for dinner, and Ruth liked a particular brand of fruity white wine. Twenty minutes at the super market and home to pick up Sadie, my black and white McNab Shepherd, and I was on my way. I'd never had a dog before, but one day three years ago I decided to take the plunge. I walked into an animal rescue center and the first face I saw was Sadie's smiling up at me. It was a done deal, and I have never regretted it. Getting my wife to welcome her into our household was a whole other kettle of fish.

The rain was still coming down in torrents. I had a moment of apprehension hoping the road would not be closed as it had been after the last big storm. Twenty minutes later I turned off the main highway unto Inlet Road. I was glad to get away from all the ferry traffic and erratic drivers. It was usually only a ten minute trip to my cabin once I crossed Toronto Creek and veered unto Niagara Cove. Today it would take me twice as long as the roughly paved road was laden with deep holes that were already overflowing from the afternoon's rain. I geared down as water was already seeping unto the bridge deck. It was only a matter of time before the road would be closed.

I had been fortunate twelve years ago to acquire my property from a client as payment for the investigation that I did that saved his business. I renovated the cabin and turned it into a comfortable two bedroom home away from home. I spent as much time as I possibly could out here away from the hub-bub of city life. Actually, I was more comfortable here than I was in the house in the city. I, along with some twenty neighbors, occupied this unique little piece of land that jutted out like a jigsaw puzzle along the coast of the Pacific Ocean.

As I rounded a corner that we locals called Blind Man's Bluff, I came upon a car in the ditch; just what I didn't want to see. I stopped, ordered Sadie to stay, and made my way down the bank. There was what appeared to be a set of footprints leading up from the car to the road. I double checked anyhow to make sure no one was in the car. I didn't recognise the car as belonging to any of my neighbors. Figuring the occupant had made it out safely and been picked up by a passer-by I high-tailed it back to the jeep. I was wet and muddy. I probably had wrecked a damn good pair of loafers. Sadie was sitting in the front seat. A kilometer or so down the road she started to bark as we both spotted a figure running at full speed ahead of us. I assumed it was a woman as strands of long hair were whipping around her. I pulled up alongside of her and rolled the window down asking her if she would like a ride.

"What do you think? Do you think I am out here for my health?" She asked caustically.

I ordered Sadie to get in the back seat and reached over to open the door for the young girl.

"And, do you think I am getting in a car with a complete stranger? How do I know that you are not an ax murderer or a rapist?" She asked obnoxiously.

"Suit yourself," I replied, " just so you know, this is somewhat of a private road, and chances are that no one else will be arriving to rescue you today, and how do I know you're not an assassin yourself?"

She held the door open while she scrutinized me "Good point; I guess I'll chance it. I'm going to get your seat all wet."

"It'll dry. What are you doing out here anyhow on a day like this?"

She closed the door. It was then I noticed that she wasn't wearing any shoes. I put the jeep in drive, turned the heater up, and continued on. She said she was looking for someone. I told her that I knew everyone who lived in Niagara so chances were that I would know the name and I could take her directly there. She said there was no need as she was pretty sure that she had already found him, and a man with a dog was probably an okay guy. Sadie had already nuzzled her head under this stranger's arm.

"What?" I asked confused.

"Adam Mitchell," she said, "that's who I am looking for."

"That's quite a coincidence as that's my name. I go by Mitch though."

"I know."

"So, why are you looking out here for me; are you looking to hire me and, if you are, why wouldn't you just come to my office in the city?"

"I did, and you had already left."

"I don't do business at my private residences, and my home out this way is not public, so just how in hell did you track me down anyhow?" I cross-examined her.

"Sometimes money talks." She said simply.

"How much did it take to bribe Archie?" I knew it had to be pawn shop Bob's son.

"Fifty bucks and my phone number."

"I'm gonna kill that little bugger!"

"Careful now Mr. Detective man; you should know better than to threaten someone."

Who was this smart-alecky girl anyhow? I looked at her sideways. "How about you tell me who you are, who sent you, and what it is that you want from me?"

"How about you take me home so that I can wring myself out, and then we'll talk?"

"Where do you live?" I asked becoming agitated.

"I'm in between houses right now, so your place will be just fine."

I had the feeling that this girl was going to be trouble. This was supposed to be a work-free weekend. I had my shackles up. "The road back into town is probably closed by now, so it appears as if I have no choice but to put up with you for the time being, but you better have a damn good reason for tracking me down. I do not intend to be babysitting a teenager who doesn't seem to know the meaning of making an appointment!" I emphasized.

A few minutes later I pulled into the carport and let Sadie out who took off for the neighbors looking for her best friend Rufus. I unlocked the back door and told my hitchhiker to drop her wet things on the bench. I realized that I didn't even know her name, so I asked her what it was.

As she was peeling off her coat, a pair of high heeled shoes fell onto the floor. "Thank God I didn't kill Mom's Asten Ardens'. It looks like your shoes might be ruined though... sorry. I'll spring for a new pair as soon as you say you'll take our case. My name is Vali; one L, one I."

I opened the bathroom door, walked in, and turned on the shower. "Okay; get yourself warmed up while I look for something for you to wear while your clothes are drying."

So, there was more than one person involved I mused to myself as I went into my bedroom to get into something dry. I looked in the other bedroom to see if Irene had left anything behind. I doubted it as she had only been up here half a dozen times since I had built the cabin. I was in luck, or should I say, Vali was. I found a pair of flannel pyjamas that looked like they would fit her. I left them outside the bathroom door and went into the kitchen to make coffee. Thinking that Vali probably didn't drink coffee I put the kettle on for hot chocolate. That was how much I knew about teenagers. I went back into the carport, retrieved the bags of groceries and wine, and put them away leaving sandwich fixings on the table. I heard the bathroom door open and close, lit the already assembled wood in the fireplace, sat down waiting for the coffee and Vali's story. For some reason I thought it was going to be a whopper.

She found me sitting in front of the fire. The pyjamas were a little big. She unwound the towel from her hair, placed it on the back of a chair and sat down opposite me. I was curious about how she knew who I was when she had decided to take me up on my offer of a ride, and so I asked her. Her answer was a little disturbing.

"Because I have a picture of you, and when I peaked in the car door I knew it was you and that I would be safe."

"Did you get a photo of me off the internet, and how did you know that you'd be safe?"

"No, it's a real photograph. My mother gave it to me."

"Oh, your mother has a picture of me…does she have a name?"

"Of course she does; it's Tess Fulton."

"I've got a pretty good memory for names, so I am pretty sure that I have never come across anyone by that name." The phone was ringing. I walked into the kitchen and took the receiver off the hook.

Vali threw me a curve ball before I could even say hello.

"Perhaps you knew her by the name Mayria Joseph."

I was shock and stuttered. "Mya… Mya's your mother?"

She nodded and asked me if I was going to answer the telephone.

I could hear Irene talking, but I was oblivious to anything she was saying.

She yelled. "Mitch, what is going on there, who are you talking to?"

I snapped out of my momentary stupor. "Sorry, I was caught up in a conversation with a young lady who I picked up down by Blind Man's Bluff. She put her car in the ditch, so rather than take her back to the city I brought her here. The roads are in no condition to be driving anyhow."

"Is she visiting someone local?"

"No, as a matter of fact, she's here to see me." I looked over at Vali. She was smirking.

"What for, how old is she?" Irene asked suspiciously.

"Oh, I don't know, sixteen or seventeen."

"You are going to take her home aren't you?"

"Not tonight."

"Mitch, you can't have an under aged girl spending the night with you! What are you thinking?"

"I'm not thinking anything...I'll ask her if her intentions towards me are honorable ...Vali?"

The look on Vali's face was priceless.

"Mitch!" Irene yelled outraged.

"Talk to you in a day or so okay, and don't worry, I've handled a few teenage girls in my time so I think I've got the situation under control." I hung up before she could drill me any further.

"I gather that was your wife...you didn't tell her you loved her." Vali said chuckling. "I take it she doesn't trust you...especially with young gals. Do you really think I'm that young?"

"Now that you are drying out I can see you might be a tad older than I first thought. Coffee, tea or hot chocolate?"

"You forgot to add "or me." I'm twenty three and I'll have coffee; black, one sugar please."

I poured two cups of steaming brew and handed one to her. I couldn't contain my curiosity any longer. "How is your mother?"

"Well, she was alive and kicking the last time I saw her which is a miracle in itself as her so called imbecilic husband has tried to kill her three times."

I was alarmed to say the least. "What, how...surely you jest, three times?"

"Yup, they've all been investigated by the police, but there is not enough evidence for an arrest. It is all "circumstantial" they say. She was hospitalized all three times. In fact, she is supposed to be in the hospital right now undergoing psychiatric evaluation."

"But, she isn't?"

"Do you think I was going to leave her there under **his** doctor's care? No way Jose; I sprung her, and she's safe for the time being...'til he gets back in town I guess."

"Where is she Vali?"

"For all I know you are one of his lackeys, so until I get proof that you're not, and that you are going to help us, I cannot tell you where she is."

"Do you know how preposterous that is? You wouldn't have come looking for me if you thought I was working for him, and who the hell is **he** anyhow?"

"His name is Brian Fulton, and he is an unscrupulous son of a bitch!"

"The industrialist Brian Fulton; he's your mother's husband, and he's trying to kill her?"

"His company was bankrupt before Mom came along. She financed him because she is too trusting, but now he wants all her assets and will stop at nothing until he gets it all."

"Okay, I get the picture, and we will address it later. Right now I would like you to elaborate on the fact that you have a picture of me that your mother gave you. It must be very old because I haven't seen your mother in a very long time. Do you have it with you?"

"As a matter of fact I do. Have you seen my purse?"

"I suppose it's by the door; I'll get it for you." I said setting my cup down.

I found where she had thrown it. It was water-logged. "I hope there is nothing of great value in it because it's wringing wet."

She joined me at the sink. "Damn; let's see what's salvageable."

She opened it and dumped the contents into the sink. "I guess these cigs are toast." She said dumping the package along with some make-up into the garbage.

I laid a towel out on the counter for her to spread out the papers from her wallet and anything else that looked half decent.

"Here it is!" She said jubilantly. "Luckily Mom had it in this little plastic casing. "What do you think...it's you, right? You haven't changed all that much."

I laughed, but I wasn't laughing on the inside. I was staring at the girl beside me in the photo. It was Mayria. It was taken on her seventeenth birthday, December the 19th, 1985, the day that changed everything for us, the day we declared our love for each other, the day we promised each other that we would be together until the end of time. That 'end of time' only lasted four months. I had only seen her once after that...it was the day she married my best friend.

I traced her face with my fingers. "She was so beautiful." I murmured wistfully.

"She still is Mitch. You were close weren't you? What happened?"

"It was a long time ago Vali. I can't say that I see much of her in you."

"Yeah, unfortunately I got my dad's features instead. Perhaps you knew him as he was from Sommerset too, and you must have known my two brothers father, Bobby Jones."

"Bobby was my best friend. He's the one who gave me the name I have gone by since I was seven years old. There were two of us named Adam in our little gang, and so to differentiate, he started calling me Mitchum which eventually was shortened to Mitch. If I have the time frame right, I think that your mom married Billy Reid shortly after Bobby was killed, so I'm assuming that Billy is your father."

"You would assume right. My father is a con-man, and he played on my mother's vulnerability. She got pregnant after a one night stand. She married him just so I would be legitimate. It wouldn't have mattered to me, but it did to her, something I never understood. When I was twelve, or so, and had come home from spending a few days with my father, I told her that I never wanted to see him again. She said it was important that a child know their biological parents whether they wanted anything to do with them or not, and someday she hoped to rectify that. We never spoke of it again, and to this day I don't know what she meant, unless…"

She left the thought, whatever it was, dangling in the air. "Unless what Vali?"

She seemed to be studying me. "Unless you're my oldest brother's real father…"

I shook my head. "I don't know where you would get that idea from because I am not, and what makes you even think that your mother and I had that kind of relationship? I left Sommerset in April of 1986, and your mother married Bobby that year around Christmas. Your brother was born a year later when I was in Australia, so you can just put your assumptions aside. Perhaps your mother was referring to someone else. Anyhow, it is of no consequence as to what is going on today. Now, where were we?"

"How would you know when my brother was born anyhow because as you say, you were in Australia, and just one more question; were you in love with my mother…you may as well confess because I will know it when the two of you meet eye to eye."

I nodded smiling. "To answer your first question, a friend sent me a copy of the birth announcement that your mother had sent to her when I was living in Brisbane. After that, I was pretty much unreachable for almost two years as I did the celebrated Walkabout. I didn't even know that Bobby and most of his family had been killed in the airplane crash until two or three years later. And yeah, I loved your mother; everyone did."

"Including your best friend whom she chose over you…is that what happened?"

"If you are through dissecting me I would like to get on with the matter at hand, that being the alleged attempts on your mother's life."

"Talk about evading the question. I thought a Walkabout was for young boys looking to find their manhood, or their purpose in the universe."

"Well, young lady, you are absolutely right in your description of the Australian Walkabout. I guess I too was looking for where I fit into **the** plan. I had itchy feet, and I thought a journey through the wilderness might help to quench my thirst. By the way, it didn't. At the end of my sojourn from civilization I realized that happiness isn't a place, but that it lives inside all of us and one has to discover it for them self."

"Very philosophical Mr. Detective. My mother could have learned a thing or two from you, and perhaps she did. She never found true happiness, or love though, and believe me, she tried. In my mind, she is still searching, and I will tell you why I think that. I could really use a cigarette; may I have one of yours?"

"I don't smoke. I have a feeling that what you have to say may take some time so how about we have a bite to eat while you talk." I suggested.

"Why is the ashtray over there filled with butts then?"

"Because my neighbor visits and is a smoker; I just haven't dumped it."

Vali followed me into the kitchen and sat at the table. I placed an assortment of cold cuts, cheeses, and condiments in front of her. She took the lids off the jars, and opened up the package of freshly baked rolls that I had bought at the bakery, and proceeded to butter two of them.

"How about a beer then?" She asked.

"That I can do." I said opening the fridge and taking out two bottles. "Hope this brand is to your liking."

"It is now. The only thing missing from this little picnic is a jar of Mom's homemade pickles."

"Your mother makes pickles?" I asked surprisingly.

"She does; she has a greenhouse and grows cucumbers, tomatoes, and the like as well as orchids and geraniums. We have two florist shops in Seattle you know. You will see how this greenhouse comes into play later on. So, a brief history leading up to today...do you know that along with Bobby's sister Aileen, Mom was the sole legatee of the chain of Legend Hotels and the fortune that the family had amassed? I believe there are hotels in twenty or so different countries now. Anyhow, neither Mom nor Aileen wanted to assume command. Aileen was too grief stricken, and Mom had two little boys to contend with, and she had no mind for business. Anyhow, Aileen's husband Floyd was suddenly thrust into the corporate world. He was a struggling musician and was used to one night gigs and smoky bar rooms. He had made it quite clear when he and Aileen married that he wanted no part of the family business. But, you know the saying, "The best laid plans of mice and men, etc. etc." Anyhow, long story short, he did what had to be done to assure the stock holders and partners that the company was not going to crumble, and that it would continue to operate in the same professional way that it had before the untimely death of the Jones family. Aileen did take her place alongside Floyd and they convinced Mom to do the same. She was barely twenty one when she was voted in as CEO of the Paris franchise. Apparently, they all felt more secure with someone with the name Jones at the helm. At least that is what she thought. Anyhow, what I am basically saying here is that she has money, and a lot of it. Before and after my birth, a mistake I am sure, and she paid Billy off to divorce her, we moved from one Legend hotel to another in places like London, Amsterdam, New York, Ottawa, and Greece where she met Andris Anastopoulos at an antique auction. He invited her to come to his villa in Mykonos which she did, and two weeks later they were married. We lived there for almost two years. Andris had some title and had money of his own, so he was not after Mom for her riches. He loved her, but she tired of him, and they too divorced. The boys were nine and seven then and needed permanent schooling so we went to England where she bought a farm. We lived there for five years. There were no men in her life that I remember. I was four at the time. So, suddenly I am nine and we move to Canada. Any questions so far?"

"Questions, hell yes!" I grabbed two more beer. "How long was Mya married to your father, and how did they get together anyhow? You said she tired of this Andris fellow; what does that mean exactly; was she not in love with him?"

"By the way, my mother goes by the name Tess or Tessa now. She had always been Mayria Jones, but she told me once that she used to be called Mya. She did not elaborate on why she had abandoned the name. I'm guessing it was your name for her?"

I squirmed a little.

"I guess you were still bumming around in Australia when your old home town had a memorial for Bobby and his parents, and uncle. You must have known all of them, right? That is when she and Billy got together; consoling each other I guess."

"Bullshit! Billy hated Bobby from day one, so he wasn't grieving. But, your mother was there and she was vulnerable... oh yeah, I can just see how he comforted her. Sorry, I shouldn't be speaking that way about your father."

"He's never been much of a father to me Mitch, so I do not take offense. I haven't seen him for three years, and rarely even talk to him. As I said, I was very young when Mom was with Andris. He was very good to us according to the boys, and wanted to have children with her. When I was about thirteen I asked her why she didn't stay with him. She said he didn't want to have any more children, and that he didn't know the words to her song, and he probably wouldn't know how to slay dragons...Mitch, what's wrong, what did I say?"

I had gotten up so quickly that I knocked my chair over. I righted it and tried to laugh it off saying that I remembered her mother and her enchantment with the mythical winged beasts. It had just taken me back for a moment.

"I think it's a lot more than that Mitch." Vali hinted. "Are you by any chance the dragon slayer she was referring to, and do you know her song?"

"I doubt it. She was just a kid when I knew her so I'm sure she lived with one foot in a fairy tale, and dragons were right up her alley of fantasy. To answer your question; I did know Bobby's family. I only remember meeting the uncle once or twice. He left Sommerset when we were just kids. I guess I was about sixteen, no, seventeen because Bobby and I were in grade twelve. He came to live with my family when his parents picked up and moved to Paris. The uncle wooed his brother into entering a business deal that couldn't fail, and obviously it didn't as it is the legendary Legend Hotel chain. Bobby went off to join the family that summer, but didn't stay. He said it wasn't for him at the time, and enrolled in business school in Vancouver. Upon completion he returned home and went to work for a local business. We remained close. I left Sommerset, and next thing I know he and your mother are married. I guess he was persuaded to join up with the family's endeavours in France, and two years later he meets his waterloo. That's all I know. Now, shall we continue with the business of the day?"

"Okay, but first I want to know what you meant to her. She wouldn't have gotten all weepy when she mentioned your name and said that she was sure you would help her for old time's sake. One doesn't have that kind of a reaction to someone's name if they didn't mean something to them. What happened thirty years ago Mitch?"

"All right," I said sitting back down thinking that maybe it was time to tell the story even if it was to a stranger who just happened to be my old sweetheart's daughter. I was pretty sure Vali wasn't going to stop with the questions anyhow. "are you aware that your mom and her parents only moved to Sommerset in 1985 from the Boston area, so we did not grow up together. I had been working in the Yukon since June of that summer with my uncle on his gold claim, so I did not meet her until I came home. It was August twenty ninth. I remember the date as it was my Grandmother Lylah Jayne's birthday. I went over to see her, and this girl, whom I had never seen before, answered the door. She was quite insolent. She said she supposed I was Adam and that it was about time that I got there as my grandmother had been waiting all day for me. It was one in the afternoon. She ushered me into the living room where I found my grandmother sitting with her swollen ankle up on a hassock. She had fallen down the front steps a few days earlier. Your mother's family had moved into the house next door. Mayria spent most of her days at my Grandmother Lylah's house helping her around the house, doing her shopping and just visiting with her. I was grateful to her for that because my own family mostly left my grandmother to fend for herself. Anyhow, Mayria says that they were about to have tea and would I join them. Without waiting for an answer she scurried off into the kitchen. It was then that Lylah told me about her. She laughed when she told me her name. "Can you believe that her mother named her after the wind...Mayria Tessa Joseph?" I asked her what she meant. "You know," she said, "the rain is Tess, the fire is Joe, and the wind is Mayria...you know, "they call the wind Mayria."

"Well, I didn't, but I remarked that she kind of reminded me of the wild, wild, wind. So, that is how I met your mother, and yes, we did have a relationship, but it didn't work out."

"I've heard that before about her name. It's true what you said as she is definitely tempestuous. Was it your fault or hers that you broke up?"

"Let's just leave it at that okay? I'll leave it to your mother to fill in any other details. How about we get back to why you think your stepfather is trying to kill her?"

"I don't just **think** that he is trying to kill her, I **know** he is; I just can't prove it. After the last bout of poisoning my brothers said that it was time to hire a private investigator, and that is when we first heard your name, and here we are. Tell me what you need to know. After, if you figure you can't, or don't want to take our case, I'll understand. Maybe you will recommend another PI though. Money is no object."

"Dessert?" I asked as I walked over to the fridge and opened the freezer door. I extracted a package of Belvedere, shook one out, stuck it behind my ear, and tossed the package to Vali.

She smiled. "I knew you were holding out on me. Got a light?"

"Sure you want that cancer stick lit up...I prefer mine sans the fire." I opened a drawer and pulled out a Bic lighter. "May I do the honors?"

"Promise you won't tell my mommy?" She inhaled deeply. "Aah, just as good as sex."

I shook my head. I liked this girl. I poured myself a cup of coffee. Vali said she would stick with the beer. I beckoned her to follow me into the living room. We sat opposite each other next to the fire. Sadie curled up between our feet.

I leaned forward. "Tonight you are going to give me the low down, everything you know or even think you know. No monies need change hands."

"What happens tomorrow if you think we have a case?'

"You take me to see your mother. Now, start with the day she met Brian."

"It was on a Caribbean Cruise for singles. Deanna, Mom's assistant at Goldenrod, one of her florist shops in Seattle, talked her into accompanying her. Mom didn't want to go because she had sworn off men a few years back. She was convinced that the cruise was all about pairing people up. She didn't even meet Brian until the fifth day out at sea. He was seated next to her at the Captain's table. She said they barely talked, but they ran into each other at the tennis court the next day and ended up becoming partners in a double's match. This became a daily exercise even though they were both terrible at the game and always lost. Dinners and dancing came next. They were not physically or romantically involved according to her, and I tend to believe her. Anyhow, they parted ways at the terminal in Seattle. He asked her if he could call her sometime, and I guess she said yes. Two weeks later he showed up at Goldenrod. She started travelling back and forth to Vancouver to attend social events with him. Before that she would make up excuses as to why she was going to Vancouver as she had been doing so for some time. Now, she didn't need an excuse because of Brian. She already knew about his business, but did not know right away that it was at the point of bankruptcy. Without consulting with any of us, she entered into a partnership with him which saw her investing a million dollars in his company. A few months later she confided in me and said he had asked her to not only be his business partner, but his partner in life. She was happy, and they got engaged. I had left college because I was bored with it and was working full time at the flower shop. In fact it had done so well under Mom's management that she went ahead and purchased another shop across town which she intrusted to me. About a month before the wedding she came home in an emotional state. I'm not sure why I am telling you this, but somehow it seems relevant to her state of mind even then. She took to her bed. I assumed something dreadful happened between her and Brian. I was not the least bit upset as I had already formed an opinion about him, and it was not positive. But, I was wrong; the wedding was still a 'go'. The next day she was back to her cheerful self. I asked her why she had come home from Vancouver in such a dither. She laughed, and said that she had visited a little tea shop where for twenty dollars one could receive psychic counselling, and also have their fortune told by the resident gypsy. The psychic told her nothing she didn't already know, and that was that she was professionally, and financially secure. She did not predict anything earth shattering in her future. However, the gypsy who read her palms had a few more revealing things to say. She had told her that she had numerous fine lines which indicated that she had a complex and sensitive personality. Her heart line had started out strong, but had many breaks and crosses. Mom says the palmist said that she felt mom's pain for all that she had lost. She said the line did seem to repair itself, and that mom should be patient. Her life and head lines were all positives. Then they looked into the crystal ball. She saw Mom standing in a wedding dress holding a bouquet of orange roses, and she appeared very happy. Then she took Mom's hand and asked her what was going on as the ball had suddenly and violently turned stormy. She'd asked her what had made her hands go from warm to cold, and her eyes to fill with tears. Mom had laughed and said that she'd had her fortune told many times and always with the same end result. I asked her what she meant. These are her exact words. "I'm happy, and then I'm not; that's the story of my life. I always had hopes that one day I would be complete again, but that day I saw the sign, and then I saw them, and I knew that dream was gone for good. The dragon was guarding the door again, and I knew he was never going to let me in. Sorry Dear, I didn't mean to upset you." I asked her if she had been looking out the window, or was it all just in her mind. She said she hoped she had the sense to never go back to that tea shop. I asked her where it was. She said it was on Bourbon. I must say that I was a little upset by the whole episode. I mean; a tea shop, fortune tellers, a sign, and a dragon? Just a minute, Bourbon Street, Bourbon... could she have meant Bourdon? I've heard that name before...hell, I've been there! It's the street your office is on. Oh God, there's a dragon on the pawn shop sign isn't there? She went there to see you didn't she? You're the reason she used to come up here aren't you? What happened Mitch?"

"There is a dragon on the sign, and there is a little tea shop across from my office, and perhaps she was there. If she came to see me something changed her mind because she didn't make contact with me, not that day, or any other. I never saw her then, and haven't for thirty years." I was struggling to keep my composure because it was not the time to reveal my dormant emotions regarding her mother.

"Perhaps if she had of made contact she wouldn't have been pushed down the stairs or poisoned with thallium or potassium chloride by her Machiavellian husband."

"You have to be friggin kidding me...thallium?"

"I wish I was."

"How the hell did she come in contact with something that's been banned for years?"

"Remember how I told you that the greenhouse would come into play? The house Mom bought is a heritage house and has an old glass conservatory in the back yard. Traces of thallium were found in it after 'her accidental poisoning' as it is referred to by the hazard crew, and cops who investigated. Her clothing and exposed skin showed exposure to it, and was viewed as not unusual because evidence of rat poison was found in the greenhouse. The concentration found in her bloodstream and urine registered much higher amounts. It was suspect as to how she would have come into contact with/or/ ingested the thallium. The grounds and main house, plus outbuildings had no positive readings for the element. Her mental state was brought into question because of the other two incidents, those being the fall down the stairs, and the overdose of potassium chloride. The question was raised if it was possible that all of these 'accidents' were attempts of suicide."

"You don't believe that do you?"

"Not for one bloody second! Her life may not be perfect, but she still loves it and us."

"Thallium is known as "The Poisoner's Poison" if I recall correctly. I need to do some research on it, and then we will compare notes on what I find, and what you know. So make yourself comfortable while I query the internet."

"Okay, and if we agree that Brian was behind all these so called accidents, then what?"

"We prove it, and when we do, your mother will be free of yet another dragon."

Vali was curled up on the chesterfield when I returned an hour later with a handful of notes. She had a copy of Wild Life B.C. in her hands. She showed me what she had been reading; The Secret Life of the Lynx.

"It says the author is one Adam Mitchum...is that you Mitch?"

"It is."

"So, is detective or photo journalist your day job?"

"When I weary of the week's events I take a hiatus and go up to the cabin in the woods, grab my camera and venture out into the wilds for day trips. Some days I find a captivating audience and sometimes I don't. When I do, I write an article and send it in for consideration. It's a hobby."

"You have another cabin? Well, you can't actually call this a cabin...where is it?"

"It's up the road, halfway between here and Lillooet."

"Thanks for clearing that up. That could be anywhere from here to Timbuctoo."

I laughed. "It's up the road a fair way. Maybe I will take you there some time. Now, let's discuss the poisonings."

"I would be honored Mitch." She smiled. "Should I start at the stair ordeal?"

"Yes, if that is where things first went down."

"Mom and Brian were married on April 2nd, 2013 just five months after they met. It should have been on April 1st because it certainly was an April Fools' joke. She started having bouts of pain in her abdomen in December. On the twelfth Brian took her to the hospital. The doctors concluded that it was her appendix. She had surgery that evening. In actuality, the inflamed appendix wasn't the only problem. She had a cyst on her ovary that had burst and was probably the cause for most of her pain. So that was mended, plus a few other problems and the appendectomy. Needless to say, she was looking at a six week recovery. She couldn't climb the stairs to the bedroom so she spent the first two weeks in the bedroom off the kitchen which Ivy stayed in periodically."

"Sorry to interrupt, but who is Ivy?"

"Her initial role was as an occasional housekeeper. When Mom came home from the hospital Brian suggested that she take on more duties like cooking and assisting Mom in her personal well-being. Their relationship blossomed into friendship. Mom trusts her explicitly and confides in her. You will like her. She emigrated from Panama with her husband and daughter fifteen years ago. She lost her husband to a massive stroke, and necessity forced her into the work field. When Mom became ill she gave up all her other jobs so she could become a full time nurse and companion to mom. Mom calls her a Domestic Goddess."

"It sounds like she will be a trusted source of information."

"She will be, and she doesn't care much for Brian. So, Mom was sleeping in the downstairs bedroom, and Ivy was sleeping in the pull-out bed in the den. One night Mom snuck upstairs to her bedroom. At three in the morning Brian found her lying halfway down the stairs. He says he was awakened by her screaming. He yelled at Ivy to call 911. It was found that she had overdosed on pain pills. Mom said she only took two, but more were unaccounted for, and her stomach contents said otherwise. She says she heard Brian calling her to help him and that she got up to find him, but remembers nothing after that. At first I thought she had fallen, but now I think she was drugged and then pushed."

"There is no evidence to support that is there Vali?"

"No, but Mom recalls that the milk Brian gave her that night tasted sour."

"Does she still take these pain drugs?"

"I don't believe so because she says she has no pain."

"Okay; how was she poisoned with potassium chloride?"

"Six months or so after her surgery she started having muscle cramps, stiffness and numbness and unusual mood changes. She was diagnosed with a potassium deficiency and was prescribed an oral potassium supplement. It seemed to solve her problems until she started having gastrointestinal problems which included diarrhea and vomiting. Ivy rushed her to the hospital when she found Mom exhibiting signs of a heart attack. She had an abundance of PC in her system. How it was administered is the question. Mom swears she never took more than the recommended dosage of the prescription. Hence the subject of her sanity came up as it is supposedly a method of suicide."

"PC is also used in fertilizers as potash. Is there any way that she may have ingested or inhaled a lethal dose through dust or dermal contact in her greenhouse?"

"I don't think so as none was found, but that leads us to the thallium scare last spring. Just when it seemed as though her health had finally returned to normalcy, she developed a skin rash and her hair started falling out. She complained of headaches and stomach pain, but carried on as if none of this was unusual. One day she was late coming down from the glasshouse for an appointment. She wasn't answering the phone so Ivy went up to see what was keeping her. She found Mom passed out on the dirt floor. Ivy couldn't rouse her so she called 911. Of course, Brian wasn't home, and I was in Seattle. So again the question arose: How did she come in contact with so much thallium? Did she ingest it deliberately or accidentally, or had her skin and clothing been exposed to a bizarre amount of the poison? As you mentioned, it is another popular way to commit homicide or suicide."

"How did your step-father react to all of it?"

"Please do not call him my step-father! My father may not be much of a role model, but he is a saint compared to that phoney baloney asshole!"

"I will not make that mistake again." I said apologetically.

"Good. He promised us that he would be more vigilant of Mom's well-being. That lasted about two weeks before he was jetting off to some business appointment leaving Ivy in charge. He suggested that we should think seriously about having Mom admitted to a facility for psychological evaluation."

"So, he believed that Mya was suicidal?"

"Well, it's one way to control her purse strings isn't it?"

"Perhaps; I'll have to look into their financial arrangements unless you know what they are."

"Not for sure I don't, but Mom is very generous, and openly told me that she had invested the million dollars that I mentioned earlier into his company. Lord knows how much more he has conned out of her."

"How is her health now Vali?"

"I see a light in her eyes that I haven't seen for a very long time. I first noticed it when Frankie suggested that we hire a private investigator, and she gave us your name. She literally lit up."

"I doubt that I have anything to do with her renewed spirit Vali. Let's leave it at that for the night and see if we can get some sleep as it's going to be a long day tomorrow. Just one more question; was Brian married before?"

"He was, but I don't know when."

"Is she still alive, or are they divorced?"

"He doesn't talk about it, but I gather from Mom that she is dead."

"I will have to look into it. It could prove interesting if there were suspicious circumstances regarding her death."

To say I was a bundle of nerves was putting it mildly. I had tossed and turned all night playing what I was going to say to Mya over and over in my head. Nothing came out sounding right. I, honest to God, never thought that I would ever see her again. I mean, why would I? She was a globe trotter, an icon in the hotel business, and probably dined with kings and queens. Hell, she had actually married and divorced a Spanish royal. Good for her; she did well. I could never have given her fame and fortune, never mind a child. According to her daughter, she was not happy, and never had been. I didn't believe that for one minute and surmised that Vali had been embellishing on the truth because she had this romantic notion in her head that I had been the one who had slain dragons for her mother. I hadn't revisited that fairy tale for a very long time. I was happily married, so there was no reason to.

There were times when I thought about Mya, but hell, I also thought about a few other old girlfriends now and then, but, had I named my boat after them? Damn. Mya could never see it. Shit, I was screwed. Come on man, that's never going to come to light. You'll see her, and find a way to prove her husband has tried to kill her multiply times without having much to do with her. Yeah, that would be best. She'll have to stay in hiding for a while anyhow.

The next morning had dawned clear and sunny. I took that as a good sign. Neither Vali nor I were in the mood for breakfast. I told her I'd buy her lunch at my favorite diner after we had talked with Mayria.

We stopped at my office where I grabbed the one burner phone that I kept in reserve for emergencies. I put in a call to Jake Daniels, my right hand man. If he was still in town I'd ask him to meet me in two hours at Millie's Restaurant with two more burner phones.

"Where are you Jake?" I asked when he answered groggily.

"Right here Boss."

"Aren't you supposed to be on the island with Michelle this weekend?"

"Haven't got there yet. You need something Mitch?"

I told him what I needed, and asked for Shane Darcy's number as I knew he wasn't busy, and that I didn't want to bother Mel.

"New case Boss?"

"Yeah, it just came up."

"You need surveillance or whatever... I'm your man Mitch, you know that."

"Maybe; what about Michelle?"

"Work comes first. I need an excuse to get out of a boring weekend, so you're it!"

"Thanks for making me your scapegoat. Appreciate it Jake, but have no idea what it's all going to entail. I'll know when I see her. I might just abandon the whole thing, but I've already promised her daughter...hell."

"You all right Boss? Sounds like you're a little apprehensive. Is it someone you know?"

"Someone I used to know. If you're on board then I need you to tell Artie when you pick up the phones that I need a tin lizzie and a new ID. I am still working on the particulars. See you at the diner around noon. Thanks in advance Jake."

"Ten-four; sounds serious Boss. See you at the diner. Anything else, just give me a jingle."

Back in the jeep I passed the phone to Vali and told her to call the convent. She waited on the line for a good five minutes while Sister Constance was tracked down. I hated listening to one sided conversations. I got the gist of it...Mya was anxiously waiting for us.

"All systems go Mitch." Vali said as she hung up the phone.

"Didn't you want to talk to your mother?" I asked edgily.

"I didn't need to. You told me to have as little as possible phone contact with her, remember?"

"That phone can't be traced. You sure that I take the 233 exit?"

"Yes, I'm sure. Are you nervous about seeing mom?"

I shot her a dubious look wondering if my anxiety was obvious. "Should I be?"

"How the hell do I know? You have given me limited information on your mysterious relationship. I have no clue as to how she is going to receive you, but she asked me to find you, so as far as I am concerned, all is good."

"There was nothing mysterious about our relationship young lady. It was a long time ago, and maybe we won't even recognise each other."

"Yeah, go with that Mr. Detective Man." She laughed. "I'm going to catch a nap. Stay on Highway 62A until you reach Rockwood Crossing; turn right, no sorry, left. Mary Magdalene Convent is seventeen miles down that road. You can't miss it."

"How about you driving and I take the nap?"

"Sorry, I can't drive a stick shift."

It was my turn to laugh. "I think you could drive an eighteen wheeler with one eye shut."

"Hope we never have to find out."

Vali curled up in the seat and I was left alone with my thoughts. Why was I so anxious? Did I really think Mya still thought of me as the guy who jilted her? Well, I guess I had… so would it bother me if she did? I rationalized that it shouldn't as that was another lifetime ago. She wouldn't have wanted to hire me if she still held a grudge would she? And, why would it be a problem for me? I was a happily married man, and Mya's and my new relationship would be strictly professional, so that was that.

Forty minutes later I came to a stop in front of a solid wood gate. There was a call centre on the post to my right. Before I could speak a man's voice inquired as to my business.

I stated my name and that I and my companion were here by an invitation from Sister Constance. The gate opened slowly.

Vali sat up. "Wow, I really did sleep! See, over there," she pointed, "that's the visitor parking lot. Were you surprised to hear a man's voice behind the intercom?"

"Well, I know single women have a man's voice on their answering machine, so I guess nuns are no different. I guess they feel a man's voice carries more clout."

"Are you serious...these are God's Ladies! They are already protected. Come on; race you to the front door."

I was almost thankful that I hadn't had children. I caught up to her at the front door. She shook her head and called me a spoil sport. She rang the doorbell, and then knocked with the giant doorknocker. She looked at me and smiled.

A young girl, a novice I assumed, opened the door for us and saw us into a vestibule. She asked us to be seated saying that she would make Sister Constance aware of our arrival. Vali paced nervously for two minutes before she pulled me up.

"Come on Mitch." She coaxed.

"Shouldn't we wait until we are summoned?"

"They know we are here...come on...."

You would think it was Vali who hadn't seen her mother for thirty years. I took a deep breath. At the end of the long hallway I got my first glimpse of my old sweetheart. She was holding hands with someone in a white uniform whom I thought might be our old friend Connie. Mya was dressed in a long knee length black sweater and black leggings. They were walking slowly. As they got closer, Mya's pace quickened. Connie let go of her hand, gave her a little push, and I guess uttered a few words of encouragement. Mya was smiling. A sunbeam from an open window bounced off the brass candleholders that lined the lengthy corridor. It landed on Mya and turned her dark brown hair golden. I don't know what came over me, but all I could think of were the words to a song that I used to sing to her. I never could get the words right, but they were something like how fine she looked, and that I wanted to make her mine. Mya would laugh every time I sang it to her. I wondered what she would think if she knew the words were running through my mind right now. When she was but four feet in front of me she reached her hands out to me. Our eyes met, and she said my name. I took the final step towards her and took her hands in mine.

"Oh Mitch, I can't believe you came." Tears welled in the corners of her eyes.

I pulled her into my arms. "I think this is a better way to greet an old friend."

I wanted to tell her that she was the most beautiful being I had ever seen, but I didn't. Everyone said my wife was beautiful, and she was. She was the day version of Mayria, blonde, blue eyed, silky white skin, tall and leggy. Mayria was bronzed, dark hair, green speckled eyes and petite. Her voice was soft, yet throaty and sensual. Her hair smelled like rain water... not five hundred dollar an ounce perfume. I pulled her away from me so I could get a good look at her.

"Do you know how good it is to see you looking so healthy? I was worried after what you have been through, but you look wonderful and are a sight for very glad old eyes."

"So are you Mitch. Here", she said pulling Connie into our fold, "you remember our Connie don't you?"

"Sister Constance, I presume. Is it kosher to give a lady of the cloth a hug?"

Connie laughed. "It most certainly is Adam Mitchum! It's been a long time."

"That it has been. I'm happy that you found your calling, and I want to thank you for being a friend to Mayria in her hour of need. I'll take over from here." I turned to Mya. "Are your belongings all packed?"

She asked me why and I told her that she was my responsibility now, so I was taking her home.

"She can't go home Mitch! The boys aren't even here yet!" Vali interjected.

"I didn't mean her home, I meant mine." I explained.

"She is safe here so why take the chance of moving her? Do you have a plan or did you just come up with it right now because you never mentioned taking her to your place before."

"Do I have a say?" Mya asked.

"Of course you do." I said presenting my reasoning. "At this point I have no idea how far Brian's reach is so I don't want you out of my sight. You are probably perfectly safe here inside these walls, but I need you to trust me, and trust that I know what is best. Besides, we have a lot to talk about…what do you say?"

"I'll go with you Mitch." Mya said hesitantly. "Are you okay with that Vali?"

Vali sighed. "What's your wife going to say about you bringing a strange woman home, or is she used to you bringing all your clients home?"

"Irene has nothing to do with my business, and do you really think that I would be taking your mother to the house in town?"

"You want to take her to the cabin? No, no that's too desolate! Come up with another plan or she is staying right here."

Connie suggested that we go into a private room and discuss the situation.

"Can you just get her things Connie; thanks. Vali, you hired me to look after your mother, and that is what I intend to do. If you think I am going all macho on you, maybe I am, but this is who I am, so suck it up and let me do my job. Now, are you with me or not?" I demanded.

"I don't even know what I am agreeing to, but you had better have a working plan all tied up with a shiny new ribbon before my brothers get into town." Vali relented.

I nodded. "It's already in the works Honey. Let's get a move on." I took Mya's arm. "We'll wait in the car for you while Connie collects your stuff."

I opened the heavy oak door. Vali put her hand on my shoulder. I turned to face her. "What?"

"I wouldn't be so apprehensive if you didn't have a past with her. You better treat her with kid gloves...you don't want me on your bad side."

"Warning taken; give me a little credit will you? There's no way in hell I am going to wrong your mother again."

Her eyes questioned me, I assumed at the word 'again'."

I asked Mya if she wanted to sit in the front or back seat. She said she would sit in the back with Vali. I opened the door for her. Before she got in she asked me if Vali had filled me in satisfactorily regarding her situation. I said that she had.

"I want you to know that you are not obligated to take my case. There may be no resolution as the evidence is slim to nil, and it may have an unfavorable conclusion."

I wasn't sure what she meant by that. "If there is evidence to be found then I will find it. I have a motley crew and we won't leave one stone unturned. Do you trust me Mya?"

"I do Mitch. You can't possibly know how wonderful it is to see you. I'm afraid I had a sleepless night worrying about what your reaction would be to seeing me."

I smiled. "Oh, I think I do as it was the same for me. Thank-you for making this so easy for me Mya. I have a lot of explaining to do."

"You don't owe me anything Mitch."

Before I could answer Vali arrived and said "Let's get this show on the road."

She climbed into the back with Mya, put her hand on my shoulder and warned me again about what would happen to me if I put her mom's well-being into jeopardy. I laid my hand on hers and told her that I was trembling. She called me a smart Alec.

"Takes one to know one." I countered.

I winked at Mya in the rear mirror; she smiled. She entertained us with what life was like in the convent. Just as we pulled into the Diner, she surprised us by saying that maybe she had missed her calling. Vali laughed. I didn't respond. As we pulled up to to the Diner, Jake was entertaining two young women standing by the 'hitchin post', a subtle reminder of horse days gone by. He tipped his cowboy hat to them and sauntered over to the car eyeing Mya and Vali in the back.

He opened Vali's door and spoke in his genuine Southern drawl. "The daughter and the mother I presume. You done good Boss."

"My number one man ladies... Jake Daniels. Don't take anything he says too seriously, but when it comes to business, he is unbendable." I said opening the door for Mya.

Vali asked Jake if he carried a six shooter. He laughed and told her that if she hung around long enough she would probably find out. Vali took his arm and they swaggered into the diner.

Mya shook her head. "That young man doesn't know what he's in for."

I laughed taking her hand. "I think she may have just met her match."

It had been a long time since I had walked hand and hand with a woman. I liked the feeling. Cherie, the diner's owner met us at the door. She hugged me and asked how I was.

I hugged her back and said that I was a hungry man, introduced her to Mayria saying that she was a very dear friend of mine. It had not gone unnoticed that Mya and I were holding hands.

Cherie greeted her warmly. "Any friend of Mitch's is welcome here. Jake and his young lady friend went on ahead to your usual table."

"That young lady is Mayria's daughter"

Cherie ushered us to the back of the diner. "I see the apple hasn't fallen far from the tree." She winked at me and said she would send my favorite waitress over.

A minute later Karley sauntered over, pencil behind her ear, notepad and menus in her hand. As always she was chewing gum in a lady-like way. "Well, lookie here, my two favorite men in the whole wide world. Now, where on earth did you find these two gorgeous gals? Ladies, I hope you know that your reputations are going to be kaput if you are seen running around with these two scoundrels."

Mya placed her hand over mine smiling playfully. "I'm afraid you're thirty years too late for that warning Karley."

"You have to be kidding... thirty years?" She said astounded. "You must have been a babe in arms."

"Relatively speaking, yes." Mya's eyes were twinkling as she smiled at me.

My God, she was openly flirting with me! Be still my heart. What to say; what to say? Karley knew I was married. Delicately, I made the introductions, articulating that Mayria and I hadn't seen each other since 1988. Then I added that she had a very special place in my heart. Then I wondered why I said that.

"How wonderful is that Mitch! I'd love to hear more of your story; another time maybe? I'd better get back to my job before Cherie kicks my hinnie. May I take your drink orders?" Karley exclaimed finally doling out the menus. "You boys want the usual?"

Jake said Vali and him would have the light beer on tap. I asked Mya if she wanted a diet Pepsi or iced tea. She said the tea would be fine. I chose coffee over beer.

Vali said, "Ummm." grinning at me.

"Ummm, what?" I asked.

"Just observing." She answered.

Mya was tittering quietly behind the menu. I lowered it asking her what she found so amusing.

"Nothing." She answered. "I can't decide what to order; what do you suggest Mitch?"

"That depends on how hungry you are."

Jake said that he and Vali were having the Mountain High Crunchy Chicken burger. I concurred. Mya said that was too much for her and asked me to choose for her. It didn't seem like an unreasonable request to me. Karly returned and set our drinks down. I ordered the burgers and a half order of the sesame chicken noodle stir fry for Mya, and an extra small plate. I got the look from Vali again, but ignored her.

"Okay, so this is what's going to happen after we leave here. Vali, you are going to go with Jake, and he's going to take you to Artie's where you can pick up your car. Then he is going to follow you home and spend the night at the house with you. Are you good with that?"

Vali said she was, but Mya had questions.

"Just a minute; who is Artie, and why does he have your car Vali?"

"Artie's the company's mechanic, and Vali had a little fender bender on her way to find me yesterday." I informed her.

"Were you injured, and what car were you driving Vali?"

"Don't worry Mom, it was the old blue, and no, I wasn't hurt. I'm not sure I can say the same for your shoes though."

"Minor problem." Mya turned to me. "Now what's this about a company, and just how much of a mechanic is this Artie? Are you mixed up with the mafia Mitch?"

Jake was wide-eyed and on the verge of laughter. I wanted to laugh myself, but thought better of it. "I'm not connected Mya. Besides being a damn good auto mechanic Artie is my "go-to" man for merchandises associated with the business like the burner phones and surveillance equipment. I haven't the room to house everything and so I rent space in his storehouse. It's a company because I'm not a one man business. Anything else? I'm a little surprised that you would think that I'm not legit."

"How would I know...remember, it's been thirty years. Why does Jake have to stay with Vali? Are you concerned for her well-being?"

"At this point in the game I have no idea what Brian is capable of, and Vali might just prove to be a pawn in his plot to get what he wants from you. So yes, I am uneasy about her being left alone. Jake will see that she is safe and besides the house needs debugging. Sorry Jake, I realise that this is all news to you but you said you wanted "in". If you have given it some thought and decide that it's not..."

"Let me stop you right there Boss. When have you ever known me to welch on a job? You have to admit that the last few cases have been pretty boring so this one looks like it is right up our alley. Protecting this gal sitting next to me is not going to pose any hardship at all. Miss Mayria, you can rest easy as I will guard your daughter with my life."

"Jake, I don't believe Brian would harm one hair on her head as he knows what she means to me, but thank-you. Just know that she can be a handful." Mya said smiling at Vali. "She's quite the spitfire."

"Thanks Mom, it beats being apathetic."

"I also doubt that Brian has the house bugged Mitch, but if this is how you operate...okay."

"Maybe you have a different perspective on the attempts on your life Mayria because so far all I have to go on is what Vali has told me. Are you saying this is all for naught?"

"I'm sorry; I can't wrap my head around the thought that the man I married wants me dead."

It was obvious that Mya was having trouble coming to terms with her husband's scruples. I put my hand on hers just as Karly arrived with lunch. I told Mya that we would discuss it all later.

I doled out a dozen French fries unto the extra plate and set them down in front of Mya. She thanked me and said the stir fry looked delicious. I picked up the pickle that was sitting on top of my burger and took a bite.

"I bet your pickles are a lot tastier than these." I offered Mya a bite.

She laughed. "I see my daughter has been telling tales again." She made a face saying that the pickle was bitter.

"Okay, **what** is going on here?" Vali demanded.

Mya arched her eyebrows. "Is there something wrong with Mitch offering me a bite of pickle?"

"I'm not referring to the pickle Mother. Explain to me how Mitch knows what you like to drink and you let him order for you, and what's this with the French fries?"

"Yeah", Jake chimed in. "the fry thing was a little weird. Come on you two, come clean, you've been seeing each other for a while now haven't you? I see the way you look at each other... thirty years, my ass!"

"Actually, it's twenty nine years and five months Jake. Mitch always gave me twelve of his fries, twelve exactly, and I always drank Pepsi or iced tea. I guess some things never change."

"You have to see it from our point of view Mom; it's strange."

"It was just a moment Honey, just a moment, a remembrance from another time, another time when we *were*."

"When you were what Mom?"

"I think your mom meant to say 'when we were young'." I added.

"Well, it's like you have never been apart. Before this week is out I vow I will know everything there is to know about you two!" Vali promised fervently.

"It's as your mom says; a moment from yesterday."

"Okay for now." Vali agreed. "But Mitch, why do you have to go all the way up to your cabin? You can stay at the house as we have lots of room."

"I could, but I would like some alone time with your mom, and then there's Sadie."

"Oh, so there's another woman waiting at the cabin for you?" Mya asked teasingly.

"There is Mom, and you are going to love her." Vali said cheekily.

"Well, we will see about that, won't we?" Mya's smile was magnetic.

All I could do was smile back.

Half an hour later we were ready to leave. The girls went to the ladies room and I gave Jake a few more instructions. Outside I confiscated Vali and Mya's cell phones and gave them to Jake for safe keeping. He would leave them with Artie. I sent him and Vali on their way.

In the jeep Mya asked me how long to the cabin. I told her about an hour and a half from where we were, depending on traffic of course. I asked her to tell me about Bobbie Jr. and Frankie. The first thing she said was that Bobbie did not like being called Junior. I said that I would keep that in mind. Frankie was twenty four and had just completed several years of technical training at a technical institute in Seattle. His interests were in graphic and video game design. She said he worked best on his own, and was the quiet and cool member of the family. He had always stayed on the straight and narrow and had never given her one minute of worry. He was just like his father. Bobbie was the hot head, and was always getting into trouble at school, and was usually the instigator of schoolyard fights. Joining the Airforce right after graduation was a blessing as it supplied the discipline that she had apparently been remiss in providing. I already knew that he was an airplane mechanic stationed in Germany with the

Canadian Airforce. I listened as she elaborated on his career. He was unattached as far as she knew, but then the boys had always been a little secretive about their love lives, so she couldn't say for sure. He had never minced his feelings regarding the choices she had made. He had pretty much given up on her ever being satisfied with just one man. I guess she caught my look of disdain because she was quick to defend herself.

"I may be a little trampy Mitch, but I have never had more than one lover at a time. Sorry, that is more than you need to know, but I suppose it's good that you know that I am not an angel, a honky-tonk one maybe." She giggled a little.

If I had been harbouring a saintly image of my former sweetheart it vanished sorrowfully right then and there. I felt compelled to ask her what she meant.

"I lose interest fast Mitch, but Brian wouldn't give me a divorce, so I had to seek out other ways of getting rid of him." She giggled again. "That may have backfired a little."

"Are you saying that you were thinking of doing Brian in?"

"You mean murder...don't be silly, of course not! I just wanted out of the marriage. It had been so easy with Billy and Andris, so I thought all I had to do was ask Brian and he would comply as did the others."

"You could have taken him to court citing one of few dozen reasons for interference you know."

"I didn't, and don't want the hassle. Anyhow, enough about me; let's talk about Mitch."

"There isn't much to tell. I would say that my life has been rather boring compared to yours."

"I would not say that my life was exciting. It was composed of board meetings, arguing over policies, living in hotel suites, and finding suitable nannies for the children. That is the legacy that Bobby left me. I did not like the corporate world one iota, and am glad to be done with it."

"I hadn't realized that you had severed ties with Legend Hotels?"

"I'm on the cusp. Brian says I am making a big mistake, and wants me to sign over my powers to him. I've seen the hole he has dug for Fulton Enterprises so I've refused. I am in the process of selling my holdings off...that is, if I live long enough to do so."

"Don't talk like that Mayria! I'm going to get you through this, just wait and see. We haven't even got started yet."

"Time will tell. Weren't we talking about you?"

"What do you want to know...how and why I became a PI?"

She laughed. "Way before that...start with the day you left Sommerset, and oh yeah... me."

There was definitely bitterness in her voice.

I skipped the events of the first year and told her about my years working as an assistant to a game warden in the Australian Outback. "After my five year stint was up I bummed around the U.S. for a few years touring around Arizona and Nevada doing odd jobs when I needed money. I came back here and worked on road construction for the next six or so years, and took some courses to become a private eye. There was a hell of a lot more work and time involved to receive my "unrestricted" P.I. license than I had imagined. This certainly was not any career that I ever thought I would have, but it works for me, and I can't imagine doing anything else."

"Is that what you think I am interested in...how you got here? Heck no, I want to hear all about the other women you left behind. The string must be pretty long?"

"Oh, so you want to dissect my love life? Sorry to disappoint you, but it pales in comparison to yours. I was momentarily engaged to a gal in Australia, but it turned out that she was only interested in becoming a Canadian citizen. She planned on coming home with me and having my child which would keep her here and allow her to bring her true love over. That was a laugh; the child thing I mean. Next one was only looking for a meal ticket and was too much of a drama queen for me. That's it."

"No, it's not! You met Irene and fell madly in love. I'm happy for you Mitch. I'm envious of your wife, and sad that I never found another "you" for myself. I'm going to close my eyes for a bit if you don't mind." She said dismally and turned her head towards the window.

I didn't ask how she knew my wife's name. I wanted to say something comforting, but I couldn't think of anything to say that wouldn't sound sanctimonious so I just put it away for the moment. Instead I told her that she was going to miss the most scenic part of the trip. She replied that she would see it tomorrow. I took that to mean that she was done with talking. I had felt warmth and tenderness from this woman when we met at the convent. She had stirred up feelings of nostalgia in me at the diner. Then she had painted herself as a harlot when she described her love life, and now here she was curled up with her arms wrapped around herself like an abandoned child. I wanted those arms around her to be mine, but the odds of that happening weren't rational. I feared that there were many complicated personalities hiding behind that beautiful face of the woman who was still a young girl to me. I had to remind myself that I was happily married.

Chapter 2
Confessions

I unlocked the door, showed Mayria into the living room and told her to make herself at home while I called my neighbor to tell him that he could send Sadie on home. I laid my cell phone on the coffee table and went out to wait for her. She was already waiting at the door. We greeted each other as usual, rough housing a bit. "Come along, I have another fair damsel for you to meet. I'm sure you'll get on with her just as you did her daughter."

I found Mya punching numbers into my cell. "What are you doing?" I asked a little too stern.

She dropped the phone and backed away. There were tears in her eyes. "I only wanted to call Vali." She sobbed.

I walked over to her and apologised for yelling. "That's not one of the burner phones Mya. I'm sorry, I shouldn't have left mine lying around. Let me get you one of the disposables...do you just want to let Vali know that you arrived safely?"

"I want her to come and get me." She said bluntly.

"Come and get you...what do you mean?"

"I can't stay here."

"Why? I thought we were clear on the reason I wanted you here. What's changed your mind?"

She looked at me blankly. "I can't be here with you."

I sighed. "Oh, I see, it's all coming back to you now isn't it? You were just putting on an act at the convent and restaurant pretending that you were glad to see me, but now that we are alone you are remembering how much you hate me aren't you?"

She tried to look at me but couldn't quite make eye contact. "I promised myself that I wouldn't go back there...back to nineteen eighty six and the day you left me. I guess I've kept it inside for so long and sooner or later I am going to address it, so it may as well be now. I did come pretty close to hating you after it was all over and done with. When I went back to Sommerset I decided to put you out of my life forever. I finally admitted to myself that you had never loved me and you were never coming back for me. I was just one of your many conquests. You had never even tried to contact me, and so I decided to get my revenge instead and marry your best friend. I'm sure you found out somehow, but it didn't matter because you had written all of us off. I should never have asked Vali to ask for your help. I made a mistake. I'm sorry I have wasted your time. Seeing you is much more difficult than I thought it would be. I gave you a pretty bleak but honest picture of myself and my relationship with men. They were all disposable. Maybe I learned that from you as…sorry that isn't fair. I don't want to ruin my memories of my few months with you by lumping you along with all other men, and that is probably what I will end up doing when you disappoint me in one way or the other. I do not want to involve you with my problems after all, so is it okay if I go home?"

What did she mean by after it was 'all over and done with' and she'd gone back to Sommerset? I'd file it away for later.

"No, it is not okay if you go home. I fear for your life. I made the mistake of a lifetime with you once, and I won't make it again. Will you sit down please, and let me try and make amends… thank-you. We can't go forward until we deal with the past. You are my responsibility now…just as you were thirty years ago. I am ashamed of the way I left you. I have no excuse except that stupidity is at the top of the list. You're wrong because I did love you and three weeks after I had left I became painfully aware of how much I missed you. Thirty years later…I guess it's time I came clean; not just for you, but for me also. There is no excuse for the way I left you, but this is how it went down. I didn't give you the full itinerary before. You can shoot me afterwards. My travels had taken me to Constantine Algeria. I couldn't get a flight out of there for three days, and so I hopped aboard a train heading for Algiers hoping to catch an earlier flight home. That was a mistake I have regretted most of my life. I met up with two blokes on the train, one from England, and one from Ireland. We became fast friends and they tried to sway me into going to Australia with them, but I was dead set on heading back to Canada and you. I did join them for a fare well drink after I booked my flight for the next day. To make a long story short, we got involved in a bar-room brawl and spent the next nine months in an Algerian prison. Fortunately for us, we were given leniency, so the judge said, and sent only to a minimum security work prison for six months. It was made clear to us what would happen to us if we tried to escape. The only thing that kept me sane was knowing that you would be waiting for me…egotistical idiot that I was. We were allowed a phone call, but I chose not to call anyone thinking that no news was the proverbial good news thing. It became clear to me later that not contacting anyone was a grave mistake. Our six months turned into nine months anyhow for what reason we never found out. I guess they just liked us."

Mya was struggling with what I had just told her. She started sobbing and wringing her hands.

"It happened, but I did make it back to Sommerset on December the twenty ninth." I said as if that was some solace.

She stuttered. "That…that was the day Bobby and I got married."

I didn't break it to her gently because the way that I saw it was that the truth was the truth no matter how painful it might be. "Yup; I sat at the back of the church and watched my girl say "I do" to my best friend."

She got up and stood looking down at me. Her eyes were on fire. "Liar, you weren't there! You're just saying that to hurt me… to hurt me again…why, why would you say such a thing?"

I tried to take her hands, but she pulled away from me. "I'm sorry Mayria. I couldn't hurt you then, and I certainly don't mean to hurt you now, but it's true, I was there."

She fought back tears. "I do hate you now. If you had of been there, and you loved me like you said you did, you would have spoken up, so I don't believe you!"

"You looked happy and I knew that Bobby could give you everything you deserved. I was just a bum. I not only lost you that day, but I found out my grandmother had died also, so it was a two for one sort of day."

"You came to my wedding, and no one saw you…how could that be?"

"I was careful."

"Things would have been so different if you had only let me know you were coming home and that you still cared for me. I wouldn't have become the ruthless, emotionless person that I am. I have made mistake after mistake, and I won't make another one. I need for you to let me out of this contract before I destroy your life. Please Mitch, if you ever cared for me, do this now before it's too late."

She tried to get up, but I grabbed her hands firmly and pleaded with her.

"Please stay. I doubt very much that you are in any way shape or form the person you describe. I see a beautiful, vibrant woman, and a loving mother. I want to help you and hope that it will make up for some of the hurt I caused you. We may never have lasted together Mya, and I could never have given you the children that you are so dearly devoted to so it all worked out best for you in the long run."

"What are you talking about?"

"I guess that bout I had with the mumps when I was fifteen left its' mark on me. I have never been able to father a child,"

She pulled away from me and stood staring into the dark fireplace. She was trembling.

"You're cold; here let me lay a fire for you." I said gathering a handful of kindling.

"It's okay; I'll go and find a sweater, and I won't be here all that long anyhow."

"I haven't even brought your suitcase in yet, and besides we'll need a fire for later. I very much want you to stay Mayria."

"Maybe you won't want me to if I decide to tell you the real reason why I wanted to hire you."

"There's another reason..." I asked stunned that there could possibly be one.

She stepped back as the fire roared to life. "I just presumed that you and your wife didn't want children; was I wrong?"

"I always thought I would have children, but it never happened. I guess it wasn't important as neither Irene nor I ever did anything about it. I just blamed it on the mumps, and she was all right with that. I can't say that we would have been great parents anyhow as she is always working, and I am up here as often as I can be. I don't know if we would be able to or want to adjust…still there's a void in my life, but it could be something else entirely. My girl Friday has two children and I do enjoy spending time with them. I have to admit that I enjoyed my time with Vali yesterday, and wonder what it would be like to have a teenage…excuse me, young lady like her for a daughter."

"Do you think she looks like me?"

"There is something about her, the eyes, I think. She definitely has your fervour. Something just dawned on me…you said you always just thought that I didn't want to have children…why would you think that, and how would you know that I didn't have any?"

"You would have no way of knowing this, but Bobbie Jr. was born in Toronto. Bobby Sr. had some business to conduct there and I came with him against my doctor's orders of flying so near to my due date. Anyhow, all was well. Bobbie was born in Toronto, and is a Canadian citizen. He always talked about joining the Canadian Armed Forces so we moved to Edmonton Alberta in 2002 where we could hopefully make it all happen. Bobbie was almost fourteen. Although we moved around some for the next four years and went back to the farm in England every summer, he never changed his mind of joining the Canadian Armed forces. In 2006 he was accepted into the Air Force. Every time I found myself in Canada I thought about looking for you, but didn't try very hard as I was sure that you would be happily married with a brood of children. I did find Constance and I did ask her if she had kept in touch with you. At that time she didn't know where you were and I didn't delve further into tracking you down. She thought you might still be in Australia as that was where she had last heard from you. The years went on and then one day I received a letter from her saying she was taking her vows to become a nun. She told me that she had heard from you and that you had married a lawyer and had your own private investigating business, but hadn't seen you. She said she had asked about children and you had said there were none, and never would be. She said she lost touch with you again during her preparation for the Sisterhood. I found your web page and read all about you and your wife, and that was that. It wasn't until three of four years ago when Vali, Frankie, and I moved to Seattle that I decided to check up on you again. You still had no children so I didn't think you would be interested. I decided not to approach you, but then this thing with Brian has come up, and here we are."

"What do you mean by "this thing" with Brian? Are you not taking what happened to you, not once, but three times, seriously? And, what does my not having children have to do with anything? What do you mean when you say I wouldn't be interested…interested in what?"

"I am not afraid of Brian. If he truly wanted me dead, I would be dead, but I am no good to him dead. There is no way he can get his hands on my money unless he wins at proving that I am mentally unfit. I suppose that is a real possibility."

I assured her that wasn't going to happen. I wanted to ask her if they had a pre-nuptial agreement, but decided this was not the right time.

She walked over to the window and stared outside. I had a hundred questions that I wanted to ask her, but I let her have a few minutes to consider whatever it was that she wanted to tell me. She asked if she could have a drink. I figured she meant alcohol so I asked her what her pleasure was. She said anything would do. I went into the kitchen, took down two of my best glasses, filled them with ice and coke, and added a generous amount of rye.

She took the glass from my hand being careful not to touch me. "Did you hear me say that I left Sommerset after you did?"

"Yes; where did you go, and why?"

"Tracie Bond left town about the same time you did, so rumors ran rampart…they've run off together, poor sweet little Mayria, he sure played her for the fool…"

"Jesus Christ Mya… I had no idea. Do you know how much I hate myself right now?"

"There's no need; that's all been taken care of. Anyhow, I had reason of my own to leave."

She emptied her glass and asked for another. I obliged thinking that she must need liquid courage to tell me whatever it was that was making her so edgy.

"I went to my Aunt Ann's on Bowen Island." She said as though it was the obvious thing for her to do.

"The reclusive aunt, the one that your family shunned...why on earth would you go there?"

"You remember that? I went to hide my shame."

"Shame, because of the rumors?"

"No, I wasn't that shallow. My aunt took me in and didn't pass judgement. I guess you might say that we bonded. I'll make this short. I helped her around the farm and she helped me make the biggest decision of my young life. On the morning of August the twenty ninth, twenty nine years and five days ago today, my Aunt bundled me up and put me in her rickety 1950 unlicensed truck. We boarded the ferry, and she took me to a hospital in Vancouver where at six thirty seven that evening I gave birth to a six pound, eight ounce baby girl."

The air seemed to have been sucked out of the room. Mya downed her drink, put the glass down and rubbed her hands together as if she was erasing all signs of what had happened. I was dumbfounded. The silence was deafening. My throat was dry. What should I say? What could I say? She spoke before I could.

"So, you can just erase all that garbage of not being able to father a child. I'd like to get my luggage now and take a shower, or you can just phone Vali to come and get me, your choice, whatever you want."

"A daughter...I have a daughter? You were pregnant when I left? Why didn't you tell me... why, Mayria, why?" I managed to stammer.

"You obviously don't remember what went down that day. I had full intentions of telling you that I was pretty sure that I was pregnant, but you took that out of my hands. You came to my door and called me out unto the porch. You said it wasn't easy for you to tell me what you had to, but you did anyhow. Without any explanation you said you were leaving town and had no idea when, or if, you would ever be coming back. You said I was too good for you, and that I would find someone who was more deserving of me. You kissed me on the cheek, smiled, turned around and walked away. I tried to ask you what had happened, but you just kept walking, and you never looked back. So, even now, twenty nine years later, I don't know what I did to chase you away unless you suspected that I was pregnant, and didn't want to deal with it."

I swallowed hard. "God, no; I had no idea. It wasn't you; you did nothing wrong. I was twenty and had done nothing with my life. I had no ambition, and had no intention of furthering my education. I had a piss poor outlook on the future. My job was menial and I had whittled away at the college fund Gramm Lylah had set up for me. I was petrified that I was going to end up like the rest of Sommerset's misguided youth. I didn't know what to do about you because you were my one ray of sunshine. I fell hard and fast for you. You were never just one of "my conquests" as you so labeled yourself. I convinced myself that it couldn't last and that it was only a matter of time before you came to your senses and left me, so it was better that I get out before it was too late. It was wrong of me, but apparently I was a selfish bastard. Like I said, I came home to make amends, but I was too late, and now you tell me I have or had a daughter. Vali never mentioned a sister, so am I to assume that our daughter didn't make it?"

Her voice softened. "I don't know if she lived Mitch, but I have always believed that she did. Vali and the boys don't know that they may have a sister. No one does. The only person I told was Bobby. He was going to help me find her. That was one of the reasons I pursued him. He had money and connections. I made quick work of that little Miss Midge Field he was dating; another one of your old girlfriends. I guess you guys got your kicks passing us girls around."

"It wasn't like that Mya. I hate that you thought of me like that."

"Oh, I know, boys will be boys."

Her mood went from one of condemnation to grief-stricken. "Doesn't matter, it's all ancient history. Anyhow, Bobby died before we even got started on tracking Lylah Jayne down. I've looked for her for twenty-nine years, and I am still looking. I got to hold her for two minutes...two minutes to wrap her little fingers around my heart. She was so beautiful Mitch. She had dark hair and big brown eyes, and a wayward curl...just like you have. I changed my mind; I couldn't give her up, but the nurse took her from me and placed her in the arms of Thelma and Art Robinson. I called for them to bring my baby back, but I couldn't move. The nurse had given me a tranquilizer. The last thing I remember as they walked out the door was me yelling at them that her name was Lylah Jayne."

"You named her after my grandmother?" I went to her and took her in my arms. I don't ever remember crying before, but I did then. Our tears mingled together as I asked her if that was the real reason she wanted my help. She said it was. I told her that together we were going to find our little Lylah Jayne.

She cried into my shoulder. "I don't see how Mitch. I have nothing to go on. All the papers of consent were lost when my aunt's place burned to the ground, and then she died three months later. I have been told over and over again that I don't have a leg to stand on because I gave up my rights. But, if she wants to find me, then she can. I have been waiting and hoping that her adoptive parents would have told her the truth, but I guess not, or else she just doesn't want to find me. I don't remember what hospital I gave birth in, the nurse's name, or even the adoptive parents name, so I have come to the end of the road. Perhaps I shouldn't have told you because now you are always going to wonder too. I'm sorry, I'm so sorry Mitch...I gave our little girl away to strangers."

I walked her over to the sofa. I wasn't sure if she would ever stop sobbing. I handed her a box of tissues. I lifted her chin and was seduced by her sad emerald green eyes.

"Look at me Sweetheart, there, that's my girl. The adoptive agency hasn't dealt with me yet, and I will stop at nothing to track down Lylah Jayne's records. Hold on...you said you don't remember the names of the adoptive parents...then who are Thelma and Art Robinson?"

"That's their names Mitch!" She said excitedly. "How could you know that?"

"Those are the names of the people who you said walked off with Lylah."

"I haven't been able to recall their names for all these years Mitch...is this good?"

"It is; I'm very proud of you Mya. I'm going to start a name search immediately. Tuesday morning I will have my secretary on it full bore. The agency provided you with counselling didn't they? I have a feeling your parents didn't know?"

"No one knew Mitch. I didn't tell anyone, not even your grandmother. There was no agency; it was a private adoption. Does that make it harder?"

"Maybe just a little. My God Mya, you were just seventeen, and you basically went through this all by yourself..." I was overcome with emotion. "I should have been there for you."

She took my hand and looked into my eyes. "You're here now, aren't you?"

I knew then what I had been rejecting for the past twenty four hours, and that was that I still cared deeply for her. Feelings that come back that fast are feelings that never went away in the first place. I would have to keep all this to myself for a while...if I could.

"Yes, and I am not going anywhere. Now how about that bath? I think it'll relax you."

"I wouldn't have imagined that you would have a bathtub in this," she waved her hands around, "in what you refer to as a *cabin*."

"That's exactly what it was when I bought it twelve years ago. I cleaned it up before I brought Irene to see it. One look at it and she told me that I was plum crazy if I thought for one minute that she would ever spend even one night up here. It was fairly new in our marriage then so I was a tad naïve about her personal requirements. We resided in a noisy small two bedroom town house at the time so I had thought that weekends fixing the cabin up would be a refreshing change from the city, but I was wrong. I went ahead and with the help of a contractor, and Jake and Mel, and it became what you see today."

"It's lovely Mitch; it's very homey and yet cozy. It's to Irene's liking now I assume."

"You would be wrong. She is not an outdoor person unless it is on the deck of a cruise ship. She doesn't like hiking, or sitting around a campfire or roughing it; and that is what life is like here according to her. God, that she would ever cook a hot dog or s'mores over an open fire. There is no dishwasher, or a Jacuzzi, or half a dozen high end restaurants right around the corner. She has come back to check it out but it's still not up to her standards so we usually spend weekends apart, not that our weekdays are much different, I'm up here enjoying the outdoors, and she's in the city working."

"Do you still live in the townhouse?"

"No, we have a sprawling ranch style house which is way too big for two people, but it has a large fenced yard for Sadie so I let Irene talk me into buying it."

"What kind of lawyer is your wife?"

"She's a corporate lawyer."

"Are you happy Mitch?"

I wondered if my voice had conveyed that I was discontented with my marriage, a fact that I hadn't been willing to address until now. "I'm as happy as anyone can be I guess."

"Then I am happy for you Mitch. Thank-you for saying you will help me track down my daughter. For the first time in almost three decades I will be going to bed with hope in my heart." She spoke softly, kissing her fingers and then laying them on my lips.

I smiled. "*Our* daughter." I wanted to kiss more than her finger tips, but didn't. I was through trying to convince myself that I was happily married.

I retrieved Mya's suitcase, overnight case, and the burner phones from the jeep. I knocked on the bathroom door. "Are you decent Mya?"

She laughed huskily. "I've never been decent a day in my life Mitch."

"All righty then; I'll leave your things just inside the door."

Some people like a Scottish, French, or other such brogues, but give me a throaty, sensual woman's voice any day. Hers was a lot deeper than I remembered. I flipped open my laptop and punched in **Thelma and Art Robinson** into the Google "people find" search engine just in case they were a couple of some notoriety. They weren't. Maybe, just one or the other...nope. Okay, I'll try a phone book, but for what city? Suppose if they weren't even from around here? Shit, I needed a lot more information. Hopefully, Mya would be able to provide it.

The bathroom door opened. A somewhat timid Mya stood there wrapped in my terry cloth bathrobe. "I hope you don't mind if I borrow your robe Mitch."

"Hell no." I walked over to her and picked up her bags. She followed me to the guest room.

She wrapped her arms around herself even tighter. "It's cold in here."

I dropped her luggage. "Sorry, the door has been shut all day. I'll turn the space heater on."

"I don't want to stay in here Mitch."

"I didn't mean that you should. Let's get you out by the fire."

"I meant that I don't want to sleep in here…"

"Okay, will you be more comfortable in my room?"

"I will feel safer, but only if you're with me."

"I think I can arrange that."

"I don't mean anything by that Mitch. I'm just…"

"I know," I said, "you're just a little jittery. This isn't exactly the protected area like the convent, but you are in safe hands."

"From the moment I saw you, I felt safe. You know "safe in the arms of love"…oh, I'm sorry; I didn't mean it like that." She exclaimed apologetically.

Could she possibly mean that? I'd give it a shot.

"I've had this stirring deep inside of me ever since Vali told me who her mother was. I tossed and turned all night. Half of me was excited about seeing you while the other half was dreading it because I was afraid I'd see hatred in your eyes. Do you want to hear something funny?"

She smiled and nodded.

"I almost didn't make it inside the convent. I'm pretty confident and nothing much affects me emotionally, but there I was; legs like rubber, and butterflies in my gut. Then I saw you walking down that endless hallway, and all I could think of was that song I used to sing to you. You know "you look so fine, I think I'm losing my mind, obey do, whatever.""

"Oh Mitch, you still don't know the words!" Her laugh was contagious.

The towel she had wrapped around her head fell off. I reached out for it and purposely pushed her hair away from her face. It felt like silk. She placed her hand on mine.

I continued. "And then, you were only a few steps away from me, and you extended your hands to me, and our eyes met. All my doubts and fears washed away. Then we had those moments in the diner just as if it was yesterday. I think I may still know the words to your song Mya. The only question is; do you want me to sing them to you?"

She pulled away from me running her fingers like a comb through her hair. Her voice was low and emotional. "It was yesterday Mitch, yesterday, twenty nine years ago. I'm not that girl anymore. I've been around the block a time or two...hell, who am I kidding...a dozen times."

"Do you think I haven't?"

"It's different for men."

"Like hell it is! Don't tell me that you are of that persuasion that men can get away with anything, but women are judged morally on their choices?"

"Sort of, but because I have always had the means to support myself and the kids, I never went looking for someone to take care of me, or had to stand on a street corner. I fell in and out of love half a dozen times; at least I told myself it was love, but of course it wasn't. I don't have that many scruples Mitch, but I do have one rule...I don't get involved with married men."

"Suppose if you just happen to fall in love with one?"

"I just told you that I really don't know what love is so that isn't going to happen."

I nodded. "Okay, got you. You are in complete control of your feelings. You can turn them on and off like a faucet. Good to know."

"Yes. You and I can be friends, and parents in search of our daughter, but that is all."

"Who said I wanted more?"

"I think your marriage may be a little rocky at the moment, and that maybe you looking for a little excitement outside of the marriage bed, am I right?"

"Apparently you haven't been listening to a thing I said about my life with Irene."

"I have Mitch. You need to put more of an effort into making her understand how important your life up here is."

"How much effort did you put into saving your marriages?"

"They weren't worth saving."

"But you know that mine is? The woman I once loved comes back into my life, and she wants me to look the other way and pretend that neither of us still have feelings for each other. Hell yes, I can do that. Come on, I'll make you something to eat."

ππππ

Chapter 3
Mayria

I followed Mitch into the kitchen feeling like a puppy who had just been reprimanded by her master. Sadie tagged along after me settling down on the scatter rug in front of the sink. She wagged her tail looking up at Mitch. He extracted a slice of ham from the plastic wrap and let her eat it out of his hand telling her that she was a good girl. I didn't have a tail to wag, but I wanted him to reward me and tell me that I was a good girl too, so why was I fighting him?

He placed all the fixings for a sandwich on the table. "Sorry, this is rude of me...perhaps you need something a little more substantial? I could unthaw some meat sauce and put on a pot of spaghetti...why are you looking at me like that?"

"This is fine Mitch as I'm still full from lunch. I'm not used to seeing a man who knows his way around a kitchen."

"Somebody has to do it, and I kind of like to eat."

"I take it that she doesn't cook?" I didn't think it was necessary to say her name.

"Doesn't, tried once or twice early on...big mistake. I understand that you can vegetables."

"I pickle; cucumbers and beets, that's it. There is no hot water baths or pressure cookers involved. I cook if I am so inclined to do so."

"The greenhouse where you grow these veggies almost killed you didn't it?"

"It was no fault of the greenhouse. I only grow cucumbers and tomatoes and flowers. I buy the beets from a farmer."

I smiled as he carefully tipped my glass and funneled a bottle of beer into it. I had just downed two glasses of booze so I asked him if he was trying to get me drunk. He raised his eyebrows and asked me why I would say that.

"That's how you got me into bed the first time isn't it?"

He seemed shocked. "I don't remember it like that."

"Did you think I was easy then Mitch? I can't imagine what you must think of me now." I said pensively.

"I thought you were the most beautiful and amazing girl I had ever met. I came home to find you in my grandmother's house whirring around like a blustery wind. You reprimanded me for being late and left the room implying that it was in my best interest that I should join Lylah for tea. I had never had a cup of tea in my life before, but I did that day. I thought you were rather rude and wondered how my grandmother tolerated it. While you were gone she explained how you had been helping her all summer and said you definitely lived up to your name. By the time I left there I realized that I liked tea, and the girl my grandmother referred to as the girl who had come into her life like a wild, wild, wind which suited you seeing your name was Mayria. She had explained your name to me based on the lyrics of the song. But, back to your question…no, my dear, you were anything but easy. You were tempestuous, just like the rain, fierce as fire, and unpredictable, just like the wind. I have a feeling that nothing much has changed today. I envy and pity all the men who have loved and lost you. Thanks to my stupidity, I am number one on that list I guess.'

He passed me the mustard. I shook my head.

"You still don't like it?"

"No, I don't like it, but I like you Mitch, and I probably still love you." Oh God, I'd said it.

He stared at me. Neither one of us could believe what had just come out of my mouth.

"Why in God's little green acre would you say that? You've been going on about how we can only be parents looking for our daughter, that you never get involved with a married man, and then you do an about face and say you love me…what's up with that Mayria?" He was irked.

"Can't I just say I love you and not mean anything by it?"

"You said "still."

"Well, I did love you once, and maybe there's still a little bit lingering on. I love that you want to help me and that you genuinely want us to find our daughter. I love the interactions that we have been having. I love that you offered to cook for me. I love listening to you speak; your voice captivates me like it always did. You are kind, yet forceful. I have to be careful how much I let you into my life because I cannot go down that road again, and yet, I don't want to leave any door unopened. On second thought I want to take it back; it's in my best interest to take it back. Your wife is crazy for not loving you."

"I don't remember saying that she didn't love me and no **backsies!"**

I smiled. "And, you love her, yet you have basically nothing in common, and I'm assuming not much of a love life?"

"You would assume right."

"Why do you stay in a marriage that isn't satisfying?"

"We share expenses, she isn't hard to look at, that is when I see her, and who wants the hassle of a divorce?"

"Just ask me; I've had two, and heading for a third, and then I might just be looking for a fourth man to marry, and then divorce."

"Anyone in mind?"

"Yup."

"Anyone in particular?"

"As long as he is brawny, has kind eyes, a silver-tongued voice, soft, yet strong hands, and I'm particularly attracted to a man with an unruly curl in the middle of his forehead, and he shouldn't already be married. Most importantly, he must be able to slay dragons."

"Is that all? Are you expecting a dragon to drop by anytime soon?"

"One is always lurking about waiting for me to try and open the yellow door again."

"And, if you do open the door, what might you find behind it?"

"I am not sure. When I was a young girl I dreamt that there was this yellow door that I couldn't open because there was this huge menacing red dragon barring the entrance. I had to see what was behind the door, but I could never get by the beast. Then one day this handsome knight, disguised as a white dragon, came by and had it out with the red dragon, and I was finally able to see what was beyond the door."

"A knight eh…well, don't keep me in suspense, what was behind the yellow door?"

"Love. It didn't last though. I am constantly searching for it again. Every time I think I have found some semblance of it, the door closes again. I guess a first love can never be duplicated if only one of the participants was involved in what was supposed to be an everlasting affair."

"That would be you, because according to you I left town and you, and never looked back. You think I have no memories of you, right?" He asked pushing his chair back. His eyes were cold as he looked down at me.

"I'm sorry; I'm not suggesting that you don't remember me. I just think…"

"Quit thinking for me! And quit batting your long eye lashes, tantalising me with your carnal voice, and suggestively hinting at some sort of tryst. Yet, when I make the smallest suggestion of it you shut me down."

"I don't bat my eyelashes." I said defending my womanly mannerisms.

He laughed brazenly. "You've been flirting with me all day Lady. I defy you to deny it."

"I haven't meant to be."

"Bull; you know exactly what you're doing!"

He stood up and asked me what I had on under my gown and robe.

"What?"

"You know; are you wearing panties?"

I think I blushed. "Yes, why would you want to know that?"

"Because we are going for a walk; that is, if you are all done flirting with me for the moment?"

"Do you consider a little harmless banter flirting?"

"Yup: wait here while I find you some socks and a pair of long pants."

"What?"

He left me sitting at the table wondering where and why he wanted to go for a walk. He returned with a pair of socks, a pair of jogging pants, and knee high boots. He set the boots in front of me, put the socks on my feet and lifted my legs into the pants. I told him that they were too big. He suggested that I lose the housecoat and tuck my nightgown into the pants. He helped me and then pulled the elastic cinch tight. He held onto me while I slipped into the boots. I asked him if they were Irene's boots. He said he had bought them for her, but of course seeing she was never here, they had never been worn. He walked over towards the back door, took a coat off the rack and helped me into it. I couldn't imagine what I looked like. Sadie was sitting at the door wagging her tail.

Outside Mitch instructed me to hold on to him as it had rained the day before and the ground might be slippery. He shone his flashlight in front of us as we descended down a slightly inclined rugged path. A cool fog had invaded the late afternoon air as darkness was quickly setting in. Two minutes later we were in front of what appeared to be a two car garage. Mitch unlocked a small door to the left of it. He flipped a light switch and I found myself looking at the stern of a fairly large boat. The building was not a garage, but a boathouse.

"You got the boat you used to talk about." I commented shivering a little.

"I did."

He led me to the portside and pulled on a tarp until it revealed writing in big bold red letters.

The
Wild Wild Wind

"That's a good name for a boat." I stammered.

"It is. Come along, I want you to see the rest."

Again he took my hand and led me to the starboard where there was a name engraved on it.

Mayria

I was overwhelmed. It was my name, *my* name…I felt like I was going to collapse.

"Well?" Mitch asked as he steadied me.

"It's not my name is it?" I managed to ask.

He laughed. "Of course not; do you think that you're the only Mayria I have ever known?"

"How did you explain it to your wife?"

"She's never seen it, and she never will. She doesn't like the water or boats, unless it's a cruise ship of course. It wouldn't matter if she did anyhow."

"She's never seen your boat? She's never taken a cruise with you?"

"I bought it shortly after we were married. She calls it 'Adam's Folly'. I have to agree as it was a dilapidated piece of junk. I had it towed out here, built the boathouse, and started the labor of love restoring it. I was guaranteed that the mechanicals were in good working order. I guess I will find out when I get her out on the water."

"You haven't tried it out yet?"

"Nope; waiting for a first mate to accompany me."

"Do you have one in mind?"

"A few names come to mind...auditions are still open." He said winking at me.

"How well does it pay?"

"That would depend on her aptitude, but the benefits will be worth her while."

"So, it's going to be a "her"?"

"Most definitely. Come on; let's see if the interior is to your liking."

We walked around the bow and climbed a set of portable steps onto the deck. Mitch turned on the flood lights. I followed him as he toured me from the bow around the narrow walkway to the stern. He said that someday he might consider applying for a license to fish the tidal waters. We ended back at the bridge. I asked for permission to inspect the wheelhouse.

He opened the door. "I'm impressed that you know another word for the navigation house."

"I've been on a few yachts before."

"I bet you have." He said rather Machiavellian-like.

"Just what are you implying?"

"Sorry, I didn't mean anything. I know your third husband had a seafront villa in Spain so I just assumed he would have had a yacht."

"He did, and his hobby was cruising his friends and guests around every weekend. They were nothing but oceanic cocktail parties. Hobnobbing with the privileged and social climbers was not to my liking. I soon tired of it all, collected the children, and moved back to England where I bought a farm. Life was simple there. I should never have left."

"How would we have met up again then?"

"It was inevitable." I ran my hands leisurely over the instrument panel. "Is this all you?"

"Mostly; the dashboard pattern was intact, but everything needed replacing." He sat down on the captain's chair and motioned for me to take the other swivel seat, and asked me what else I would like to know.

I replied that I wanted to know everything.

"It's 10 meters, roughly 32 feet. It's fully loaded so it's classified as a "live aboard boat". The interior is mostly hand crafted wood, the hull is fiberglass. It has twin diesel engines, diesel generator, 50 amp shore power, bus heater and air conditioner, 2 heads and 1 cabin. Can sleep 6- 8 depending on weather and comfort level. Cruising speed is 15 knots with a maximum of 28 knots. Anything else?"

"That's quite sufficient for now. Do I get to see the galley?"

He got up. "Right this way Ma'am."

I followed him out the door and towards the rear again where we descended into the living quarters. The first thing that caught my eye as we reached the bottom was a yellow door to my left. It seemed out of place as I could see into the u-shaped galley and nothing else was painted yellow. It was all light cherry wood with white walls and blue trim. The floor was a blue tile. I asked Mitch what was behind the yellow door. He said I would see later. There were several small skylights and portholes in the galley. It was so much more than I was expecting.

"Who made the cabinets?" I asked expecting for him to say that he had contracted them out to a professional cabinet maker.

"Don't look too close as there are flaws. That corner one was the biggest challenge." He said humbly.

"Mitch, it is all extraordinary! You are so talented. Where did you learn how to do everything?" I exclaimed wandering around the kitchenette opening and shutting cupboards. The table which could be raised or lowered sat in the middle of a cozy blue upholstered seating arrangement. Mitch said that it converted to a double bed. Bunk beds and a lavatory made up the remainder of the room. I marveled at the sea blue tiled floor. I felt like I was walking on water.

"Did you make the bunkbeds too?"

"I did with a little help from Jake and Mel. They helped me with the heavy lifting and were instrumental in the laying of the floor. Is it just wishful thinking that our daughter might come with grandchildren?"

"Oh Mitch! I almost wish I hadn't told you about Lylah Jayne. Now there are two of us agonizing over the possibility that she is alive."

"Don't you ever regret telling me Mayria! I only wish that I had known sooner. I hate that you were all alone for all these years with the angst."

"I had Bobbie and Frankie and Vali so I was never alone. True, our little girl was always in my thoughts, and sometimes it was painful because you were there too." I wiped a tear from my eye.

"I guess thinking of me left a bitter taste in your mouth."

"Not always. Sometimes when I was unusually blue I would conjure you and me living happily together like in a fairy tale."

"Were there dragons?"

"Of course not silly; you banished them all."

"It's pretty obvious that you passed through my mind too or else why would I have named the boat after you? The inscriptions I wanted perfect, and so I found a calligrapher on line. Do you think she did a good job?"

"Yes; everything is just romantically lovely. I will say it again... Irene is a fool. You need to drag her out here and let her see what a craftsman you are!"

His silence and blank look indicated that I had touched a nerve.

I asked if I could see what was behind the yellow door now. Mitch said I wasn't ready and started up the stairs asking me if I was coming.

"What do you mean by saying I'm not ready." I tried turning the knob but it wouldn't budge.

"Why is it locked?"

"It's not locked. I told you that you weren't ready to open it. Come on, you're shivering."

"I don't understand." I said defiantly.

"You will." He said hurrying me along.

I climbed gingerly down the steps grumbling all the way. Mitch waited until I was safely down before he extinguished the lights. I didn't wait for him but walked around the boat mumbling "Good night Mayria, whoever you are." He yelled at me to wait for him but I kept going, stumbling as I climbed the rutted hill. The warm air from the cabin welcomed me as I kicked the boots off. Mitch arrived to find me struggling to unzip the coat.

"Why didn't you wait for me?"

I threw the coat on the floor and stomped off to his bedroom. I sat on the bed and removed the pants and socks and climbed into bed. He appeared at the doorway and asked if it was safe to come in.

"Suit yourself." I said contrarily.

His eyes twinkled as he sat down on the bed. "Are you mad at me?"

"What was your first clue?"

"Is it because you couldn't open the yellow door?"

"Well, obviously there is something in there that you don't want me to see, and it is none of my business anyhow. For all I know you are keeping a woman in there against her will."

"Oh, I want you to see, and you will in due time, three days from now I am hoping." He said in his most charming voice.

"Is that a puzzle that I am supposed to figure out? What does three days have to do with it?"

"We need to get to know each other again, and we need to decide what it is we actually want from each other. I'm hoping that after three days of living together we'll have all the answers."

“What do you mean, living together? Are you suggesting that we stay here?”

“No, I’m moving in with you.”

“Just like that, you’re moving in? How do I explain it to the kids and Brian?”

“It’s a no brainer Mya. You hired me to find proof of his attempts on your life, so what better way to do it then to be living in the house and be your body guard day and night. The kids will be on board. Do you really care what Brian thinks? I’m assuming that you don’t, and that the house has many bedrooms, and that one will be in close vicinity to yours. Surely you didn’t think that I was going to leave you alone?”

“Is this your usual mode of operation…sleeping with your client?”

“Whoa there Sweetheart…who said there was going to be any seduction going on?”

“Wishful thinking I guess.”

“There you go again…conjecturing. Didn’t I just say that we needed time to get to know each other again, and don’t forget that this is also a working arrangement, and you don’t get involved with married men anyway.”

“I see you get to make all the decisions.”

“Only when they involve your safety. Now how about I go and make us the sandwich we never got to eat and a hot drink.”

“My feet are cold.”

He looked at my socks lying on the floor and asked why I took them off.

“They were itchy.”

He said he’d heat me up a towel which he did, and wrapped it around my feet.”

“You never answered my question.”

“What question was that?”

“The one about what or whom you are hiding behind the yellow door.”

He grinned. “Well, I can guarantee you that it is not a dragon. I thought it would be more fun to keep you wondering.”

“I am not wondering; as I said before it really is none of my business.”

"But *you* are my business." He winked and left again.

I could hear noises coming from the kitchen so I got up and listened at the door. Mitch was talking to Sadie as he prepared the sandwiches. "Well, what do you think Girl? You like her eh? What's not to like? Yeah, she's going to be a hand full. I'm not too sure I'll be able to handle her, but I'm going to give it a try. Cripes, you know what this means...I'm going to have to get rid of the dame in the boathouse."

I cupped my hand over my mouth to keep the giggles from escaping and slid back into bed. Mitch returned a few minutes later with our supper and two cups of steaming tea to which he had added a generous amount of brandy. It smelled delicious, and tasted even better. I wanted to tell him that I loved him again.

"Let's talk." He said pulling up a chair close to the bed.

"Okay, about what?"

"First thing is how I am going to pass myself off to Brian. I can't go in as myself, so tell me, does he know all your relatives?"

"Nothing much has changed in thirty years Mitch. He has never met my parents or my sister. In fact I have very little to do with them. Shelley is living in Mexico or Peru with her artist husband and my parents are in a retirement home in Boston. They never call or write. We last visited them four years ago just because I still wanted the kids to know their grandparents. They are just as affectionate to them as they were to me and Shelley, so we are done with that."

"What about your two cousins, the Wilkinson boys? You were close with Peter right?"

"I was, but for all I know he is dead."

"Okay then, Peter it is. I'll be him, your long lost cousin."

"You want me to call you Peter?"

"No, I think it's best if we stick with Mitch. Did anyone in the family ever ask you for financial help?"

"No, I offered, but no one wanted or needed anything so that was fine by me. Are your parents still living Mitch?"

"They are. They moved to Sherbrook to be close to Annette and her family. They are in a retirement facility also."

"Did they come to your wedding?"

"We were married at the courthouse with Irene's lawyer pals as witnesses. I hadn't met Jake or Mel yet, so afraid I had no close buddies at the time. Irene has not been on speaking terms with her family ever since I have known her."

"How sad for us all; it must have been the age we were raised in."

"Maybe, but it's easy to see that you didn't inherit any of your parents lack of nurturing, and I like to believe that I too am capable of that kind of devotion."

"My children are my world Mitch. I don't know how I could have done what I did..." I drifted off because I knew I couldn't say what was really on my mind, but Mitch had caught the inflection in my voice.

"Could have done what Mayria?"

"Lots of things, but mostly for being such a middle-aged fool and taking one last stab at finding happiness with a man I wasn't in love with."

"I hope that's not your final decision regarding love Mya."

I smiled and asked him if I could call a friend. He leaned forward. "Always, my Dear. Now, let's discuss poisons."

"What about them?"

"What side- affects do you have from them?"

"I don't have any."

"You don't have any...I find that hard to believe."

"Well, you can believe it. I am perfectly healthy. I have blood tests done every other week to prove it. My hair has all grown back; I don't have constant headaches or leg pains anymore. My appetite is good, and I sleep fairly well. How do I look to you?"

"Pretty damn good I must say. For someone who has endured two different poisonings and a fall down a flight of stairs you don't appear to have any visual or emotional scarring. You seem to be unconcerned about the possibility of some of these symptoms reappearing...why is that?"

"The "poisoner" knew exactly what my body could tolerate. I wasn't meant to die...only to suffer. There is no possibility of me ingesting or inhaling any of those substances ever again."

"I'll be keeping an eye on you for any signs of disturbance in your psyche. How about pain pills...are you still taking them?"

"Then you are going to be a very busy man for I have many temperaments, and no, I take nothing stronger than a Tylenol."

"That brings us back to the subject of you and me. It's pretty obvious that we still have feelings for each other. I'm not wrong about that am I?"

"I've told you that I loved you, and that I wanted to be your first mate, so that should tell you how I feel."

"When did you tell me that you wanted to be my first mate?"

"I don't remember; on the boat maybe, or maybe I just inferred it."

"Well, it's in the record books now, and I shall hold you to it unless after three days you find that you can't stand the sight of me."

"That's not going to happen Mitch. The house is plenty big, and if I so desire to get away from you I can. When was the first time you thought that you may still have feelings for me?"

"I guess they never went away. Why else would I have named my boat after you? For certain it was the minute Vali said your name. As I said before the anticipation of seeing you was unnerving, but then I saw your face..."

I covered my mouth to keep the laughter in.

"Don't worry; I'm not going to sing. I gave that up years ago. I never had the desire to sing to anyone else."

"I hardly doubt that."

"It's true, but all the songs are still in my head, and I think I still know the words to *yours.*"

My laughter immediately turned to blubbering.

"Hey," Mitch said, "don't cry."

"Then quit saying things like that." I said sniffling.

"It's the truth Mya. Anything I tell you is truthful; I will not lie to you."

"I'll try to be honest with you too Mitch."

"Are you saying that you haven't been so far?"

"Pretty much, but there are always things that should be kept secret."

The phone rang. Mitch ran to answer it.

"It's Vali." I said. I listened, but couldn't make out the conversation. Mitch returned and said that it was the landline and not the burner phone. His neighbour had called to check up on him as he had seen lights on in the boathouse.

Just as Mitch sat down, the phone boomed again. It was a harsher jingle. "Where the hell is it?" Mitch yelled as he ran to find the phone. I heard him swear and then a strange conversation as he returned limping to the bedroom. The phone was on speaker.

"Yes, you heard me swearing. I stubbed my toe looking for the damn phone."

"Why didn't you have it with you…where were you?" Vali questioned.

"In the bedroom." Mitch was shaking his head.

"Where is Mom?"

"In the bedroom."

"Why are you in the bedroom…Mitch, what's going on?"

He passed me the phone smirking.

"Hi Sweetie, how are you? Has Frankie's plane landed?"

"Mom, are you with Mitch?"

"You know I am Vali."

"You know what I mean Mom."

"Actually, I don't."

"I'll spell it out then…are you and Mitch in bed together?"

I was feeling mischievous. "Not yet Dear."

"MOM! Put Mitch back on the phone."

He looked at me coolly and whispered, "Thanks a lot."

He took the handset form me. "Your mother is being facetious. We are just sitting here making plans. Your mother was cold so she is in bed with a warm towel on her feet. Anything else?"

"Take me off speaker Mitch."

I shook my head.

"There, are you happy now?" He said winking several times.

"She's very vulnerable Mitch. Please don't promise her anything you can't deliver. I know you two have a very complicated past, but its best if you leave it at that for now, okay?"

"You can rest easy Vali; I will not do anything to hurt your mother. We are sorting through our feelings. It will take some time, but whatever the outcome is it will be consensual. Right now we are just enjoying each other's company. You will be able to witness the unfolding of our relationship with your own eyes. Are you good with that?"

"For now."

"Good girl; what did Jake uncover at the house?"

"Nothing; he said that he couldn't detect any bugs. He and Shane are setting up surveillance in and around the house."

"How did you get to the airport?"

"A funny little fellow brought me and is sitting a few feet away from me."

Mitch laughed. "Must be Poco; he's a good lad. I'll pass you back to your mother so you can say good night and tell her you love her."

"Thanks Dad, I'll do that." Vali said cheekily.

Mitch passed the phone back to me. "Give Frankie a hug for me. I'll see you all tomorrow...Mitch says before noon. Love you."

I apologised to Mitch about her innuendos. He replied saying that she was my daughter and had the right to be concerned about my well-being.

"She already assumes that we are sleeping together so..." I teased.

He left the room and returned with an oversized pillow and placed it in the middle of the bed.

"There that ought to keep you on your own side." He smirked.

"Very funny. Do I at least get a good night kiss?"

He gave me a quick peck on my forehead. I asked him if that was what he called a kiss these days. He said it was as much as he dared. He retreated to his side of the bed. I asked where Sadie was and he said she was sleeping by the fire in the living room. We talked a little about nonsensical things before we both drifted off.

My dream had ended. I glanced at the radio clock. It was three a.m. I knew exactly where I was. I turned over and threw the pillow that had been separating Mitch and me on the floor and cuddled up to him gently placing my arm around his midriff. He raised it up and kissed my hand and told me to behave myself. I said I would.

I awakened to a wet nose nudging my hand. Two little brown eyes were staring at me. Standing behind her was another set of brown eyes. In his hand was a steaming cup of coffee.

I sat up and took the cup from him. "I like your alarm clock." I said smiling.

"Yeah, I do too. Are you comfortable there on my side of the bed?" He asked grinning.

"I am, and I was."

"Good. Now drink up, have a shower; breakfast will be ready when you get out."

I scurried out of bed, wrapped his robe around me and slipped my feet into some very large slippers he had set out for me. I followed him and Sadie into the kitchen.

"I don't eat breakfast Mitch."

"You do now."

"Mitch…"

"Skedaddle now, times a wasting." He said pointing me towards the bathroom.

I looked down at Sadie asking her for help, but she only wagged her tail. Mitch snickered. Just before I closed the bathroom door I heard him whisper to her that it was a damn good thing that he had locked the yellow door.

I quickly showered without washing my hair. I had forgotten to bring clothes in with me so returned to Mitch's bedroom and rustled through my suitcase not remembering what I had packed for my stay at the convent. I pulled out an oversized white blouse and rust colored ankle length skirt. It would have to do. I arrived back in the kitchen to find Mitch ladling an egg out of a pot of boiling water. He placed it in a little glass and set it in front of me.

"Sorry I don't have any egg cups but this shot glass seems to do the trick." He quipped as he proceeded to cut up two pieces of nicely browned toast into diagonal strips. He placed them on a small plate, passed me the pepper, and placed it all next to the egg. Then he poured me a glass of orange juice and sat down to his own breakfast of scrambled eggs.

"It's been thirty years Mitch." I blubbered.

He placed his hand on mine. "Somethings a man never forgets."

"I could have had scrambled you know."

"No, you couldn't have. Do you think you have room for one more?"

"I think you should give it to the damsel you are holding captive in the boathouse."

Mitch's eyes were wide with amusement. "Damn it, I knew I couldn't get away with anything with that dog around."

We arrived at Artie's sprawling establishment at nine thirty. It was situated in the hub of an industrial part of the city that I didn't know existed. It was basically hidden from view from the street by a circumference of Lombardy poplars and a six foot high fence which I was sure was electrified. Mitch pulled up to a locked gate and punched in a code mumbling that he guessed Artie wasn't up yet. He parked alongside a white Cadillac at the back of the building. There were a few dozen other vehicles parked further up the yard. Mitch instructed me to stay in the jeep with Sadie. He said he'd only be five minutes. I asked why I had to stay behind.

"Because I asked you to, that's why." He answered.

"I don't feel safe here." I retorted.

"You are safer here than anywhere else. Just do as I ask please."

I crossed my arms in compliance. "Yes Sir. I liked you a lot better this morning."

"Nothing has changed Mya; I'll be right back. Do you want me to lock the doors?"

"No thanks, I've seen this movie before."

He looked at me quizzically. I motioned for him to go. I watched him enter the building by a side door which also had a code lock. Damn. I got out anyhow hoping that it was the same code that I had seen him punch in at the gate. Just for fun, I pushed on the door, and to my surprise, it opened. I found myself inside an immaculate structure composed of everything related to a mechanical business. I must have triggered an alarm because a shrill siren was threatening to deafen me. Sadie was howling. A door opened and Mitch came out shaking his head.

"Whatever made me think that you would stay put?" He scolded as he walked past me and reset the alarm.

"Jesus Christ Mitch!" A voice bellowed from another door.

I gathered that it was Artie. He was a white haired man of about sixty attired in sloppy overalls. He did not have a shirt on underneath. A middle-aged woman with flaming reddish hair dressed in a flimsy red nightgown and peignoir joined him. She towered above him. I was pretty sure I was looking at a "Lady of the evening." As she descended down the stairs I saw that she hadfurry blue heeled mules on her feet. She walked straight over to Mitch and threw her arms around him. She was very bosomy.

"Mitch, you old scallywag; where have you been? I see you've been holding out on us!" She said turning and summing me up.

"Sorry we disturbed your Sunday morning Doll." Mitch looked accusingly at me.

I felt my face flushing. He asked this woman he had called Doll to take me off his hands for a few minutes while he finished up with Artie. He then proceeded to introduce me as Mya, to his friends. I managed to say a curt hello and apologised for setting the alarm off. I glared at Mitch saying I would wait in the jeep.

He grabbed my arm as I stormed past him. "I shouldn't have left you alone Mya...please just go with Doll."

"Do you know how tired I am of you ordering me around?" I said harshly.

"I do. I'll make it up to you I promise. Look after her for me Doll." He wiped a tear from the corner of my eye.

I felt an arm around me. "Let's let the men do their thing Honey. Come, I have a fresh pot of coffee brewing."

I snivelled and followed Doll. There was a fully modern apartment on the other side of two more doors. I couldn't decide whether it was a trailer or a modular home. It was immaculate just as the garage was. It definitely had a feminine touch. Was I wrong...were these two in a permanent relationship? I scolded myself for thinking that she was a prostitute.

"This is quite a treat Mya...Mitch bringing a lady here I mean. I know you are not his wife as I have met her. Well, actually I didn't meet her, just had the occasion to observe her once while I was at the court house to pay a fine. And, you sure aren't her Honey!"

She placed a dainty cup in front of me and offered sugar and cream. I shook my head "no." I explained that Mitch and I were just friends and that he was doing some routine work for me.

"Work that requires a false identification, surveillance equipment, a run-down jalopy...yeah, routine, my ass. Excuse the French. I know every case that Mitch has ever worked on and never have I heard the anxiety in his voice as I did on the phone yesterday, and **NEVER** has he brought a beautiful woman here... so what's the scoop?"

"If I had of stayed in the vehicle you would never have seen me..."

"Aah, but I did, and I saw the way he looked at you. Are you denying that there is something going on between the two of you?"

"He's married, and so am I."

She laughed heartily. "As if that makes any difference. Are you by any chance pregnant?"

"No; why would you even ask such a question?" I was a little insulted.

"I guess by the oversized clothes you are wearing...so dowdy for such a pretty lass."

"They are my convent clothes." I answered sharply. Who was this woman anyhow to assume that I was pregnant?

"Oh, my God, you can't be that nun friend of Mitch's?"

"You know about Connie?"

"Connie?"

"Sister Constance; and I can assure you that I am definitely not her."

"Mitch has mentioned her; sorry again."

Doll got up and placed a large plate of freshly baked muffins in front of me. I thanked her and said I wasn't hungry as Mitch had made breakfast. Again, I got the inquisitive eye.

"It appears as if he tells you everything so I may as well admit that I spent the night at his cottage. We haven't seen each other in thirty years. We probably would never have met up with each other ever again, but I got myself into a bit of a mess with my husband, so my daughter hired Mitch to help me. He took me up country because he didn't have all the particulars of my case and thought I might be in danger. We spent the night talking, and now here we are. That's it, there is no more."

"So, where to from here; is he putting you in protective custody?"

"So to speak I guess. He's moving in with me and my family until he digs up some damaging information on my husband. Jake is also staying at the house." I added that so she would think that Mitch's staying with me wasn't something else.

"Well my dear, you are in very good hands. Mya, is that short for something?'

Without thinking, I said it was actually Mayria, but Mitch had always called me Mya.

Doll stared at me for a moment. Then she got up, went to the door, crossed over to the other door that led into the shop, opened it and yelled. "Get in here you two...right now!"

I had no idea what was going on with her. Mitch arrived breathless. He looked at me.

"What the hell Doll? Are you trying to give me a heart attack?"

Artie arrived and said the same thing. Doll asked him if he knew who I was. He said "Yeah, Mitch's new client, Mya."

"You fool! She's not Mya, she's Mayria... Mayria, from the boat! You know; the wild, wild wind Mayria!"

"No shittin..." Artie slapped Mitch on the back.

I glared at Mitch and then turned my best smile on for Doll and Artie wondering why I had volunteered so much info. "I think you are both reading too much into the name. Mitch assured me that I am not the only Mayria he has known. It was a pleasure to meet friends of his. Thank you for the hospitality Doll. It's time to get me home Mitch."

"You are so welcome, but we haven't really had time to get to know you....can't you stay just a little longer?' Doll probed.

I shook my head no.

Mitch thanked them and said he would be in touch in a few days.

I was already heading for the door where I had set the alarm off when Mitch caught up to me.

"Wrong door Hon." He said pointing to another door on the far side of the garage.

"How many damn doors are there in this building anyhow?" I shouted.

I had no idea why I felt like crying.

Chapter 4

The House on Marlborro

I opened the passenger door for Mayria, and the back door for Sadie of the 1959 Chevy coup. Neither of them budged. I knew that Mya was peeved at me, but Sadie never failed to jump in a vehicle even if she wasn't invited. Mya walked around me and proceeded to get into the back seat. Sadie willingly followed her.

"I may as well get my money's worth and take up your limousine service seeing you are already in my hire. 211 Marlborro Drive please, and be light with the gas Sir."

I closed her door tipping my non- existent hat. "At your service Ma'am."

We had only gone a few blocks when she asked me if I had a gun. I glanced at her in the mirror and told her I had several. She asked me why.

"I have a shot gun which I purchased to scare rodents at the cabin. Turns out Sadie and the vagrant cat are the only deterrents I needed. I have a 30 odd 30, a hunting rifle given to be by an old miner up the valley, and a Smith and Wesson semi- automatic hand gun."

"Are you carrying?"

I grinned. "No, I'm not."

"I would feel much better if you were."

"I thought you weren't afraid of Brian."

"I'm not; it's for your safety."

I could hear the trepidation in her voice and thought I had better squash her concerns before we reached the house. I pulled into a used car lot, climbed out, and opened the back door and coaxed her out, and into my arms. She broke into tears.

"I'm sorry Mitch; I didn't mean for them to know who I am. I'm sorry, I said too much."

"I'm pretty sure that they already knew Honey."

"How...why...who else knows my name is on your boat?"

"Originally, just Shannon and Mel. There was no way they were ever going to meet you so...I guess I had to tell someone why I named the boat Mayria, and they are two of my best friends. Doll and Artie showed up unannounced one day when I was at the boathouse and saw the name. I did not elaborate; just said that the name was romantic. I guess they put two and two together when they saw us together. No harm done Honey."

"But, we are not together Mitch, and we may never be. I know what I want because I have known for a very long time, but it's all new to you, and I don't love Brian, but I am pretty sure that you love Irene..."

"Whoa there...what I feel for you is not new. Yes, I do have feelings for Irene because I wouldn't have stayed with her this long if there wasn't something there, but she has never set my heart on fire like you do. I've only been with you for one day and I know it is you I want to spend the rest of my life with. I won't settle for mediocre anymore. I'm *in* love with you. I want us to take all these wild and intense feelings to the limit. From the moment Vali spoke your name I experienced an excitement that overpowered me. Please just give me these few days to make things right; can you do that Mya?"

"Three days, three weeks or three months; it's all for naught anyhow."

"What are you saying?"

She pulled herself away from me. "It's all just a dream Mitch; a crazy dream. I know you are not going to leave your beautiful, elegant and intelligent wife for someone like me. I bet she's athletic too. I don't know what possessed me to even consider that you might want to have some sort of life with me. Lordy," she smacked herself on the forehead, "where is my head anyway? Did I expect that you could just pick up again after thirty years with this dowdy ole woman?" Her laughter was ugly.

"I have just told you that I am in love with you...what is it that you don't understand? You're right; I don't know where your head is. Where is the girl who said she wanted to be my first mate and cuddled up to me in the middle of the night? And, don't ever put yourself down...you know the old saying that no one can hold a candle to you...well, it's true; no one can. You are more beautiful than you were at seventeen, and brains, come on; you are gifted in so many ways. Do you think I don't love you because

I didn't made love to you last night? Do you think I didn't, and don't want to? Keeping my distance from you, is, and will be the hardest thing I have ever had to do, but I am also respectful of your rule."

"I don't have any rules."

"Remember, you don't get involved with married men."

"Well, that rule is all shot to hell pretty much isn't it? You will always be married so I guess I'll take my chances that you won't break my heart too badly."

"I'm not always going to be married Mya, and I sure as hell don't plan on breaking your heart. We just need to let things unfold. Are you going to be patient for these three days?"

"I'll try, but I'm afraid that at the end of three days, you won't want me."

"Suppose if it's you who won't want me?"

"Then you had better take advantage of me right now."

I laughed. "Oh Honey, if I was only agile and devil-may-care like I was thirty years ago…"

"I'm sure you are still agile, and hopefully, still have a little devil left in you."

"Then put your fears and tears aside and come and sit with me in the front; it's a bench seat you know so you can get as close as you want, and I can still drive with one hand."

She chose not to sit close to me, and said it was best if we just move on to her house at 211 Marlborro. I asked her for directions. She said she couldn't help me as she had no idea where we were. I turned around and drove back to the main thoroughfare. She didn't recognise anything. I figured she was just being obstinate and told her so. She said she didn't drive so she never paid attention to anything. I asked her to call Jake and get directions, but all of a sudden she knew where we were and proceeded to direct me. I swear we passed the same shopping mall twice but didn't say anything. Finally, Marlborro Drive was before us. I asked her which way, right or left. She told me to guess.

"Quit playing games with me Mya." I warned her angrily. "I thought we just had this all settled. Make up your mind once and for all; do you want me or not? Do you want my help or not? Tell me now before I get anymore invested in you. I can just as easily turn around again and go back to the cabin, or I can drop you off right here and let you fend for yourself…"

"I think that would be best. You won't have to get your hands dirty then."

"They are already tainted with temptation of adultery, so no worries in that department."

I made an uneducated guess and turned left. Mya did not correct me. A minute later I pulled up to an open wrought iron gate at 211 Marlborro. I asked Mya why it was open. She replied that it always was. I said that would be my first task then to make sure that everyone knew that it must be locked at all times. I got out and examined the situation. The gateway pillars did not have a security device of any sort. I asked her if it was broken. She replied that there never was one as the neighbour was safe.

"Okay, a safety catch will have to do until we can have a proper functioning system installed. I'll put a call into Artie from the house."

"Is there anything that man doesn't do?" She said sarcastically.

"Not that I know of."

"I think you are being over cautious."

"You do eh? What's with you wanting me to carry a gun all about then?"

"I'll agree to the security system if you agree to carry a gun."

I wanted to shake her. "One minute you appear not to care about anything, especially me, and then the next you pretend to be worried about my safety. I'm at my wits end with you Girl."

"I'm not pretending Mitch. I'm just safeguarding myself against failure."

"You don't think I can protect you do you?"

"It's not that." She turned her head away.

"Then what?"

"You and me; I'm afraid we will crash and burn, and I will be left dejected again. I'm not stable enough to endure another heartache."

"Look at me Mya. It's time you quit doubting me and believe in my love for you. It's not going away so quit trying to discourage me. Nothing I say seems to register with you. Have you forgot about our daughter?"

"Never!"

"Okay then, let's get on with the plan. Quit worrying about my safety. I'm pretty good at what I do, and I'm not going to walk around with a gun stuck in the back of my pants like the cops and gangsters on television. I'm not going to wear a holster or a bandolier, so where do you suggest I put it?"

"You're a detective so I'm sure you will think of something." She got out of the car gesturing me to park behind the yellow convertible.

I had the sinking feeling that we should never have left the solitude of Niagara. I caught up to her at the back door of her stately home. "So, this is how the other half lives." I remarked.

"I'm pretty sure you're already living that life Mitch."

"Before we go in I need to hear you say that you love me."

"None of this would be so hard if I didn't love you. I'm sorry I am such a conundrum."

"I love you just the way you are even though you are driving me crazy."

She kissed me hard, and then quickly pulled away and opened the door into a very large entryway. I said that Sadie would be very comfortable here. Mya bent down and proceeded to wipe Sadie's feet, one at a time on a scatter rug.

"She is welcome anywhere in the house."

"And, you will be here to wipe her feet every time she comes in?"

"No silly; she'll learn to do it herself.

I laughed. We walked in to four pairs of eyes smiling or questioning; I couldn't tell which. They were all sitting at a large table in the kitchen. Vali was the first to get up to greet us.

"Well, how did the rest of the night go for you two?" She asked cheekily.

"My virginity is still intact if that's what you are wondering." Mya replied brazenly.

I just shook my head, but was not one bit embarrassed by her audacity.

Vali laughed as did the woman whom I figured was Ivy, Mya's best "everything". She kind of hugged me. Then I was introduced to Frankie. He shook my hand.

"It's a pleasure Sir." He bent down and said hello to Sadie. "A little bird told me your name, and you are most welcome to live here Sadie Dog." He turned back to me. "I see you have already been introduced to Mom's mettle Mitch. I hope you won't hold that against her."

I wanted to reply that wasn't what I wanted to hold against her at all, but smiled instead and replied that I was slowly getting used to her chutzpah.

"I understand from Vali that you and Mom had some sort of romantic relationship a long time ago that may have ended catastrophically ...was she as sassy then as she is now?"

"So your sister has been telling tales out of school again I see. Well, let me tell you..."

I interrupted Mya. "No, let me reply to this because you will just undermine our involvement with each other. I will be as honest as I can be. Thirty some odd years ago we fell in love. We were young, but very much in love. Your mother was tempestuous even then... yet somewhat shy at the same time. I had never met anyone like her. She was just as gracious and beautiful then as she is now. It was me, and me alone that sabotaged our relationship. Our two worlds have collided over the last twenty four hours. We have discovered that we still have feelings for each other, and I think she may have forgiven me." I took her hand and surprisingly, she didn't pull away. "Before we can move forward and dwell into these renewed emotions we have a lot to contend with so we are respecting each other's boundaries." I hoped that only I could hear Mayria snicker under her breath. "As you all know I'm here to protect her, and hopefully find some proof that Brian has attempted several times to kill her so he will be forced to agree to an amicable divorce. I am also married, so anticipating the same result. The most important thing though is keeping her safe. I think we all agree on that. The rest will all work out, I am confident of that. We may have been separated for thirty years, but our feelings for each other never went away, so please be patient with us, and we hope you will give us your blessings. I can't very well be presented to Brian as a PI, so from now on I will be known as Mitch Wilkinson, Mya's cousin. I will be living here if that is all right with all of you. Any questions?"

"I feel safe here with Jake and Frankie, but having you here Mitch just doubles that, and Mom needs you. It ought to be fun watching you two keep your distance from each other though, so good luck with that." Vali chuckled. "But, I for one will be cheering for you."

Frankie stepped forward, winked at his mom, and shook my hand again. "Sounds good to me. We are amateurs at this sleuthing thing so look forward to your guidance Mitch. So far you're looking pretty good in my eyes. I wish you luck in taming Mom, and keeping her under wraps."

Mya smacked him lovingly and smiled at me. "I'm not sure what you mean by that Frankie. You should know Mitch that my sons think I'm the black widow of romance, so I guess time will tell if you are going to be the next victim in my labyrinth of victims."

"I think I will take my chances, but thanks for the warnings. Now, how about that tour of the house that you promised me?"

"Not before I fix you something to eat." Ivy quipped.

"Mitch made breakfast, so we are good Ivy." Mya stated.

"But you never eat breakfast..." Both Ivy and Vali said in unison.

"Yeah, well I was coerced, and I wasn't going to let the dame in the boathouse get both perfectly cooked soft boiled eggs. Are you coming Mitch?" Mya teased me propelling me out of the homey kitchen.

I turned around shrugging my shoulders like I had no idea what she was talking about to the four faces staring at us. "See you in a bit guys; looking forward to comparing notes with you and Jake, Frankie.'

The house was as I had expected, large and tastefully decorated which I assumed was all Mya's undertaking. She ushered me from room to room not pointing out anything of significance. She just stated that this was the dining room, the den, Ivy's room, or

Brian's office which Frankie had taken over for the time being. She had a little more to say about the living room.

"Brian calls it The Great Room. It's great all right; so enormous that if you took all the furnishings out you would have a dance hall. By the way, I had nothing much to do with the decorating or choosing of furniture. I have wanted to move stuff around to make a cozier sitting room, but just never got around to it. I'm hardly ever in here anyhow; there is no reason to be."

"I agree, it's rather baroque. I think we will be spending quite a bit of time relaxing here with everyone so just tell me how you want it arranged and it will be done."

She smiled graciously, and pointed to sofas and small tables and said that should be all that was needed, and that she would work with me later on the new arrangement. The formal front entrance came next. It was out through two heavily curtained French doors at the north side of the living room. She unlocked the glass doors and we stepped into a long corridor. Mya said only people who didn't know any better used the front doors. I wasn't quite sure what she meant by that. Near the end of the hallway was a set of stairs and a side door. Mya explained that it was a private entrance to the suite that Jake had set headquarters up in.

She reversed direction. I followed her back through the living room and the round room, for lack of a better word. It was a lobby-like room in the middle of the house. It was empty except for a large table with a humungous vase of fresh flowers adorning it. Mya called it "a round-about" as it was a directional to all the other rooms. Mya started up the stairs to the bedrooms.

"Just a second," I stopped her, "what's that room back there behind the stairs?"

"Perhaps it's a secret room."

"Secret or not, I still need to see it, and then we'll tour the basement."

"I don't go into the basement. There is nothing there but a games room and two bedrooms and a tiny workshop."

"Why don't you ever go down there?"

"I don't like it, and I don't play games."

"Good enough; now the secret room please."

She started up the stairs saying she didn't have the key on her.

"You don't play games eh?"

She ignored me. At the top of the stairs she pointed down the hall. "The last room is Vali's and the hall that veers off to the right is the inside entrance to the suite. The next two bedrooms are Frankie's and Bobbie's, and this is the master." She opened a solid wood door into a massive room with one king sized bed. She shut the door quickly and we moved on to the next door.

"This is my room. If you like you can have the end one next to me. It views out onto the street which you might like for viewing. It does share a lavatory with my room, but I will use the one that connects with Brian's room. You may choose one of the bedrooms in the basement if you like. That's the end of the tour." She said curtly.

I put my hand gently on her shoulder. "What's wrong Honey; have I said something wrong?"

She placed her hand on top of mine. "No, it's not you, it's this house. I hate it."

"It's a lovely house Mya; it's just not a home yet. We can make it into one, don't you think? Your kids are here, and you and me; that's the important thing, and that we're together again. How about a little kiss before I meet up with the kids?"

She brushed my hand off her shoulder and reprimanded me. "You made the rules Mitch so play by them!"

I told her that I loved her as she walked away from me and that I was definitely taking the room next to hers. She gave me a "thumbs up" over her shoulder. I glanced into the room that was going to be mine and the bathroom that I would be sharing with her. Both entrance doors to it had locks. I took comfort that Mya had referred to the bedrooms as his and hers. I caught a glimpse of her entering the secret room as I descended the stairs.

I sought out Frankie mulling over papers in Brian's office. He shook his head indicating that he had found nothing of interest. We joined Vali and Jake in the rec room. They had nothing to add. The search of the house, upstairs and down, and even the attic didn't reveal any suspicious activities that could incriminate Brian.

"There has to be something somewhere guys...what are we missing?" I queried.

"His business offices I guess." Vali offered.

"Yes, I have been thinking about that. I suppose they won't be open seeing that tomorrow is a holiday will they?"

"I can't speak for the industrial office on Mackenzie, but I know for sure that his uptown office won't be open because his secretary told me so."

"When did you have occasion to talk to her?" I asked.

"She came by to visit Mom in the hospital. I think Brian had her keeping an eye on Mom."

"Is she loyal to him?"

"I think she has a crush on him...why, I don't know, so yes, I think she is loyal."

"So it will be a fight to get her to open up his office for us? Does *she* have a name?"

"It's Carmen, and there is no way that she will unlock his door for us. I hardly doubt that much business is conducted there anyhow."

"Maybe not, but we need to check it out. Would she open the door for Mya?" I asked.

"Talking about me are you?" We all turned our heads. Mya was sitting halfway down the stairs. "What exactly am I the topic of?"

I got up and walked towards her. "We were just wondering if Carmen would let you into Brian's downtown office. So far nothing is showing up here on his computer, so he may have all his transactions on one at the office." I sat down beside her. "If not I guess Jake and I will have to case the place and decide how to break in. How tight is the security in the building? I really don't want to wait until Tuesday and take our chances with Carmen, so perhaps tonight would be a good time to go and chat up the sentinel if there is one. What do you think?"

She seemed to be pondering the thought. No one spoke. After a minute she eyeballed at me and nodded. "I've always wanted to be in on a clandestine mission so yes, let's go."

Before I could protest she put her finger to my lips. "I believe I know all the guards and they know me, so it won't be all that secret, so not to worry about getting caught. The elevator is locked on holidays and weekends. The office doors will also be locked, but the same ID card opens them all so a break-in won't be necessary."

She was smiling mischievously when I asked her if she was saying she had a key, and why didn't she tell anyone. She brushed herself off and rose.

"No one asked. I'm going to take Sadie for a walk and introduce her to the neighbourhood. See you all later."

"Hold on one minute young lady; you are not going anywhere without me!" I said loudly and affirmatively.

"Well, you had better bring your gun because it is a pretty rough neighbourhood." She flounced off up the stairs.

Jake was laughing. "Just holler if you need any help Boss. Meanwhile we'll formulate our plan for later."

We arrived at the Davis Block a few minutes before midnight. Mya, unbeknownst to any of us, had brought a flask of whiskey with her. She passed it around and told us all to take a generous sip before we got out of the car. I asked her what that was all about. She said we'd see. I was not one to refuse a swig of aged Scottish spirits. The rest of our merry little band followed suit. Mya did not imbibe. We followed her inside the building and up to where a watchman sat at a desk in front of a dozen or so computer screens. He turned when he heard us.

"Well, hello there Mrs. Fulton, what brings you out so late on a holiday weekend?"

"It is not of my doing Carl, but these well-oiled relatives of mine..." she turned to us, "stand back, your breath is most offensive...sorry Carl. Anyhow they insist upon seeing our offices; why I can't imagine as there is nothing to see, but I'm tired of arguing, so here we are. Do you want me to sign in? Her voice was soft as black silk.

Carl laughed and said that it wasn't necessary and wished her good luck. He said he would unlock the elevator. She said there was no need, and produced a key card. Then she gave him a know-it-all wink. I swallowed hard. Damn that girl; flirting was supposed to be reserved for me. Inside the elevator Vali asked her mother why she looked so self-satisfied.

"I'm sure I have no idea what you are implying. I have every right to be here you know." She pushed the button for the fourth floor.

We stepped out of the elevator and stopped to read the information panel of business offices.

"When did your name get added to the business Mom?" Vali asked curiously.

Mya didn't answer as she was already halfway down the hall. We joined her as she was entering her key card into the offices of Brian and Tessa Fulton Enterprises. There were several sub headings. The one that caught my eye was 'Specializing in Chemical Manufacturing'.

"Have at it kids." She said opening the inner office, and then sitting down at the desk whose name plate said Carmen Santos. She motioned me to pull a chair alongside of her.

I asked her what she was looking for.

"Well, I am pretty sure that Ms. Santos is having an affair with my husband, so if all else fails I can use infidelity as my reason for suing for divorce. You can go through all the drawers and the file cabinet while I check the computer."

"It would help if I knew exactly what I was looking for." I uttered.

"What kind of a gumshoe are you anyway?"

"I have assistants to do that kind of grunt work."

"Well, I'm the boss tonight, so get busy."

"I might just have to reassess this case to see if it merits my commitment."

"You still owe me two more days, so quit bellyaching and get to work and earn your keep."

After ten minutes I closed the last drawer not finding anything of any importance in any of them. I got up and squeezed her shoulders. "You damn well better be worth all of this abuse."

"There's a lot more to come I promise if things work out."

"And, I promise **you** that they will. Now, what makes you think that Brian is having an affair with his secretary?"

"Well, he's a man, so I am sure it was somebody, and she's handy."

"Explain yourself."

"I've been out of commission, so to speak, for two and a half years, so figure it out...you're a man." She said tiresomely.

I rotated her chair so that we were face to face. "Are you insinuating that all men cheat when sex isn't available to them with their partner?"

"I'm not insinuating anything, just stating a fact."

"So, in other words, you think I cheated on Irene also because our love life was a failure?"

"If the shoe fits..."

"It doesn't, and if you hadn't of shown up on my doorstep I wouldn't be envisioning adultery."

"Such an ugly word...adultery, don't you think? I much prefer infidelity. Anyhow, you're not cut out for it so your integrity is safe, and besides I don't get involved with married men..."

"Yeah, well that bridge has already been crossed so you don't have a leg to stand on." I turned her chair back and caressed her neck and kissed the top of her head.

She sighed and said she wished we weren't so virtuous.

An hour later we returned to the house on Marlborro. Frankie had downloaded everything from both computers unto his devices while Jake and Vali had searched Brian's offices. Mya was content with Carmen's and Brian's personal day journals. Jake photographed what she thought to be incriminating evidence of an affair. Ivy had left us a note saying that she had left snacks for us in the refrigerator. Vali placed them on the table with a big pitcher of milk. Mya excused herself saying she was exhausted. I followed her upstairs to her bedroom door.

"You're upset with what you discovered in those day-books aren't you?" I asked.

"If you're suggesting that I am distressed to discover the truth about what I had been suspicious of, the answer is no. I told you that there has been nothing between Brian and me for a very long time."

"And, when there was…was it good?"

"Are you asking me about my sex life with my husband?"

"I guess I am."

She slammed the door in my face. I heard her turn the lock.

Vali placed a big jar of homemade pickles in front of me and asked if her mom was all right when I sat down to join them at the kitchen table. I opened the jar, popped one into my mouth, and nodded my approval stating that they were better than any I had ever had before.

"I think you were right when you said that you thought that Brian was carrying on with Carmen. Your mom thinks she found evidence of it tonight."

"That wouldn't upset her; it must be something else. Did you two have an argument?"

I frowned. "Not that I am aware of, but your mother is a puzzle and I'm not sure I will ever be able to put all the pieces together."

"How long have you known the new Mayria…not even two days? This last poisoning changed her in ways that I can't wrap my head around. It messed with her psyche Mitch, and to tell you the truth, I'm feared for her mind-set."

I patted Vali on the hand. "There is nothing the matter with your mother's head so you can quit worrying about that. She's emotionally troubled by something you don't even know about, plus I believe she has health issues that she won't talk about. First thing is to get her in for a complete physical as soon as possible, and the rest we will work on day by day."

"What do you mean by saying that she is troubled by something I don't know about…what?"

"Sorry Vali; can't talk about it." I said ending the conversation.

"Mitch…"

"Sorry Hon, I'm working it out with her; all will be resolved in time. First thing though is getting her away from Brian." I rose. "Get some sleep you guys, and we'll collaborate in the morning. Jake, I want you out at the main warehouse first thing Tuesday morning. In the meantime, I'll do a little investigating myself to find out just what chemicals are being used out there and why, and if it was thoroughly explored by the authorities who ruled that thallium was an accidental poisoning."

I wearily climbed the stairs. Not wanting to go to bed with a heavy heart, I nonsensically tried the connecting bathroom door to Mya's room. It was unlocked. I turned the knob and whispered.

"Are you awake Honey; can we talk?"

She had her back to me, but turned over, and said she was sorry.

I walked over and sat on the edge of the bed. She had been crying. I told her that I was sorry too for being so insensitive. "We are going to be all right; you believe that don't you?"

She nodded and asked that if she put a big pillow between us could I lie with her for a while. I said I didn't see why not. I rejected the pillow and folded her into my arms. She told me that I smelled of garlic. I told her that I had been eating her pickles. She said, "Ummm…" and fell asleep a few minutes later. I returned to my own room chastising myself for sticking to the rules.

I returned from my early morning walk with Sadie to find an unfamiliar car in the driveway. It was only seven thirty, rather early for a visitor. I dismissed the idea that Brian had returned three days early because the vehicle was a compact 1996 Buick, and certainly not his style. A stunning young lady was sitting at the kitchen table with the family. A little girl with twinkling big brown eyes and a mass of dark curly hair sat on her lap. Everyone seemed to be captivated by her. I reckoned she was around three years old, but really had no idea. Ivy introduced the duo as her daughter Bebe and granddaughter Melanie and that Mellie, as she was called, would be spending the day with us as Bebe had several job interviews. Apparently, all commerce didn't take Labor Day off. I said hello thinking that Mya must still be sleeping as she was not present and wondered if she knew about the baby sitting arrangement. My answer came almost immediately as Mya made her entrance. The delight and surprise on her face answered my question; she had not known about the visitors.

The little girl jumped off her mother's lap and ran to Mya who scooped her up and danced around with her. Mellie giggled and plied Mya with kisses. I watched in awe realizing that I had indeed missed out on the joy that a child could bring. Mya surprised me and sat down next to me asking if I had met her Goddaughter. I said I had…sort of. Mellie hid her head in Mya's bosom.

"I'm very pleased to meet you Mellie. I hope we can be friends. I never had a little girl of my own so you are going to have to show me all the things a little girl likes to do." I said softly.

She lifted her head and asked me if I was Tessie's daddy. I think she meant husband.

"No Darling," Mya said smiling at me, "his name is Mitch, and he is my very, very special friend. Do you think you might give him a hug?"

She obliged Mya, and for the first time in my life I felt the delight of a child's tiny arms around my neck as I hugged her gently. Mya had tears in her eyes.

And so the day had begun with an unimaginable captivation.

I spent most of the day behind closed doors with Frankie and Jake analysing the boring data from the two computers from Brian's offices while Ivy, Vali and Mya spent an enjoyable day of frolicking with Mellie. We were called in for lunch at noon. I needed a longer break and told Ivy that she was relieved of dinner preparations as I felt like barbecuing. I asked Mya if she would join me in a run to the market for steaks. She said that I was a big boy and could manage myself as long as I brought her a T-bone. She wasn't about to leave her Godchild. I was on my own as someone had to safeguard the girls, and that was Jake. Frankie chose to return to the doldrums.

Bebe returned at three saying she had been hired at a retirement home as an activity co-ordinator. Apparently, that had been her vocation in Panama before she married an American. No one mentioned her husband, or how she ended up in Canada. She and Mellie stayed for dinner much to everyone's delight. Frankie appeared to have a genuine fondness for Bebe and her daughter, and it appeared as though it was a mutual admiration. This was definitely not the first time these two had met.

We ended the evening in the newly assembled living room by socializing with everyone's personal choice of alcoholic beverages. Beer was Frankie's and Jake's poison; mine was whiskey. Vali was the bartender and brewed up a concoction of Long Island tea for the girls. There was no talk regarding the reason we were all here. It was just laughter and story- telling. At eight thirty the merriment was halted by the rude ringing of the telephone. Ivy pulled the portable out of her pocket. Before answering she looked at me and said that she did not recognise the number on the call display. I told her to answer. She did and frowned. She covered the mouthpiece and whispered that it was Brian and that he wanted to talk to Tessa who was shaking her head "no". I encouraged her to take the call as we needed to know what his plans were. She scowled and took a deep breath. I made sure the speaker was on.

"Hello Brian." Mya spoke in a subdued voice.

"Thank God you're home Tess! I've been so worried about you. The phone just rings and rings, and you're cell seems to be turned off...where have you been?"

"Here and there."

"That doesn't tell me anything! Why didn't you stay at the hospital?"

"I didn't want to be poked and probed and analysed by your sleazy shrink because I am not crazy, contrary to your belief."

"I don't think you are crazy Tessa, just confused from the damage the thallium and potassium chloride did to your body and head. You have to admit that you haven't been rational for some time now?"

"I do not admit anything. I am going to hang up now as I have a house full of guests."

"May I inquire as to whom you are entertaining in our house?"

Mya laughed obscenely. "'Just the usual suspects, Ivy, Vali and Frankie, and then Jake and Mitch dropped in." She winked at me.

"Who are Jake and Mitch, and what are they doing there?"

"Not that it is any of your business, but Mitch is my cousin, and Jake is Vali's friend. They are probably here to take advantage of me and steal all my money just like you did." She snickered and smiled at me. I was having a hard time not laughing.

"No need to be so flippant Tess. I love you and am concerned for your well-being. I'm sorry this damn merger is taking so long.

If I could I'd be on the red eye home to you tonight, but I can't pass up this deal that is going to secure our financial future."

"Mine's already secure. No need to hurry back on my account; toodels."

"I love you Tessa."

I told her to tell him that she loved him. She balked and pressed the disconnect button. She then asked Vali to make her another drink. Half an hour later she said she was going to be sick.

I managed to get her upstairs and into the bathroom before she heaved. She sat on the floor with her head wrapped over the porcelain bowl groaning and moaning. I placed a cold washcloth on her neck and rubbed her back. Ten minutes later I managed to drag her to the bed where she flopped down on her stomach and was out for the count. I was able to get her blouse off and loosen her bra. I yanked her jeans down being careful not to pull her panties off, covered her up, planted a kiss on the back of her head and told her to go to sleep. Just as I reached the door she turned over and spoke lethargically.

"I'm glad you are here Mitch and that I don't have to stalk you anymore."

I walked back to her, but she was out again. I made my decision then.

I took my place back on the sofa that Mya and I had been sharing, and asked Vali what kind of a concoction she had made for her mom. She gave me a taste of hers; it was potent. She then passed me Mya's glass and told me to take a sip which I did. It tasted like cola. Vali said her mother's drink was one tenth as strong as hers and Ivy's. She said it wasn't the alcohol that had made her mom sick, but that it was Brian's phone call.

"You may be right." I agreed. "I'll check in on her before I hit the sack, but I think she will sleep the night. Anyhow, I'm out of here early tomorrow morning and won't be back until sometime in the afternoon. Frankie, you should take the day off, and Jake I am going to need you here keeping the girls out of trouble, okay?"

"That's my plan Boss." Jake answered.

"I'm not trouble Mitch." Vali asserted.

"No, you're not, but you did bring a new kind of trouble my way didn't you?" I got up, ruffled her hair. "It might just be the finest trouble I have ever had the pleasure of participating in."

"I can only hope that it turns out that way." Vali beamed.

I said my good nights, called Sadie, and checked in on Mya. She was sound asleep. Next morning I was up at the crack of dawn, wrote a note to Mya telling her I would see her later in the day. I signed it "Mitch" and folded it up, unfolded it and added "love" to Mitch. I ripped it up, rewrote it saying that I hoped she was well, and that I was sorry that I would be away most of the day, but I would be thinking about her every minute. I ended it by saying "Be good Sweetie. Love you, Mitch."

After Sadie's and my extended walk around Central Park, I decided to go to my office and leave some instructions for Shannon. At seven thirty I decided that she was going to have a thousand questions regarding Mayria and our daughter so I best do it in person. I picked up the phone and placed a call. It was answered on the second ring.

I parked behind Irene's red Buick, walked around the house to the back yard, opened the gate, and let Sadie in. I had expected her to go to her doghouse and collect her Frisbee, but she chose to stay with me. Irene opened the door and we followed her into the kitchen. I took my usual seat at the oak table. She placed a tray of bakery offerings and coffee in front of me. I asked her how she had been. She called Sadie who only wagged her tail and chose not to move. She would leave me in a heartbeat if it had of been Mayria or Vali calling her.

"It's been a little lonely around here Mitch. I expected you home yesterday."

"Lonely; I wouldn't think you would even notice that I wasn't here. I told you I had a new case. I suppose you do too as that's why you are working on a holiday." I said taking a sip of coffee. It was a fairly simple procedure to brew a pot of coffee. I had told her a thousand times; eight cups of water in the reservoir, six measures of coffee in the basket, hit the start button. How could she screw it up every time? Don't get your shirt in a knot over rotten coffee Mitch; keep your cool.

Irene was immaculately dressed as always. A blue silk blouse was neatly tucked into her tan linen slacks; a matching jacket sat on the back of a chair awaiting her exodus. Her choice of jewellery, a single strand of pearls paired with a pearl bracelet and earrings complimented her ensemble. The rings I had bought her twinkled on her left hand. A guilty sensation passed through me for a fleeting moment. It passed quickly as I pictured Mya rushing towards me at the convent. Hell, what a conundrum... Irene had done nothing wrong, and yet, here I was about to upset the apple cart.

"Of course I notice that you're not here. You know lawyers don't have holidays Mitch. Have you been up at your cabin all weekend? I tried calling you there yesterday, but there was no answer. Your cell phone is out of action too...are you undercover Mitch? I was hoping that you could do some leg work for me this week?"

"I'm not available Irene."

"How about Mel or Jack, are they available?"

"Do you mean Jake? No, as a matter of fact they are all tied up with me. I may be able to spare Poco for a day or two."

"I don't like him."

"Okay then. Do you want me to see if Mike Smithson has an agent he'll hire out?"

"A rival agency...really?"

"Sorry, that's the best I can do. Are you in a hurry, or do you have a few minutes?"

"Can't it wait until tonight? You are coming home tonight aren't you?"

"No, I'm not Irene, not tonight, or tomorrow..."

She interrupted me. "It must be a whale of a case if you can't even come home at night. How long are you anticipating it will take? Are you at liberty to disclose the bare bones? I have tickets to the symphony on Saturday. It would be nice if you could accompany me."

"Okay, I may as well get to the reason I am here. There isn't going to be any symphony, and I will not be calling this home anymore. It never was much of one anyhow; the cabin is my home. I want us to dissolve our marriage Irene."

She stood up smoothing her skirt out. "What…are you saying that you want to live up at your cabin permanently?"

"Not exactly; did you not hear me say that I want to dissolve our marriage?"

"You don't mean that you want a divorce do you?"

"I am. It can be simple, or just as hard as you choose to make it."

"Why? I have seen no signs of your discontent. It can't be another woman because I would know, so what is it?"

"How would you know if there was another woman Irene?"

"I would smell her on you."

"Well, you would have to be close enough to me to be able to do that now wouldn't you?"

"I know we haven't been close for a while, but I would still know."

"Up until a few days ago I would have said no, there wasn't anyone else. Truth of the matter is that I have been discontented for some time now. I just accepted the monotonous day to day of our existence. We spend a few hours together every week doing nothing but discussing our jobs. Me, only listening with one ear closed to your everyday crisis, and you not paying any attention to anything I say. We don't have the same interests, we hardly ever have meals together, and we certainly don't have a love life, so what the heck is keeping us together anyhow?"

I saw a light in her eye. "Who is she Mitch?"

There it was…who is she? "No one you know." I wanted to add: As if I would have anything to do with any of your condescending friend or attorney colleagues, but I didn't.

"How long have you been unfaithful to me Mitch? Has your cabin become your love nest?"

"I have not been physically unfaithful Irene; not in the past, and not even now."

"I don't understand then…"

"However, there is someone who I want to share the rest of my life with. Her name is Mayria. We were in love many years ago, thirty to be exact. I foolishly left her to search for another meaning to life. You know about my stint in the Algerian prison…

well, that was right after I left her and Sommerset. I did go back for her, but she had married my best friend, so I left and never saw her again until three days ago."

"Well, that can't be the girl you rescued last week because you said she was a teenager... were you lying?"

"No, that was Vali. She is Mayria's daughter."

"So this woman comes with a ready-made family, the family you never wanted."

I ignored the remark. "Actually, there are two sons also; one is here and the other will be joining us tomorrow."

"Joining you for what?"

"It's of no consequence to you or factors into my decision of wanting out of our marriage contract. I may have gone on living in this pedestrian existence forever if Mayria hadn't come back into my life, but she did, and I want to spend the remainder of my days with her." I stood up. "I know this is not what you expected to hear when I asked you to meet me here today, but I wanted you to know of my intentions right away."

"That is so very kind of you." She said sarcastically. "And, I suppose you thought that I would readily agree to a separation and give you permission to move in with your old lover while you explore your new found feelings?"

"I'm not suggesting a separation Irene. That would benefit no one. I am moving out, lock, stock, and barrel. I will take nothing that doesn't belong to me, or anything we bought together. You can keep the house if you so desire, but I will not continue paying half of the mortgage. You make more money than I do so it will be no hardship for you. I will give you a few days to decide how you want to proceed. I won't contest anything you and your lawyer friends come up with. I assume you will be asking Jonah Meyer to represent you?"

"I know you have some savings Mitch and that property of yours is probably worth a small fortune! She probably knows all of that too. I would think that you would be smarter than to fall for the oldest trick in the world."

I laughed. "You're suggestion that I am being enticed by a femme fatal who is after my riches is absurd, and I will tell you why. For one thing, I am far from being rich, but she isn't. Enter her name into one of your search engines and find out who she is. Her full name is Mayria Tessa Joseph. You will find her under Mayria Jones, part owner and former CEO of Legend Hotels. She may be currently listed as Tess Fulton, wife of industrialist Brian Fulton." I was feeling self-satisfied so I gave her a quick wink. "I will be unreachable by phone for the rest of the day and night. I left you my contact information on the table. Don't think too long or hard on this; let's just get it over with."

I thanked her for the coffee and headed for the door.

"That's it? Just like that you want me to agree to a divorce so you can have a clear conscience when you and your old lover take to the sheets again...wait a minute, is she your new client? Is she why you can't come home at night? Not for one minute do I believe that you're not already sleeping with her!"

"Believe what you want Irene, I really don't care; I'm done."

She followed me out the door yelling that we were not done and if I thought that she was going to make it easy for me then I was in for a rude awakening. I closed the car door on her loud shriek, "My God, **what** are you driving?"

I waved and drove out the driveway. I hoped it was the last time. Yeah, there wasn't anything of value for me to come back for.

It was almost three in the afternoon when I arrived back at the house on Marlborro. I found Vali and Jake vigorously polishing Jake's truck. A trickle of water was running down the drain in the driveway. I parked beside the truck and asked where Mya was. Vali said she was in the greenhouse.

"Alone?" I asked.

"Yes Dad," Vali replied cheekily, "we can see her from here you know."

"Okay, what are you two up to?"

"Babysitting mother."

"Funny; I am here so you have the rest of the day off."

"Maybe we will head out to the valley and check out the factory then." Jake suggested.

I liked how he never questioned me about where I had been, or where I was going.

"It can wait until tomorrow. I'm taking Mya out so everything is on hold for the day."

"And, just where are you taking my mother?" Vali queried.

"Now wouldn't you like to know Missy?" I winked at her. "And, by the way, it's an overnighter. Have a nice day."

Jake wished me good luck. I replied that I didn't need any as luck had already found me. Sadie had already found Mya and the two were walking down the hill. Mya was waving at me.

"Hey good lookin," I said cheerfully, "wanna go for a ride?"

Her eyes flickered. "With you?"

"Yes my dear, with me."

"Should I change?"

"No, I like you just the way you are."

"Clothes, I meant."

"No, you're good."

She popped in the house to tell Ivy and Frankie that she was going for a ride with me. She came out and tossed me the keys to her yellow sports car, waved to Vali and Jake telling them that I was taking her off their hands.

"Have fun Mother." Vali called blowing her a kiss.

"Are we going somewhere fun Mitch?"

"Perhaps. I guess you don't want to be seen in the old Chevy anymore eh?"

"It's not that Mitch," she stated letting Sadie into the back seat before getting into the passenger's seat, "this car needs a run."

I laughed. "Do you want to drive?"

"Oh no, it's too powerful for me."

I asked her why she bought it then. She said it was a gift.

"From Brian, I presume."

"Sort of, but I paid for it, so..."

"Speaking of sports...do you like them?"

"I didn't realize that we were talking sports. But, if you mean like basketball and football, no."

"How about hockey?"

"Is that the game where kids and grown men and women dress up in colorful outfits, socks up to their knees, big padded pants and long sweaters, wear helmets on their heads, and funny shoes with sharp blades on their feet, carry a funny long stick, and chase a little black thingy on water that has turned to ice trying to bat it into a small net all the while trying to keep it away from other guys dressed in different colors? Is that what you call hockey?"

Laughing I said, "That's probably the longest explanation I have ever heard. I think we are talking about the same thing though I have never heard it described quite that way before. We have a very good National Hockey League team here, and I was hoping you might like to go to a game with me. If you do, I'll look into acquiring tickets."

"If you mean the Vancouver Canucks, then we may as well use my tickets?"

"You have tickets?" I asked rather surprised.

"Yes, season tickets. I bought them when they went on sale last spring. They were supposed to be a birthday present for Brian, but I don't like him anymore so he isn't getting them. Would it bother you that they were originally meant for him?"

"Hell no, I'm not one to look a gift horse in the mouth!"

"Oh, are we going to the cottage?" She squealed with delight as I turned off unto Inlet Road.

"Do you know how happy you make me Mya?"

"You make me happy too Mitch."

I pulled the car over to a wide spot, stopped, and told her that I was going to need a minute. She asked for what. I got out and walked around to her door, opened it, unhooked the seat belt and pulled her out and into my arms.

"For this." I answered kissing her passionately.

"Oh, I never thought you'd ever kiss me like that again! What took you so long?"

"Well Sweetie, the house is a little crowded, and I did tell you that I would give you three days. Besides, I was pretty sure once I started kissing you I wouldn't be able to stop."

"Three days isn't up yet."

"Believe me Honey, they are. As far as I am concerned they were up the minute I saw you."

She wrapped her arms around me. "For me too Mitch, but there are all these obstacles..."

"You mean like being married to other people? You're done with Brian aren't you?"

"I am most definitely!"

"Good; I told Irene that I want a divorce today, so I'm done too."

"You did; is that where you were all day? What was her reaction?"

"I was only there for ten or fifteen minutes. I think she might fight it."

"Of course she will, and so will Brian. We are going to have a battle on our hands Mitch."

"Do you love me Mya?"

"I do."

"And, I love you, so nothing else matters. We are consenting adults so what say we get on with our lives the way we want to live them, and to hell with the rules."

She kissed me. "Wherever we are going, let's get a head start today."

"That's my girl." I buckled her back in her seat, and climbed back behind the wheel. "I'm sorry; I haven't even asked you how you are feeling today? Any ill effects from the *tea*?"

"None. Did you undress me last night Mitch?"

"Why do you ask?" I said devilishly.

"Well, when I woke up, I only had panties on."

"Very nice panties they were too."

She hit me playfully.

"Well, I wasn't going to leave you in soiled clothes. It's not the first time I have seen you naked you know?"

"That was a long time ago Mitch. I don't have the body of a seventeen year old girl anymore."

"It looked pretty good to me. You said something cryptic as I was leaving...something like you didn't have to stalk me anymore...what was that all about?"

She turned her head away from me. "I must have been delirious."

"Did you come looking for me more than that once Mya?"

"I don't want to talk about a despondent time in my life when I am so happy right now."

"I'll say it just once more; I wish that you had contacted me."

"It wasn't our time Mitch."

Maybe she was right.

Mya and Sadie were both out before I had even come to a full stop. I laughed. "You'd think that dog hasn't been here for a week."

"Well, three days probably feels like a week for her. Something sure smells good. Your neighbors must be cooking up a feast."

"Remind me to introduce you to them after."

"After what Mitch?"

I took her hand. "Wanna go for a walk?"

"With you?"

"Yes silly, with me."

We walked down what passed for a road to the shoreline. The lane was overgrown with weeds and rocks that the rains had unearthed. The only time it had been driven on was when I had to transport boat parts. I had pretty much finished doing that awhile back. Mya was unusually quiet. I asked her if she was all right.

"Oh yes, I am just taking in the quiet and the beauty. Is this cement ramp how you will get your boat into the water? Will it have to be towed?"

"It's called a slipway. I had it professionally designed for the "Mayria". Time will tell I guess. I've built it up high enough so that I can get a trailer under it to transport it back and forth to the water. It'll take a fair amount of man power. If it's not a slam-dunk I might just have to have it towed to a dock in a marina somewhere down the road."

"It will work out Mitch. I can hardly wait to be out on the open sea with you."

"Me neither, but first we have a little business to conduct."

She asked me what kind of business. "Monkey business." I answered.

Chapter 5
Beyond the Yellow Door

"He propelled me towards the lower door of the boathouse, opened it, and told me he had a surprise for me inside. I followed him wondering what he was up to. He stopped at the top of the stairs that led into the galley. "After you my dear." He crooned.

Gingerly, I made my way down. I came to a halt on the last step as I caught sight of something sitting outside the yellow door. It appeared to be a child's stuffed toy.

"What is it Mitch, or should I say, what is it doing here?"

"Why don't you see for yourself?"

Puzzled, I approached it and broke out in laughter when I discovered that it was indeed a child's stuffed creature. I picked it up. There was a tag on it stating that his name was Snap, and that I should press one of his buttons. I did, and a bright red, blue eyed miniature replica of a fiery dragon came to life and said that it loved me.

Clutching it to my breast I turned and smiled at Mitch. I didn't have to say a word. He took my hand, covered it with his, and placed it on the doorknob. He asked me if I was ready to see what was behind the yellow door. We opened it. It was pitch black inside. Mitch flipped a light switch. When my eyes adjusted to the dim radiance I saw that there was nothing in the room but a bed and a small night table.

"So, this is where you keep the "other woman"? I said coyly. I could smell the sweet aroma of freshly picked roses.

He laughed enthusiastically. "I see that you have been eavesdropping on my conversations with the dog. If you will take a closer look you will see that this room is meant for you. I didn't know it at the time, but I sure as hell know it now."

He walked me over to the bed. The floor was covered in a carpet of rose florets as was the coverlet. Above the headboard was a banner that read: "Reserved for my First Mate."

I don't know why I was apprehensive. I was trembling slightly. "There is no name on it."

"Is that what is troubling you? I think you know what name belongs on it…here, I'll fix it."

He opened the drawer on the nightstand and extracted a red felt pen, reached up and wrote my name on the banner. He looked at me for my reaction. Again I was glib, and asked him if he had brought me here to seduce me, and did he consider himself divorced now.

"Yes, to the divorce question. Seduction is so one sided. I thought our feelings were mutual?"

"They are Mitch." I stammered.

"Good because I didn't think that I had misinterpreted you. After all, you're the one who has been trying to get me into bed for the past three days…"

That brought a smile to my face. He took me in his arms, brushed some of the rose petals off the bed and laid me down gently. "I'm going to kiss you now."

π π π π

The earthquakes that had ravished my body had been quieted. I was left in a state of absolute elation. Mitch was so quiet and still beside me that I was reluctant to move or speak. Suppose if I was the only one who had felt the rapture?

Finally, he spoke. "I think I just died and went to heaven."

"I heard singing." I countered.

He had turned and we were face to face. He stroked my face, wound his fingers through my hair and in a deep, sensual voice asked me if it was his voice that I had heard, and was he singing my song.

I smiled. "I've been waiting a very long time for someone who knew my song."

"And, I've been waiting a long time to sing it. You're going to have to be gentle with me because I'm not too sure my heart can take too much more torrid love making."

"I'll be sure to stay clear of you for a while then."

"How long do you think that will last?"

"I don't know…half an hour?"

"Well, I am going to need some substance, so what say we go up and tackle that roast that is waiting for us at the cabin?"

"Do you mean that those whiffs of delight that I smelt were coming from your kitchen? When did you have time to cook and do all of this?" I asked.

"I told you that I was only occupied with my ex for a few minutes. I shopped, drove up here, got the dinner ready, spread the flowers, and went back for you."

He got out of bed and tossed me my clothes.

"I don't remember getting undressed." I confessed.

He said he didn't either. I grabbed Snap, closed the yellow door saying that I'd be back. I did not need to leave my little dragon to guard it.

Mitch took my hand. "Just in case you need to hear it Mayria, I *will* still love you tomorrow."

Mitch sat a platter of rack of lamb surrounded by baby potatoes, julienne carrots and silvery little onions on the table. Garlic and rosemary wafted up tantalizing my taste buds. A crisp garden salad sat by our plates. He filled my wine glass with a red Zinfandel that intoxicated the senses like some exotic spice. He dimmed the lights and lit the candles. We clinked glasses.

Mitch said; "To us."

"To this day never ending." I said wistfully.

Mitch's appetite did not match mine. He sat smiling watching me eat as I had a second helping of everything. I did not feel self-conscious at all, but felt like I might burst.

"I'm stuffed Mitch. I need to undo my jeans. Next time you whisk me off and feed me a three course dinner please bring me a change of clothes."

He laughed. "There just might be something on the bed for you."

"What have you been up to now...should I be leery?"

"Suit yourself, or you could choose to be uncomfortable, or sit around in your undies which would suit me fine."

"I'm going, I'm going..."

On the bed sat a Walmart bag. Good, it wasn't anything too expensive. I opened it and found another bag which I opened and extracted a pair of slippers. Thoughtful. Next bag contained a Japanese Kimono. Beautiful. I smiled thinking I knew exactly what was in the next bag; it would be a sheer negligee. Wrong.

"Oh my God Mitch, where did you find these?" I called out to him. He didn't answer. I knew he was smiling and waiting for my grand entrance. I didn't keep him waiting.

He was standing at the sink washing dishes. I undid the kimono sash and wrapped my arms and body around him. "How do they feel?"

"Just like they did thirty years ago. Do you like them?"

"I love the kimono and the slippers, but these Baby Dolls…I have no words. Where on earth?"

He turned around and eyed me. "As you can see, I only shop at the finest department stores so if you aren't happy with cotton I am sure I can exchange them for something silky."

"Don't even think about it; I love them. I didn't think they were being made anymore. This kimono is to die for, and it **is** silk."

"The dragons don't scare you do they?"

"What?" I took a closer look and realized that the kimono was patterned with fiery dragons.

I shook my head. "This is all so déjà vu…"

"Except for you standing before me in these little pyjamas, nothing is the same Hon. I did not go looking for pj's from the eighties. I was going to buy you a sexy gown, but there they were staring at me just like the damn dragon was. The kimono design was just a bonus. Now, how about grabbing a dish towel and help me finish the dishes?"

I hugged him again. "When we are married I will cook for you."

He turned again and with that crooked smile he had a way of concocting and looked at me with wide eyes. "Marriage; are you thinking we are going to get married?"

"We will." I pronounced

"I don't know about that. You see, I had a wife, and it didn't work out satisfactorily, so I don't think I am marriage material.

And, another thing, how do I know that you won't tire of me like you did all the others and toss me aside breaking my heart? Hardly seems worth the risk does it? It might just take the passion out of a good romance."

"There is not a chance of that happening. I'm an old hand at the marriage game, so not too worry as I will have you habituated in no time. Now get to work so we can play again."

"Yes Ma'am."

After we finished cleaning up Mitch asked me if I would be all right while he ran next door with the remains of the supper. I assured him that I would be as long as he left me with a gun and Sadie. He asked me if I wanted the rifle or the pistol. I said it didn't matter. He unlocked the gun cabinet in the hallway and passed me the pistol relieving it of its magazine. I asked what good it would be to me without bullets. He said he didn't trust me with a loaded weapon. I asked him why. He said it was possible that I might just shoot him.

"Just give me a reason... give me a reason." I vowed.

He said he'd never give me a reason, winked, and left. What to do, what to do while he was gone. I struck a match to the laid firewood, watched it roar, and rummaged through a wicker basket of magazines. They were all the same, "Wild Life B.C." Wonderful. I rifled through a few. One caught my eye; an article called Sourdough Sam by naturalist Adam Mitchum. What...this can't be my Adam. Just a minute, wasn't Sam the name of his uncle that he used to go gold panning with? I turned to the page and read the article. Then I picked a different publication and read how a fox had outwitted him. There were various intriguing pictures of the little fox. After three days of tracking Mitch finally got the award winning photograph. I put all the magazines, except for that one, back in the basket when I heard the door opening.

"Honey, I'm home; don't shoot."

"See any vixens out there?" I asked innocently.

"Strange question, but no, the only vixen I have ever come across is sitting right here."

I pulled the magazine out from behind my back and pointed to the sassy fox. "What about this one...was she worth the hunt?"

"Assuming she was a lady, she definitely was, but not near as much fun as the lady I'm pursuing right now is." He grinned as he took me in his arms.

"Well Honey, this hunt is over because I am yours; no hunt involved."

"Aah, I was looking forward to chasing you through the woods."

"Maybe another time; right now I want to know how you came to be a writer for a wildlife magazine."

"I really didn't have any aspirations in doing so. I was up at the other cabin chopping wood when a mother deer and her two fawns came wandering by. We stared at each other for a while. I asked them to stay put while I grabbed my camera. I guess the opening of the door startled them because they bolted. From then on I always carried the camera with me. One day I put some words together with a photo of a lynx while I was in the office. Shannon found it and told me I should send enter it in this contest she had read about. I told her not to be silly. She went ahead and did it anyhow. I did not place in the contest, but the article was published, and so started my little hobby."

"Good for Shannon. I am looking forward to meeting her. What did the other woman in your life have to say about it?"

He laughed. "Do you mean Irene? If I remember correctly it was something like, "So this is what you do up there in the wilderness? Doesn't sound like you at all. Is it a popular magazine? I hope you received a big fat cheque." I told her I didn't do it for the money. I never showed her another article, and she never asked if I wrote anymore."

"Pooh on her. I am so very proud of you Mitch and I am going to read every article in every magazine. In fact I'd like to bundle them up and take them into town for the kids to read."

"Vali already knows. We have so much on our plates right now Sweetie, so maybe another time okay, and when it is all over, I'll take you to the wilderness cabin."

ππππ

I was nervous about meeting Mitch's neighbors. I suppose I didn't want a repeat of my uncomfortable encounter with Artie and Doll. Ruth and Harvey seemed genuinely pleased to meet me. Harvey said that they could now quit speculating on who the mystery woman was. I jokingly asked if they thought that Mitch was keeping me hostage in the boathouse. Ruth had laughed and said no, but they knew that there was a woman who wasn't his wife who he was keeping time with. She said Mitch had denied that there was, but now here we were, and indeed the woman was me...the Mayria from the boat.

Mitch had hurried me out saying that we had an engagement in the city that we couldn't be late for and that we would all get together soon. As soon as we were in the car I asked him who she was. He replied that was the same question that Irene had asked about me yesterday.

He didn't volunteer any more information, so I was going to have to try and get him to omit that he had lied. "You told me that you never cheated on her, and you also told me that there wasn't anyone else in your life...have you been lying to both of us?"

He didn't answer right away. I thought he was trying to come up with an answer that would be acceptable to me. Had he never entertained the thought that once I met Ruth and Harvey the question of a mystery woman would arise? His answer was not what I was expecting at all.

"There is another woman, but she isn't real."

"What the hell does that mean?" I asked flabbergasted that he might have an obsession for someone he had manufactured in his head or worse... someone he could never have.

Mitch pulled the car over. He looked at me pathetically. "It means that I don't know who she is. She comes to me in dreams. She is a figment of my imagination."

"That doesn't sound like you Mitch."

"Yeah, well tell that to my subconscious. You sound just like Irene."

"Don't ever confuse me with **her!**"

"Sorry."

"It's okay. How long have you been dreaming about this entity?"

"Three years or so I guess."

"Do the dreams upset you?"

"Well, I don't usually remember dreams, so yes, I guess they do. This young woman who comes to me is woeful and seems to want me to help her. When I try to follow her, she disappears, and I wake up."

"How old do you think she is?"

"Your age."

"I am almost forty eight. I don't consider that as being young."

"You were, thirty years ago."

"So the girl in your dreams is seventeen, and you think it's me?"

"No, she is older. Hell, I don't know because I never see her face clearly, but there was definitely something familiar about her."

"Have you told anyone about these dreams?"

"Just who do you think I would tell?" Mitch asked irritably.

"I'm just trying to help."

He pulled back out unto the road. "Well, you're not, and I think you think I'm making the whole thing up because I really do have a mistress."

I reached over and touched his hand. "Honey, I am sorry that I gave you that impression. I do believe you, and I am pretty sure you don't have a mistress…oh… I guess that is what I am now isn't it?"

"I don't consider you my mistress because I'm in love with you…oh hell, I guess you are."

"Does that make you my master? Now, back to your dreams… they can be powerful and overwhelming, especially recurring ones. I am going to offer you a hypothesis. You may reject it, or you might think that it has some validity. Three years ago I came looking for you with the intention of telling you about our daughter. Strange things happened to me in that tea- shoppe that day…" I stopped and covered my face with my hand not believing what I was about to say.

Mitch stopped the car again and reached for me. "What is it Mya…just say it, just say it because we are both thinking it."

I stuttered. "Is it possible that I somehow transferred my thoughts and emotions to you? It makes sense because that is when you first started having the dreams, and yet, it makes no sense at all. Did I channel you, or did Lylah channel both of us?"

"I don't know where you get some of these fangled-dangled notions from, but I have been wondering if she is the girl in my dreams ever since you told me about her. I don't believe in all this mumble jumble supernatural occurrences, but I'm definitely stepping up my search for her. Are we both crazy Mya?"

"Perhaps."

I thought Mitch was taking a shortcut until I realised that we were on Bourdon Street. I had a moment of panic when I spotted the dragon on the pawn shop sign across from the tea shoppe. "I don't like it here Mitch."

"Honey, it's my office. I want you to meet Shannon and Mel." He said pulling into the lot.

"It's where I had a breakdown." I confessed.

"When…you've said that you came by a number of times?"

"You know damn well when! I'm tired of meeting your friends…I'll wait here for you."

He came around and opened my door. "I'm not leaving you out here, so put on your happy face. What you experienced before is done and gone and has no bearing on today. It can't be the dragon logo that has you frightened because surely you know by now that they have no power over you. We'll talk about it later, but I need you to come with me now." He took my hand.

"They won't like me." I stammered.

"Probably not, but they'll make the attempt because I'm their boss."

I put up my hand up to hit him. He grabbed it and asked me if I really wanted to do that. I said that I did. He laughed and told me that we could continue squabbling when we were alone.

"I'm so tired of you bossing me around that I could spit!"

"So un-lady-like. How about if I let you be the boss later tonight?"

"I so liked you better at the cabin." I walked past him and marched into his office. Two people were standing by an opened window. I assumed they were Shannon and Mel, and had been watching us. I sat down in a chair.

"Hi, I am Mayria, the girl from the boat, the girl Mitch walked out on, the mother of his child, and the love of his life!"

Mitch entered shaking his head grinning from ear to ear. "I told you guys that you'd love her didn't I?"

Shannon ordered Mel to get me a glass of water. She bent down and embraced me. ""It's my greatest pleasure to finally meet someone who has domination over this thick headed man."

"Be careful there, you're talking to the man who signs your paycheck." Mitch said jokingly.

"Don't be intimidated; I'll pay you double if you can find our daughter." I exclaimed.

"I did hear you right…a child, how, when?"

"I'm pretty sure you know *how* Shannon." Mitch said winking at her, and then me. "I guess the plan was to lead up to the part where I tell you that Mayria and I have a daughter, but I see I was beaten to the punch." He was still smiling. "I just found out myself five days ago so I am still reeling. Here is what we know."

We spent the next half hour filling them in on our relationship that dated back thirty years. Shannon cried when I emotionally retold the story of my pregnancy and the birth of Lylah Jayne. Mel noted all the facts, little that there were. He said that he was already on it. Mitch told them that my children didn't know yet as we didn't want to give them false hope so it had to remain a secret. They both encircled us with hugs when we were leaving. Shannon said that Mitch was a second father to their children so she knew he was going to embrace a child of his own. He replied that my two children had accepted him already and he was off to meet the third, so fingers crossed. I left knowing I had made two new friends.

We parked the car and walked hand and hand up the walkway to the house.

"What the heck is all that commotion coming from the back yard?" I asked.

"I'm sure I have no idea, but it sounds like they're having fun." Mitch offered.

As we rounded the corner I let out a squeal. "Good God, they're in the pool! I bet this was Vali's idea. Can you imagine the power bill for heating it?"

Mitch laughed. "Guess you had better think twice about selling off Legend Enterprises...hey, who's the new kid?"

I squealed again. "It's Bobbie!" I thrust Snap into Mitch's hands and ran up to greet my eldest calling "Bobbie, Bobbie, Bobbie." I threw my arms around him. He picked me up and twirled me around and around.

"I missed you too Mom .You know I am going to get you wet?"

"I don't care. I am so happy to see you, but you're four hours early."

"Yeah, I was able to catch an earlier flight." He was looking over my shoulder. "Now, this wouldn't be the new man in your life would it?"

Mitch had joined us. "Yeah, I am, and if I didn't know who you were I would take exception to you throwing my girl around." He extended his hand. "Talk about déjà vu; it's like thirty years ago and I am looking at my best friend." He said as he shook Bobbie's hand heartily.

Bobbie pumped his hand. "It's a pleasure Sir. Just out of curiosity, would that be the same best friend who married your girl?"

"It is, and it is all water under the bridge. I'm only sorry that it ended the way it did. Your father was one of a kind."

Vali had joined in the love fest. She relieved my dragon from Mitch. "For me...you shouldn't of Dad. What **do** you say Bob; is he all I told you he was?"

Mitch reclaimed Snap. "His name is Snap, and he's your mom's as I am sure you know. How about Bobbie and I get to know each other before you throw the "Dad" word at him?"

"Oh funny, Snapdragon; you gotta love it hey Mom?"

"I never thought about it, but you're right, it is comical."

Mitch said he didn't see what we found so amusing about the name.

"Snapdragon is a flower Honey, and my dragon's name is Snap, so Snap Dragon...get it?"

He shook his head and said, "Whatever."

Bobbie told Mitch that he would soon discover if he hadn't yet, that Vali and he were usually on the same wave length. He ruffled his sister's wet hair. "I assume that having three grown kids suddenly thrust into your life must seem a little intimidating, especially one like my presumptuous little sister here."

"I don't intimidate easily." Mitch stated. "Vali and I came to an understanding the first night we met, didn't we Hon?" He put his arm around her. "Sometimes she disagrees with me, but she usually comes around to my way of thinking. You got to love her swagger though. So far Frankie and I have seen eye to eye, and I trust that in time, you and I will also. Mya's well-being is all that matters. For the record, if I had of been lucky enough to have a daughter..." Mitch seemed to drift off. I knew he was thinking about Lylah Jayne. He scared me for a second, but caught himself, and said, "I'd want her to be just like this kid here."

She reached up and gave him a big kiss on his cheek. "I love you too old man."

"See what I have to put up with?" Mitch grinned from ear to ear.

I said I was going to have a quick swim and invited Mitch to join me. He declined saying him and my eldest needed to get to know each other. Bobbie grabbed two beers from the cooler and they moseyed off towards the patio.

A few hours later Frankie and Jake cranked up the barbecue and we feasted on burgers, corn and cold slaw, and ice-cream sundaes for dessert. It was family fun. I let the boys talk me into playing a few hands of poker in the recreation room. It wasn't very often I got to spend time with all my children, so I donned a sweater and joined them all in the underground room. At ten p.m. I'd had enough and said I was going to bed. Mitch said he best go with me to make sure I was safe. There was much razzing from the group regarding Mitch's reasons for following me. We stopped outside my bedroom door.

"Your room or mine?" Mitch asked.

"I've been in your bed so I think it's time you were in mine for the whole night."

Once comfortably in bed I asked him how he'd made out with Bobbie. He said, "Okay, I guess."

"Just okay; didn't it go well?"

"I didn't say that. I get the feeling that he is more cautious than the other two."

"Cautious; about what?"

"Honey, I don't know. Maybe he doubts that my intentions towards you aren't as idealistic as you make them out to be. I think he doesn't like the fact that I am married."

"He said so?"

"Not in so many words. He doesn't want you to be hurt again."

"He thinks you are going to leave me again?"

"I don't know. Maybe he was referring to one of your past loves."

"There are no past loves except for you. Nobody else hurt me. I was the one who did the walking away. I am going to have to talk to him."

"Leave it be Mya. We just met; he'll come to see that I'm thoroughly committed to you."

"There you go again!"

"What do you mean?"

"Bossing me around, telling me what to do. I've a good mind to kick you out of bed."

"This should be fun; let's see what you got."

"Damn it, you exasperate me!"

"Yeah, but I also appease you so how about a little bit of loving for the wounded crusader who tames dragons for you."

"I may surrender, but the war isn't over."

He laughed. I wasn't winning any battles, but I was happy not to.

Mitch had only been back in my life for five days. They were the happiest days of my life that didn't involve my three children. Now, if only the fourth child would show up...I fell asleep not anticipating tomorrow as Brian would be back, but surely the rest of the day would bring some pleasures.

Thursday had started out pleasantly. Everyone was busy. Jake and Vali were off on their quest to find some damning evidence against Brian at the industrial plant. Bobbie and Frankie were finalizing and condensing data from Brian's files and computers. Nothing that had been uncovered proved his guilt in my poisonings. I was not at all surprised. There did seem to be enough evidence of his affair with Carmen to take to court. Mitch had gone to check in with Mel and Shannon. He said he'd only be a half an hour just in case Brian was able to catch an earlier flight as Bobbie had yesterday. I shooed him out telling him to take as much time as he needed to tracking down our number one priority.

Ivy had taken on the chore of upholstering some ratty kitchen chairs for her daughter's new apartment. I was to be her assistant. Mitch had only be gone a few minutes when she asked me what our number one priority was. The front doorbell chimed. We looked at each other, made a face and ignored it. I told her it was probably just Mitch trying to be funny. On the third ring, Bobbie came out of the den and asked me if I wanted him to get it. I shrugged my shoulders saying that no one of any importance ever used the front door. He returned telling me that I had a visitor and that he had ushered her into the living room. I sighed, put the tacks down and sauntered in to see who had the nerve to be bothering me. Lord help her if she was a salesperson.

She was studying a Goya painting. She was definitely not a hawker because no salesperson I knew could afford Louis Vuitton four inch heels. She was tall and slim with shoulder length buttery locks. I knew immediately who she was. She turned when she heard me and asked if I was a fan of Goya. I told her that my husband was.

"Right, you have a husband, but you want mine to add to your collection don't you?"

"Mitch isn't here Irene; you just missed him. You may wait for him if you like, but I won't wait with you. Please excuse me."

"From everything I have read about you, I would think that you'd have the gumption to face up to your lover's wife."

"I think for both our sakes we should not be engaging in pleasantries that will surely erupt into something unpleasant." Again I turned to leave the room.

"I did not come to see Mitch. I came to see you and ask you to give him back to me."

Oh God. I motioned for her to take a seat. As if on cue, Ivy entered with a tray containing two large mugs of coffee and small pitchers of cream and sugar. No china cups and saucers here in this fancy house. Irene took a seat at the end of the sofa smoothing her knee length skirt out. She crossed her legs at the ankle and reached for a mug, adding a drop of cream. She picked the cup up with her left hand; deliberately, I was sure so that I could see her wedding rings. They were beautiful, and I was envious. She thanked Ivy.

"By the size of this house I imagine you have half a dozen servants."

I ignored the barb. I sat on the edge of the sofa. "I can only imagine what it took for you to come here today and confront your husband's mistress as you label me. It's important that you know that we did not renew our love until after he made his intentions known to you."

"Well, that is comforting. What does *your* husband have to say?"

"My husband and I are divorcing so it is of no consequence what he might think. You asked me to give Mitch back to you, but I cannot do that. Mitch is his own man, and I do not own him. However, if I had that ability, I would not return him to you because you do not deserve him. You did not nurture him. You had no idea what his dreams were. You did not take part in his life. You're love life was jaded to say the least. Do you know that he built that cabin, which is not a cabin at all, but a very cozy cottage, hoping you would spend weekends with him? Have you seen his boat? It is a work of art. He is a master craftsman. You don't, but I do. Mitch and I have each lost thirty years of laughter, tears, love, and family, so no, you cannot have him back."

I gave her the floor for rebuttal.

"Maybe I have made some mistakes along the way, but he never complained or asked me to change my ways. We never argued. We were happy until you came along and wormed your way back into his life on the pretense that your husband is trying to kill you. Women like you are a dime a dozen, and I will not stand by and let you bamboozle a good and honest man!"

I hadn't mentioned that Brian had tried to kill me, so Mitch must have told her.

"What you think of me does not factor into this Irene. Mitch *is* an honest and good man and that is why he made his intentions clear to you regarding his feelings for me. He deserves more from life than you are willing to give. I have not heard you say you love him…"

"I do love him, and I know he loves me! You're just some little dalliance, and he will soon tire of you. He's like every other man having a mid-life crisis pretending that having an affair with some trollop will bring his youth back. And, for your information, Mitch is sterile so if you had thoughts of having a child with him that is not possible." She laughed vulgarly. "You're much too old anyhow." She eyed me up and down. "Whatever does he see in you?"

I bit my tongue. I wanted to tell her that I satisfied him in bed, and I wanted to laugh in her face and tell her that we already had a child, but it wasn't the right time. I stood up. "Sticks and stones Irene. I wish you no ill will. I will see you to the door as this confrontation is over."

She followed me hissing that I hadn't seen the last of her, and there was no way she was going to give Mitch a divorce. Ironically, just as I opened the door, Mitch pulled in the drive and parked next to her car. The look on his face when he spotted her was one of disdain.

"What are you doing here Irene?" He yelled. "You all right Mya?"

Irene laughed haughtily. "I didn't harm one grey hair on her head Dear, but then I am not through with her yet, or you for the matter." She turned and waved to me. "Thanks for the chat."

Mitch opened the car door for her, said a few words that I couldn't hear and shut the door quietly. He was such a gentleman. I met him half way down the steps. He kissed me before her car was out of sight and asked again if I was all right.

"I guess my mind was somewhere else because it took me a few blocks before I realized that I had passed her car parked on the street. Sorry, I took so long getting back, but I got stuck behind a slow moving tow truck. She wasn't looking for me was she? She wanted to catch you alone. Damn her!"

"I am hardly alone, and no harm was done. We'll talk about it later. I guess you didn't have time to get to the office so there is no news on Lylah?"

We sat down on the top step, and he gave me some good news. It was in a long text that Mitch had received just before he had left the house. He opened his phone so that I could read it. The gist of it was that Shannon and Mel had tracked down a tentative relative of Art and Thelma Robinson after hours of phone calls to every Robinson they could get a listing for. They had hoped that they had struck gold with a phone number in the Courtenay directory for a June Robinson. Mel had called her and she had said that the names sounded familiar, but she couldn't place them. She gave them another number for her husband's aunt who in turn gave him a number for Dick and Dora Chorney saying she thought Dora's sister had married an Art Robinson. That proved to be another dead end, but did lead to half a dozen more contacts all over the island. Just when Mel thought he had exhausted all his leads, he hit pay dirt in Nanaimo with a Richard Halliday. His wife Maureen, had a cousin by the name of Thelma Robinson, or so he thought. Unfortunately, Maureen had been in a serious car accident and was in the ICU unit in the hospital. Richard himself was house bound with a multitude of health problems so he was unable to visit her. His daughter would be arriving on Saturday and he would pass the information on to her. So, it sounded like a plausible lead, but was still a wait and see game.

"See why I have people to do the leg work? I don't have the patience for all that mumbo jumbo. I'm not in the mood for company, and I'm sure you could use a little solitude also after that altercation with Irene. I promise it won't happen again." He pulled me up. "Is there any way we can sneak upstairs without being discovered?"

"I like your way of thinking. Jake and Vali aren't back yet so we can go through his suite."

"Won't it be locked?"

"I'm sure the lady of the house knows where the key is." I took his hand. "Come on before the kids get back and spoil our plans. And Mitch, I am not upset; Irene did not intimidate me. Did you tell her that Brian was trying to kill me?"

"Nope, pretty sure I didn't. What did she say?"

"Something to that affect. Wonder how she found out then. Doesn't matter, let's go."

At four forty five we made our way back downstairs. Vali and Frankie were setting the dining room table. I sat down in the kitchen and remarked to Ivy that I was hungry.

"Dinner is at six or thereabouts when Mr. Fulton arrives." She stated.

"I'm hungry now, and I do not care to dine with Mr. Fulton."

"You will wait and dine with everyone else Tessa. We are all putting on a front for your benefit. It would be gracious of you to stick with the plan and be considerate of us. Next time, don't expend all your energy upstairs doing what suits you and leave us with all the work downstairs."

I opened the fridge door. Mitch shut it. "Ivy is right Honey. You can wait a few minutes longer can't you?"

"This is my house, and I will eat whenever and whatever I want, and I want to eat now!"

Ivy passed me a piece of celery that she had been chopping. I said "Thank-you, but just so you both know, I don't like being told what I can and can't do; one boss is enough."

"Who is that one boss Honey?" Mitch asked devilishly.

"Wouldn't you like to know?" I walked over and put my arms around Ivy and told her that I loved her.

π π π π

Chapter 6

Storm's a-Brewin'

I took my seat beside Mya at the dining room table. She had chosen Bobbie to be at the head of the table by the patio doors with her sitting directly to his left, then me, Vali and Jake. Brian would take his usual place at the other head of the table. Ivy would be seated to his left and then Frankie, Bebe and Mellie. Mya had asked Ivy if she minded sitting next to Brian. Ivy replied that it was better her than she.

Frankie met Brian at the back door. We heard a low growl coming from Sadie. I arose to discipline my dog, but Mya said that Sadie knew what she was doing, and to let her be. I figured she was probably right and let Frankie handle it.

Brian entered with a flourish. "Well, that was some greeting! I thought you'd be waiting for me with open arms Tessa? How about a little kiss then?"

Mya snorted. "In your dreams."

He laughed whole- heartily. He greeted Ivy and Bebe, Frankie and Bobbie, and then his eyes shifted to me and Jake. "Okay, own up, who's the cousin, and who's the boyfriend?" He nodded to Vali. "I suppose this strapping young fellow is your new beau?"

Jake stood up extending his hand. "Jake Daniels at your service Sir, good to meet you."

Mya snickered under her breath. I nudged her.

Brian took Jake's hand and pumped it. "I think you may have hit pay dirt this time Vali. Do I detect a southern drawl there Son?"

"Yes Sir; I am Texas born and bred, as they say, but am proud to say that I have been a Canadian citizen for five years."

"Good show Son." Brian's gaze settled back on me, "So, I guess that leaves you as the long lost cousin?"

I didn't move a muscle. I was not going to suck up to him; that was Jake's job, and he was much better at kowtowing than I was. "Not lost, just misplaced for a while." I smiled innocently.

Mya put her arm on my shoulder and spoke robustly. "Mitch was my best friend thirty years ago. How we lost touch is a calamity, but we have taken over right where we left off. Take fair warning, he is very protective of me, so if you still have plans of doing me in, or having me committed…you've been forewarned."

Brian appeared to be genuinely injured. "That was never my intention Tessa. You underwent a personality change and I was concerned. I thought talking with a specialist would help. Doing you in…are you suggesting…can we please discuss this in private later?"

"There is not much to discuss, and I am not suggesting anything, I am stating it outright." With a wave of her hand she dismissed him coldly, and asked Ivy if we could get on with dinner.

Jake and Vali followed Ivy out to the kitchen. I was sure Jake was having a good chortle.

Her indifference didn't seem to fizz on him. Brazenly he chose to vex her. "I know you are a much better hostess than how this table is set Tessa…where's the wine? Frankie, will you get some suitable glasses from the credenza? Be back in a jiff folks."

"It's lasagna for Christ's sake! Do you have to have booze with every friggin thing?" Mya yelled at him as he exited the room. "I'm so sorry Bebe I forgot…come here Baby," she said holding her hands out for Mellie, "Tessie didn't mean to yell."

I told her she was going to have to settle down. Bobbie asked her if she needed to go for a walk. She said no, she just needed to hold Mellie. Bebe walked her daughter around the table and put her on Mya's lap. She assured Mya that no harm was done, and kissed her on the cheek. Mellie asked her if that man was Mya's daddy. I think she probably meant husband.

"No sweetie, he is not. Do you know what would make me happy?"

"What?" Mellie asked sweetly.

"Tessa is my old name and I don't like it anymore. My real name is Mayria, but everyone calls me Mya…do you think you can call me Mya too?"

"But Grammama and Mama call you Tessie."

"I know honey, but I want them to call me Mya or Mayria too. What do you think?"

Calla turned to me. "Mitchy, what do you call her."

I was surprised that she remembered my name. "I call her Mya."

"Okay, I call her Mya too. Can we eat now; I'm hungry."

Mya was beaming. "You bet we can. Uncle Bobbie is going to get your plate and you can eat right here beside me and Uncle Mitch."

"I didn't know he was my uncle too. Is Mya right Mitchy?"

"Mya is always right." I winked at her.

She giggled and said, "He winked at me Mya."

The food was on the table. Mellie told us she wanted lots of butter on her bread. Mya told her it was already buttered and toasted, but more butter sounded good.

Vali took her seat beside me. I asked her where Jake was.

"Brian commandeered him into accompany him to the wine cellar wouldn't you know it?"

I hadn't been aware that there was a wine cellar. I'd have to have a look see for myself.

Vali looked around me. "Are you all right Mom?"

"I am. I'm just honkey dory because everyone I love is here," Mya frowned. "with one exception that is…"

Brian and Jake arrived carrying four bottles of wine. Brian looked at Mya and asked if it was safe for him to pour the wine. Without waiting for an answer he made his way around the table with a bottle of Tuscan red. Jake was in charge of the Sauvignon Blanc.

Brian stopped behind me. "The red I assume?"

I held my glass up for him. "Sounds good."

Mya covered her glass with her hand as he moved on to her. "I know Honey; you're waiting for the blush." She didn't respond.

I didn't like him calling her honey, but there wasn't anything I could do about it at the moment so I spoke for her instead. "She has one of her headaches and is abstaining tonight, right Mya?"

"Yes, and it is increasing in magnitude by the second."

As soon as Brian was out of ear shot she squeezed my leg and said "I love you," out of the corner of her mouth. I muttered that this was not the time for her to be flirting with me. She laughed. Mellie asked her what flirting was. Mya hushed her and whispered something to her. Mellie motioned me to bend over and whispered in my ear. I couldn't make out her words but was pretty sure they weren't meant for anyone else to hear. Then she giggled and put her hand over her mouth. Bebe asked her what was so funny.

"Shh it's a secret, right Tessa? I forgot the other name."

"Yes, it is Sweetie. I'm Mya, remember?"

Mellie said she did and asked me if I could butter her more toast. My thoughts went back to wondering about Lylah Jayne and the possibility that I might have a granddaughter.

Halfway through the meal Brian asked us if we would join him in a toast. I was surprised that Mya chose to take part. However, when he spoke of family and friends, she lowered her glass saying under her breath that they were not his and never would be.

When I had first been introduced to the house I hadn't noticed any photographs of Brian or Mya on display anywhere. Photos of Mya's three children adorned the mantelpiece and her bedroom dresser. Ivy had opened a drawer in the dining room sideboard when I asked where their wedding photo was. I had lifted it out and examined it thoroughly. Mya's knee length dress was a pale peach color. She held a bouquet of roses that matched. She had an elusive smile on her face, and a very large diamond ring on her left hand. I had never seen her wear it. Brian was dressed in a casual tan leisure suit. He towered over his bride by a foot or more. To me, the broad smirk he showed to the camera was one of victory. I'd replaced the picture unsure if the smile on Mya's face was one of contentment or contempt.

When Brian had first bounded into the dining room full of pomp and gusto I despairingly realized that he was a force to be dealt with. He was a good five inches taller than me, and outweighed me by at least twenty five pounds. All I could hope for if push came to shove was that my four years of amateur boxing that had been my pastime down under years ago would give me some advantage. Maybe it was time I found a friendly gym to find out if I had any skills left. Hell, this was not my wheelhouse. A man never wants to admit that his competition is better looking and brawnier than he is, but I was in his presence and my bravado had weakened. I had to remind myself that Mya loved me, not him.

The men were treated to Cuban cigars and cognac on the terrace after dinner. Mya suggested that Ivy should go play with her granddaughter while she and Vali do the clean-up. I offered to stay and help but she shooed me out saying it was "women's work." I laughed at that.

"Be on guard Mitch; I have this feeling that he will be testing your every word." Mya warned.

"And, I'll be watching him for any tell. He's taken to Jake and won't even know that he is being scrutinised. We've got it covered Babe; don't worry."

We ended the evening in the living room with Brian laying out the blueprints that were intended for the addition to his factory. I feigned interest, but left the interrogational up to Jake and Bobbie. Frankie had told us not to wait up for him when he drove Belle and Mellie home. Mya and Vali had helped Ivy into bed after she had polished off the remainder of the white wine and was feeling its effects.

I was proud of Mya for not bombarding Brian with interjections regarding his plans. He asked her several times what she thought. She was uninterested and said they would discuss it another time. At ten fifteen she excused herself saying that her headache was still raging so was going to bed. I bowed out also stating that it had been a long day. Brian said he'd see Mya to her room. She said it wasn't necessary, but he followed along behind us. Without further ado Mya entered her room and slammed the door. Brian and I heard her lock it.

He shrugged his shoulders and laughed brashly. "That cousin of yours has a temperament, but she always comes around."

I said good night and continued on to my room. I left the door ajar as Brian was still talking.

"Come on Sweetpea, open the door. Just a little kiss, that's all I ask."

I heard another door slam. He laughed again. "You win Tess. Have a good sleep because we have a lot to discuss tomorrow. I promise you'll be delighted with my surprise."

I waited until I heard him descending the stairs before I closed the door. I turned; Mya was standing in the bathroom doorway. I asked her what she was doing. She started to undress.

"Are you deliberately trying to sabotage us? What if he'd followed me and caught you in my bedroom? Quit playing with fire Mayria! We're almost there so be a good girl and go back to your room."

She started to button up her blouse. "Well, it would be all over then wouldn't it? Never mind; if you don't want me, I'm sure I can call Brian back."

I crossed the room in two steps. I put my hands heavily on her shoulders. "Don't you ever say anything like that **ever** again!"

Her bottom lip was quivering. "I won't." She whimpered.

I removed my hands thinking I may have been pressing too hard. "Sorry; I didn't mean to hurt you. How would you like it if I said that I was going to drop by my old house and see if Irene was up for a quickie?"

Her eyes filled with tears. "I wouldn't Mitch; I'll go now."

"I think not. Get undressed and get into bed. I'm not letting you out of my sight." I fished one of my shirts out of a drawer and passed it to her. "Put it on in case you have to leave in a hurry."

"Why would I? All the doors are locked. I wouldn't have called him Mitch. You know I can't stand him…you don't trust me do you?"

I folded the covers back. "I've seen the way he looks at you. It wouldn't surprise me one bit if he has a key to all the doors, and wouldn't even think twice about breaking the door down."

"He wouldn't do that." She said self- confidently

"Never underestimate a desperate man. Move over, that's my side." I partially undressed and climbed in beside her. "Come here." I said pulling her into my arms.

She rested her head on my chest and slid her hand under my shirt. "I've been thinking Mitch."

"Well that's scary." I chuckled.

"Irene is right."

"Right about what?"

"I'm a homewrecker. I took the man she loves away from her and…"

I sat up. "Stop right there! We have already talked about this. You did not break up my marriage. You know that I was yours from the moment I saw you at the convent. It took a little finagling, but we are right where we want to be except for the matter of the spouses. It's all going to take care of itself, so stop feeling guilty. You say she loves me; perhaps she does, but she never told me so every day like you do, nor I her. You're my girl, and you know it. Now lie down and go to sleep."

"I do not feel guilty, just sorry for her loss. She's going to make it difficult for you Mitch."

"So be it. It's nothing I can't handle, especially when my reward is you."

Friday had been an uneventful day up until late afternoon. We had a few more hours to confront Brian. Trouble was that we had nothing to challenge him on. Jake and Bobbie had come up cold again last night. If Brian was hiding something he was doing one hell of a good job. Jake had managed to sneak into the wine cellar. There were no false doors leading to clandestine rooms. There was nothing down there but wine. I had never failed to come up with evidence before. Had Brian defeated me at my own game? Was he not responsible for Mya's poisonings, or was all his boasting and mawkish behavior a smokescreen for something more sinister? I had until tomorrow to figure it all out. Was I too close to the situation because of my love for Mya? No, Jake was here, and he had not suggested that I take a secondary seat, so we would proceed as planned with him doing the questioning. The straws had all been drawn and none led to Brian's culpability. Damn! A storm was brewing outside and in my head.

I decided to give Rory Adams a call. He was one of the chief detectives at the Vancouver Police Department. We had collaborated on half a dozen cases and had become friends. I grabbed a cigarette and a beer from the fridge and went out to the patio. I was tempted to light the cig but didn't have a match so tucked it behind my ear as usual. Rory was on a lunch break so something was going my way. It had been a month or two since we had last spoke so we talked for a few minutes about mundane things. As soon as he asked me how Irene was the conversation changed direction. I told him how Mayria had come back into my life and that I had asked Irene for a divorce. He wasn't all that surprised because he knew I had a ho-hum marriage. I asked him how he had known and I hadn't. He laughed. He was on his third marriage so had seen all the signs. I asked him if he had ever had any dealings with a Brian Fulton. He said he knew who he was, but knew nothing more, and why was I asking. I told him that I had been hired by the family to investigate him and prove that he had tried to kill his wife who just happened to be my old sweetheart Mayria. We had run into stumbling block after stumbling block and hadn't been able to find any prove of his culpability. I was hoping that maybe he had come across some dirt on him. Rory said he'd run his name, but it sounded like I had already done a thorough job investigating so chances were that there was nothing to uncover. I related the poisonings. There was an immediate change in Rory's attentiveness.

"Christ Mitch, why didn't you lead with that?"

I had him.

It was four-thirty. The ladies were in the kitchen cooking up a storm. The smell of fried chicken was wafting through the air. Bobbie, Frankie, Jake and I were in the living room chatting Brian up still hoping to catch him in some incriminating lie.

We were called into dinner when Brian held us back. He winked and said that he had a surprise planned for Tess so we shouldn't be too surprised if they disappeared upstairs right after dinner. He was pretty sure that she was going to accept his proposal, but he needed some privacy to seal the deal. I lost my appetite wondering what the hell he had in mind. Mya had been jittery all day anticipating what was to come, I suspected. I had the uncanny feeling that it wasn't going to end well. Vali commented that she had never seen me eat so little. I made some dumb excuse of having eaten too much at lunch. True to his word, right after dinner, Brian asked Mya if she was ready to talk. Her eyes said that she wasn't, but she nodded. He took her arm and led her towards the stairs. I stood up. Jake cautioned me to let it play out.

"He's not going to do anything with all of us down here Mitch. Mom can handle whatever he throws at her." Vali said unconvincingly.

I paced the living room like a caged animal. Jake kept vigil at the door ready to pounce if need be. The mantel clock ticked loudly. Fifteen minutes turned slowly into forty. "This is taking too long; I'm going up." I announced.

Bobbie put his hand on my arm to stop me just as Mya appeared at the top of the stairs. I did not like the look in her eyes as she descended. As soon as she had joined us I said that I needed some air. "If anyone's interested, Sadie and I will be at the dog park."

Mya asked sheepishly if she could join me.

Brian immerged buttoning up his shirt.

"If you like." I replied coldly.

We didn't speak for the four block ride to the park. I let Sadie out and turned to Mya. "Are you going to tell me what happened up there?"

"I can't go through with it Mitch. I can't bring any charges against him." She said pitifully.

"Oh, so that's how it is, you feel sorry for him and you want to give him another chance. I guess you've changed your mind about a divorce, and me also? What did he promise you?"

"He wants me to go on a holiday with him to Japan. He didn't promise me anything. I haven't changed my mind about anything Mitch."

"You came out of the bedroom looking pretty dishevelled, and Brian had the look of satisfaction on his smug mug. Did you do the happy dance for him?"

"What are you implying?"

"You know exactly what I am inferring. Did you part the sheets with him?"

She didn't deny it or cry asking me how I could accuse her of such a thing. She opened the door and got out. "I told you I was a tramp and that I bore easily. Good thing for you that you discovered who I really am before your wife agrees to a divorce. Brian loves me unconditionally, and so I will take my chances with him until something better comes along. I'm sure there is another dragon slayer out there somewhere. For a minute I thought it was you, but wrong again. Ha, look at me…I'm closing the door on you this time, but then you weren't in it for life anyhow. Have your lackey and equipment out of my house by end of day."

What just happened? I called Sadie and caught up to Mya, stopped and opened the door for her. She didn't acknowledge me and cut through somebody's yard. I lost sight of her as she disappeared into a grove of trees. I continued on down Marlboro not seeing her emerge anywhere. I parked at the bottom of her drive for fifteen minutes before I realized that I wouldn't be able to see her enter the house anyway. I decided to give her a little time before I burst into the house spilling the beans. She had decided to abandon the mission for whatever reason so our plans were all shot to hell. There was very little that we could confront Brian with so I may as well confess that his wife and I were not cousins at all, but lovers. I'd had it with his "holier than thou attitude" anyhow. I backed up and screeched out of the drive thinking it might be a good idea if I cooled off first.

I had been sitting in Artie's beat-up rattletrap staring across the street at my former residence for a while. I had no idea how or why I had ended up there. Was I contemplating reviving my marriage if Mya was indeed through with me? Hell, I was better than that! Just because Mya and I might not work out did not give me a license to promise Irene something that I could not deliver. Anyhow, I was deeply in love with Mya, and it was all just a little misunderstanding. What an asinine middle-aged fool I had been. Sadie was whining, the sound of thunder was echoing in the distance, sirens were blaring, and the mobile was ringing snapping me out of my despondent stupor. Reluctantly, I opened the glove compartment and extracted my cell. I guess

I hoped that Mya would be on the other end. I must have fallen asleep because the phone's display was blinking 7:30 P.M. It was already dark.

"Mitch; thank God, where are you?" Vali cried. "Please tell me that Mom is with you."

"She's not Vali. I haven't seen her since the dog park." I said apathetically.

"What do you mean? Didn't you drop her off?"

"No, we had an argument."

"Oh God, that's why she left."

"She's not at home?"

"No, she's gone Mitch; she's gone."

"What do you mean exactly?"

"She came in the house saying you were going to the office. She said she had a splitting headache and was going to lie down. Brian was sitting with the boys explaining his plans for the future of the company again. He told her he would check on her in a few minutes. She asked him not to as she was going to have a shower, take a Tylenol, and lie down and didn't want to be disturbed. I had the feeling that something was up with you and her so I waited about fifteen minutes and went up to see her. Her room was empty except for a wet towel on the floor, and a note on the bed. It said she was feeling overwhelmed and needed some quiet time to herself, and that we shouldn't worry."

"Did she tell Jake to collect all our equipment and vacate the premises?"

"No; what?"

"I guess she changed her mind."

"What are you talking about Mitch; changed her mind about what?"

"About me; she told me to leave."

"She loves you Mitch; she must have been upset."

"Yeah, she was upset all right, and I didn't help matters any. Did you check the greenhouse? She's probably up there doing what appeases her."

"Of course I did! She wouldn't have left a note if she was just going there, and her car is missing! It's dark, and she doesn't like to drive in the dark."

"Did she take the old blue?"

"No, her sports car. You know she hates driving that thing so that is what has me so worried, and Mitch, her sleeping pills are missing."

That revelation brought me to attention. "Damn, you're right, that car scares her, and it's dusk and storming. How do you know the sleeping pills are missing?"

"I just do, and it's not the first time Mitch."

"The first time for what

"That she's tried to kill herself."

My mouth was dry; the lump in my throat was constricting my breathing. "What are you saying...no, don't even suggest that!"

"I've been putting things together Mitch. She's not afraid of Brian, and there is no evidence to be found incriminating him so..."

Suddenly, everything made sense. "Don't say another word; I'm on my way."

"Where are you going?"

"To the cabin. I'm hanging up now."

"Hurry Mitch, hurry."

Even after all these years I still enjoyed my forty minute jaunt to Niagara Cove once I left the main highway. Tonight I had the feeling that Mayria's life depended on my swiftness. I made the trip in less than thirty minutes hoping that the old Chevy coupe wouldn't let me down. I talked nonstop to Sadie trying to calm myself. Lightning lit up the road ahead of me. The wipers were working overtime. I cursed. I half expected to round Dead Man's corner and find Mya's car in the ditch just as I had Vali's. I wasn't at all convinced that Mya was at the cabin or even knew how to get there. My heart started beating again when I pulled into the Cove and saw her yellow sports car in the drive. The house was dark. I unlocked it and scanned every room knowing full well that she wasn't in any of them.

Chapter 7
The Poisonings

I opened the back door and saw a dim light coming from the boathouse. Sadie barked and ran ahead of me. I always left the key under a moss covered rock. Obviously, Mya had taken notice.

I found her curled up in a fetal position in the bed behind the yellow door. An open prescription bottle sat on the overnight stand. I took a deep breath and lifted the coverlet. I put my hand on a warm body. "Thank God." I whispered.

She turned over. "You came for me Mitch."

I crawled into bed with her and took her in my arms. "I should never have let you get away. I'm so sorry for what I suggested."

"I didn't sleep with him Mitch. He wanted to, but I couldn't. I love you Mitch."

"I know you do Honey, and I love you. What were you thinking coming way out here in the dark and storm all alone?"

"I thought you would be here, but you weren't. Where were you?"

"No place in particular, but I'm here now. We have to go up to the house so that I can call Vali. She's worried sick about you as I am sure everyone is.

"Can't you call her from here?"

"No reception; and I don't even have a phone."

"I'll wait here."

"No, you're coming with me. It's cold in here, and we are both wet so we need to change and warm up." I coaxed her into getting up. I put her shoes on her and asked her if she could stand. She said of course she could. I picked up the bottle and asked her how many sleeping pills she had taken.

"There just peppermints Mitch."

I checked the bottle; they were indeed peppermints. I hugged her and asked why they were in a prescription bottle. She said it was the only thing handy.

I managed to get her down the steps and outside. Sadie met us at the door and ran circles around us as we climbed the hill stumbling at every footfall. I tried to laugh, but it came out as sounding more like a cry. My heart was tied up in knots knowing that this beautiful creature clutching onto me had tried to take her own life, not once, but maybe three times, and that I was probably the cause.

I sat her in the big armchair and wrapped the afghan around her. I cursed myself for not laying the fire before we had left last Wednesday.

"I'll have it warm in here in a few minutes." I promised her throwing wood and Firestarter into the fireplace. "I'll turn the electric on and make you some tea, and then we'll talk, okay? First I'm going to get you out of your wet clothes."

"I've done a bad thing Mitch." Her voice was filled with anxiety.

"I know, and we are going to fix it. Do you believe me when I say that everything is going to be all right, and that the sun will shine again tomorrow?"

She said she did. I kissed her and told her that I loved her again.

I put the kettle on and placed a call to the land line at the house on Marlborro. Vali answered on the first ring. I assured her that her mother was okay. I heard her relaying the news to the rest of the family.

"Brian wants to come and get her."

"Did you tell him where we are?"

"No, but he's insistent. Can't you hear him?"

"Put Bobby on the phone Vali."

"Okay."

"Mitch, is she really all right?"

"She is. She's cold and scared, but I've got everything under control. What has Vali told you?"

"Just that Mom isn't herself, whatever that is supposed to mean."

"She's emotionally distraught Bobby, but she's my responsibility, not Brian's. I promise that all will be revealed tomorrow. Brian is no longer a suspect...do you understand? Brian is not behind the alleged attempts on your mom's life. We were wrong; we were all wrong."

"I don't like where this is leading."

"Sorry Son. I need you and Jake to keep it together until morning. Can you do that?"

"Yeah, we will. Tell Mom that we love her."

I hung up the phone and checked on Mya. I went to find some dry clothes. I dressed quickly in a pair of kakis and pullover. I found Mya's pyjamas and grabbed my housecoat for her. Undressing and dressing her was a chore as her body did not want to cooperate. I asked her why she hadn't taken her wet clothes off before climbing into bed in the boat. She said she didn't know that she was wet.

The kettle was whistling. I made her a lavender blend tea. I figured I needed something a bit more substantial. I placed the cup of tea on the floor beside the fireplace and knelt down beside her. She asked if I hated her. Her eyes were moist. I knew I was as close as I had ever been to breaking down, but I'd have to hold it all together for a little while longer. I pulled her down on the floor beside me and rocked her liked a baby. She was my baby. I wanted to pick her up and put her in the car and drive until we found eternity. I told her I loved her more than I did a minute ago.

"I tried to put her out of my mind Mitch. I really did try, but when I moved to Seattle I just had to try one more time. I was so close to where I had lost her."

She didn't have to say anymore. Her guilt of giving up our daughter had ruled her life. She was never going to have closure until Lylah Jayne was found. That was my job, and I'd die trying.

She said through sobs that not only had she lost our baby, but she had lost me now too.

"You haven't lost me Honey. I'm right here, and I am not going anywhere."

"But I am Mitch. They are going to lock me in a rubber room and throw away the key."

"No one is going to do that Mya. Why would you say that?"

"Isn't that what they do to people who are mentally insane?"

I held her away from me so I could see her face. "You are just as sane as I am, and probably more so. You kept everything locked inside for so long that it reached a boiling point and you couldn't stand the pain anymore. You wanted to make it all go away didn't you, and the only way you knew how to do that was to escape into another world, so to speak. You are not the first one to rely on opioids to ease the pain of mind and body. What I don't understand is why you deliberately ingested the potassium chloride and thallium. Did you think that they would take the place of the pain pills somehow or...were you really planning on killing yourself?"

"You know what I did?"

"I never once suspected that you were responsible for the poisonings...not until an hour ago. The question is why, and did you hope to die?"

"I knew the consequences. I knew just how much my body could tolerate. You will find all the information on my computer. I'm the one who did all the research. I told you that the poisoner knew exactly what they were doing didn't I? I wasn't trying to kill myself Mitch; I was punishing myself."

"We'll get back to that in a minute. We checked your computer thoroughly thinking that maybe Brian had used it. There was nothing on it except for a few e-mails and unrelated internet queries. You knew that Frankie is an expert on computers, and he found nothing, so how did you manage to erase the files that you researched?"

"They are not on that computer."

"Where are they then? Did you borrow one from a friend, or did you go to a library?"

"I don't have any friends Mitch. I bought another laptop; it is under my bed."

I was mortified. "There are five of us Mya, five of us, and no one thought to look under your bed. The most important case of my life, and I almost blew it. I'm ashamed to say that I was neglectful...Brian could have very well hidden information there..."

"You would have just found out sooner that I was crackers wouldn't you?"

"That's why I know you are not crazy because you knew exactly what you were doing all along. A person with a severe mental disorder would not be so methodical. I'm in no way qualified to address the guilt you have carried with you for thirty years, so we are going to have to get you some professional help. I think the first step is that you need to forgive yourself. Can you do that for me Honey?"

"I will, as soon as we find Lylah. I don't want to lie on some psychiatrist's couch and relate thirty years of remorse to a stranger, so you can forget that. I won't hold you to anything Mitch. I love you, but I am unstable and won't saddle you with my problems. I need to set you free."

"Set me free? Do you think I am some bird or something? You can't set something or someone free if they don't want to go, and I'm not going anywhere. I have told you that a dozen times so it's high time you started to pay attention. Furthermore, if you kicked me out of your life, your self-punishing would just start all over again wouldn't it?"

She smiled slightly. "You are probably right because you were always part of my depression."

"Good to know." I said acknowledging my guilt. "Have you warmed up…good; more tea? How about I make us something to eat? Scrambled eggs and toast good enough?"

"Okay; I guess I could eat. I should help you."

"You stay here by the fire. We'll continue with this after we eat." I told her I loved her again.

Twenty minutes later she put her plate down. She asked me how much I knew.

"I really don't know anything for sure Mya."

"Where do you want me to start?"

"Wherever you're comfortable."

"I always dreamed of finding Lylah, and Bobby was going to help me. I already told you that. But he died, and I had to put it on the back burner because I had two little boys to care for. Then Vali came along, quite unsuspectingly. I doted on her never wanting to let her out of my sight. She did not replace the daughter that I had given away, but she filled that emptiness in my heart for a while. All of a sudden the boys were teenagers and I decide to leave the tranquillity of the farm in England and move back to Canada. It was up to me to get a start on making Bobbie's dream of joining the Canadian forces possible. A new Legend Hotel had recently opened in Toronto, and wasn't doing well. I inserted myself into management because I could, and I needed something to occupy my days with. Five years later Bobbie joins the Airforce. I believe it was 2007 or '08. Shortly after, Frankie, Vali and I moved to Boston. For some unknown reason I wanted to be near my parents. They lived in their own little world and didn't have time for us so a year later Vali and I moved on. Frankie stayed for another two years attending college. You know most of this already Mitch."

"Some of it, yes. I know Bobbie was born in Canada, but where were Frankie and Vali born?"

"Frankie was born in France, and Vali was born in Sommerset."

"You went back there…why?"

"I guess I thought that it was the right thing to do as her father was there."

"Did you think of staying there?"

"No, there were too many memories there so we left shortly after she was born."

"Am I one of those memories?"

"You and your grandmother were, and are, my memories. Perhaps I had this make-believe notion that you would be there. I didn't know where you were, but with one breath I hoped you were happily married with a half a dozen kids, and then in the next breath, I hoped you weren't. There was nothing left there for me."

"It doesn't do either of us any good saying that I wish I had kept track of you, but I wish I had. Hindsight is really twenty/twenty isn't it? No amount of apology will ever make it right."

"I could have searched for you sooner Mitch, but maybe I was too proud and afraid of rejection again. Anyhow, it's all in the past. What happens next is up to you. I have no choice but to admit what I did to the children, and in so doing, I will have to tell them about Lylah Jayne. Are you all right with that?"

"Yes, and we will do it together. They do not need to know all the gruesome details of the poisonings. After you have finished re-counting the rest of your story to me I will come up with a way to soften it. Now where were we…2010, I believe. I can't believe we haven't talked about this before."

"Maybe I didn't want you to know. Anyhow, we bought a small motor home, and Vali and I toured the USA for almost two years. One day I woke up and told her we were moving back to Canada. She said she hoped it wasn't Sommerset because if it was she was going to have to decline. I said it was Vancouver. We stopped in Seattle because Frankie had relocated there. I discovered that I could take either the train or ferry from Seattle to Vancouver and vice-versa in less than three hours each way so I chose to stay in Seattle. Of course, flying would be quicker."

"Can we go back a bit? I'm a little embarrassed to ask, but was it when you were touring that you had all those meaningless relationships?"

"You needn't be embarrassed as I broached that seedy part of my life on the first night at your cabin. I had sworn off men by the time Vali and I hit the road; she had too, so it was strictly mother and daughter. I do not wish to comment on my decadent search for love in Toronto any further. It is not a part of my life I want to revisit."

"I wasn't going to press you for depictions Mya. I hope you know that. I was just curious as to the timeline. We all have things in our past that we would rather forget. Please forgive me for broaching the subject. I never will again, and I never want you to refer to yourself as 'trampy' ever again…understood?"

"I suppose that depends on how often you ask me if I slept with Brian."

"Do you want to slap me, or should I do it myself?" I offered her my cheek.

She smiled impishly and put her hand on my cheek and caressed it. I kissed her fingers as they travelled across my face. She sat back and asked me if I knew why she wanted to be close to Vancouver. I told her I imagined that she was planning on taking up the search for Lylah again.

"It was because of you Mitch. I knew you lived there. I knew you were a private investigator...heck, I knew everything about you. I found it all on the internet."

"I knew everything about you too, that is up until about 2012 or so. You seemed to disappear after that, or at least from the tabloids. If I had of known you were living in Seattle..."

"You would have done what Mitch?"

"Well, I had already named my boat after you, so I'm pretty sure I would have looked you up."

"Hmm; so much time wasted, so much time. If only I had of confronted you on one of my many visits to Bourbon Street..."

"How many visits were there Mya? And, just for your information, it's Bour**don** not Bour**bon**."

"I like Bourbon better. I don't know; half a dozen, two dozen maybe."

"Damn; and I never saw you once!"

"You almost ran over me once."

"What? When? Hell, I remember a woman walked right behind me a year or so ago as I was backing down the drive. I thought I may have hit her so I jumped out, but she had already crossed the street and climbed into a bus. Are you telling me that was you?"

"I don't know; it might have been me. I guess it all depends on how many women you have almost run over. On the other hand, maybe I wanted you to hit me, but chickened out."

"Oh God Mya, I wish I had of...just lightly, though. Was the bus the way you got around?"

"Sometimes I took a taxi. If I was feeling overly adventurous I would drive myself."

"I thought you hated driving."

"I do, but I had to spell Vali off regularly when we were travelling, so I grin and bear it."

"Are you ready to get this inquisition over with so we can go to bed?"

"I don't think of it as such Mitch; it's my acknowledgment of my self-punishing. You are the only one I can bear my soul to...I hope you know that."

"I do, and I am grateful that you trust me enough to do so."

"Admitting to you how reckless and selfish I was may help me heal. I had always been reasonably healthy so when I started having stomach pain after marrying Brian, I was scared. I feared that I might be pregnant. Thank the heavens that I wasn't. Recovering from major surgery was painful and boring. I hated being confined to downstairs. I wanted to sleep in my own bed. One night I took two, maybe three of the pain pills that had been prescribed for me. I was three weeks or so into my surgery recuperation so I had figured that with a little help with the pain I could make it up the stairs, and I did. I was awakened from a deep sleep by Brian calling out my name. He was yelling that he had fallen down the stairs. I imagine I was in a stupor of sorts, and rushed out to help him. I remember standing at the top of the stairs, and then the lights went out. I woke up in the hospital. Not only had I incurred damage to my previous incision, I had a concussion, a badly bruised hip and tailbone, and injured my left leg. So, I was back in the bedroom downstairs again and terribly unhappy."

"I understand that Brian and Ivy found you, right?"

"Ivy was in the den with the television on. She had heard nothing until Brian yelled for her to call 911."

"I believe the consensus is that you were pushed?"

"There is no proof, and I had self-medicated, so an overdose was the official verdict. Ivy was in charge of the pain pills from then on, but I found a way around that."

"I'm almost afraid to ask how."

"You don't have to ask because I am going to tell you. I called in an order to a grocery store that delivers and hoped that Dick Dyson would be the delivery boy, and he was. I had specified that I needed the items delivered immediately. Ivy had stepped out to run a couple of errands while I was supposed to be sleeping. I wasn't sure how much time I had, but I managed to get myself into the wheelchair and wheel myself to the back door. Dick arrived. I asked him if he or one of his buddies could procure some Percocet, or a reasonable facsimile for me. He balked at first. I explained my situation and pulled five one hundred dollar bills out of my pocket. I told him there would be more upon delivery. I told him that it had better be clean and to deliver it only to me. I left how he was going to disguise it up to him. That evening he arrived with a shopping bag with several get well gifts from his mother. I thanked him with a handshake that contained another five hundred dollars. Ivy asked me if I knew his mother. I said I didn't, but I supposed that Dick had relayed my tribulations to her and she had replied in kind."

"That was very risky Mya. Marijuana would have been safer." I said in a scolding voice. I didn't want to admonish her too much or she might decide to quit talking.

"I tried it, but didn't like it. I knew it was risky, and I was lucky that it wasn't laced with anything deadly. I never had to resort to back street drugs again because of the potassium deficiency."

She moved away from me and tossed the afghan on the floor. She reached for my drink and downed it in one gulp. I told her that was straight whiskey.

"You can make me another while I make use of the facilities, please and thank-you."

I cracked a tray of ice and filled a glass for her going a little easy on the liquor. She noticed.

"I want you of sound mind for the next few minutes. I don't want an intoxicated brain confusing the facts." I said in an apologetic voice.

"It wouldn't make any difference because believe me, it is all etched in my mind. I hadn't been to see you for almost a year. When I was well enough I asked Ivy to take me for a ride. I told her there was this charming little tea house over on Bourbon that I had discovered strictly by accident. Ivy didn't like driving any more than I did, but she reluctantly agreed. It was noonish, so I thought I might catch you going out for lunch. I just wanted to catch a glimpse of you, but I didn't. I went home down heartened again."

She knew how to make me feel deflated even if there was no reason for me to do so. I sighed and asked a futile question. "Did you ever think of picking up the phone and calling me?"

"I did, several times, but Shannon always answered and I hung up."

I wanted to tell her that her actions were that of a teenage girl, but didn't. It was if she had read my mind.

"I know it was childish of me, but down deep I guess I wasn't really ready to have you see me, or me you. I did see two men come out of your office once. I know them now as Jake and Mel. I can see by the look in your eyes, and on your face, that you are wondering what the hell you got yourself mixed up with, and that no amount of unadulterated pleasure is worth objecting yourself to my craziness ...just say the word Mitch, and we can go back to being strangers."

I shook my head. "Okay, I will say it. You are crazy...crazy if you think anything you did is going to make me walk away. I do not feel threatened by any of your admissions. It is just the opposite; you have inflated my ego. To know that you risked your health to seek me out is overwhelming. Do you want to go on or call it quits for the night?"

She shook her head. "I'll be brief. It wasn't just when I came to Bourbon Street that I thought about Lylah and you. I cannot explain why I suddenly felt such a need to find her; it was just something I felt. I can't expect that you would understand it; maybe it's just a mother thing."

"I do understand Mya because I feel it now too...the urgency to find Lylah. There is no doubt in my mind that she is the girl in my dreams, and that she is in danger."

"Oh, what have I done to you Mitch? I've got you chasing windmills..."

"As long as I am chasing them with you it's okay."

She kissed me, picked up her drink and relocated to the sofa. It was a good idea as I had pins and needles in my legs from sitting on the floor for so long. I chose a chair opposite her.

"About a week or two after my visit to see you, I began having stomach pains and cramps again. I thought that maybe the pain pills were the cause, so I let up on them. The pain didn't go away, and I became irritable and weak. I didn't want to eat as everything made me want to throw-up. Unknown to me, Ivy had made me an appointment to see a doctor. She had randomly chosen one on-line. She made a good choice. When I started having breathing problems Ivy rushed me off to see her. I was diagnosed with a potassium deficiency and was put on KCL, potassium chloride tablets. I had to eat healthier and Ivy saw to that. The dried apricots and prunes and bananas I could tolerate, but broccoli and lentils were another thing. I started to feel better quite fast, but then I realized that the severe pain had kept me from obsessing over Lylah. I decided to quit taking the pills because the physical pain was better than the emotional roller coaster I had been riding before. I researched potassium chloride and soon found out that extra doses of it would have the same effect as being deficient. Ivy had trusted me to administer the tablets so it was easy for me to take an extra one, and then two extra, and on, and on. I wanted to be numb again, and screw the pain."

"Oh God Mya, you're breaking my heart." I plunked down beside her and took her into my arms. "You could have died before I even knew...Where the hell was Brian all this time?"

"I don't know; working, or out of town, or in a love nest with some bimbo. Anyhow, you know the rest. I over dosed and was rushed to the hospital again. When asked why I was taking more than the recommended dosage, I lied and said that I wasn't aware that I was. I was kept under observation for a week until Vali arrived and took responsibility for my care. I was on the straight and narrow," she paused and laughed, "so to speak for a while."

I was holding her hand. "There is nothing funny about this at all Mya. I have kept my tongue...but why in hell couldn't you just have called me and told me about Lylah? You could have died; she might already be dead..." I got up and looked down at her.

"I disgust you don't I?" She asked glumly.

"I don't know what I am right now. I know I am scared because I have to come up with a reasonable lie for the kids to accept..."

She tugged on my sleeve. "No, you don't Mitch! It's up to me to tell them, and I am going to tell them the truth just as I am telling you."

"Like hell you are! We are going to sugar coat it as much as we can. We are going to be married, so they are my family too. I won't have them thinking that their mother tried to kill herself even if it wasn't her intention. It wasn't just our daughter; it was me who set everything in motion, so you are going to let me handle it. Now get on with the self-punishing courtesy of thallium that was viewed as another suicide attempt." I wanted this night to be over.

"I was never consciously trying to kill myself Mitch. How could I? I was just punishing myself because I gave her away, and I was so afraid of you rejecting me again."

"You had no way of knowing that I wouldn't, but after thirty years did you not once think that maybe I was living in some hell of my own?" I pushed her hand away. "It doesn't matter because I am here now, and you are my responsibility... now, and forever. I am going to make all the decisions going forward, and you are damn well going to go along with whatever I come up with...are you clear on that?"

She said she was and could she have another drink. I told her "no" and to quit stalling.

"Okay." She said sheepishly. "Vali was in charge of my KCL and pain pills, and I went back to feeling remorseful again. I had been neglectful of the plants in the greenhouse so they had all died. Vali took me to a nursery where I restocked. It was last spring. I have a gardener whom I think you have met who looks after the lawns, hedges and perennials in the front and back yards. His name is Pete. One day I found him unloading a bag of fertilizer. I approached him and told him that my plants weren't doing so well so maybe I was using the wrong fertilizer. He came up with me to the greenhouse and suggested that I try what he used. He gave me a small bag of it and a fifty pound bag of planting soil. He had me read the bag of fertilizer so that I was aware of the dangers of overuse. It had a list of elements including arsenic and thallium, and a warning that it was harmful when misused. He cautioned me to always wear a long sleeved shirt, gloves and a mask, and to always make sure that there was lots of ventilation when I was using it or any other fertilizer. He showed me how to mix it with the planting medium and how to mix a small amount into the soil of already planted flowers and vegetables. I followed his directions at first, and then I guess I got careless…"

I interrupted her. "You guess? Did you or didn't you ignore his warnings?"

"I honestly don't know. Sometimes I forgot to wear gloves, and I hated the masks. When summer rolled around I quit wearing protective clothing as it was too hot. I would go up early in the mornings to beat the heat. There was a time I became concerned that maybe the tomatoes and cucumbers could be toxic if eaten so I pulled out my lap-top and researched thallium and arsenic. I was satisfied that they were safe. I had also read all the warning signs of thallium poisoning. A few weeks later I started to experience some of the symptoms. I convinced myself that I had unconscionably transferred what I had read into my addled mind. I was still able to function though I had a headache every day, and was tired all the time, and my legs ached. I wasn't fixating on you and Lylah anymore when I was in pain, so that was a good thing. I suspected that it was the ingredients in the fertilizer that was causing my discomfort, but if I got any worse I wouldn't use it anymore. I felt that I was in control. I kept visiting the greenhouse daily until I developed a skin rash and a scaling on my hands. I quit fertilizing, but I guess the damage had already been done. It was all accidental, but of course because of my previous history it was looked into as a possible suicide attempt. My greenhouse and the yards were thoroughly examined. There were only trace amounts found in the greenhouse and very minute amounts in the yard. How so much was found in my system was a mystery, but it was finally deemed that I was highly susceptible to the metal, and that it had been absorbed into my body through my skin and as an inhalant. Apparently, very small quantities are lethal and therefore doses are easy to transport, conceal, and mix. The kids were highly suspicious that Brian was behind both the poisonings and I let them believe that he might be. He had refused to give me a divorce so I threw him under the bus. My conscience got the best of me and I can't frame an innocent man even though he disgusts me. There is no sugar-coating the truth

Mitch. You do believe that I wasn't trying to kill myself don't you? If I had of wanted to commit suicide, I would have just stuck my head in the oven."

"Stop joking! I wish you would quit treating that what you did as an everyday occurrence. Did you ever come to see me… that's a laugh isn't it, during that time?"

"Yes, of course I did."

"When was the last time?"

"A few days before I was last hospitalised."

"So you were already sick then?"

"Yes, I had fears that I might be dying, and I needed to tell you about Lylah."

"But, you didn't; why?"

"It was the end of June There was a sign on your office door that said the office would be closed for two weeks for holidays. There was no emergency forwarding telephone number."

"So, you were actually going to make contact with me? Never mind, it doesn't matter. It never happened because I wasn't available. When I was, you were in the hospital recuperating from thallium poisoning. I let you down again didn't I?"

"No, you didn't. None of this was your fault, so get rid of that notion! The damage was already done. There wasn't anything you could have done."

"So, why didn't you contact me after you got out of the hospital?"

"I didn't want you to see me like that. I was in pretty bad shape. I needed time to recuperate. I was constantly at the hospital having my blood and urine measured to confirm that I was on a decreasing trend. I was treated with a substance called Prussian Blue. I had to have the treatment until my urine concentration returned to a safe reference range. I was lucky as it happened relatively fast. Apparently, it can take years or is never achieved."

"You consider yourself lucky do you? For three years you have either been in pain, in the hospital, recovering from a fall down the stairs and subjected to two different poisons. It hasn't been much of a life has it? You still have excruciating headaches don't you? All of this could have been avoided if you'd only told me about Lylah." I was trying to keep my voice on an even keel but I was failing. "Suppose if Brian was really trying to get rid of you starting with the accident on the stairs? It would have been easy for him to put extra crystals of potassium chloride in your milk or tea at night, and how about an extra handful of tainted thallium in your potting soil…did you ever consider that?"

"No, why would I? He loved me then, and he loves me now; he wouldn't do anything to harm me. It's very easy to fake a headache Mitch, and Brian's presence forces me to do so."

"I see you have taken a complete turn- around. He's your golden haired boy who wouldn't harm a hair on your head, never mind that he has been cheating on you by your own admission. You went along with the kids to blame him just to calm them didn't you? It had nothing to do with finding me did it? I'm beginning to believe that you never had any attention of telling me about Lylah, that is, if there really is a Lylah." I hated myself for insinuating that she still had feelings for Brian, and that maybe Lylah didn't even exist, but I needed to enflame her. By the way she reacted to my accusations, I think I did.

She was in tears. "How can you say such a cruel thing? If you want me to hate you again then you have just accomplished it!"

"Good, there is still some fight in you. Now, go put yourself into bed while I take Sadie out for a walk. By the way, did you know that the bag of fertilizer is missing from your greenhouse?"

I knew the whole story of the poisons was true because what kind of a devious mind could create such a fabrication? I was ashamed of myself for badgering her. I was probably going to have to get down on my hands and knees and beg her to forgive my arrogance. I was good at sucking-up; I'd been taking lessons from Jake.

ππππ

Chapter 8
Aftermath

He was giving me orders again. I wasn't sure how long I was going to put up with him doing so. I knew that I had mood changes, but so did he. Sometimes he sympathised with me, and other times he questioned my intentions and sincerity. He was definitely wary of Brian even though I had absolved him of any wrongdoing. I was curious as to why he had said that the fertilizer was missing. I picked up our glasses, washed them, dried them, and put them in the cupboard. The back yard light was on. I couldn't see Mitch or Sadie. It was still raining. There was nothing left to do but go to bed. I wondered if he would choose to sleep elsewhere.

Five minutes later I heard the door close and Mitch sending Sadie to her bed beside the fireplace. He came in the bedroom towelling his wet hair. He stripped down to his briefs. He asked me if I was going to move over. I rolled over to the far side of the bed. If he so much as touched me I knew I would break into tears again.

"Well, not that far! Get back over here."

That order I didn't mind filling. He said it had been one hell of a day and we had better get some much needed sleep, and be prepared for whatever tomorrow had in store for us. He bent down and kissed me lightly and said goodnight. He kissed me again, a little longer and said goodnight again. I said goodnight and was about to turn over when he kissed me again. This time long, and passionately.

"Do you want to make love? It's either that or a cold shower." He said it like I had to choose.

"I always want to make love with you, but if you would rather take a cold shower I'm okay with that too. I wouldn't want you to feel like making love with me was some sort of duty, or an apology for what you said about Lylah."

He turned the lamp off and pulled me close to him. "I'm sorry Babe. I know I don't always come off as a compassionate person, but believe me I am sympathetic to everything that you have endured. Can you forgive me for my blunders? I have never gone through anything like this before. Every case I have been involved with has been just that...a case that had no personal consequence for me. If I fail at this one then I'm going to fail both us, and there will be no coming back for either of us. It's no excuse for my imprudence but..."

I stopped him. "Thank-you; I needed to hear that, but I don't want you to feel like you are walking on eggs by expressing your opinions and asking me sensitive questions. I'm a big girl, and if I feel you're a little too overbearing than it is my problem and I will try and deal with it. I've never been in this situation before neither Mitch, so yes, it is overwhelming. You're not the only one who is afraid. I'm terrified that you will tire of me and realize that I am way more than what you bargained for. Love may not be a road you want to travel down with me."

He hushed me with a kiss again. "Nope, not going to happen, and I will go down any road with you no matter how rocky it may get. Now what say we get on with the business at hand?"

I was up before Mitch the next morning. I put a pot of coffee on, grabbed Sadie's leash and took her outside for a walk. The rain had let up, but the ground was wet and muddy. I kept her in the grass so she wouldn't get too dirty. Once back inside I wiped my feet on the inside rug and encouraged her to do the same thing while I toweled her off. I heard a muffled laugh. Mitch was standing at the kitchen sink with a mug of coffee in his hand.

"I see it, and I still don't believe it."

"I told you she would learn didn't I? Want to pour me one of those?"

He handed me a cup. "I must say that this was an added pleasure waking up to the smell of coffee that somebody else made besides me."

"Someone at the house always makes coffee."

"I mean at my old residence."

"Surely Irene make it for you once in a while?"

"Periodically, but she usually forgot to put actual coffee into the pot, so it was undrinkable."

I smiled. He told me to sit down as he had the story that we were going to tell everyone all worked out. I listened carefully. He asked me if I was in agreement. I said I was.

Three blocks from home Mitch called Jake on his cell. He asked him to have everyone seated in the kitchen, and that it might be wise if he and Bobbie flanked Brian. We stopped outside the door. Mitch asked me if I was all right. I nodded that I was. He winked at me and said, "That's my girl." We walked in the house hand and hand.

Before Mitch even finished wishing everyone a good morning Brian was on his feet demanding to know what was going on and where had I been.

"Sit down pal; let's hear them out." Jake suggested by putting his hand on Brian's shoulder.

"Not before that charlatan gets his hands off my wife!" Brian roared. "He's no more Tessa's cousin than I am the king of England!"

Mitch sat me down between Vali and Ivy. He placed his hands lovingly on my shoulders. "You're right about that Brian; you are definitely not the king of England, and I am most definitely not Mya's cousin. However, we did know each other thirty years ago. We were sweethearts then, just as we are now."

Brian was on his feet again. He kicked his chair over in an attempt to come around the table to get to Mitch. Jake and Bobbie both took hold of him and suggested that he remain seated. Bobbie righted the chair and forcefully sat him down. Jake opened his vest to reveal a gun in a holster strap. Brian went berserk.

"So, you are all in on this charade? This imposter has been screwing my dear sweet little wife and you are all okay with it! How long Tessa, how long?"

I looked up at Mitch and he nodded. That meant it was time for me to confess. I had to get one last barb in first. "Not as long as you have been carrying on with Carmen, or all the other women who fell for your line of bull. Unfortunately, I was one of them."

He tried to interrupt me, but Jake tapped his chest and shook his head. Brian closed his mouth.

"We, my family and me, hired Mitch, who by the way is a private investigator, to prove that you have been trying to kill me."

"That's a fucking lie! I never tried to kill you...where in the hell did you get such a crazy idea? From your little slut of a daughter..."

Jake slugged him so hard that he fell to the floor. He picked Brian up by his collar and threatened him under his breath. I think Brian finally got the word that Jake was serious.

I continued as if nothing had happened smiling as Brian rubbed his jaw. "Mitch and I have renewed our love for each other." I patted his hand. "He is the only man I have ever truly loved. I had been looking for him for a very long time. I found him, but I couldn't bring myself to approach him with the secret that I had been harboring for thirty years. It was slowly eating away at me. The only time I could put it out of my mind was when I was sick. The pain seemed to numb me, and I could tuck Lylah Jayne into the back of my mind for a little while."

The room was silent. It's true what the old proverb says: "You could have heard a pin drop."

Mitch knelt down on the floor beside me. My eyes were filled with tears and sobs were racking my body. Ivy and Vali both had hold of my hands. It was as if they knew what was coming. Mitch asked if I wanted him to continue for me. I told him that he had better. He stood up still holding on to me. He directed his words to my children.

"This lady is the bravest woman I have ever met. Thirty years ago I made the biggest mistake of my life...I walked away from her. I loved her, but I was young and foolish. I have thought about her often...hell, I even named my boat after her."

There were a few hushed "Whats?" from the room.

"One week ago, she came back into my life and lit it on fire again. You all know that I am married, but never had any children. I had a severe bout of the mumps when I was a teenager and I always figured it made me sterile. Then along comes this woman and tells me that I am crazy because I fathered a child with her thirty years ago."

He let that sink in. Vali and Ivy were crying. Frankie and Bobbie both came over to me and hugged me. Frankie said he was so sorry.

I found my voice. "Don't be my darling. This story *may* have a happy ending. I did give birth to Mitch's child on August 29th, 1988. I named her Lylah Jayne after Mitch's grandmother who was like a mother to me. I was seventeen with no visible means to support myself, less a child. I'm afraid I took the easy way out and gave her up for adoption, so she may very well be alive.

"Oh Mom," Vali wept, "we can find her. We can find her can't we Mitch?"

"Yes Honey, we can. Mel and Shannon have been working on it around the clock for days. We are almost there...God willing; you will have a new sister soon. How does that sit with you all?"

They were all talking at once wanting to know more, and how could they help. The telephone rang. We let the answering machine get it. It was Dr. Graham's office saying they had a cancellation and would Vali like the appointment for Tuesday at ten thirty. She shook her head, grabbed the phone, and said she would have to pass.

I asked her why she did that as she had been waiting to have her tooth repaired for ages. She said she couldn't because that was the day her sister might be arriving. I laughed a little telling her it wasn't going to happen that quickly. I asked for the phone, redialed, and accepted the appointment for her. This would be something I would come to regret.

Brian was seething. "You are all a bunch of blithering idiots! Especially you," he directed his wrath at Mitch, "believing that I tried to kill her, and that you're the father of *her* bastard child! She's been around the block a few dozen times..."

Jake grabbed him by his collar. "One more word of filth from you and you're a dead man!"

"Take your grimy hands off me and get out of my house!"

Jake would have slugged him again if Mitch hadn't stopped him. "Take a breather Jake; I'll handle this."

He let go of me and laughed maliciously at Brian. I noticed a bulge under his shirt as he rose. Could it possibly be a gun?

"*Your* house; is your name even on the deed? We both know the answer don't we? That's not the issue here though; your attempts to murder Mya are. Shut up; it's not your turn to talk!

She's the woman I love, and one more word of disrespect from you is going to land you in the hospital...comprehend? Now, let's get down to brass tactics. You can deny your innocence as much as you like, but facts don't lie. Want to show him what we've uncovered Frankie? You know that he's somewhat of an aficionada when it comes to computers don't you?"

"So, what's that got to do with me?" Brian asked caustically.

Frankie gathered the data from the dining room bureau and sat it down in front of Brian.

"What the hell is all this mumbo jumbo?"

"Some facts we acquired from your computers."

"I'll have your license!" Brian attempted to pull his phone out of his pocket.

"Who are you calling there buddy?" Jake asked.

"Don't call me your buddy, asshole! I'm calling my lawyer. I see you amateurs don't even know that it's illegal to open someone's personal computer without permission. How the hell did you get by the security? Just a damn minute, did you say com-**puterS**? What have you done Tess?" He was so angry he was spitting.

"Make the call, and while you are doing that I will call my pal Detective Rory Adams who heads up the Criminal Intelligence Unit with the Vancouver Police department. He's been doing some digging into your tarnished business practices. I have thrown him a bone or two about your suspected involvement with Mya's poisonings. He's ready to pounce, and these files are just what he needs. Oh yeah, we had a nice little tour of your offices and factory. Security is a little lax wouldn't you say Frankie?" Mitch said gloating.

Brian shuffled the papers and threw them in the air. "I don't need to read any of this garbage. There is nothing anywhere that can indict me...oh, I see, you've doctored the books."

"Just took a little professional liberty. One thing has me stumped though; why did you remove the fertilizer from Mya's greenhouse?"

"What the hell are you talking about?"

Ivy had retrieved her camera from the drawer behind her and passed it to Mitch. He showed Brian the images that Ivy had captured. "A day ago Ivy remembered that she had photographed Mya in the greenhouse, and also of your comings and goings after Mya had been hospitalized with thallium poisoning. This first one is of Mya holding a potted orchid. You can see the time stamp at the bottom, and the large bag of potting soil behind her, and a bag of fertilizer on the counter. You can even read part of the "Danger" tag. Next one was taken after the forensic team had investigated the greenhouse. You can see the yellow incident tape is up. Ivy was curious and visited the crime scene and snapped another picture. You can see the bag of fertilizer is still there. Why it wasn't confiscated by the team is a mystery, but then...see here...there you are entering the greenhouse, carefully ducking under the tape. You emerge with a large garbage bag, load it up in your truck and drive away. Ivy revisits the greenhouse, and lo and behold, the bag of fertilizer is gone. Again, why did you remove it? Did you suddenly realize that your fingerprints might be all over the bag that almost caused Mya's death? Was it a triple dosage of thallium? Come on, fess up. It's a heavy metal so surely every gram has to be accounted for or did you doctor *your* books?"

Brian was looking a little pale. "There is no collusion on my part. I wouldn't harm one hair on Tessa's head...I love her." He looked at me pleadingly. "You know that Tess; how could you accuse me of wanting to kill you?"

"I asked you for a divorce, not once, but at least a dozen times. Your answer was always the same; "I'd sooner see you dead than give you a divorce." And then I got sick. First it was with an overdose of potassium chloride and then the thallium. Doesn't leave much to the imagination now does it?"

"You know damn well that is not true Tess! If I said something like that it was a wisecrack. We all say things we don't actually mean."

"Well, I still want a divorce, so we have a proposition for you." I gave the floor to Mitch.

"How does this all sit with you Brian?" Mitch asked standing over my soon to be ex-husband.

Brian laughed. "Is this all you got; not much for a private dick is it?"

"May not seem like much to you, but paired with what Lieutenant Adams is formulating it'll be enough to tie your businesses up for some time. Oh yeah, did I mention that the government is most interested in your dealings with the Chinese? For two days now we have listened to your ravings about your multi- million dollar contracts with them, and your innuendoes that it's not quite on board legally...did you think we weren't paying attention? What you got there Frankie? Are you saying you recorded it all?"

"You are all a bunch of sons of bitches! You might think you have some trumped up evidence against me, but none of it is admissible so let's put an end to this dog and pony show and tell me what the hell you want." Brian demanded.

"Delighted to; you can take your chances and spend endless hours of denial with the feds or fending off charges of attempted murder, or you can take our sweet deal. One signature and *this* all goes away." Mitch picked up the documents off the floor and placed them in front of Brian. "Take a closer look, especially at the copy of your ex- wife's death certificate. Was her death really accidental, or did you have a hand in it too?"

I gasped. Mitch had not informed me that he had that information. I was surprised at Brian's calm reaction to the accusation.

"You've really hit the bottom of the barrel haven't you by bringing a distressing time in my life into this? Not that it is any of your freaking business, but Lola died an agonizing death from a rare disease, and that is all I will say about that." Brian got up. "Whatever your so called deal is, I will take a pass. It's been a deplorable pleasure gents. If it's all right with you Tess, I'll collect a few things and take my leave until you get rid of the vermin."

He scooped up the papers saying his lawyer would get a kick out of the misinformation.

Mitch still had an ace up his sleeve. "It's time to give Rory a jingle Jake. May as well dial up Les O'Halloran too; should be some party; a cop, a lawyer, and an informant."

Brian shot daggers at Mitch. He sat back down and asked what the deal was. He hadn't balked when Mitch had mentioned Detective Adams before so it must be this Les fellow who had Brian do an about face.

"It's straight forward; no lawyers or court involved if you don't contest the settlement agreement. The assets that need to be addressed are personal property, real estate, automobiles, and investments and bank accounts. It is advisable that you agree to the terms which are: Both of you leave the marriage with what you came into it with. Mya keeps the house and property and furnishings as they are legally hers, and you did not contribute monetarily to any of it. The artwork you purchased is yours and will be shipped to you along with anything else that you brought into the marriage. She wants nothing to do with your businesses so she waves all rights to any of it. She stipulates that her name is to be removed from all properties. Her yellow sportster and blue Buick sedan remain with her possessions. Your fleet of vehicles remain as your assets. The business account is to be dissolved. Mya wishes no compensation from the profits if there be any. There was no personal joint account so it does not factor. If you are in agreement with this marital settlement, and that you do not contest the divorce, then all that is left is for you to do is sign this legal document dissolving the marriage. You do not need to be present when the decree is presented to the court if you chose not to be. Any questions?"

"I take it you moonlight as a lawyer?" Brian asked Mitch sarcastically as he read over the document.

"It's a simple procedure. I had a paralegal do the paperwork and she will meet us at the courthouse Monday morning, 9 o'clock sharp. Can we count on seeing you then?"

Brian picked up the pen and scribbled his signature. "Sure, what the hell; I've nothing else scheduled for that morning so may as well get a divorce. Is this what you want Tess, or has this charlatan filled your head with promises that he has no intentions of keeping? By the way, how long does this quickie divorce take?"

I answered frowning. "It could take up to a year, but I'm hoping it is granted immediately."

He winked at me. "A lot can happen in a year you know Tess."

I knew that Mitch was ready to wallop Brian as did Jake and I. Jake nudged Brian and said that it was time to go, but first he owed Vali and me an apology for his disrespectful remarks.

Brian made an effort to bow to Vali and me. "No hard feelings ladies; I just call them as I see them…sorry for the vulgarity if it offended you."

I waited until the four men with Brian in tow had exited the house. Ivy and Vali started preparing lunch. I asked what I could do to help. She told me I could make a fresh pot of coffee as Mitch would surely be ready for one. I filled the carafe with water and carefully measured the coffee, adding a half scoop extra. I muttered. "I wouldn't want Mitch comparing my coffee making to Irene's."

Ivy asked me what I had said.

"Mitch will probably want something a lot stronger than coffee. I'm going to take a shower as I suddenly feel dirty."

"Don't be too long, lunch is in twenty minutes." Ivy called out as I reached the stairs.

Mitch was buttoning up a clean shirt when I came out of the bathroom. I asked him if he felt dirty too. He said he didn't, just a little sweaty, and asked me why I did.

I opened my underwear drawer and extracted a frilly pair of black panties. I dropped the towel and searched for a camisole. "Are you just going to sit there and stare at me?"

"Yup, do you mind? I'll even throw in a buck or two for the performance." He solicited playfully.

I pulled an oversized caftan out of the closet and yanked it on over my head. "Wouldn't matter if I did because you pretty much do as you want anyhow?"

"Hey, where is this coming from? Are you mad at me?"

"Where did you put your gun?"

"It's in a safe place. Is that what's got your goat?"

"It had better be locked up so I can't get my hands on it."

"Okay; I feel some sort of hostility here. Are you not pleased with the outcome of the day? Is it aimed at me or Brian?"

I walked to the door. "Why did you not feel the need to inform me of the information you presented to Brian? Accusing him of killing his bedridden wife was hitting below the belt don't you think?"

"No, weren't we accusing him of trying to murder you? I didn't think bringing suspicion of another death into the picture was unreasonable."

"Of course you didn't. Are you forgetting that Brian had no hand in my poisonings?"

"I'm still not convinced of that, or the fall down the stairs."

I threw my hands in the air. "As usual, you are right, and you can make up my mind for me. I guess I am safe for the time being so I won't require your protection anymore. We may as well get the matter of payment settled. Make me out a bill, and don't forget the night-time overtime. Do you want cash or a cheque?"

He either thought it was time for a joke or else that I was baiting him. He laughed and said he would take it out in trade. I gave him a rude gesture, told him he couldn't afford me, and walked out. He wasn't laughing anymore.

"Come on you two, food is on the table!" Vali yelled from the bottom of the stairs.

I did not take my usual spot that would have had me sitting next to Mitch. Instead I chose the other side of the table and slid in between Bobbie and Frankie.

Mitch sat next to Vali. She looked at him suspiciously out of the corner of her eye, and then at me. I ignored her questioning stare. Everyone knew something was up, but no one said anything except pass the salt, or I'll have a bun please. I pushed the food around on my plate. Bobbie commented that he hadn't had a potato pancake since the farm so that led to some reminiscing from his siblings. I put on a smile for their sakes. Mitch got up and got a beer out of the fridge offering one to everyone else. They all declined.

"I told you didn't I Ivy?" I said rather triumphant.

Vali put her fork down. "Okay, what the hell is going on with you two? You're not sitting together fawning over each other like usual; you won't even look in the other's direction, so what's up? What could possibly have happened in ten minutes?"

"Your mother is upset with me." Mitch offered as a reason.

"Everything went according to plan didn't it? Brian is out of our lives and agreed to a divorce, so what *is* the problem?" She looked directly at me.

"Mitch chose to keep me out of the loop…again. We are supposed to be a team, but he bosses me around like I am a child, and thinks he knows my mind better than I do myself. I had no idea about some of the things that went down today. Yesterday we were in full agreement of what *we* would be presenting to Brian, but that all went amuck, and Mitch went off on his own tangent. What I found most deplorable was his insinuation that Brian had killed his ailing wife." I started to get up. Bobbie asked me to sit down and give Mitch a chance to explain. I crossed my arms.

"She's right. I'm guilty of everything she said. I think she wants me out of her life." Mitch said glumly locking eyes with me.

"I never said that. You want them, *my* children, to take your side so whatever you say they are going to believe your take on it because their mother has made one mistake after another. They know you are not a mistake."

"Do you think I'm a mistake Mya?"

I shook my head.

"Then listen to me Honey." His eyes were pleading with me. "No one is going to take anyone's side here. I love you, and I love your family. For thirty years I wandered and looked for a close facsimile to what I had left behind in Sommerset. Yeah, I found women, I even married one, but there was always this problem… none of them were you. From the moment Vali mentioned your name, I knew I was in trouble. You know very well what happened next. We discovered we still had deep feelings for each other, and now here we are in some sort of a lover's quarrel which I will take full responsibility for. I can bare my soul here to all because I want them to accept me and trust me with your love. I already think of them as family, and hope they will come to think of me as so one day also. This last week has been the happiest in my life. I actually feel like I have found my tribe, and a home. Tell me what to say or do please Mya because I don't want to lose any of this life you have shared with me in the last week."

"We already consider you as family you know that Mitch... Mom?" Vali pleaded.

"Will you stop treating me like a baby?" I asked Mitch.

"But Honey, you are my baby...sorry; yes, I will do my damndest." Mitch got up and invited me to go with him so he could apologize for his sins of the day.

"You're coming back aren't you? We want to hear more about thirty years ago and Lylah Jayne. You're not going to fire him are you Mom?" Vali questioned.

"And the boat; I want to hear about the boat. Can we see the boat?" Frankie pleaded.

Mitch took my hand at the end of the table and asked me where I would like to go to talk. I said I didn't care, and where did he suggest. He said it was my decision. I asked him if he was going to allow me to make all the decisions from now on. He asked me what I thought.

"I think you will come up with a way to make me believe I did." I steered him towards the stairs muttering that we may as well get away from inquiring ears and eyes.

He agreed. "You know if we decide to keep on living here we should install an elevator?"

"Do you want to take the elevator?"

"She said it as if there was an elevator." He supposed.

"There is. Have you not seen it? It's right beside my private room."

He followed me down the hall. "I thought that was a linen closet."

"Yes, I could see how you might think that as all our linen closets have up and down buttons on them." I stepped inside the stuffy enclosure.

"Are you being sarcastic?"

"Who me?"

He asked me why I wouldn't have mentioned the elevator before, and then something clicked in his head as the door opened unto the top floor next to another linen closet.

"Why wouldn't you have used the elevator instead of the stairs the night of your fall?"

"Did I mention that I was probably stoned and didn't know what I was doing?"

"Sorry; I wouldn't have thought that you'd forget that there was an elevator in the house. You favor your left leg so I imagine climbing the stairs still causes you pain. The elevator seems like a safer and sound solution."

"If it bothers me I'll let you know, but I need the exercise." I said as he opened the bedroom door. "Are you sure that you still want to live here with me?"

We sat on the edge of the bed. He looked into my eyes, kissed my forehead and asked me the same question. I said I did and that it didn't matter where we lived.

"Good, because I want to continue living with you too, and your right, it doesn't matter where we live, just as long as we are together. I am going to try and be the man you deserve Mya. Tell me what you don't like about me beside the fact that I am bossy, have a smart-alecky mouth, and treat you like a child. Tell me, and I'll do my best to change."

"If you change you won't be the man I adore and love. I'm the one who has to make adjustments. I know I fly off the handle easily and usually for no reason, so I should be apologizing to you. No one has ever cared for me the way you do, so sometimes it's hard for me to realize that you are doing what you do and say for my own good. I put you in an unimaginable position when I told you about Lylah Jayne. I had lived with the nightmare for thirty years, and I sprang it on you on our very first night. You never once questioned that you were her father. You didn't judge my decision to give her up. You blamed yourself. I knew what kind of a man you were then, and I know it now. I don't want you to change anything, but I will try and make it easier for you to manage me."

He pulled me away from him. "You're kidding right…manage you… as if anyone could? I love you just the way you are, just like your name says; Mayria, a wind so strong that she blows the clouds and stars around."

I laughed. "You've kind of mixed up the words, but your famous for that aren't you? The girl in the song is spelled differently you know?"

"An R, a Y, what's the diff here and there?"

"Not much I guess. We should get back downstairs and pacify the family before they come a knocking don't you think?"

"They are going to think we made up in bed you know?"

"We weren't gone that long. Do you think Vali and Jake are lovers?"

"You want my honest answer?"

"Yes, of course."

"Then no, they aren't. Not saying that they aren't considering it, but Jake is still on the job, and co-habituating with a client is taboo."

"How is it okay for you to sleep with me then?"

"I'm the boss, that's how."

"Oh, so this is a common practice of yours then?"

"You're the first, and the last; you know that Mya."

"I do; just checking. Let's not go overboard with that "boss" thing okay?"

"How will I know when I've exceeded my limit?"

"When you get the look."

"Which is?"

"You'll know."

"I think I may have already got it once or twice."

Mitch and I spent the rest of the day answering all the questions about our past that the kids threw at us. I did not confess to my poisonings because Mitch had made me promise not to. He would share the guilt with me so there was no need to upset the kids. He was especially sensitive when he spoke of his leaving me, his incarceration, and coming home to find me wedding his best friend. He said it broke his heart, but he knew Bobby was a better man than he could ever hope to be and that the proof was in his two sons. They said that I deserved all the credit as I was the one who raised them and Vali to be who they were today. Mitch agreed and asked if he had their approval to be a surrogate father as he planned on being a permanent fixture in their lives because he was going to marry their mother just as soon as possible. They gave us their blessings adding that I had better not blow it. Laughter followed and then tears when I had to divulge my anguish at making the decision to give Lylah up. Mitch hugged me and said that was all going to end in a few days. Bobbie regretted that he wouldn't be here to welcome his new sister. The evening ended with Jake asking my permission to date my daughter. I had answered that I thought they were sort of already dating. He had said: "No ma'am, I've been on the job." Mitch winked at me. I said yes of course, and that I already considered him as one of the family.

After hugs and kisses, Mitch decided that we should celebrate by having a barbecue up at our 'other home' on Sunday. Mel and Shannon, their two children, Bebe and Mellie rounded out the other guests along with his country neighbours. Artie and Doll were in Nevada so unfortunately couldn't come. It was a beautiful late summer day, and I was sad to see everyone leave at the end of it. Mitch and I spent the night in the cabin. I was dreading the next day because it meant I would have to see Brian again. He did make an appearance at the courthouse and as usual exhibited an air of superiority. As he took his leave he turned around and said to me. "See you around Tess." Of course, he had to have the last word. I did not reply. Mitch and I walked out hand in hand, and I had hope that the last hostile hurdle regarding Brian was finally behind me.

Tuesday, September 13th, 10:50 a.m.

Jake had driven Vali to her dentist appointment. Mitch had gone to his office to check on a new case and any news regarding Lylah Jayne. He had wanted me to go with him, but I didn't want to hang around waiting for two o'clock to roll around as that was when we were to hear from Mr. Halliday regarding Lylah. He said he'd only be gone for an hour or so. Ivy and I were trying to finish upholstering the kitchen chairs for Bebe. Frankie was straightening up Brian's old office as he would be taking it over when he moved back here in a month. He had accepted a job with a local computer company. I was sure that Bebe and Mellie were the main reason he had decided to relocate. Bobbie was packing as he was leaving for Germany on Wednesday. I was sad that he had to leave so soon.

Ivy and I had taken a break and were sitting having tea. The phone rang. Ivy answered it, covered the mouthpiece saying it was Brian. She asked me if I wanted her to say that I wasn't home. I took the phone from her.

"What is it now Brian?" I asked annoyingly.

"And, how are you this fine day Tessa?" He purred.

"What is it?" I asked again.

"Just wondering if you know where your daughter is?"

Momentarily I thought that he had found Lylah. No, he couldn't have…

"Yes, I know exactly where she is; what's it to you?"

"Are you sure Tess? I'll call you back in five minutes after you have checked with her bodyguard." He hung up.

I scanned the wallboard for Jake's cell no. and dialed it. "Jake, is Vali still with the dentist?"

He said as far as he knew she was. "Go see Jake, go see, hurry, hurry."

"You sound worried; what's up Mayria?"

I could hear him arguing with the receptionist, and then a door opening.

"Holy shit, what the hell?"

"What is it Jake; what's wrong?"

"The dentist and his assistant are lying on the floor, unconscious I think. There's a heavy stench of chlorophyll in the room…Vali is not here. A door is open into a hall…following it… down a flight of stairs…another door open leading into a back alley. Damn!"

I heard him order whoever was with him to call the police and ask for Detective Rory Adams.

"It's Brian, he's got her; call Mitch, you're probably next." He yelled.

I hung up. Ivy was begging me for information that I didn't have. I picked up the phone on the first ring. "You son of a bitch… what have you done with my daughter?"

"Tell you what Tess; you get your skinny ass down to Jimmy's Quik Mart and you can have her. She's too much trouble anyhow, oh, and make sure you come alone. Go to the back…tick, tock, times a wasting; she's not looking so good." He laughed sadistically.

I scribbled Quik Mart on a grocery list, grabbed a set of car keys, and ran out the front door. Thankfully the keys were for the old blue. Ivy was screaming at me, but I didn't stop. I peeled out of the drive and headed south not too sure if I even knew where this market was. Three times through a round-about before I got my bearings and headed down to a run- down mall which housed a bowling alley and an arcade, and a grocery out-let. One had to have a good imagination to get Jimmy's Quik Mart out of the remaining letters left swinging from a rusty sign. I pulled around to the back beside a car which Brian was leaning up against. There was another vehicle parked a few feet away. My hand was on a large wrench as I flung open the door demanding to know where Vali was. He told me to lose the wrench. I didn't know that I knew so many swear words. He laughed. I had never wanted to kill anyone before. He waved to the other car. Two men got out and dragged my daughter towards me. I reached for her still cursing.

"Not so fast there Sweetheart…what have you got in exchange?" Brian taunted. "Put her in the car boys." He ordered pointing to my car.

I started to move. A hand clasped over my face and I knew that no bartering was going to take place…I was the intended target.

Chapter 9

Mitch's Challenge

I put my coffee cup down. I'd been reminiscing past cases with Shannon and Mel for the past hour, but it was time to get on with the business of today before I had to pick Mya up. We were awaiting a call from Mr. Halliday, or his daughter Jennifer. Maureen Halliday was supposedly a second cousin to Thelma Robinson. Hopefully, she could confirm that as soon as she had recovered from surgery. Unfortunately, the surgery that had been scheduled for the past Saturday had been cancelled due to unknown circumstances, and was to have taken place yesterday. Jennifer had called Mel after her father had relayed to her that he needed to talk to her mother regarding Thelma. She herself had no information of Thelma's whereabouts, but was fairly sure that she was on the island and might be in some sort of care facility. Jennifer lived in Alberta and had not been home for a few years. She said her mother and Thelma were not close, and she did not remember if there was a daughter. She didn't have anything else to add, but said that she would be in touch as soon as she knew anything. Unfortunately, Mel had only given her the phone number here so Mya and I would be returning back to the office for two o'clock. I told Shannon to catch me up with new directives, and to instigate a call-forwarding application.

She nodded, and chuckled. "Mrs. McNaughton's cat has gone missing again. She stipulated that she wants only *you* to find "Puffy" again."

"Not going to happen. Make whatever excuse you think will satisfy her as to why I am not available. I think Poco can handle this one. What's next?"

"There's another request from Inland Insurance for fraud surveillance."

"Do you want it Mel?"

"You may need me to do some leg work in finding Lylah yet, so hand it off to Shane Darcy. He likes that kind of thing anyhow."

"Right; I'll leave it to you to make the arrangements then."

Shannon asked me if I knew Wallace Davis. I asked her what his problem was.

"It's a she. She's a friend of your wife's." Shannon smiled cheekily.

"Strange name for a woman; what's her problem? Is she a lawyer by any chance?"

Shannon pulled a newspaper out of the recycle container. She folded a page over and handed it to me. "She's an actress; you know her better as Dazie Wall."

I looked at the article and her picture. I handed it back to Shannon. "So, what does she want?"

"You know her then?"

"She's been at the house a time or two."

"Did she flirt with you there too?"

I glanced at Mel who was smirking. "What's going on here? What's with this flirting thing?"

"Short memory Boss… surely you remember her inviting us all backstage after her performance last year at the Orpheum?"

"Well, let's say, it's one performance I wouldn't want to see again."

"You mean her blatant suggestive flirting with you?" Mel winked.

"I don't remember it as such so you guys can quit with the implication. Now, again, what does she want?"

Shannon was still smiling. "You, I think." She pushed a button on the recorder.

I listened to a sultry voice. "Adam Mitchell, please."

"I'm sorry, Mr. Mitchell is not available. May I take a message?" Shannon asks.

"Surely, you have another contact number for him? I can guarantee you that he would want you to relay that number to me."

"I am sorry ma'am; I don't even know who you are. Mr. Mitchell has left strict instructions that he is not to be disturbed. I can put you in touch with one of our other personnel if you like."

"This is a highly sensitive matter, and my business is with Adam, and only Adam. It is imperative that I speak with him immediately! Do you understand?'

"All I can do ma'am is to relay the message to him when he checks in. If you will give me your name and contact information I will make sure he receives it."

"Did I not tell you that I am a personal friend of his wife?"

"Do you mean of the wife he is divorcing, or the woman who will be the new Mrs. Mitchell?"

"Who the hell are you to be making such an obscene hypothetical remark?"

"I'm the woman who is keeping Mr. Mitchell's personal phone number from you. Have a good day, and if I can be of further assistance..."

Shannon stopped the recording. "You don't need to hear her profanity Mitch. Sorry, I just couldn't resist. If you think it might be important, I'll dial the number that came up."

"I think we'll let that one go." I hugged her and had a laugh with her and Mel.

"I'm glad my husband is skinny and has a receding hairline so the women clients don't take much interest in him."

"Thanks Hon. We can't all be rugged and flawless like Mitch now can we? Just as well, what happily married man wants gorgeous women like Margaret Downing and Sharon Ruff offering up their room keys to them?" Mel jested.

"Are you guys through with your imaginary analyses yet? I think I better find something a bit more challenging to occupy your minds with."

"Just out of curiosity Boss, what did Mayria have to do to turn your head?" Mel implored.

"She said my name."

"Oh Mitch, that is so profound." Shannon blubbered. "I so want the two of you to make it together, but I am concerned that her moralities will prove too much for her."

"What the hell does that mean?" I demanded.

"I think it is *your* morals that she is more concerned with."

"Where is this coming from Shannon? You know damn well that I don't have any morals. Is this what you two were talking about so seriously on Sunday? What exactly did she say?"

"Besides Mel, you are the most ethical person I know! It's all evident in the cases you take on. Neither of us would be working for you if you were a sleaze ball, so there! Yes, we had a heart to heart during your baseball game. You had just waved to her from first base. She waved back and asked me if I thought you were happy. I said that you were the happiest I had ever seen you. She said it must be so hard for you to be in love with two women."

I interrupted her rather boisterously. "That's hogwash; she knows I'm in love with her, and only her. She knows it Shannon."

My cell rang. "Do you think it's her?" I asked jokingly. It was Jake.

"Slow down Jake; I can't understand…what…what…Oh Christ! I'm on my way." I grabbed my keys and headed for the door.

"What's going on Mitch?" Mel stopped me.

"It's Brian; he's got Vali, and he's going after Mya!"

"I'm driving." He took the keys from me, and told a wide eyed Shannon to mind the store.

In the car Mel asked me what Jake had said? "That's it; just that Brian had Vali and to get to the house right away as he was going after Mya. He told me to hurry. That's the second time in the past week I've been told to hurry because Mya's life may depend on me. I let my guard down Mel. I became complacent with getting him to sign the divorce decree. I believed it was over."

Mel told me to call Rory. I told him that Jake had probably already called him, but I punched in his mobile anyhow. It went straight to voice mail. I dialed Mya's cell; it didn't even ring. I dialed the house number. Ivy answered crying.

"She's gone Mitch. I'm so sorry I couldn't stop her. She grabbed her purse and ran out of the house as if it was on fire."

"What car did she take?"

"The old blue; the boys are in the sportster."

"What's the mobile number?"

Bobbie answered halfway through the first ring. I asked where they were. He said he hadn't a clue. They'd been through the same round-about four times already because they thought they'd caught sight of their mother's car, but they had lost it. He asked me what the hell was going on as all Ivy had yelled at them was that Vali was in trouble and Mya had gone after her. I told him what I knew trying to keep calm.

A cruiser, sirens blaring, roared past us. Rory was at the helm. Mel followed it into the drive on Marlborro. Ivy was waiting for us with a slip of paper with an address on it. She said it must have fallen off the counter. I told Rory of my conversation with the boys who thought they were on Mya's tail but had lost her. Rory told me to get them back on the phone.

"Punch this into your GPS." He directed Bobbie. "Jimmy's Quik Mart; Quik with a K. Didn't register... okay, it might be defunct. Can you get back to the round- about...good. Take the west exit unto Henderson...good. Okay, stay on it until you come to Division, take a left and keep an eye out for a rundown mini mart. We're on our way, keep this channel open. Mitch, Jake, you're with me."

We squealed out ahead of Mel and two other police vehicles that had shown up. Two minutes later Bobbie let us know they had found the mart. "Nothing here; Frankie's driving to the back...there it is, Mom's old blue. I'm getting out...oh God; Vali is in it...she's unconscious. She's breathing, but her pulse is very weak. Mom's not here. We need an ambulance."

Rory said that one was already on its way. He asked me how I was holding up.

"You don't want to know." I answered knowing full well that everything that was said in the cruiser was being heard and monitored by ears back at headquarters. He nodded and requested additional prowl cars be sent to the Quik Mart, and ordered a kidnapping alert, descriptions unavailable at the moment. Jake offered up his phone as he had photos of both Mayria and Brian. Rory pulled into the mart next to the old blue, and relayed information to the command centre. Jake was out and holding Vali in his arms before I even had my door open.

Frankie and Bobbie had backed off releasing their sister to Jake. Their faces registered shock and anguish. I walked over and placed a hand on Jake's shoulder. He said he was going to kill the bastard. I told him that he was going to have to stand in line. I bent down and kissed Vali's forehead telling her that she was going to be all right.

"She has to be Mitch. She's what I have been looking for all of my life." He looked up at me. A tear escaped from his eyes. "I love her Mitch."

Vali's eyelashes fluttered. I swallowed hard. I had never seen this side of my best friend before. I told him to hang in there... what else could I say?

"Find her Mitch, find Vali's mother."

"That's the plan Buddy." I walked over to where Mya's sons were talking to Rory. He had calmed them somewhat. "Give me a minute guys...I've got a head rush; I have to sit."

Bobbie helped me over to the decaying sidewalk. I collapsed and put my head between my knees. I had never felt this woozy ever in my life before. A few minutes later the light headiness started to fade. I attempted to get up, but hands held me down.

The ambulance had arrived and the attendants were loading Vali. Jake yelled that he was going with her. I waved him on. Rory called an EMT over to check me out. I gawked at him.

"Just being cautious Mitch. I can't afford to lose you right now." He said somewhat apologetic.

I was given the okay and told it was probably a panic attack. I felt like I had been unmasked.

Rory said that everything was in place. He'd already dispatched officers and cruisers to the dockyards, and other ports and marinas in the district. He said that he'd follow me to the house where I could drop off my car, and then we'd head down to The Keg Marina. I asked him why. He said he had a hunch. That was supposed to be my job; acting on hunches. I told him Arte could pick up the relic. I climbed in his cruiser and said, "Let's go."

"Speaking of Arte...get him on the horn will you?"

He motioned for me to get back out. I gathered he didn't want any ears listening to our conversation with Arte. I asked him if he was trying to get me into trouble, and that Mya already thought he had connections to the mob. He laughed and asked me if she had met Doll, and did she know who Doll's father was.

"Doesn't matter; your girlfriend isn't here is she? Do you think she would object to Arte's help in finding her? We need him; you know as well as I do that he has associates who know people who can infiltrate places we can't."

"He's not going to be sympathetic with me working with you, but no, she would not object."

"He'll have to suck it up; you too. Do you want to find Mayria or not?"

"What kind of a dumb ass question is that?"

"Then get off your frickin high horse and put a call through to the man who might just be able to give us the information we need!"

I hit the 3 button on my phone and pushed the conference button.

He answered on the first ring. "Jesus H Christ Mitch; how in the hell did you lose her already?"

"You've heard?"

"Yeah, I heard. I don't have a police scanner for pleasure you know. So, give me the dl."

"Brian's goons, I'm assuming, sprayed the dental office with some sort of inoculant. Jake's pretty sure the smell was from chloroform because it was still lingering in the air. He went out the open door which led to a back alley, and no sign of Vali. I guess you have put it together that she is Mayria's daughter? The dentist and his assistant were tied up on the floor. Jake can't recall whether they were gagged or not because his only concern was for Vali. She has been found and is in the hospital, but no sign of Mya. Detective Adams was called, who by the way is sitting next to me. Do you have an issue with that?"

"Damn right I do! I thought I heard a hissing. Are you on your way over?"

"No time, but I need your help."

"Tell me what you need."

"Don't have a shit fit; I'm passing the phone to Rory. Be civil."

"Have you ever known me to be anything but? Put him on; anything for you Mitch."

I listened intently to the two way conversation with respect for the two men who were on opposite sides of the law. Not that Arte was involved with any criminal activity that I was ever privy to, but he was not one to sit back and let an injustice go unpunished. He had connections inside and out, with the high and mighty, and with the common street snitch, and many owed him for services rendered. I had never met Doll's father as he lived in Reno Nevada, nor had I ever asked what his business there was, but I had a darn good idea. Rory hung up with a self-satisfied smirk on his face. He nodded and said he thought the alliance was going to benefit us all. I wanted to tell him that this was probably going to be a one- time thing, but who knew, stranger things have happened. We climbed back in the cruiser. Rory didn't start it. I asked him if he had changed his mind about going to the marina.

"No, but Arte peeked my curiosity. I know you said no one but the family knew you were going to the office, or that Jake was accompanying Vali to the dentist. Are you sure about that?"

"It's like I said. Brian knew about Vali's dental appointment because he was sitting at the kitchen table when she got the call. No one outside of the family knew I was going to the office."

"Think about it Mitch. Did you get any phone calls or messages yesterday, or on the weekend?"

"Nope; Shannon had everything under control. I had my phone turned off most of the time anyway. If Mel or Shannon had any news regarding Lylah they would have tracked me down."

"Who the hell is Lylah?"

"She's Mya's and my daughter…"

"WHAT?"

Ten minutes later Rory knew as much about my daughter as I did.

"So, it's not likely that she fits into Mayria's abduction, right?"

"I don't see how. Brian knows about her, but if we haven't found her yet I don't see how he could have."

"Let's hope not as we don't need another pawn. Now, back to the phone calls; you're absolutely certain that you didn't get any or make any? Irene and you are not in divorce talks?"

"No, but I did receive a text from her Sunday or Monday saying she wanted to see me. I might have texted her that I'd be in the office this morning."

"You *guess*...what the hell Mitch? Why aren't you asking yourself these questions? Has your common sense gone out with the wind?"

"Yeah, with the wild, wild, wind."

"Give your head a shake Brother. You told me earlier that Brian wouldn't hurt Mayria because he loves her, but I am not convinced you believe that."

"Too much time has gone by Rory; she's long gone. She's gone with the wind; the wild, wild, wind."

"What the hell is with you and this wind thing?"

"Ever hear the song "They Call the Wind Mayria"?

"So she reminds you of the damn wind, so what? It's time to quit wallowing in the quagmire! I don't even know who you are right now. I've never met Mayria, but she's got her claws in you but good, so I have to ask you, is it at all possible that she went willingly with Brian? Is it possible that your affair was more one sided than you want to admit?"

"Yeah, willingly at the bunt end of a cattle prodder...she hates the dirty rotten bastard! Don't take my word that she loves me as much as I love her, ask her kids and Jake. It's my fault she's gone. I let my guard down. I didn't know what the power of love could do, but I do now. You're right; I've let my blame blind me. It's not Brian I am worried about, it's Mya. She will try and escape from him, and will stop at nothing to get back to me. I'm afraid it won't end well."

"Okay, you sold me Bud; let's make sure it's a happy ending. You and me are going to be walking hand and hand to bring her home."

"Thanks for the call back to reality. Let's get on with it."

Rory nodded and told me to call Irene. I hesitated. He asked me if I still considered her family.

I saw what he was getting at so I placed the call.

She answered breathlessly on the second ring. "You picked a fine time to call me Mitchell!"

She always called me Mitchell when she was annoyed with me like when I bought the derelict boat, or refused to go to the opera with her.

"What's going on there…is that a fire alarm I hear? What's that beeping?"

"How the hell do I know? Fire, bomb threat, hostage taking… all I know is that we have been ordered to evacuate." She answered in a panicky voice.

I asked her where she was. She said she was still on the stairs. I told her to get out and I'd meet her at the Gavel Pit as we were already in the vicinity. Rory was on the phone getting information regarding the evacuation. We stopped at the courthouse so he could check it out for himself. I walked the two blocks to the bar. Irene was sitting at a booth with her drink of choice, a Lime Rickey in her hand. The drink always looked refreshing, but it didn't do anything for me.

I sat across from her. She told me I looked like hell. I told her there was a reason for that.

"Yes, I'm sure there is. Too many late nights with your new squeeze I presume?"

I ignored the question and asked her if she had been to see a lawyer yet.

"Not yet Deary, I've been too busy, and I am not in any hurry to ease your guilt."

I waved to the waitress and ordered two coffees. "There is no guilt Irene."

"What's with the two coffees? Are you nursing a hangover?" She laughed wickedly.

I ignored her insinuation again. "If you didn't want to talk about the divorce why did you want to see me?"

"To tell you…what's *HE* doing here?"

Rory had slid into the booth beside me. He reached across the table and took a sip of her drink and made a face. "Nice to see you too Renee." He winked at her. "What's new; any ideas about who would want to blow up the courthouse? How about a kidnapping… any thoughts on that?"

She hated being called Renee. She glared at Rory, but answered his questions. "I'm sure there are a thousand felons who would like to see the courthouse and every lawyer in it perish. I do not know anything regarding any kidnapping. Why would you be asking such a stupid question?"

"Were you at court all morning? Do you have witnesses who will testify to that?"

"Are you questioning me?"

"Do you know Brian Fulton?"

"What…Fulton? Isn't that your girlfriend's husband Mitch?" She said mockingly.

"I'm asking the questions Renee. Do you know him or not?" Rory demanded.

"I do not, and just suppose if I did…what then?"

"Well then I suppose you would be a suspect in the kidnapping of his wife." Rory said almost triumphantly.

She looked at me wide-eyed. "Is that true? Has your lover gone back to her husband? Your ego won't let you accept it so you've reported her as being kidnapped, is that it Mitch?"

I nodded. "Yup, sounds like something I would do. Did you ever consider that Rory?"

He laughed. "Yeah, but you have a solid alibi so I had to dismiss it."

Irene grabbed her purse, stood up and threw two ten dollar bills down on the table. "Coffees on me boys. It's been a pleasure. As for the kidnapping, I cannot comment as I know nothing about it. Perhaps it's all a smoke screen and is just as I said. She wasn't abducted at all, but just decided that her husband was a better option. Karma's a bitch isn't it Mitch? Next time you want to talk leave your friend and his sense of humor in the gutter where they belong."

I held my tongue as she wasn't worth the effort. "Have your lawyer call mine. You and I will not be meeting or talking again. Have a nice day." I called the waitress over and paid for our coffee as Irene headed for the door. Rory wanted the last word.

"You may be in your arena in court Renee, but you're in mine now, so watch your step because I'll be watching you. Oh, and by the way…it's advisable that you don't leave town."

She had a comeback, but the door closed on her choir of expletives.

I took my place back as shotgun in the cruiser. "I see you and my ex still have a feud raging."

"I will never forgive her, or her cohorts for the role they played in Captain O"Rourke's heart attack in the Manchester/O'Neil affair."

"I thought as much. You know she only talked about it once, and that was to say that justice won out, and that the fraud squad was finally put in its place."

"I was leader of the pack back then so I guess it was me she was actually referring to."

A call came in that there was a disturbance at the Keg Marina. Rory gave me the look, hit the siren and we blew through traffic. There were already two other squad cars in attendance. One of the officers came over as we drove up saying that the problem had been dealt with. Rory asked for detailed information. It had something to do with one old gent disagreeing with a newly docked boat regarding his rights as a permanent resident. I left the discussion to find Rolph and Gerta who were the resident caretakers of the marina. They had already received a bulletin on Mya's kidnapping, but had nothing to offer as no one fitting her or Brian's description had rented a slip. They did relay the particulars regarding the disagreement between the two men in detail. The permanent resident was a seventy year old gentleman of Vietnamese descent who lived on a small fishing boat. Apparently, last night a large yacht had snuck in alongside of him which was an intrusion of his privacy. This gent, whose name was Fam approached the yacht owner demanding that he pull away from the dock and find another place to moor. Rolph was called in to mediate when Fam and Juno's, the yacht's captain, erupted into a fisti-cuff. Rolph had rented the space, W39 out to a Dr. Zang Lu for three nights. He had informed Rolph that he himself would not be arriving with the yacht, but that his trusted assistant would be ferrying the boat. He would be joining the crew on Thursday. According to Rolph and Gerta, the brawl ended up with the two of them rolling around on the sidewalk. Everyone from the marina had joined in to cheer Fam on. It was quite a sight to see pint-size Fam duking it out with his Chinese opponent who out- weighed him by at least a hundred pounds. The cops had been called, and everyone had been sent back to their quarters. The operator of the yacht left not wanting any more trouble. He had said his boss did not believe in violence. Gerta said that the yacht was a compliment to the marina. I asked her what she meant and she told me to take a gander at it. Rory had shown up and was now engaged with Rolph. I wandered down the wharf to W39. I stopped short of it and stared at the portside. The whole side was consumed by a massive silvery gold and green dragon. I walked to the starboard; same thing. The dragons were breathing fire. I knew it was an omen...an omen of what was to come. A cold chill ran up and down my spine.

"That's one honkin dragon!" Rory exclaimed as he caught up to me. "What's the junk's moniker?"

"Jeudanzee."

"Whatever that means."

"It implies that it is a fire breathing flying dragon, and has powers over the oceans."

"How the hell would you know that?'

"Dragons are Mayria's antagonists, and sometimes friends."

"That still doesn't explain how you can translate the name of a Chinese vessel. Speaking of Chinese, this supposedly owner of the rig, a Dr. Zang Lu has a ring to it. I've got to get back to the precinct and run the name along with a few others. I've got someone at city hall running a check on every vehicle Fulton has ever owned hoping that a boat of any sort pops up."

My phone jingled. It was Jake; Vali was awake and eager to talk.

"Let's head over to the hospital first and see what she's got." Rory suggested.

Vali broke into tears the second she saw me. I wrapped her in my arms telling her everything was going to be okay. She buried her head in my chest.

"I'm so sorry Mitch; I let him get me, and now he has mom. I'm so sorry."

I lifted her chin and made her look at me. "This is not your fault, understand? If anyone is to blame, it's me. I should never have left her alone. None of us thought that he was so conniving. From the minute he walked out of the house, the wheels were turning in his head. I should have taken more notice to the way he said good-bye to Mya at the courthouse."

She asked what he'd said. "It's not so much what he said, it's the way he said it, so full of himself. He said, "See you around Tess." Then he winked, and strutted off like a peacock."

"You're going to be able to find her aren't you Mitch?"

"We are Darlin." I called Rory over and introduced him to her. "Are you up to telling us what took place at the dentist office?"

"It all happened so fast that I'm not even sure if what I am remembering is right. My head is still a little foggy."

"I'm sure it is Honey; close your eyes, and just tell us what you see."

"Okay. Dr. Graham was checking to see if the freezing had taken affect. There was a loud noise behind us. I guess it was the door being rammed. He said "What the hell...Laura, she's his assistant, "get down!" He covered his face but succumbed to whatever the haze was that was descending on the room. I felt something moist on my face and then a hand covered my mouth. I was wearing the safety glasses so everything was dark. I tried to bite him, but I couldn't as the novocaine had done its job. I felt myself sinking, but not before I noticed that the man was wearing a mask, you know one that covered his mouth and nose, a gas mask maybe. He asked me if I was Vali, but of course I couldn't answer him. Just before I blacked out I heard him say something like "What's taking you so fucking long to get them tied up Red?" That's all I remember. Why did it take me longer to succumb then it did the dentist and Laura?"

Rory told her that she done good, and could open her eyes. He looked at me and said, "Good call Buddy. It's just conjecture Vali, but the reason you lasted longer may be because you were seated, and they had been standing, but then the vapor should have reached you sooner, so I really had no idea. Can you describe the man you saw?"

She said he was very tall, balding, and had beady little eyes.

My cell jingled. It was Arte; he had some news for us. His underlings had come through with a possible four suspects. With the little description Vali had managed to recall and Arte's profiles, Rory narrowed it down to two felons known to police; a Cecil Dandridge, and Carl Anderson, aka Red.

Jake and I were both without wheels so I called Frankie and asked him to pick me up planning on dropping by Arte's and getting my jeep back. Vali wanted to come home but the doctors wanted to keep her for a few more hours. She was not happy, but understood it was for her safety. Jake stayed behind with her as she needed him more than I did at the moment.

I took the elevator down to the first floor with Rory. He said he hoped he'd have one or both of the subjects in custody by days end. He'd keep me appraised, and my best bet was to man all the phones at the house in case Brian or Mya called. He still figured there was going to be a ransom demand. I had told him earlier that wasn't a possibility as he already had the woman who had all the money. I told him that Brian wanted something besides money. Yeah, he did, Mya.

Frankie drove me over to pick up my jeep and then I followed him back to the hospital where we dropped the yellow sportster off for Jake before we headed home. Yeah home…home without the lady who belonged there. It was three in the afternoon. It felt like midnight. Ivy sat me down and fed me.

I checked to make sure that all the surveillance equipment was still functioning. We had planned on dismantling it all, but hadn't got around to it. The day dragged on, and no word from Rory. Vali and Jake made it home at seven p.m. She came straight over to me where I was sitting in her mother's love chair and cuddled up to me.

"How's my girl?" I asked her.

"This wasn't supposed to happen Mitch. She shouldn't have come for me."

I laughed feebly. "She'd walk through fire for you Honey. You know that don't you?"

"Yes, but…"

"No buts; that's what parents do for their children. If I didn't know that before, I know it now. Half an hour little girl and then you are going upstairs to bed."

"I want to stay down here with you and Jake, and the boys. I don't think I could make it up the stairs anyway."

"Then, you'll take the elevator."

"It's broken."

"Not anymore. Now those are your orders, half an hour…"

"Okay Dad." She purred. "But, I have to be awakened if you hear anything. Are you going to come with me Jake?"

"What do you think? I'm going to tuck you into my bed in the suite. I'll leave the door open into the hall because we have a full view of what's going on down here. How does that sit with you?" Jake replied.

"Are you going to stay with me?"

"You bet I am. No one will get by me again."

"It wasn't your fault Jake. I should have been safe in the dentist's office."

"And, your mother should have been safe here. Sorry Mitch." Jake said sorrowfully.

"She was my responsibility, and Vali was yours. Who would have ever dreamed that she could be abducted right in front of you, so to speak? It was a macabre plan that only a mad man would think of executing. I should have seen the wheels turning in his head all the time while we were

interrogating him. He knew all he had to do was agree to a divorce and we would let him off the hook, and then he would work on getting his revenge. I've said over and over that I don't believe he'll harm your mother, and I have to hold on to that or else I will lose my ability to concentrate and analyze. I'm missing something…just like I did in the…"

Jake interrupted me. "Don't go there Mitch! This case is entirely different."

"Is it? The only difference I can see is that I'm in love with the victim."

"What is it Mitch? Does this remind you of another case? The outcome wasn't favorable was it?" Vali asked nervously.

I gave her a hug. "Nothing for you to worry your pretty little head over." I kissed her on her forehead. "Time to get her upstairs Jake; use the elevator, and that's an order."

"Yes Boss. If anything comes to mind, I'm just a yell away."

"Going to go over the whole chain of events with Ivy and the boys...where is Ivy?"

"I guess she went to her room; I'll get her." Frankie volunteered.

What was it; what was gnawing at me? What had I missed?

Three hours later I was still no further ahead. The facts were what they were. No matter how many times we relived the day, it always came up empty of any new information. Ivy and Frankie had taken my advice and gone to bed. Bobbie and I stretched out on corresponding sofas fighting the sleep bug.

Mya and I were on my boat drifting out to sea. She asked me if I liked her rendering of the dragons. I asked her what she meant. Come see, she had said, and took me out a yellow door. I leaned over the starboard with her and came face to face with an overbearing red dragon grinning at me.

I came to and jumped to my feet. "That's it; it's that bloody Chinese yacht!"

Bobbie practically fell off the sofa. "What the hell Mitch?"

"Want to take a midnight ride with me Son?" I asked.

He looked at his watch and told me it was 3:15 a.m. Jake was leaning over the railing. I told him the house, phone, and dog were his watch now, and that Bobbie and I were on our way to the Keg Marina.

Chapter 10
Into the Wind

I was so cold. "Damn it Mitch; quick hogging all the blankets!" Was he laughing at me? I made an attempt to roll over, but the fiery pain in my head stopped me. Without opening my eyes I applied pressure to my temples. Moaning I asked Mitch what I had drank last night. Laughter again. Where was it coming from?

"Sorry Sweetpea, but your boyfriend couldn't make it. Seems he was occupied somewhere else. It's just you and me from now on."

Oh no, oh no…this couldn't be happening. I wasn't suffering with a hangover, but from the drugs Brian had given me. I remembered smelling chloroform just before the sting of a needle pierced my neck.

I forced myself to sit up and open my eyes. He was standing with his back to me. I could not fathom what he was doing, or where we were. I tried to look around, but every motion sent the pounding in my head accelerating, and the rocking didn't help any. Rocking? Oh God, I was on a boat…a boat bound for hell.

"You rotten son-of-a- bitch!" I yelled with as much force as I could muster without causing myself to have a stroke. "What have you done with Vali?"

He turned around. "Not to worry Tessa; she's sleeping it off, with her boyfriend no doubt."

"I hate you! I'm going to kill you!"

"You don't mean that Tessa, and remember hate is only one step away from love. Relax; in a few days we are going to be sailing away to Shangri-La just like I promised you."

"I'm not going anywhere with you!"

"Afraid you don't have any choice Sweetpea."

"Quit calling me that! I am not your sweet anything! You are going to beg for mercy when Mitch and Jake get their hands on you!"

"Ah, we have arrived; our own personal island for a few days before the final journey. And," he said as the boat came to a hard halt, "they'd have to find me first, and believe me, there is no chance of that ever happening."

"You don't know Mitch very well if you think that, but go ahead, give yourself false hope because it is only a matter of time before he finds me."

He laughed again. "Take a gander Honey...we are virtually on the other side of nowhere. The island is deserted, and there is nothing as far as the eye can see. No, we will be perfectly safe here for a few days. Your lover has no idea..." he reached for me.

"Get your filthy hands off me!"

"Fine; get yourself up and off the boat or I'll throw you off!" He ordered.

I didn't move. He swore and grabbed me by my feet and dragged me to the side of the boat, picked me up, and true to his word, threw me overboard. Actually, he had lowered me quite gently, but it still hurt. Luckily for me he had landed the boat on the beach so it was only a three foot drop to the sand. Maybe I had been right all the time, and that he wouldn't hurt me because he still loved me. This could all fit into my plan to escape.

"Let's get you to the cabin before I unload." He said as if he hadn't just tossed me off the boat.

"No thanks, I'll just wait here."

"I think not. Now get up or I'll put a rope around you and drag you by your feet again. It's gonna hurt a hell of a lot more when we hit those rocks though...up to you."

"Do whatever you want you sadistic bastard!"

He pulled me up. "I've got a good notion to sedate you again; but this might be more to my advantage."

He stuck something hard in my side. It might have been a gun. I didn't resist. He pushed me ahead of him and told me to hurry because he wanted to be settled before dark. I hadn't a clue as to what time of day it was as I never wear a watch. Vali's appointment had been for ten thirty, and then there were the two phone calls from Brian just before eleven, and then my hurried dash to find her. How long did that take? It didn't matter anyhow as I had no idea how long I had been unconscious. It could be three or four. The sky was no help as it was an overcast day. I had to formulate an escape plan. He had told me that there were no other inhabitants on the island, but I chose not to believe him.

I stumbled along not wanting to make anything too easy for him. Every few feet he would jab me in the back with his fist. The cabin, as he called it, was not too far from the water's edge. A boardwalk took us the last twenty five feet. He held on to me as he unlocked the door. It was dark inside. He locked the door behind us and led me to a sofa where he told me to sit.

"Are you going to behave yourself, or do I have to tie you up?" He asked authoritatively.

I didn't answer him. I guess he took that as submission.

"I'm not the monster that you think I am. In time you will come to see that I saved you from heartache and thus harming yourself again." He gave me a bottle of water and two aspirins. "Sorry if you have a headache."

I swallowed the aspirin hoping they would quell the pounding in my head.

"A few trips to bring in the supplies and put the boat away, and then I will make you dinner." He said as he went out the door locking me in from outside.

It wasn't that he was reciprocating from me locking my bedroom door on him; he didn't trust that I wouldn't run off. I had questions, but wasn't going to give him the satisfaction of knowing that I was curious about things, like this sofa. It wasn't all that old, and the throw pillows and blanket appeared to be brand new. I glanced around the room. Apparently there was no electricity as he had lit two gas lamps, and turned the propane on for the stove and refrigerator I guessed. The floor was bare linoleum. There was a small table with three chairs tucked in around it. The kitchen consisted of four upper and lower cupboards and a sink. I wondered if there was running water. My question was answered when Brian returned with a bag of groceries and a large keg of water. He also had my shoulder bag strung around his neck.

He threw it to me. "You had this in the car so I thought there might be a few things in it you could use. You might want to make yourself useful and unpack the groceries."

My answer was to pop the pillows under my head and pull the blanket over me. He left again. As soon as I heard the padlock click I sat up and rummaged through my purse. It was a pipedream that he hadn't searched my bag and found my phone. Damn it; what now Mitch? You won't be able to find me so it was up to me to find a way to get back to you.

Brian returned with another bag of groceries and a shopping bag from some clothing store I had never heard of. He told me that I might find something interesting in it, and he hoped he had got the size right. He left again. Curiosity got the best of me. Inside the bag was a pair of jeans, a sweatshirt, a sweater, nightgown and two pairs of undies and socks. His taste left something to be desired. I put the sweater on as I was cold, and stuffed the underwear and a pair of socks into my shoulder bag. Just in case...

He was gone a lot longer this time. I heard him unlock the outside door and then lock the inside one, and put the key in his pocket. Wasn't that just great? I wondered about the back door and cursed myself for not investigating while he was gone.

He asked how I was doing.

"How do you think? You've taken me away from my children, my home, and the man I love so figure it out for yourself!"

He put a pot of water on the stove saying that we were going to have hot dogs and Kraft dinner, and continued to unpack the rest of the bags as he spoke. "You should have known better than to chase after a married man Tessa. He's not worthy of you. Word on the street is that he is leaving you and going back to Irene, so I've saved you from the embarrassment and dejection."

Word on the street? How did he know Mitch's wife's name? I thanked him. Evidently he didn't hear the mockery in my voice because he smiled and started towards me. I instinctively pulled my knees up to my chest and locked my hands around them.

He laughed. "You know I am stronger than you don't you? You don't have to get so defensive because I am not going to hurt you, but if I wanted to take advantage of you I could. I could pick you up and throw you on the bed, and you would be at my mercy wouldn't you? But, I wouldn't do that because I love you, and I know you will come around in time."

He was right in front of me. "We used to have a rip roaring time didn't we Sweetpea?" He leaned forward. "A little kiss would be nice."

I took a deep breath, released my hands from around my knees and kicked him with all my might. He yelped and backed away falling to the floor holding his groin, and moaning. I realized that my feet had made contact with his manhood, and that he might be writhing in pain for some time so I grabbed my bag, the blanket, and two bottles of water, and bolted for the door.

Damn; I didn't have the key. Before I would take the chance of rummaging through his pockets, I tried the back door. It was a simple dead bolt. I slid it open, and made my escape. I could hear Brian mumbling my name asking me why, why, why?

I ran around to the front of the building. The boat was gone; not that it would have done me any good anyhow. I took off running up the shoreline to the next cabin. It looked deserted. I realized that I was an easy target out in the open and so I made a beeline for the shelter of the trees behind it. First I had to climb a twenty foot bank of rock and small brush; not an easy task for a girl in her house slippers. Luckily, I had chosen to wear my lined moccasin-like ones and not my flimsy heelless mules. I broke two fingernails grabbing on to the shrubs and rocks to help propel me to the top. Thank goodness I had a nail file in my purse. Really, I was concerned about broken nails when I was on a deserted island running to God knows where away from a crazed man who had kidnapped me?

After a few slides backward I reached the top and took shelter in some pine trees. I was out of breath and collapsed on a moss- covered terrain. I leaned against a large pine tree. Perhaps it wasn't pine, but a fir. My knowledge of the coast flora was embarrassing. I had a drink of water. I wanted to wash my hands but thought better of wasting drinking water. I dug into a zippered compartment in my bag hoping that I had some moistened wipes. I did, and I also found a small bottle of sanitizer, two sanitary napkins, several bandages, and a small packet of Kleenex. Another compartment held lipstick, lip balm, tic-tacks, two wrapped peppermints, and a half package of Juicy Fruit gum, the nail file and a little sewing kit which I knew contained a tiny pair of scissors, some safety pins and a spool of thread and a needle pack. At the bottom of my bag was a pair of sunglasses, my wallet, a cheque book, a small notepad and a pen, a small penlight on a string, plus the underwear I had thrown in. I always carried a small prescription bottle that held a few Tylenol, travel tablets, Benadryl and a couple of pain pills. I hoped I had transferred it into the bag from my purse. I had. Wow, I must have known I was going on a wilderness jaunt because I had everything I needed for survival. I laughed nonsensically. Oh Mitch, I need your knowledge of survival in the wilds. Hell, I needed him, never mind anything else. A few tears slid down my cheeks.

I dumped the sand and rocks out of my slippers, revised myself with a stick of sweet gum, and stood up. I zippered up my shoulder bag and expanded the strap on it so it would be more comfortable around my neck. I had tried to stuff the blanket in it but to no avail so I wrapped it around my shoulders. Dusk was closing in fast. I best get myself down the trail and find another bungalow that I could take refuge in for the night. I heard the distinct roar of a motor.

I stayed close to the shelter of the trees in case I had to duck behind them if I felt in danger of Brian spotting me. He stopped at the first cabin, shut the motor off, and called my name. I was hunkered down above the second and third cabins. I could see him as he got off the boat and made the walk up to the cabin. I couldn't quite make out what he was yelling, but it sounded like: "Tess, you are starting to piss me off!"

For some reason he didn't stop at the next cabin and continued on up the shore. I figured that he was gone for about ten minutes before he returned. The boat stopped again, very close to where I was. I held my breath and remained still fearing that he had one of those devices that could track a person by a sound amplifier. He walked back and forth between the two cabins before he gave up. I could hear him shouting my name over and over.

As soon as I felt that he had left, I quickly made my way along the trail hoping to find a path leading down to the third cabin. I found a semblance of one and started down it only to trip on an exposed root. I tried to keep my balance, but ended up on my butt, and continued sliding down the slippery slope. Half way down I smashed into a log. I squealed as pain shot up my left leg.

I told myself to get up and get going and to quit whining. That was all fine and good, but my leg didn't want to cooperate. I managed to get myself into a sitting position without inflicting too much pain. I felt in my bag for the penlight and shone it on the log I was up against. The log was too large for me to wrap my arms around it for leverage. I saw a large branch just below my knee and aimed for it. I slid down by digging my right leg into the soft ground and pushing with my hips. I managed to propel myself a few feet. I grabbed onto the branch. It broke. I turned the flashlight off wanting to reserve the battery power. The effort had angered the pain in my leg even more. I reached down and felt it. There was a rip in my slacks at the knee. Nothing was protruding so I was confident that I hadn't broken anything, but my hand was sticky. Sap I presumed from the tree. I smelled it; it was not sap. I shone the light on my knee. It was worse than I had anticipated. I succeeded in clearing the blood away for a few seconds from the laceration with some of the hand sanitizer before it started bleeding again. Okay, it was probably just a flesh wound. I pulled out one of the sanitary pads and tucked it into my pants at the injury. I found the scissors and used them to cut away at the cord around the penlight as I needed something to hold the pad in place. This was not going to help the pain, and I needed desperately to get into the cabin in front of me so I took one of the pain pills with a small sip of water. There was nothing else I could do. I waited a few minutes, took a deep breath and hurled myself unto the log. I screamed as I pulled myself up. I was on my feet. I waited for the pain to subside a little. It didn't, but I needed to keep going. I inched myself forward in the dark using the log as a support until I felt like I was off the hill. Never had I thought that it was so far down. I pulled out the penlight again. I could make out the outline of the cabin in front of me. I needed a walking stick so I shone the light around until I found a large limb. It would have to do until I found something better. I let go of the log and transferred my weight to the makeshift cane. Thank God it was strong enough to support me somewhat.

The back porch to the cabin had four steps leading up to the door. I was doubtful that I was going to be able to manoeuvre them, and suppose I got up there and found the door was locked. Well, it was going to be locked so I was going to have to break in. I shone the light around and discovered that the one window was not on the porch landing, and so was inaccessible to me. Ten minutes later I had made it around to the front of the building. I was confronted by more steps. I turned the light on for a second. There were at least six stairs. With the help of my walking pole and a very rickety handrail I climbed ever so carefully to the top. The pill had helped or else I had just become numb. I turned the light on again, saw two windows with a door in between. I tried the door. Nope. I rammed it slightly with the stick; no luck. I sat down on the bench to catch my breath and think. If I broke a window there would be glass all over the floor and I would cut myself by climbing in. Maybe the windows were unlocked...they weren't. I had no choice as I was exhausted. I took the cane and slammed it into the left window shattering the glass. It was as I thought; broken shards all over. Why had I even thought that I could lower myself through the window anyhow with my injury?

A beam of light emerged from the dark sky as the clouds parted. I thanked the moon and made my way down the stairs sitting on my derriere. The next cabin was only a stone's throw away. I was determined to gain entrance to it. It appeared to be more like the one Brian had taken me to. There were no steps. I felt that I needed to cleanse my wound first so I hobbled to the water's edge. I unfastened the string around my knee. The pad was blood soaked. I ripped a larger hole in the pants so I could get a better look. I decided that the pants had to go. I undid them, and let them fall to the ground. I had trouble getting my left foot and leg out of them. If I fell down I would probably not be able to get up again, and Brian would find me here in the morning. That was not going to happen even if I had to crawl.

I stepped into the water. As much as I hadn't wanted to, my bladder automatically gave way. Thank heavens I had extra panties. I washed myself with a piece of the ripped pants taking extra caution with my knee. The salt water stung it. I wondered if I had done it more harm than good. I washed what was left of my slacks, gathered my bag, the dirty blanket, and made my way in my wet underwear to the cabin. The moon went dark as I reached the door. Two dried up plants sat in ceramic pots on either side. The door was locked of course. The small cement blocks under the overhang of the roof had a welcome rug on it. I laughed. Could there possibly be a key under it…there wasn't. I was teetering and fighting to stay upright. I had one last hope. I managed to move one of the urns up and felt under it. My hand came away with a key. I turned it into the lock. The door swung open. I turned the penlight on and made a quick sweep of the room. I found what I needed… a place to lie down. I threw everything to the floor, and sat down on the sofa. With great difficulty I managed to change my underwear. Then with one quick motion I lifted my left leg with both hands and rolled over. It hurt like hell. I reached for the blanket that I had seen on the back of the couch, covered up, and closed my eyes.

I awoke to a rat-a- tap. Oh God, he's here! Rat-a-tap, rat-a-tap, rat-a-tap…wait a minute, I knew that sound. It was a woodpecker. I sighed a breath of relief, but it was soon diminished as I realized that dawn was breaking. I threw the blanket off me and swung my legs over the sofa forgetting that I had an injured leg. The pain was excruciating. While I was assessing my knee which was swollen and ugly looking, I wondered why I was in my underwear. I saw my slacks rolled up in a ball on the floor. I pulled them towards me with the aid of my walking stick. They were soaking wet. No loss I guess as I had pretty much ripped one leg to shreds last night. Hopefully, the owner of the cabin had left some clothes behind. I tried to stand, but to no avail. I manoeuvred one of the chairs with the help of my stick within reach and used it as a crutch to stand. It still hurt, but I needed to get into the bedroom. I slid the chair along the floor, stepping with my right leg and dragging my left. It was getting lighter and lighter outside. I didn't have much time. I wanted to stop at the bed and rest, but realized that I might not be able to get up again so pushed on to the chest of drawers. Every drawer was empty except for a pair of socks. I had socks. I cursed, turned around and lumbered to the next bedroom. I could see something hanging on a peg on the closet door. I'd get there, but checked the bureau first. Top drawer was full of socks. Damn. Second and third drawers were empty. The fourth revealed a pair of questionable long Johns and a long sleeved sweatshirt. I threw them on the bed and made my way to the closet. There was nothing in it but rain gear. I made my way back to the bed and sat. I took my blouse and bra off and threw them on the bed, put my blouse back on and pulled the sweatshirt over my head. I struggled getting into the long Johns. What the hell was a woman of my stature doing wearing a stranger's drawers thinking? I told myself that I was doing whatever I had to; anything that would get me back to the man I loved. There is nothing special about you Mayria; riches do not make the woman. Out here I was just an ordinary individual who had to rely on her senses to defeat the obstacles, and the man pursuing her.

I checked the cupboards in the kitchen. They held nothing of any use to me except a few dish towels which I stuffed in my bag with the rest of my worldly possessions. There were no staples of any sort. Was that a motor I heard? I opened the back door to discover four steps to the bottom. I daren't return to the front. I descended gingerly holding my breath to keep from screaming. I exhaled only when I felt like I was going to pass out.

"Help me Mitch, help me." I cried when I reached the bottom.

I heard him in my head. "This is what you are going to do Mya. You are going to make your way to the back of the forest, or as far back as you feel comfortable. Then you are going to find a nice soft spot to rest, and then you are going to tend to your leg, elevate it if you can, lie down and rest until evening. I'm coming for you."

Tears filled my eyes. "I'm scared Mitch; I'm scared."

"Are you going to do as you're told just this one time?"

I managed a little laugh. "I will. I hear the boat…"

"Get going Mayria; get going, and try not to fall again."

I could barely here the sound of the boat anymore so I figured it was safe to stop. Brian had probably searched the cabins by now and had discovered where I had spent the night. He would be on full alert tonight. I had ventured into the woods as far as I dared. I threw everything down under a very large fir tree. I really needed to pee, but wasn't sure how I could manage to squat. I walked around the tree until I found a small sapling that I figured would hold me as I crouched. I was okay until I tried to right myself. With great difficulty I pulled the long Johns up holding on to the tree with one hand, but I could not stand upright. My left leg buckled, and I fell to the ground. I laid there writhing in agony for a half hour or so. I needed a pill, but it was back at the tree. I couldn't crawl so I had no choice but to try and get back by scooting on my butt. I wished that I had put the rain pants on as the ground was littered with pine needles and the remains of broken hazel nuts that jabbed me at every movement. Ten minutes later I rolled unto the blanket I had spread out. I had not the energy to even check on my knee. I reached into my bag, found the pain pill, emptied a bottle of water, and collapsed.

The sun had come out. It was high in the sky as I woke up sometime later. I figured I had five or six hours until dark. I pulled my pant leg up. The ankle was puffy. The leg itself was only bruised, but the knee was twice as large as it should be. There appeared to be a hole in the centre of the knee cap. I imagined that it was a mass of infection and wondered how long it took for gangrene to set in. I knew not what to do. Should I wrap it or leave it open to the air? I decided on the latter as maybe the roughness of the wool was irritating it. I dug out the sanitizer and a couple of moistened wipes and cleansed the wound as best I could. I found the nail file in the bottom of my bag, popped a piece of juicy Fruit in my mouth, and tended to my broken nails. Next, I took out the notepad and pen, leaned back against the tree and started a journal of my misadventures. A black bushy tailed squirrel sat on a stump a few feet away and chattered relentlessly, scolding me for what I did not know. In turn I reprimanded him for leaving a trail of broken nuts for me to scrape my butt on. He kept me company for half an hour and then scurried off up a tree.

Suddenly, the sunny day became cloudy and a north wind rustled through the woods. I shivered. It was time for me to head back to the bench above the beach houses. I braced myself against the fir tree, and with the walking pole in front of me I put all my weight on my right leg. I pushed with all my might until I was standing. I leaned back against the tree, took a deep breath, and reached for the blanket and my bag. I hoped my yelling hadn't awakened any critters.

I laboured along slowly until I reached what I thought would provide me with a cover from being spotted. I couldn't see or hear the boat, but stayed close to the shrubberies peeking out now and then. I didn't dare sit. I heard him before I saw him.

"You are really pissing me off but good Tessa!" He yelled. "We have to be out of here early tomorrow morning, so quit this hide and seek game of yours, and get down here! Don't make me bring the dogs in! There is no way out of here except with me so admit defeat and surrender!"

I didn't move for what seemed like an eternity. I was struggling to stay upright. He must have parked the boat out of my line of sight because it started up almost immediately after his rant at me. He must have been walking the beach checking out all the cabins. I waited until I was reasonably sure that he had called off the search and had given up for the time being. I had to get into one of those cabins in front of me before complete darkness. Rain was threatening. I knew that Mitch was never going to find me, but if I could thwart Brian's plans for another day I would have some sort of victory over him. I would know that I had done all that I could.

The cabins in front of me were all a good distance apart. I theorized that they were the fifth, sixth, and seventh ones. For some reason I chose the sixth. If it was locked then so be it, and I would move on to the next, and then the next. Who was I kidding? I probably wasn't even going to make it to any of them. A loud thunder clap encouraged me to keep going. I rounded the corner of the cabin and a cheery sight greeted me. Two solar lights were flickering in the breeze trying to gain control of the night. I took that as a positive sign. I plodded up the four steps. At least there was a railing to help me. I crossed the porch and stood in front of the door waiting for it to magically open. I laughed at myself and turned the knob. It swung open. I knew in my mind that it was a trick and that Brian would be waiting for me inside. I took a wide sweep of the room with my penlight. No sign of him. I made my way from the table to the cupboards hoping to find some food. I found a can of coffee, some crackers in a sealed container and a half jar of peanut butter. I wondered if the propane was turned on as I desperately needed coffee. I checked the fridge. It appeared to be running. Inside was a bottle of water, a can of beer, and a grape soda. I reached for one of the chairs, set my bag and the blanket on it, the crackers, a knife, the peanut butter, and the can of beer, and made my way to the open door of a bedroom. I hoped that the closed other door would reveal a bathroom of sorts, but was too tired to check it out. Anyhow, it was probably just another bedroom. I pulled the quilt back. The sheets and pillow cases all looked clean. I sat and removed the itchy underwear and crawled into the inviting bed. I didn't want to move again, but knew I needed to eat something if I was going to live to fight another day. I did my best to sit up, spread peanut butter on half a dozen crackers and downed them with the beer. I left a swig to swallow a Tylenol and a travel tab. I thought the Gravol pill would help me get the sleep I needed. I lay back, shut off the little flashlight which had become my best friend, closed my eyes, and drifted off into the land of dreams and nightmares.

Chapter 11

All hands on Deck

Bobbie didn't question my reason for wanting to revisit the Keg Marina. In fact he hadn't had

much to say all night. I asked him if he was all right.

"Sure I am Mitch; why wouldn't I be? I'm military; I know the importance of being diligent, and what did I do...I let my own mother be abducted on my watch. Sure, I'm all right."

"I figured that was what was bothering you, but you have to let it go. I'm the one who underestimated Brian. It was all so easy thinking that he accepted the divorce agreement. I did expect trouble, but I didn't think he was going to be so brazen and strike so quickly. Abducting your mother never even entered my head. It appeared as if he didn't need Mya's finances anymore if we believed that his new venture was going to make him a rich man. I never completely believed that he didn't push her down the stairs, or have a hand in the poisonings, so why in the hell did I let my guard down...it's on me Son; it's on me." I said regrettably.

"Mom absolved him of any attempts on her life, so why do you still have doubts?"

"I don't know; been too long in this job I guess. I'm always suspicious... even of the truth."

"She won't blame you Mitch. I need you to be honest with me; are we going to find her before it's too late?" Bobbie asked pessimistically.

"No, she wouldn't blame me. She would blame herself for getting me involved with her problems. You probably don't know this, but she came to my office a few dozen times. She never had the nerve to confront me and tell me about our daughter though. The one time she decided she would, the office was shut down for a holiday. None of this would have happened if I had just been there."

"You don't know that for sure. She was already married to Brian then wasn't she?"

"I think so. It's all water under the bridge now, and I can't go back in time and change things. To answer your question, yes, we are going to find her, and that's why we are going to the marina. Call it intuition or whatever you want, but I know that yacht has connections to her disappearance just as I know that our daughter is in trouble."

He asked me what made me think that Lylah Jayne was in trouble.

I told him about the dreams.

I stopped so suddenly that Bobbie almost ploughed into me. I cursed and threw up my hands. He asked me what was wrong.

"I'm too late; it's gone, damn, damn, damn!" I kicked the pier where the yacht had been anchored to earlier.

"Do you think the captain would have notified the care takers? Maybe he knows something."

"Don't think criminals let anyone know their intentions."

"What's going on out there?" A voice called from the fishing boat.

"Is that you Yan...its Mitch, we met earlier today. I was interested in the yacht with the dragons on it, remember."

"Yeah, well it's gone, thank the lucky stars."

"Do you know who ferried her out and what time it was?"

"Midnight. Didn't see a thing, just heard her engine."

"Twice I am woke up. First, that thing and now you. Goin back to bed. Some of us need to sleep so they can support themselves."

I apologized, hopped aboard his vessel and passed him my business card asking him to call me if the yacht came back. My pockets were empty. Bobbie passed me two twenties which I offered to Yan. He nodded his head and accepted the money. I told Bobbie that it was time to go home.

"I like that you consider it your home Mitch. We want you to stay even if mom doesn't..."Bobbie couldn't finish the sentence.

I put my hands on his shoulders. "She's as good as home Son. I appreciate the offer, more than you know. I hate to wake him, but I have to alert Rory. Something about the owner, a Dr. Zang Lu had his shackles up. I punched in Detective Adams's number.

"This better be damn newsworthy Mitchum!" Rory answered sleepily on the fourth ring.

I explained the situation. I visualized him coming to attention. He said he would alert the coast guard on both sides of the border. He told me to come by the station at eight because he had a whale of a tale to tell me.

Sadie was waiting for me at the door when we returned. I took her for a quick run and let her sleep on the rug in Mya's room. It was 4:30 a.m. when I finally crawled into Mya's bed. I clutched her pillow to my chest and buried my face in her scent.

Three and a half hours later I was sitting having coffee with Rory in his office at the downtown headquarters waiting with baited breath for his earth shattering news which he seemed hesitant on sharing immediately. His eyes kept wandering back and forth through the windows. I asked him if he was expecting someone.

He said, "Yes, and here he is."

The door opened, and my arch enemy walked in. Rory got up and shook his hand.

"Mitch, Special Agent Douglas Phelps will be working with us on Mayria's abduction."

I stood up. "Like hell he will be! He leaves or I do." I gave Rory the ultimatum.

"Yeah, I thought you'd have that reaction. Let's hear him out before you make up your mind."

Phelps answered nonchalantly. "I'm willing to let bygones rest while we work together to find Mayria, and prosecute Brian. What do you say Mitch?"

He extended his hand. I didn't take it.

"Mitch?" Rory wanted an explanation for my hostility.

My hand was on the door knob. "This is the rotten son of a bitch that cost Maryanne Withers her life if you remember? I will not have him interfering with my case and endangering Mayria's."

"It's not your case anymore Mitch. It's a kidnapping and The FBI is taking over." Rory explained diplomatically.

"Mayria is my case. Thanks for nothing." I quipped walking out.

"Mitch!" Rory's hand was on my shoulder. "Don't do this; don't let a past incident interfere with this one."

"Oh, just as you have let the Manchester/O'Neil Affair go?"

"Touché, I get it. You have to put what happened yesterday to rest for the time being; take up your hostilities again once we have Mayria back. But now we need to work together. It's still yours and my case, and we are not relinquishing our command. Special Agent Phelps is not asking for complete control; he wants us to share information and work together. You need to hear him out. He has a tidbit about Brian that will interest you...what do you say Buddy?"

I heard her in my head. "I need you Mitch...help me."

I walked back into Rory's office, offered my hand to Phelps, and said as he took it. "For now; we can take up the gauntlet again, or not, depending on whether you deliver or not. If it has not been made clear to you already the woman in question is the woman I love. If you get in the way of rescuing her...well, jury's out on the consequences."

"Sit down Mitch. I get where you are coming from, and we'll rehash it another day. Today it is all about your lady and her husband Brian Fulton, alias B.G. Fullerton. He has been on our radar for some time now, but we haven't been able to assemble enough dirt on him to warrant an arrest. He may have just stepped into our hands this time with the kidnapping. We'll have enough to hold him on for years while we finish our investigation into a number of other crimes we believe he has had a hand in." Phelps said.

I raised my eyebrows. "First, you have to catch him, and what makes you think that he is going to co-operate with you? For one thing, he'd have to be breathing to do so. Chances of that are mighty slim."

Rory and Phelps both grinned. I think they both knew that I was serious.

"Okay," Rory said. "remember how I told you that Dr. Lu's name rang a bell? Well, how about this for a consequence? It appears as if he and B.G. Fullerton are business partners. What do you say about that Mitch?"

"I say, what the hell are we doing sitting around here; let's find him!"

Rory's desk phone rang while we were formulating a plan. He listened intently. His eyes blinked rapidly. After a few minutes he told the caller to get him the phone number asap. He hung up and told me and Phelps to sit down. He pulled a bottle of Scotch and three glasses out of a drawer and poured a generous amount in each. I knew the phone call had to be bad news.

"It's Mayria isn't it? Has she been found; is she in the hospital, is she...?"

"Take a breath Mitch. It is about Mayria, but it is not current, but may have some bearing on her disappearance. Did you know that she owns a yacht?"

"That's preposterous! She would have told me. Where is this coming from Rory?"

"I decided to extend the search for vessels owned by Brian with the alias B.G. Fullerton to several U.S. states last night, and on a hunch, I included Mayria's name with several different last names. Nothing came up under his name, but it did under Mayria's. It appears as if she bought a yacht from a boat dealership in Seattle Washington. Should have a phone number of the outfit any second."

"It was her yacht at the pier...is that what you are thinking?" I shook my head. "It can't be."

Rory picked up the phone, pen in hand. "What have you got Shirl?" He jotted something down.

"We should have an answer straightaway." He put the call on speaker.

A woman's voice, "Boats Are Us; how may I help you?"

"This is Detective Rory Adams of the Vancouver police department in Canada. I need verification that a yacht purchased from your dealership several years ago is the one in question in an investigation. Can you help me with this inquiry?"

"Certainly; I will refer you to Mr. Dennison. One minute please."

A booming voice greeted us. "Denny here, how may I help you Detective Adams?"

"I'm hoping you can Sir. I imagine that you don't sell a yacht every day?"

Denny laughed. "You'd be right on that Detective."

"It has come to our attention that one was purchased from you by a Ms. Mayria Joseph. Can your records confirm that?"

"I can as I handled the transaction myself. Give me a sec to bring it up on the computer. Ms. Joseph is not a woman a man forgets."

"How is that Mr. Dennison?"

"Call me Denny. If you have ever met her you would know what I mean. I met Ms. Joseph long before she purchased the yacht. She would come by now and then, especially when we posted a sale special or sponsored an auction. Nothing we had seemed to interest her. Finally, one day she admitted that she was interested in buying a yacht. That was a commodity that we didn't deal with on a regular basis. I guess a few months passed before one came up for bids. I viewed it and pretty much dismissed that I could resell it. On a whim, I called Ms. Joseph and described it to her. I remember our conversation. I had laughed and said that I couldn't imagine anyone wanting to buy it in its current condition. She had said that she wasn't just anyone, but she was the woman the yacht was made for. The same day she arrived with a cashier's cheque, and the deal was sealed."

"Was there something unusual about the boat Denny?"

"There sure as hell was! Encompassing the starboard and portside were colorful fire-breathing dragons. They seemed to be the selling point with Mayria. I can still see the smile on her face as she witnessed them up close. She said that all she needed now was her white knight."

I picked up the glass and downed the Scotch in one gulp.

Rory passed me the bottle. I shook my head. He carried on asking Denny a leading question.

"Did Ms. Joseph have the yacht moved somewhere?"

"Yes, it was towed to Black and Black Yachting Marina on Oceanic Way."

"In Seattle? I don't suppose you would have the phone number would you Denny?"

"It's staring at me. I don't suppose you are at liberty to relate why this boat is of interest?"

Rory scribbled the number down. "You're right about that. Thanks for the info."

"You're welcome. Let me know if I can be of further assistance."

Rory disconnected and immediately punched in the numbers of the marina. A minute later he had cut through the red tape and was talking to one of the owners. "Thanks for taking my call Mr. Black. It has come to our attention that a yacht owned by Mayria Joseph is docked at your marina. Is it still there?"

"It has occupied the same berth for two and a half years. Ms. Joseph visited regularly for the first year or so, but hasn't been around for some time. Let's see...October 19th, 2012 is the last date we have on record. Her mooring fees are always paid in advance."

"So, the yacht is still docked with you?"

"No Sir; the Jeudanzee was piloted out of here two nights ago, September 11th at 4 P.M. to be exact. Is this of any help to you Detective?"

"Somewhat, but under whose authority was it released from your marina?"

"A Mrs. Diaz arrived with a notarized bill of sale from Tessa Fulton; aka Mayria Joseph. A note accompanied it explaining that she, Ms. Joseph had married and that the Jeudanzee had become an albatross so she had sold it. She thanked us and enclosed a cashier's check for three thousand dollars for its' mooring. She owed us nothing so it was shredded."

"Seems to be aboveboard. Can you describe this Diaz woman?"

"I would say she was in her early forties, olive skin, reddish hair, long I believe, but a cap was hiding most of it. She was about five feet five, maybe one hundred and thirty pounds. She had a bit of a Spanish accent. She was very pleasant."

"Good recall Mr. Black. I wish all my witnesses had the same memory."

"It was just a couple days ago, so is still fresh in my memory. Hope it helps."

I reached for the handset. "Detective Mitchum here Sir; two questions, what was the note from Ms. Joseph written on, and what was Mrs. Diaz's full name?"

"Let me see, yes, Lorena Marie Diaz. She provided credentials proving her identity. The note which I have here in front of me has Tess and Brian Fulton, Fulton Enterprises as its letterhead. The banking institution is Coast Credit Union. My brother and I believed everything was legal, but now I'm thinking that it wasn't. Would I be right about that?" Mr. Black inquired.

"You said it left the dock at 4 P.M.; surely it wasn't piloted by Mrs. Diaz?"

"No Sir. Mrs. Diaz was accompanied by a big burly man. He was of an Asian descent. I could not detect which one. He produced his pilot's license and navigated her out of here as slick as could be. Mrs. Diaz waved to us from the deck. I'm sorry, I do not seem to have his name."

I passed the phone back to Rory as I had all I needed to know. Rory thanked him and asked for his fax as he was going to be sending a photo to him so he could authenticate or deny that it was Lorena Diaz. He hung up and asked if I had a photo of Brian's secretary.

"Sure thing Boss because I go around taking photos of every woman I come into contact with."

"I see you have your sense of humor back. Do you think you can handle this one yourself?"

I stood up. "Aye aye, Boss."

"Hold on Mitch; do you mind if I accompany you? I'd like to see the headquarters myself."

"Suit yourself." I answered Agent Phelps, not caring one way or the other. "There isn't much to see, but if you want to tag along I guess I have no objections. It's doubtful that Ms. Carmen DeSoto will even be there, but I might just need your credentials to acquire her home address. Unless you have another job for him Rory, we'll touch base in an hour or so."

"As soon as possible Mitch. I'll be on the mobile. Think I'll give the marina another look. Play nice you two."

We both sniggered. In the elevator Phelps asked me if I thought Mrs. Diaz and Carmen DeSoto were one and the same. I asked what his first clue was. He said that I had nodded my head when Black described Diaz.

"I haven't met the woman, but I have been in her office. She has a picture of herself and her daughter at her desk."

"You just assumed it was a picture of her?"

"I'm not in the business of assuming. Mayria identified her. It was her opinion that Carmen and Brian were having an affair."

"Did that bother her?"

"Hell no!"

"Is that because she was already involved with you?"

I stepped out of the elevator and proceeded to my jeep. Phelps followed asking if he had offended me. I told him that Mya's and my relationship was none of his business.

We buckled up and proceeded the five blocks to the Davis Block.

"That's where you are wrong Mitch. If we get into a situation where your involvement with Ms. Joseph puts her or you, or the rest of the team in jeopardy, I will have to pull you out...you understand?"

He was testing me. "You won't be pulling me off this case...do you understand that? I have no problem with disobeying you or Rory, and if either of you get in my way of rescuing Mya...have I made myself clear?"

"You have. It's to your advantage to work alongside of us, not against us. We all have different outlets for information, so let's make it work. I take it that Mya is your nickname for her?"

"It's the name she goes by now, and yes, it was my name for her thirty years ago."

"Adams mentioned that you two go way back. Thirty years, that's a long time?"

"It was yesterday."

"I wonder what it's like to carry feelings around for that long. None of my business I know, but how did you two find each other again?"

"Rory didn't tell you? Her family hired me to protect her and prove that her husband had tried multiple times to kill her."

"Yes; let's talk about that."

I pulled into the underground parking lot, put the jeep in park, turned and looked at him, shook my head and said, "Let's not."

He followed me into the building. I started up the stairs to the fourth floor.

"What, no elevator?" Phelps inquired.

"Sure, but I thought that those new Italian loafers you're wearing could use a work-out."

"Funny."

"Is a three piece suit standard attire for the FBI these days?" I said eyeing his pinstripe suit.

"Late meeting last night. Everything else was already packed and on the tarmac, so for now, this is it. I came directly to headquarters last night to talk with detective Adams. Actually, it was early morning so pulled an all-nighter on the computer checking data and haven't been to bed yet. Right after this tete-a-tete with Ms. DeSoto and nothing else comes up…"

"Managed before you came on scene so think we will manage while you snooze."

We stopped in front of the office. Carmen was at her desk. She rose when we entered.

"Good morning gentlemen. I tried to call you but you had already left the hotel, and I didn't have a cell number. Where is Mr. Tanaki?"

"What were you going to tell us Ms. DeSoto?" I asked.

"Just that I would have to reschedule you as Mr. Fulton is unavailable. I hope you understand."

"Do you know where he is?"

"I am sorry, I cannot divulge his whereabouts."

"No need Carmen; we know he is on the run with his ex-wife."

"You know about that? Of course, it is all over the media."

"Why are you still holding the fort down? Orders from Fulton? Are you in contact with him?"

"I'm going to have to ask you to leave." She said nervously.

"Right after we take a look around. Oh, by the way, I am Detective Mitchum, and this is Special Agent Phelps of the FBI."

I flashed her my ID holding my hand over the 'private'. Douglas made sure she got a good look at his credentials.

"The FBI", she stuttered, "why are you involved?"

He tipped his imaginary hat. "It's a kidnapping Ma'am. Can you open this door for us?"

"It's Mr. Fulton's private office." She was very flustered.

"I know, and that is why I want to take a look see. Did Mrs. Fulton have her own office?"

"No, she was never here. She had no interest in the business."

I asked her why her name was on the door then. I picked up a business card. "And, why is her name on this and the company stationary?"

She hemmed and hawed. "He wanted it that way." Reluctantly she keyed Douglas into Brian's office. "If there is nothing else?"

"Sit down Carmen; you and I are just getting started. Who are the gentlemen you were expecting, and who is Mr.Tanaki?"

"They are just people interested in the business."

"What exactly is the business?"

"Fulton Enterprises; would you like a brochure?"

"Sure, why not." She handed me a small pamphlet while I pulled out my cell. "First things first; smile for the camera. Give me a second while I forward this to headquarters."

We could here Phelps opening and shutting drawers in the office next door. Carmen was fidgeting with the necklace around her neck. I asked her how she had enjoyed her trip back from Seattle on the Jeudanzee. She said she had no idea what I was talking about.

"Cut the crap Carmen; you know exactly what I am talking about. Did you forge Mayria's signature on the bill of sale for the yacht?"

"Who is Mayria?"

I laughed. "She's Tess to you; you know, your boss's wife. So, is Carmen DeSoto your real name or is it Lorenza Diaz?"

"I have nothing to say to you without my lawyer present."

I picked up the phone and handed it to her. "Go ahead, call him. You haven't been charged with anything, but up to you if you want to waste his time. Hold on while I read this text. Okay, my boss wants us to bring you down to headquarters. He has questions of his own, and has two suspects in the abduction of Tess Fulton in custody that he wants you to identify. Have your lawyer meet us at the VPD.”

“I can’t go.”

Douglas had joined us carting an armful of files. “Miss DeSoto, or is it Diaz?”

“DeSoto.” She answered trembling.

I didn’t blame her as Phelps demeanor had changed from one of friendliness to stern commandant. He continued in a condescending voice leaning over her desk. “Ms. DeSoto, I don’t believe you know just how much trouble you are in. Forgery, fake credentials, larceny, kidnapping, are all federal crimes. It is in your best interest to co-operate with us.” He turned to me and asked for my handcuffs.

What the hell! I don’t carry handcuffs. Carmen had broken into tears.

“That’s not necessary Phelps; she’s not under arrest. Rory wants her downtown as there have been some new developments. Will you accompany us of your own free volition Ms. DeSoto?”

“I will.” She gave Phelps the evil eye. “You cannot take those files out of here.”

“Oh, sorry; my bad.” He laughed as he walked out the door with them. “Hurry along Mitchum.”

He held the back door of the jeep open for her. “After you.”

Her eyes pleaded with me. “Can I sit with you Detective Mitchum?”

Phelps laughed arrogantly again. “Did you frisk her Mitch; she may be concealing a weapon.”

“Keep your hands where I can see them.” I tried to sound authoritative without being fearsome.

I’d be glad to hand her over to Rory as he would handle her with kid gloves. It would definitely be “good cop”, “bad cop” if he included Phelps in the interrogative. I hoped to be long gone doing some investigating on my own.

Rory wasn't ready to let me vacate the premises just yet. He had Shirl escort Carmen to an interrogation room and asked me to accompany him. Of course Phelps tagged along.

The two suspects in the abduction of Vali were being questioned in two different rooms. He pushed the speaker button on each of the rooms and let me listen for a few minutes. Suspect number one was Carl Anderson. He did come by the nickname rightfully as his hair was as red as I had ever seen. The next suspect was Cecil Dandridge. He was boasting a full beard, and indeed had piercing eyes. Rory said that Dr.Graham the dentist, and his assistant were on the way to see if they could identify the assailants, and was Vali well enough to join them. I said she was. I called Jake and asked him to bring Vali down to the VPD.

One by one Vali, Dr. Graham and his assistant Nicole were escorted into the viewing room to hopefully identify the suspects. 'Red' was immediately identified by Graham and Nicole. Vali had never gotten a look at him so couldn't pick him out of the line-up. The other suspects in the second line-up had been outfitted with facial masks. Neither the dentist nor Nicole could identify Cecil Dandridge as one of the kidnappers until they heard him speak. Vali shuttered when she first saw him. She said she would never forget those beady eyes staring into hers. His voice made her tremble. Rory said he had all he needed to make a formal arrest.

Agent Phelps appeared out of nowhere, winked at Jake and me, and proceeded into interview room 1 to question Red, aka Carl Anderson, I presumed.

"Tell me I'm seeing things Boss?" Jake asked with disgust.

"Nope, it's Phelps in living color." I answered with equal disgust.

"What the hell is he doing here?"

"Apparently, he asked for the case; insisted I think is more accurate."

"Did he know that you were involved?"

"Hell yes; I'm the main attraction!"

Vali asked who he was. Jake said he was a thorn in our sides and to just leave it at that for now.

I caught up with Rory before we left and asked him to come over to the house for lunch. I figured he needed a break, but he asked for a rain check as he wanted to stay on top of the interrogations. He said he'd check in with me later. I told him to ask Carmen about a Mr. Tanaki.

Ivy had a nice lunch waiting for us. I wasn't all that hungry but knew I needed the calories in order to keep going. After I had the last bite I reiterated what had gone down that morning at the precinct. Vali's eyes lit up when I told her that her mother owned a yacht, and not just any ole yacht, but the one with the fiery dragons on it that I had been suspicious of.

"She never told me that she was even contemplating on purchasing one. I knew about her trips to the boat dealership, but I always thought that she had a crush on the owner, and that is why she kept on going back. She even dragged me with her a couple of times, but there was never any mention of a yacht." Vali was visibly overwhelmed.

"Are we talking about Mr. Dennison? Did she refer to him as Denny?"

"Oh God, are you jealous?"

"Somewhat. This was before she married Brian though, right?"

"I guess. Is that important?"

"Just trying to get a time-line on everything." I got up. "Enough of that for now. I'm going to take another look around the factory out in the valley. Call me if anything comes up."

"You're not going without me Boss." Jake insisted.

I looked at Frankie and Bobbie. They said they wouldn't let their sister out of their sight. Bobbie let me know he was toting his handgun.

No one at the factory could add anything knew about Brian's whereabouts. They were all shocked at what had gone down. Most of them had only met Mya once or twice, but had thought that she was the one who controlled the purse strings. Work was commencing, but for how long it could keep operating was the question. Its' future would depend upon how much authority the board of directors had. It did not look promising unless Mrs. Fulton returned to continue running the company as surely Fulton would be spending the rest of his life in prison if the kidnapping charge was laid. One could only hope was my response.

Rory and I touched base after dinner. He said there wasn't anything new and that every boat in their jurisdiction had been notified of the kidnapping. That meant sailboats, fishing trawlers, tugs, yachts and everything in between. The coast guard on both sides of the border were on full alert. He was of the assumption that something was going to break overnight. It didn't appear that this Mr. Tanaki was anything except a businessman.

The family decided to call it an early night. I was in full agreement. I probably wasn't going to sleep, but just the thought of lying my head down on Mya's pillow was appealing. I was on my way upstairs when my cell jingled. The call display read "Irene". Hell, what could she possibly want at this time of night?

I answered. "What can I do for you Irene?"

"I'm glad you took my call Mitch. I want to apologise for my remarks yesterday."

"There's no need. You're entitled to your opinion."

"I can't even blame my outburst on Rory. That man irks me to no end, but I guess I just wanted to lash out at you, and I am sorry for my words."

I heard the sincerity in her voice, and decided to cut her some slack. "None of this was ever your fault Irene. I guess that I had become accustomed to the platonic life that we had been living and didn't even realize that I was wasting away. What made us think that we could go on the way we were? Answer me truthfully; were you happy?"

"I love you Mitch, so my answer is yes, I was happy. I'm not now. I don't like to come home anymore because you're not here. I hated the weekends because you were always gone. I realize now that I could have prevented that if I had of been more willing to compromise."

My mind was filled with worry for Mya's safety. I had no desire to hear Irene talk about what could have been. "It's all water under the bridge now Irene. There is no sense in you trying to reconstruct a favorable outcome. My life is with Mayria now. By the way, your friend, Wallace or Dazie, whatever her name is, called the office looking for me; any idea what she wanted?"

Irene laughed sarcastically. "Well, she knows you asked me for a divorce so I guess she feels you are fair game now. Suppose if Mayria doesn't come back; what then Mitch?"

"That's not a possibility I am willing to entertain at the moment. Please talk to your lawyer as we need to end our marriage. Good night Irene."

"I am still of the belief that what you feel for Mayria is only a school boy's crush. When you come to see that for yourself I will be here waiting for you. I love you Mitch."

Just what I wanted to hear. Sleep was an elusive mistress. We were all up before the crack of dawn. Jake and Vali were the last ones up. I reached for two cups off the rack. The phone rang. I dropped the cups, and grabbed the phone. "Mya, is that you Baby?" I cried frantically.

"Oh Mitch, oh Mitch, thank God you're there!"

Chapter 12

Day Three

Damn, why did I have to drink that beer last night! Now my bladder was crying out that it was

going to burst. This better be the cabin that had a bathroom. What kind of vacation retreats were these anyhow? There certainly weren't any amenities. A bathroom was at the top of the list. These cabins were more like a prison. I knew I wouldn't make it to the outside biffy so there had better be a lavatory behind these doors. I turned the knob. It was just another bedroom. Damn! Wait a minute; what was that sitting on that dresser?

My penlight was sitting on the night stand where I had left it. There was only a trickle of light coming in through the window. I didn't have time to wait for the sun to show me the way because surely Brian was on his way. I ran my hand over the apparatus in front of me. It was some type of telephone. I found the receiver and lifted it. There was no dial tone. I had no idea how to work it. I kept feeling around for a knob of some sort. My hand stopped on top of what I recognised as an oil lamp. Matches...there must be some. The sun must have risen because the room was suddenly aflame with light. No matches, but an igniter. I lifted the globe off the lamp, pulled up the wick a tad, and flicked the ignitor. Nothing. I knew it was too good to be true. I kept trying to fire the lighter, but couldn't get it to spark. Well, I didn't need the lamp anymore anyhow as I could see. I thought I heard the boat.

There must be an instruction book somewhere. I searched all the drawers, but came up empty. This apparatus was so old it probably doesn't work anyhow, and there is no electricity or... maybe it is battery operated. Yes, but how? Wake up girl; try the red button. I did and the monitor lit up. Do I dial the operator or the phone number? Hurry up, hurry up...I couldn't remember any numbers but the land line at the house. I took a deep breath. It was still on the first ring when Mitch answered.

"Mya, is that you Baby?" His voice was music to my ears.

"Oh Mitch, oh Mitch, thank God you're there." I cried.

"Where are you Honey; are you all right?" His voice was strained.

"I don't know where I am Mitch. We got to this deserted island two days ago. I escaped from Brian the first night. He's coming for me now. I can't run anymore because I fell and hurt my leg. My knee hurts so much. I think it's infected, and I am out of pain pills. What'll I do Mitch…tell me what to do."

"Slow down Honey. I'm coming for you. Tell me what you can. Jake is tracing the call. What kind of a boat were you on and how long did it take you to get where you are?"

"Just a small boat. I was unconscious and came to just as we pulled into shore. There are a lot of cabins here, but there is no electricity, or water, or anything. I found this phone in the one I slept in last night. I don't even know how it works. I'm scared Mitch."

"I know you are Sweetie. It's a radio phone I'm assuming. It worked so that is all that is important. Where is Brian right now?"

"He's close. I've never been afraid of him before but I am now. He says he has to be out of here today. He's been yelling at me for days. I've managed to evade him, but I can't anymore. He's taking me somewhere far away, that is, if he doesn't kill me first. He's very mad at me."

"He's not going to kill you Mya, and we'll find you before…"

"You have to promise that you will find our daughter Mitch. Tell her that I am sorry that I gave her away, and that I didn't get to see her again. Tell her I love her, tell her I love her. Tell the kids I love them. I love you Mitch. I just found you, and now I will never see you again…"

I heard a cry.

"Mommy, it's me. Mitch is going to find you. I am so sorry I let Brian get me; I'm so sorry."

"Are you all right Vali? None of this is your fault or anyone else's. I'm the one who put you all in danger by marrying a psychopath. I love you Sweetie. You'll look after Mitch for me won't you? Where's Frankie?"

"He's right here, and so is Bobbie. I love you too Mommy, and you'll be back to look after Mitch yourself. Never doubt that Mommy; you'll be home soon, you'll be home soon."

"Hi Mom; we are all here. Mitch and his friend Detective Adams have been working round the clock to find you. This is the break they needed. Here's Bobbie...love you Mom."

"I love you all so much. Take care of your sister."

"Hi Mom."

"What are you doing Bobbie? You are supposed to be back in Germany." I blubbered.

He tried to make fun of the situation. "My mother was AWOL so I figured I may as well be too. Don't worry; my leave was extended. I wish I was with you to look after you like you have cared for us all our lives. We have to trust that Brian won't hurt you, and that Mitch will find you. I love you Mom, and don't you worry, we'll look after Vali until you get back home. Keep up the fight as best you can."

It had been many years since either of the boys had to hold back tears over a skinned knee or a sprained finger, but this was their mother whom they would never see again, so there was no holding back. I told him I loved him and asked where Mitch had got to.

"I'm right here Honey." His voice was soothing, yet I could hear the trepidation in it.

"He's going to be here any second...Oh God, how did this happen? What have I done to you? Promise me that you won't blame yourself, and that you'll go on with your life, and find someone new to share it with. I will love you forever, and I'll never forget the days of paradise we shared. I have to say good-bye now before he gets here and knows I called you."

"NO, don't hang-up! Keep talking. I want to hear your voice for as long as I can right now. We've already traced the phone so we know where you are. Tell me how you escaped from Brian and how you hurt yourself."

"I kicked him hard in the groin."

"That's my girl."

"It was all in vain though."

"Honey, you are giving him a run for his money, and he's probably thinking that it's time to cut his losses and cut you free. If you are hurt, it will only slow him down."

"He's not going to Mitch. I'm glad you can't see me right now. I haven't combed my hair in days, I have no clothes, I'm dirty, and my knee is the size of a watermelon."

"You would still be the most beautiful girl in the world. I am a little worried about the state of your knee though. Are you keeping it elevated as much as you can?"

"I've done everything you told me too Mitch."

"When was that Honey?"

"Yesterday. You came to me and told me what to do."

"Good; and you listened?"

"I did because you are always right."

He tried to laugh. "I was wrong about how dangerous Brian is, and I'll make it up to you..."

"I hear the boat. He's shut it off; he's coming."

"Hold off getting on the boat with him as long as you can. Rory and a helicopter are on their way to pick me up. We're gonna get there in time Mya; just hold on. This isn't good-bye Honey. I'll be able to tell you in person just how much I love you in just a short while..."

"Hurry, hurry, oh God he's here!" I cried as I heard the door bang open.

"Mya, Mya..."

Brian grabbed the receiver out of my hand. "You lose lover boy. Karma's a bitch isn't it Mitch? Ha Ha; jokes on you. Say good-bye to your mistress; it's the last thing you will ever say to her." He laughed vulgarly.

Mitch was still calling my name as Brian shut the phone down.

"So, I see you found a phone, and the cabin I left open for you. Ha Ha; guess I wasn't thorough enough though. Did you have fun running around the island for the last few days? Looks like you have a boo- boo. Did my Sweetpea fall down? Thanks for not dressing. Too bad there is no time or we would try out that bed...."

"Not while I am still breathing!"

"We'll see about that. Now get dressed. I'm out of time and patience."

"I'm not going with you! I have no clothes, I can't walk, my knee is probably septic, so just leave me here to die because that is a fate I would rather face than be with you!"

"Still got some spunk I see. You're nowhere near deaths' doorstop, so let's go. I'll carry you if I have to."

"I'm not going anywhere except to the biffy, so get out of my way!"

"I thought you couldn't walk?"

I started to make my way to the back door with aid from the chair. Brian grabbed me from behind. I couldn't move so I just hissed. He laughed again.

"You're a little too dirty and smelly so don't get yourself all worked up. You know if you had of just stayed put you could have had a nice bubble bath, and an all over body massage."

"Shut your filthy mouth and get me to the biffy or I'll pee all over you!"

He picked me up and swung me over his shoulder. I pounded on him, but he only laughed. He set me down on the rickety seat in the loo and told me to be quick. Mitch told me to stall so I was trying, but after two minutes Brian opened the door, told me to pull my panties up, and hoisted me again. I told him I had to wash. He set me down in the cold Pacific beside his boat. I was almost naked as it was so I stepped, or I should say tried to step out of my undies. I fell over and went under. I made no attempt to surface.

He pulled me up and maneuvered me into the boat setting me down on my backside. "You are getting to be more trouble than you are worth, so don't fuck with me anymore girl! Drowning you sounds like a good idea, and I may just throw your wretched body overboard once we reach deeper water. Three years I've been looking after you, three unrewarding years! Being woke up in the middle of the night to get you to the bathroom, or fetch your pills, or hold your hair back while you puked. You're a god damn malady just waiting to slow me down! Tread lightly, very lightly, and don't piss me off again! For God's sake, put some clothes on that festering body."

He threw a bag at me. I recognised it as the one from the unknown shop he had given me the night we had arrived at the island. I was wet and cold. I fished through it and found undies, a pair of jeans, and a long sleeved blouse. I struggled to put the pants on. I didn't want to cry in front of him, but I was in so much pain, and at this point nothing mattered. I let it all out screaming in agony. I guess he wasn't all that heartless because he slowed the boat and came to help me. I did not refuse. He maneuvered me into the jeans, took his coat off and zipped me up in it. He sat me in the seat next to him. He passed me a bottle of water and told me there was a bottle of aspirins in the jacket pocket. I don't know how many I swallowed before he grabbed the bottle from me.

"Oh no you don't, not on my watch Lady! How a smart person can be so incredibly stupid raises the question of your sanity again. Do you want me to send you back to your lover in a body bag 'cause it's sure starting to look like that, but I have other plans for you my sweet."

"What do you want of me?" I asked imploringly.

"Just taking back what is rightfully mine."

"I'm not yours; you agreed to a divorce. You know I love another man, so why?"

"You mean that tiny little piece of paper that I was coerced into signing? Hell, that wasn't worth the ink I used to sign it. I was always going to get you back; I just didn't know it was going to be so fast and simple. I wish I could have seen the look on your useless detective's face when he learned that I had outsmarted him." He was laughing cold-bloodedly.

I tried to get the last word. "Don't sell yourself short because you *will* see the look on his face when you come face to face with him when he finds me. It will not be friendly, I can promise you that!"

He continued laughing. "Yeah, like that is even a possibility."

I swear we were going around in circles. Even through my blood-shot eyes I knew I had seen the same rock-way leading up to a dilapidated cabin four times. I snuck a look at him out of the corner of my eye. He did not seem to be upset. He just kept tapping on the wheel to some unknown tune in his deranged head. We had met very few boats. I was beginning to wonder why there weren't more, and where was the helicopter Mitch had said was on its way? Had I misinterpreted him, and shouldn't the Coast Guard be out patrolling the waters? I tried to calm myself by reminding myself that it was a very big ocean, and that somehow Brian had been able to avoid any other craft. But, Mitch had said they knew where I was. Brian suddenly gunned the boat and took off like a bullet. He told me to hold on. Without slowing down he steered the boat right up unto that rock-way, and under a stand of trees. I pitched forward; my head hit hard against the dash. Well good, the boat isn't going anywhere ever again, and what's a few more bumps and bruises.

Brian got me up and carried me to the back of the boat where he deposited me into a man's arms. "Careful, she's hurt."

Where had this man come from? My question was answered a few seconds later as another boat pulled up to the shore. The man tried to stand me, but I pushed him and fell to the ground. Brian was yelling at him. I rolled over and begged to be left there.

"Christ Chris, can't you do anything right? Get out here Mug; I need your help."

Next thing I knew there were two sets of hands lifting me up. Brian instructed the man he'd called Mug to get me on board the other boat and look after me. He turned to the Chris guy and asked him if he was able to complete the job. Chris answered that he needed five minutes.

Mug had sat me down on the floor on a bed of blankets behind a chest and fishing gear. He cleaned my forehead, gave me a cup of tea and asked me if I was comfortable. My first impulse was to refuse the tea as it was probably drugged, but I was parched and cold, so took it from him and drank it slowly. I guess we waited the five minutes for Chris. A curtain was pulled blocking my view of anything as I heard Chris tell Brian that it was done. We were on the move again.

Brian asked Mug if he had been stopped. He said he had been, and the boat was searched so he didn't expect he'd be stopped again. He was just a fisherman, so he didn't feel they would bother with him again. He had seen several aircraft though; one was a helicopter heading in the direction of Suppression island. Was that where I was; what did the suppression stand for?

I was so very tired. I wanted to lie down.

"Is Tessa secure Mug?"

"I think she is comfy. I gave her the tea."

I think we stopped. I heard a loud boom. The three men laughed.

Brian thanked Chris for doing a good job and apologized for yelling at him earlier.

I closed my eyes. I didn't think I would ever open them again. The last words I heard was Brian yelling.

"OPEN the damn gates Clive! NOW!"

The water was so warm and comforting. I was floating in a sea of sapphire bubbles. Beautiful sable haired mermaids were whirling around me. One was braiding my hair, another was washing my feet, and another was wrapping a long silk white swathe around me. They took my hands and pulled me with them... down, down, down. The deeper we went, the murkier the waters became; darker, and darker, and deadly. Brian had made good on his threat. He had thrown me overboard and had left me to the mercy of these mythical ocean dwellers. The air was being sucked out of me. With one last breath I cried out Mitch's name. From somewhere out of the shadows, a fire- breathing, winged creature emerged. It was the dragon who guarded the yellow door in my dreams. He spoke in a voice I knew... "Get on my back Mayria, and we will fly like the wind... the wild, wild, wind!"

"Mitch, Mitch, Mitch..."

Hands were on me again. "No, no, it is all right Ms. Fulton. You have bad dream, that's all. Get the doctor Sakuri."

I looked into the dark eyes of a young lady standing over me. She was wearing a long sleeved maroon and blue silk kimono. Her hair was piled on top of her head with a decorative pearl comb in the front. She was very dainty and had small delicate hands. Her smile should have been music to my heart, but I realized as I surveyed my surroundings that I was not in Kansas anymore. I was lying in a bed of luxurious white linens enclosed inside a tent of flimsy gauze-like material. Silk screens and pictures of Japanese landscapes and people surrounded the room. I had no doubt that the young woman comforting me was a Geisha girl, and while I had been asleep had been transported to what Brian had described as Shangri-La.

I asked her what her name was. She said it was Misaki. I asked her what country we were in. She said that we were in Canada. I asked her if she knew Brian Fulton. She nodded that she did.

"My name is Tessa Fulton, but my real name is Mayria Joseph. Mr. Fulton is not my husband anymore, but he thinks he is. He kidnapped me...do you know what that means Misaki? He stole me away from my family and the man I love whose name is Adam Mitchum. I need you to contact him. Can you do this for me? You understand that I have been kidnapped don't you? Please help me Misaki."

I asked her for a pen and paper so I could give her his phone number. She stepped away from me quickly and announced that the doctor was here. I followed her eyes towards the door. A tall man with silver hair entered the room and addressed me. His voice was amiable.

"Ms. Fulton, I am Dr. Low. Your husband has asked me to have a look at your injury." He instructed Misaki to lift the covers off my leg.

"My name is Mayria Joseph. I am no longer married to Brian Fulton. However, he has not accepted that and kidnapped me because he thinks we are still married. I am his prisoner and he plans on taking me further away from my family. You must help me get away!"

He took my hands in his. They were warm and looked freshly manicured. His eyes locked with mine. "You are not Tessa Fulton?"

"No. Tessa is my middle name, and he chooses to call me that, but I am Mayria Joseph."

"I see. Let's have a look-see at your leg first; after that we will talk some more okay?"

I nodded and winched as he poked around my knee. He asked me to describe my pain. I told him that it hurt like hell and that I couldn't walk. He asked me to rate it on the scale from 1 to 10. Well, I knew pain, so it was easily a 10 if I moved, but a 5 if I remained motionless. He asked me how I had come to injure myself, and what had I done to cleanse it, and what medications I had taken. I gave him a brief outline of my trials and tribulations. He seemed to be shocked at my full disclosure. I had started with Vali's kidnapping.

"This does not sound like the B.G. Fulton I know. He has spoken of you often, but always with reverence. I believe that the trauma from your injury has caused you some delirium which has caused you to fantasize your situation." He pinched my skin. "You are seriously dehydrated which is probably the cause of your hallucinations. This is not a hospital, but fortunately I have the equipment at my disposal to do small operations. I think its best if we bring in the gurney; will you see to that girls? Thank-you. Now, how about you and I talk a little more Tessa…oh sorry, you wish to be called Mayria."

I was incensed. "I wish to be called Mayria because **that is my name**! Who are you anyhow? Just another one of his sleazy business partners I assume. You are not even a licensed practitioner are you? I'll die of blood poisoning before I let you do a hack job on me!"

He had the insensitivity to laugh. "Good, a gal with spunk! It will assist you immensely in your recovery. I am a real doctor, and you can inspect my credentials while I prepare you for the little surgery. Does that fit with your expectations Miss Mayria?"

"I am not giving you the authority to operate, so there is nothing more to say or do."

"Then it is a distinct possibility that you will succumb to blood poisoning."

"Is she giving you a hard time Zane? Tessa is very familiar with a variety of poisonings…aren't you Sweetpea? However, I am going to have to override you on your decision citing that you were of diminished capacity and didn't realize what was at stake. It's not like Dr. Low is going to be giving a full report to the medical board anyhow." He laughed. "Go ahead, take her away."

He bent down to kiss me. "Don't even think about it! Your day is coming Brian Fulton, and I can't wait to dance on your grave!"

He was still laughing. "You know I am going to rot in hell, so sorry, there will be no dancing."

The operating room was very small. I could barely make out certificates of Dr. Lows authenticity on the wall. I did not ask to examine them up close. He was going to do what he said he would so I could only hope that he knew what he was doing. I was hooked up to an IV. He said it was for hydration. My blood pressure was a little high, but nothing to worry about. He asked me if I had any allergies. I wanted to say yes to thallium and potassium chloride, but figured the odds of him giving me one of them was very low so shook my head. He said he would be administering a local anesthetic to numb the area around my knee, and that it would relieve pain during and after surgery. He asked me if I had ever had cause to take a sedative before. I told him that I did not want to be put under. He promised that the choral hydrate would only relax me, and that I should have no lasting effects from it. He then placed headphones on my ears so I wouldn't hear the scraping. I shuttered, closed my eyes, and hoped that the sedative would work.

I was aware of Dr. Low and Brian talking by my bedside later. I did not open my eyes until I was sure Brian was gone. Dr. Low smiled as the door closed behind Brian. He told me the surgery had gone well, and showed me a tiny sliver of wood that he had extracted from the perforation in my knee. It was a shard that had broken off the fallen tree that I had banged up against. He was sure it was a cedar, and was sending it off to a lab for confirmation along with my blood cultures. He said if I hadn't received help I could very well have ended up with cedar poisoning.

I understood what he had said, but was still a little groggy so didn't ask any questions. After he left Sakuri and Misaki managed to get me to drink some broth and tea. They assured me that Mr.

Fulton was banned from seeing me until morning, but that I had another visitor. I could not imagine who that could be.

She entered my room as if she owned it. She was tall and statuesque. Her long gray/black hair swirled around her as she moved. A red rose pinned at her ample bosom seemed out of place in the full length black dress and bat-wing cape that she was wearing. Her cold dark eyes were adorned with thick mascara, eye liner, and blue eye shadow. Her lips were painted a deep purple. She placed a cool pale hand on mine drumming her long pointed index fingernail on it as if she was keeping time to some ghoulish tune. Which of the evil fairy tale queens was I looking at?

She ordered the girls to take their leave from us. "So, you are the damsel in distress...no need to answer. My husband has mended you, so you can be out of my house post haste. I can see that you will be nothing but a burden to Bri. You must possess something that is not visible to the naked eye to please such a man as he. I suppose it is your chaste demeanor?"

She expected an answer, so I gave her one. I removed my hand from hers. "Yes, I am innocent of all lustful thoughts and manners, and men flock to me hoping they will be the one that will unlock the wanton woman in me. Thirty years I have travelled down the road of dissatisfaction. No man could hold onto me, especially the one you refer to as Bri. He is a sadist. He kidnapped my daughter to get to me. He cannot accept that I have been reunited with the love of my life and has taken his revenge by abducting me. His mistake is underestimating Mitch who will move heaven and earth to find me. Kidnapping is punishable by death in most countries, but unfortunately not in Canada, but the penalty will be severe. You and Dr. Low are accomplices so that does not bode well for you, does it? One phone call and you can be pardoned."

She applauded. "Well, isn't that all just too sweet? I know all about you, but you don't know a thing about me do you?"

"There is nothing that I care to know."

"Who do you think kept your husband warm when you were unavailable to him because of one of your trumped up illnesses?"

"No one that interests me. If you are one of his concubines then I am truly sorry for you, but it means nothing to me. Just out of curiosity, does Dr. Low know?"

"What goes on between my husband and me is of no concern of yours."

I am sure she would have gone on and on had Dr. Low not entered.

His voice was harsh. "What are you doing in here Regina?"

She bowed her head. "So sorry Master; just checking up on the competition."

"Say good-bye, and get on with the packing." He tapped his watch.

Regina blew me a kiss as she backed out of the room. "Good luck sweetie."

Dr. Low laughed. "Sorry Mayria; she's a bit of a cut-up. Now, how are you this morning?"

A bit of a cut-up? Who was kidding who? I told him I was fine and was he going to help me.

He gave me a pathetic look as Brian bounced in and said that he would take over now. I tried to protest, but it was futile. Dr. Low gave him some final instructions on my care and made his exit. I yelled at him that it was his duty to help me.

I was alone with Brian and scared to death.

"I see the girls dressed you in their garb. Not what I would call travelling clothes, but they will do for now. Are you going to co-operate, or do I have to take other measures?"

I did not answer him. He walked over to a window and engaged in some sort of countdown.

Five minutes or so later I heard the whir of a helicopter. He laughed and said it was just the Lu's taking flight, and that it was our turn next. Who were the Lu's? I heard yelling...it was Mitch.

"Open the door you bloody coward! If you've hurt one hair on her head..."

"Sorry Sweetpea, but it's time for me to eliminate your lover, once and for all!"

Chapter 13

Storming the Citadel

He was holding a small pistol. His voice was condescending as he aimed it at me. "Too late ole man; she's gone. I don't have time for you so let's get this over with."

"Mya, are you here?" I called out as I tried to see around him ignoring the threat in his hand. His bulk kept blocking the doorway. He stepped from side to side mocking me all the while telling me that I was a piss poor detective and bodyguard. I was pretty sure that Mya was in the room, but unable to communicate. I feared and that there was another exit.

He laughed menacingly. I knew it was now or never.

I grabbed him by his pant legs and pulled him towards me. We fell to the floor, hard. He landed on top of me. He had managed to hold on to the gun. I wrestled it out of his hands as we rolled around like two kids letting off steam in the school playground. After a few rounds he said he'd had enough fun, and that it was time to finish me off, and he wanted to do it barehanded. Just as he proceeded to choke the life out of me Rory momentarily distracted him by asking me if I needed help. Brian turned. I let out a yell, and with all the thrust I could gather I let him have it with my right hook. It made contact with the corner of his mouth. He grabbed his chin, and I jabbed him again. The man had a glass jaw, and he was feeling the blow. I pushed him off me.

"Thanks Rory, but I've got this. Send a couple uniforms to escort this piece of shit out of here."

"Ten-four."

Brian wasn't done though. He rolled over, stood up, and made his way towards the door where he stopped and pulled a switch blade out of his boot. He leered at me.

"Christ, are you one of those dumb-nuts who brings a knife to a gun fight?" I jeered. I made a dive for the gun on the floor because I thought it would be faster than trying to unfasten mine. I rolled over, grabbed the gun and took aim. Out of the corner of my eye I caught a movement above him. He heard it too, and erroneously turned his head again. She let him have it with a large ceramic urn. He collapsed like an accordion.

Two cops arrived, handcuffed him, and dragged him out.

Mya and I stood there looking at each other. Time seemed to stand still. I couldn't believe she was right in front of me. I told her she could drop the rest of the urn now. She looked down at her hands and let it fall. With one movement she was in my arms wrapping her arms and legs around me, crying and laughing at the same time.

"Where the hell have you been for four days?" I asked flippantly.

"Same place I have been for the last thirty years...trying to get back to you Sweetheart!"

It was music to my ears as she proceeded to kiss me all over my face.

"You cut it pretty close because fifteen minutes more and I would...have...been..."

She went limp in my arms. "Mya, Mya, oh God..." I yelled into my shoulder mic hoping it hadn't got wrecked in the skirmish. "Jerry, get up here!"

I carried her back into the room and laid her on the bed. There was a roll of duct tape on the bed. That's why she couldn't answer me; she had been bonded and gagged. Her lips were red and bruised as were her wrists. I asked her how she had managed to free herself. Of course she couldn't answer. Jerry rushed to my side and asked me if this was how I had found her.

"No, she was alert and talking. Hell, she cold-clocked him with an urn and then she was in my arms, and then...tell me she just fainted."

Jerry said her pupils were dilated and she was non-responses to stimuli so he figured she had been drugged. He asked me if I could get her to the helicopter. I picked her up and headed for the door that we had entered half an hour earlier. Jerry said he'd fill Rory in and be right behind me.

I raced across the field telling myself that I could make it. I had to stop a few meters short of the copter. I was all out of breath. I stumbled.

"I'll take her from here Mitch."

I released her into the arms of Special Agent Phelps.

I took a few deep breaths. The copter was whirring. Jerry reached out a hand to help me in. Phelps passed Mya to me, and said, "God speed."

I was still breathless, but managed a nod and a thumbs up. Jerry pulled the seat belt around Mya and me. It was tight, but I wasn't going to let her out of my arms. She was dressed in silk pyjamas so I'd wrapped her in a blanket to keep her from slipping out of my arms back at the house. I pulled it down and examined her hands and arms. They were cut and bruised. Curiously not one fingernail was broken. It appeared as though someone had given her a manicure.

I pulled her left pant leg up and discovered that her damaged knee appeared to be recently bandaged with surgical tape. I deemed it best not to undo. I removed the dainty slippers from her feet. I wish I hadn't as the soles of her feet were red, blistered, and weeping. There was a strong odour. I ran my hand over the surface of one foot and realized that the discharge was from a strong antiseptic. I covered her back up, held her to my chest, and caressed her face and head. I pushed her hair off her face. It smelled like vanilla.

Jerry called out to me that we had an ETA of fifteen to twenty minutes. He asked how she was doing. I told him that she was still asleep.

ππππ

Was it only three days ago that all this craziness had started? I was running on sheer adrenalin. How could I have bungled up so badly? It had been a nightmare right from the moment that Jake had called to tell me that Vali had been kidnapped by Brian and to get home to Mayria. I had been too late, and the hunt had begun. Why had I thought that Brian was going to take his licks and go away? Had I underestimated his love for Mya, or was the abduction retaliation? Hopefully, there would be some answers when he was questioned. On the other hand, I wondered if he would clam up because there was a lot more to this plot than Mya's abduction, and who then was in the helicopter?

Her frantic phone call from the island was almost more than I could handle. Thank God Vali had snatched the phone out of my hand before she heard the fear in my voice. Jake had put his hands on my shoulders and eased me back into control with calm assurance.

"Look at me Mitch. She needs you, and only you can assure her that we are coming for her. Tell her you love her over and over. You promise her whatever you have to. Rory's on his way. Suck it up Bro."

I nodded and took the phone from Bobbie. It wasn't long afterward that I had heard a loud commotion and his ugly voice laughing and telling me that I would never see her again. The line went dead. We weren't going to make it in time. Nobody could convince me that we would.

Jake and I had climbed in the helicopter that had set down in the back yard. I was glad to see that Jerry Dean was the pilot as he was also a paramedic. Rory was on the radio all the way to the island which I learned was Suppression Island. Apparently, it had been an internment camp for Japanese Canadians in the 1940's. The travesty of injustice sickened me. I knew now why Mya had thought that the cabins were poor excuses for summer holiday lets.

There hadn't been any signs of movement that we could see from the air. Jerry set the copter down on a sandy beach. Four officers, including Agent Phelps, touched down to the right of us. Two patrol boats had also been dispersed. It seemed like an overabundance of man power to take down one man... one man who had already flown the coop with Mayria. There was always the hope that he had left her behind. Ha, did I really believe that?

Rory and I found the cabin where Mya had phoned from. The radio phone was indeed a relic. Rory turned it on. Nothing happened. He proposed that Brian had broken it when he had slammed it down. I shrugged and continued my search of the building. The bed had been slept in. I found remnants of crackers, a jar of open peanut butter, and an empty beer can. Well, at least she had feasted. I reprimanded myself for my warped sense of humour.

I found a pair of men's long-johns on the floor. I couldn't imagine that she had worn them, but if not her… The question was answered a few minutes later as I was asked to identify some clothing found in another cabin. The articles were disturbing. What was left of a pair of bloody tan slacks, and a dirty sweater were balled up on the floor by the chesterfield. I thought that the slacks were hers, but couldn't say if the sweater was or not. In one of the bedrooms a bra and panties were lying on the bed. They were probably hers. I guess she had tossed them for some reason. I didn't want to think what that reason might be. I understood now why she had said that she had nothing to wear. I had heard that phrase from Irene a thousand times, but it always fell on deaf ears as I knew that woman's closet was filled to capacity. But, here was Mya, a lady who had to don a pair of man's underwear to stay warm.

Rory met me outside cabin 6 with a large shoulder bag that I recognised as Mya's. He gave it to me and said he was leaving a crew here to search the whole island. He had commandeered one of the speed boats and said that we were going to take to the waterway. Jake and Jerry were going to continue with air reconnaissance. I took a quick look inside of Mya's purse. Her wallet contained three hundred dollars, a cheque book, and several credit cards. I had never thought that money was behind the abduction. I flipped a little notebook open. As soon as I realised that Mya had written about her trials I put it back. I didn't need anything distressing to distract me and remind me that it was because of me that she had wound up here. I took my place scouting the small islands for any signs of disturbance.

Rory sounded the police siren which brought several fishing boats to a stop. No one had seen anyone matching Mya's and Brian's description. They had already been boarded by the Coast Guard earlier. Good to know that they were out there searching. We were looking for the age-old needle in a haystack; one little boat in a chain of a thousand islands. Rory and the Coast Guard had their forces concentrating in the Gulf Islands at the southern end of the Strait of Georgia. They were looking for anything suspicious. I was sure they would uncover grow-ups that had never been in their radar before plus a host of other illegal activities.

I was aware that British Columbia's coastline stretched from Washington State to Alaska which is a distance of over 25,000 kilometers. However, Suppression Island was in the southeast, so the search was only extended south of that. Still a formidable task.

After an exhausting five hours of stopping at small inhabited isles and questioning dozens of people we decided to pull the plug and leave the search up to the Coast Guard for the time being. Rory radioed for a car to pick us up at the Keg Marina. I asked him why there? He said he wanted to have another talk with the dock-master about Dr. Lu.

I told Rory that I was going to take a little stroll to get my land legs back while he talked to Rolph and Gerta. He thought it odd that I didn't want to be in on the questioning. I shrugged and walked down to berth W39. I was staring into the water fifteen minutes later when he found me.

"What's up Mitch? What's bothering you?"

"It was right there, right there." I said pointing. "The bloody yacht was right there! I had the gut feeling that it was somehow connected to Mya, but I did nothing about it. I should have sat on it Rory...I should have sat on it."

"And, I should have dug deeper the minute I heard the name Zang Lu, but I didn't. You gotta let it go for now Buddy. You're still raw from our discoveries on the island. How about we commiserate over a jug of beer down at the pub?"

"I should get home to the kids."

"Jake has probably filled them in by now. My stomach's reminding me that I haven't eaten yet. Pretty sure that you haven't either, so how about a juicy burger with that beer?"

"Yeah sure, anything to shut you up."

It had been another long night without answers again. I checked in with Rory at 7 a.m. the next morning to see what he had planned for the day. He had said that we were going to concentrate our search more intensely on the small islands and coastline again right up to the U.S. border. He was assembling a team as we were speaking and to get my ass down to the mobilizing area pronto to get outfitted for combat. I thought he was being a little melodramatic as Brian was only one man, wasn't he?

The situation had changed in the twenty minutes it had taken me to get to the police station. Rory had taken a call that the switchboard had forwarded to him. The caller had asked for me stating that he had crucial information on the whereabouts of Mayria Tessa Fulton. The caller had said that I needed to check out the residence of Regina Lord at 1872 Hemming Island.

The crew, 18 of us, were outfitted with Kevlar, shoulder mikes, and firearms. I chose to wear an ankle piece. Rory stated that it could be a trap or a ruse. Phelps suggested gas grenades and flash bangs. I objected strenuously asking him if he was crazy because Mya was supposedly in the dwelling. Rory said that we didn't have any proof of anything so would proceed with caution. He, Phelps, and I would be taking the helicopter piloted by Jerry Dean whose medical training may be needed. The rest of the crew was sent out on patrol boats to navigate the coastline, and would provide back-up when radioed to do so. Two and half hours later we were beginning to think we had been sent on a wild goose chase to an island that didn't exist. Rory was on the phone non-stop to headquarters. They had failed to come up with any coordinates because sure enough there was no record anywhere of the existence of the island in question. Jerry said we were running low on fuel. Rory ordered the water crew to keep searching as we had to return to refuel. I figured we had circumnavigated every little island a dozen times over. Just as Jerry was making a turn to the north, a small helicopter appeared out of nowhere and headed east.

"Put it down Jerry, put it down! Over there, over there in that field! We were hoodwinked into trying to find a non- existent island. Why weren't we suspicious of this huge property? " Rory said angrily.

"There was some sort of camouflage over that area. It must have become unmasked in order for the heli to take flight." I said trying to ease his feelings of self-blame.

Phelps agreed because there was no way we could also have missed the break in the seawall.

"Suppose if she's on that bird Rory?"

"Hold on Mitch, there's no sense jumping to conclusions. Air control is on it as we speak."

Jerry set us down in the field 500 yards from the walled building. We made our way to the front of the property where Officers Cruz and David were waiting for us. They had seen a breach in the wall which appeared to lead up to an entrance. We climbed the steps cautiously. Phelps was ready to ram the door. I put out my arm to stop him and rang the doorbell, and told them all to step back. Two young women in colorful Asian dress answered. I put my finger up to my lips. Fear radiated in their eyes. Their eyes darted to upwards.

"Is Mayria up there?" I asked.

They nodded, bowed, and said that I should hurry. We heard a commotion coming from somewhere down the way. I left my comrades to investigate, and went to find my girl.

ππππ

I lifted my head off the gurney to find two green speckled eyes smiling at me.

"Hello Beautiful. I've been waiting for you to wake up."

Tears filled her eyes. "Don't I know you from somewhere?"

I kissed her. "Yeah, you do, but apparently I am no Prince Charming because my kisses couldn't wake you up."

"I'm awake now, and you are my prince Mitch. You were dealing with someone more menacing than the evil queen, but you found me...did the girls call you?"

I wiped her tears away with my thumbs. "You mean the Geisha girls?"

"I thought at first that they were Geisha, but I think they are too young. It takes years to become a Geisha you know, and they weren't wearing that ghoulish make-up."

"Oh, you know all that do you? They took good care of you didn't they?"

228

"They did, and Dr. Low fixed my leg."

I hadn't been expecting Zang Lu's name to pop up. "Dr. Lu, what was he doing there?"

"It's Dr. Low, not Lu. How do you know the name even if you are pronouncing it wrong? I don't know what he was doing there…oh wait, I do; it's his house, his and Regina's."

"You know Regina?"

"Do you? Is she mixed up in this too?"

"Not necessarily; we'll see how she fits in when all the pieces are assembled. We'll talk about it later with Rory okay? By the way Hon, thanks for saving me."

"Saving you; how did I do that?"

"Well, for one thing; you're here, safe and sound, and you cold-cocked Brian which saved me from shooting him."

"Is he dead?"

"No, but he's going to have a very big headache. How did you ever lift that urn anyhow?"

"I didn't see that you had a gun, and he was going to hurt you. I wanted to kill him you know?"

"I know Honey. I'm glad you didn't though as I wouldn't want you living with that for the rest of your life."

"I would have managed. Speaking of headaches, can you ask the nurse for an aspirin?"

"Sure can. Are you ready to see the kids?"

"Is Lylah Jayne with them; did you find her?"

Mya was almost out of the bed anticipating seeing her long lost daughter..

"Hold on a minute; you're not going anywhere." I said holding her back. "Listen to me…we haven't actually found her yet. I've been a little too busy, but Mel and Shannon have been on it. It's looking like they have found Thelma Robinson, so as soon as you are feeling up to it, we can make the trip to Nanaimo."

"What has kept you so busy that you didn't have time to look for our daughter?" She asked in an accusatory voice.

I didn't take offense, but laughed and asked her if she was kidding.

"No."

"I've been a little consumed with finding her mother you know."

"Oh, sorry; I'm so sorry I caused so much trouble."

"It's too late for that. I knew you were going to be trouble from the moment I saw you, but there wasn't anything I could do about it because my heart had a mind of its own. This kidnapping was nothing you did, or didn't do. It was my mistake. I underestimated how much Brian loved you..."

She stopped me flat. "Love...what he did to me had nothing to do with love!"

I was afraid to know just what he had done to her. It was my turn to apologize. I climbed up on the bed with her and took her in my arms. "You're right, it wasn't love. It was my fault though, and I will always regret my leaving you alone that day."

It was like she hadn't heard a word I'd said.

"You said "had"."

"Had what?"

"You said that your heart *had* a mind of its own, but it doesn't now?"

I shook my head. "Oh Sweetie, my heart is yours; never doubt that. All I want to do is to hold you and tell you how much I missed you, but we are both exhausted and emotional and we need to take a break from misinterpreting our words right now. I'm going to get you the aspirin and your kids. I love you."

"Don't go Mitch. I need to feel that you are real, and that this isn't all just a nightmare like when the mermaids were trying to drown me."

I kissed her long and lovingly. "Does that feel real to you? Believe me when I tell you that you are safe. It wasn't just me who rescued you; I could never have done it by myself. We'll have a full account of each other's last few days later okay? But, what's this about mermaids wanting to drown you?"

"I guess it was a bad dream, but so real at the time. As I was being led into the darkness of the netherworld, a beautiful creature emerged. It was you disguised as a dragon. You told me to climb on your back and together we would ride like the wild, wild, wind. You saved *me* Mitch."

"I've graduated to a dragon now, have I? I'm very happy that I was able to save you, but I hope you won't need saving anymore. Funny how dragons keep turning up in this soap opera though."

"What do you mean?"

I didn't want to bring the dragon yacht up at the moment so was relieved when Vali opened the curtain and asked if she could come in.

Mya reached her arms out to her. "Come here Baby, come and see your mama."

It was a tearful reunion. I excused myself and said that I'd send the boys in after they had a few minutes by themselves. Mya thanked me and reminded me about the aspirin.

I met up with Frankie and Bobbie in the waiting room. They asked me how she was. I told them what they wanted to hear, and sent them in.

Jake was more attuned to me. "What is it Boss?"

"I honestly don't know Jake, but somethings not right with her. She's been through one hell of an ordeal. I guess if she was all cheerful and acting as if nothing happened I would be suspicious that she was putting on an act for my benefit. I fear that something is haunting her, and she can't bring herself to talk to me about it."

"She will Boss; just give her time. Like you said, she's been through hell. Rory's on his way, and wondering if she is up to a few questions. What do you think?"

"Yeah, he might be just what the doctor ordered if he keeps things light. Speaking of doctors, I have to go track hers down. Go and give her one of your cheery smiles."

"Sure thing. I'd like to see her for myself. I'll say a quick hello and see you back here."

Rory arrived to find me hunched over with my head in my hands half an hour later. I'd sent Jake on a coffee run to a shop across the street from the hospital. I thought Mya might like her favorite brew, and a vending machine's excuse for coffee was not acceptable.

"Catching a few winks are we Bud?"

I looked up. He told me I looked worse than he felt. I laughed.

"I thought you'd be all smiles and bubbly now that you've got your lady back, so what's up?"

"Just exhausted I guess. Here's Jake with the mocha; hope it takes as good as it smells. Shall we mosey in and see if Mya's up for a little talk?"

Rory said he just wanted to meet her and that he'd play it by ear and hoped that she might volunteer something on her own. Vali stopped us and said that the doctor was with her mom and that we should give her fifteen minutes or so. She and the boys were going home to prepare for the homecoming. I told her not to go overboard.

Vali kissed me on the cheek as usual. Then she hugged Rory. She was still emotional.

"There are no words to thank you two for finding Mom and bringing her home. We are all so very, very grateful." She sobbed.

Rory told her it was all in a day's work, but that a little more effort had been put into it because she was my lady.

I concurred. "It wasn't just a job for me, you know that Vali. I could never have found her on my own, but thanks to Rory and the VPD, the ordeal is over. I'll see you at home soon as the doc springs her."

"I know Mitch. Whatever would we have done without you?"

"Chances are none of this would have even happened if..."

"No, you don't! You don't get to take any blame. It was all Brian, all Brian. I hope he rots in prison...he is going to be convicted isn't he Rory?"

"Yes, he is Vali, have no fear about that. By the time we have amassed all the charges against him, he won't have a hope in hell of seeing the light of day ever again."

She smiled. "Good; take me home Jake."

"Mr. Mitchum, Mayria is all set. Her vitals have returned to an acceptable level. We are just waiting for the lab's bloodwork results. I am confident that they will be also be satisfactory, and that you can take her home within the hour."

I thanked Dr. Nelson. I wanted to ask her if she thought that Mya was going to have any lasting emotional disturbances, but talked myself out of it. She was an ER doctor and not a psychologist, so probably wouldn't have voiced an opinion anyway.

Mya was sitting up on the edge of the cot with her legs dangling over the side. I walked over to her, kissed her, and introduced her to Rory. She extended her hands to him.

"I am so happy to finally be meeting Mitch's partner in crime." She radiated an aura of joy.

I had never seen this side of Rory before. He was downright charming. He took her hands in his and asked her if he could hug the bravest woman he had ever met.

"You certainly may, but I have to forewarn you that Mitch has somewhat of a jealous streak."

Rory laughed. "Not to worry, I know how to handle him, and believe me when I say that I had to ride roughshod over him a number of times when he fell by the way stressing about you."

I recognized that mischievous look in her eyes. "Were you worried about me Mitchy?"

I passed her the coffee saying I hoped it wasn't too cold.

"Mitchy...yeah, it suits you ole boy" Rory razzed.

He stepped back and took a good long look at Mya. "So, this boo-boo on your forehead and these scratches on your arms are all you have to remind you of your retreat on the island?"

"And this." She pulled up her pant leg.

"That looks a little more significant. What happened there? Did Dr. Nelson fix you up?"

"I fell down a hill and landed against a fallen tree. Turns out that it was a cedar and a piece broke off and embedded itself in my knee. Dr. Low said it could have very well developed into cedar poisoning if it had of been left unchecked."

Rory glanced at me with a question in his eyes. "Dr. Low; is he on staff here?"

"No, he was at the house Brian took me to. I think it was his house."

"Not that I doubt you Mayria, but is it possible that it was a Dr. Lu, and not Low?"

"I see you are with Mitch on this. I don't know who your Dr. Lu is, but the one that operated on me was Dr. Low...Dr. Zane Low."

"Zane, not Zang?"

"Correct, at least that is what name was on a licence that was on the wall in the operating room. There were many more documents, but I could only read the one, and his wife called him Zane."

"There was a wife? Do you recall her name?"

"Of course I do. Her name was Regina as I already told Mitch. He said her last name was Lord. I suppose she never took his name. Anyhow, she is definitely someone I will never forget. Even though I only had the pleasure of her company for a few minutes. I don't mean that literally as she kind of scared me."

"Why was that Mayria?"

I believed that Mya was unaware that she was being questioned. "Do you know your fairy tale characters Rory?"

He laughed. "Guilty, I do not."

"I will enlighten you then. You can look her up when you get home. The name is Maleficent; the mistress of evil from the fairy tale Sleeping Beauty. Regina was her splitting image."

"She sounds scary." Rory commented.

Mya winked at me, and smiled demurely at Rory. "I didn't think that your subtle line of questioning would include me giving you a lesson on a fairy tale. Carry on, but no need to camouflage your objective. It's not the first time that I have been interrogated you know."

Rory shook his head. "You've got yourself one smart lady here Mitch. I want you to know Mayria that I really had no plans on questioning you at this time, but you sort of played right into my hands."

"Are you sure about that? Perhaps it is you who played into mine."

"From one detective to another, I think you've been had." I said grinning. "She's a woman, and what we take as their charming demeanor is sometimes just trickery."

"Right you are Darling: how do you think I landed you?"

"I think that is best left to the bedroom." I answered anticipating being alone with her.

"Okay then Ms. Mayria, if you don't mind, I have a few more queries. I will be brief. Curious if Regina was also of Asian descent?"

"You're asking because of the Japanese girls?"

"No, not Japanese, but Chinese like her husband."

Mya smirked. "You are barking up the wrong tree Detective. Dr. Low is Scottish. I have no clue as to what Regina's nationality is, but she did not have the Scottish brogue."

Rory scrolled through his phone until he found what he was looking for. "So, this man is not your Dr. Low?"

She laughed. "Definitely not!"

"Could he have been wearing a disguise?"

"I hardly doubt it, but maybe your man was the one in disguise. On closer look, I would say that this gentleman was half the size of Dr. Low. Do you have another photo of him standing?"

"Unfortunately no, this is the only photo we have of him."

"I don't know who this Dr. Lu is to you, but I can say with certainty that your man and Dr. Low are not the same person. At some point you are going to ask me for his description so I will save you the effort. He was definitely fair skinned. He was lean, and had greying, well- kept longish hair, his eyes were hazel, and he was about two inches shorter than you two."

"You are an excellent witness Mayria; thank-you for your keen observances. If Low and Lu were one and the same it would have solved a piece of the puzzle. To your knowledge, did Brian ever sign his name as B.G. Fulerton?"

"Not that I know of, but if it is important I could have Frankie checked all the documents at home, or his secretary, Carmen Santos might know. I could ask her if you like."

"Oh no, you wouldn't want to do that!" Rory exclaimed.

Mya looked back and forth at Rory and me. "Why?"

"She's a person of interest that's all." Rory stated.

"Oh, because she was not just his secretary, but his mistress… is that why?" She looked at me.

"Let it go for now Hon; you've been through enough for today."

She cut me off before I could say anymore. "Don't patronize me Mitch! You have no idea what I have been through, so don't try and shut me up! I was the unwilling victim of a crazed man who wanted me for his demented perversions so I have every right to know everything that you two know, so tell me how Carmen is mixed up in this, please."

I had been admonished, and rightfully so. I had been living in a fool's paradise believing that Brian hadn't abused her, but she had just dispelled that hopefulness. I would have to quell my own emotions for now and do everything to support her. "She's right Rory. You may as well tell her because she'll get it out of me sooner or later."

"Right, I think you can handle anything we tell you. First, will you answer a question for me? Thanks. I would like to know what Fulton's plans were for him and you. Did he tell you where he was planning on taking you, or how you'd get there?"

"Not really. He just kept saying that we were going to sail away to Shangralai."

"Aboard the Jeudanzee?"

Mya was genuinely shocked. "What...where did that come from?"

"It's okay Honey, don't excite yourself. We know about your yacht." I said trying to calm her.

"How could you know that I had a yacht? Never mind; I guess you know everything about me don't you? I suppose that Mitch has filled you in on all my past transgressions, but my buying the yacht was not a criminal offense, so how does it figure into this? Anyhow, she's not mine anymore; I sold her."

"Mitch didn't tell me anything Mayria. He was just as surprised as me when it came up in our investigation. To whom, and when did you sell it?"

"I don't see how or why it would come up in the investigation. I sold her to a woman named Lorena Diaz a few weeks ago. I figured Mitch had a nice boat so I wouldn't be needing it."

"Thanks for verifying that Mayria. How did she find she out it was for sale?"

"I have no idea as I never advertised it for sale anywhere. To tell you the truth I had forgotten that I even owned it. I had bought it on a whim strictly because of the dragon ornamentation. I only stepped foot in it when I bought it and again when I left her at the marina. She must have saw it moored there. I never asked her any questions as it wasn't important, but apparently, it is to you."

I asked her if the kids knew about it. She said no, but Brian did. I was a little surprised and asked her why she had told him and not me. It was the wrong thing to say.

Her eyes told me she was displeased. "Have you told me about everything you own and everything that you have discussed with Irene? We've only been together for two weeks, so I hardly doubt it. I was married to him for three years, and contrary to public opinion, we had some good times, and had plans. When he talked about buying a large boat of some sort I told him about the Jeudanzee. He said he'd like to have a look at her, but that day never came unless he went to view her and never told me. Have I committed some sort of crime by not telling you Detective Mitchum?"

I wanted to crawl under the bed. "I was out of line Mayria; I'm sorry. I guess my green-eyed monster just made an appearance."

Rory stepped in. "I'm going to give you two some privacy and check on security so we are all set for when you get your walking papers. It's been a pleasure Mayria."

She took the hand that she offered. "Are you saying that I require security?"

"Your abduction and rescue are front page news my dear. The paparazzi are hungry. You may choose to give interviews at a later date, but today is not the day."

"Thank-you Rory. Before you take your leave, I have some more names for you. Sorry, I don't have the last names, but there were two chaps that were with us after we changed boats. Their names were Chris and Mug. They seemed to be close acquaintances of Brian's."

"I will see what comes up on the data base. I'm looking forward to talking with you again Mayria as I'm sure you have a wealth of information in that pretty little head of yours."

Mya was all smiles again. "It will have to wait for a few days though as I am going to be very busy the next few days finding the daughter I gave away thirty years ago."

"Mitch told me about her, Lylah Jayne right? I have no doubt that you will find her, and wish you all the best in your quest. Remember that you have been through a gruesome ordeal and are healing, so don't overtax yourself. I'm sure Mitch will see to that." He said he'd see us in a bit.

We were alone again. I had been put in my place when she hadn't included me in the search for our daughter. Should I ignore the slight and apologise again for my crude question regarding the yacht? Or should I continue on as if everything was all right? Who was going to make the first move? I guess it had better be me.

"How much trouble am I in Mayria?"

"I don't know Mr. Mitchum; what do you think you deserve?" She answered grim-faced.

"I think you should reprimand me, and then you should tell me that you forgive me, and that you love me."

She smiled a little. "I'm sure that I can come up with a suitable punishment, and that I can forgive you because I do love you, and then I suppose I will let you boss me around again."

I took her hand. "Thank-you. I'm not your boss Honey though I might act like I am sometimes, and I need reminding of that. I've never loved anyone the way I love you, so it is difficult sometimes for me to realize that you had a life before me. You are very headstrong, and I know I can be intimating, but I don't mean to be. I thought I'd lost you Mayria." I was very close to losing control.

"I thought I'd never see you again either Mitch. I'm having a hard time believing that you are really sitting here beside me, and that this is not just part of one of my dreams."

"Are there any dragons waiting in the wings?"

"Oh, they are always around, and I never know what form they will take. Thanks to you and Snap, they are not so scary anymore. I think we have to decide where we want to go from here Mitch. This chapter of my life was not in my repertoire and made me realize that I need to take a closer look at the choices I have made. My expectations of others may be more than they are capable of expressing. Lylah Jayne may not want to know me, and you may not want to continue on with our relationship. I need to accept that I can't always get what I want. You understand what I am saying don't you?"

"No, I don't, but here is not the place to be discussing anything. Can we table it until we get home? Yes, I do mean *home* because wherever you are is my *home.* These last few days have been hell because you haven't been there. If you don't want me there just say so, but know that I am not going without a fight, is that clear? You are my lady, and I'm your man so don't ever make a mistake about that. I fear there is something about me that is troubling you. For the life of me I have no clue as to what that could be, but you need to come clean with me so we can put all this nonsense to bed."

Before she could say another word a nurse showed up with a wheelchair and told her she could go home. I was about to call for a taxi when Rory showed up and said that our carriage awaited us at the back door. It was in the form of a bright new cruiser. We were its first passengers.

Mya asked Rory if he could join us for a late lunch or early supper whatever one wanted to call it. "Actually, if I know Ivy and Vali, it will be more like breakfast."

"I would love to, but will take a rain check as I need to get home to Bernice as I haven't seen her for a few days."

Mya asked if that was his wife. He laughed and said that it was one of them.

"I guess you and Mitch are more alike than I thought as you both have women problems."

Mya was silent most of the way home. Rory dropped us off and wished us good luck with our daughter again, and said he'd see us soon. I wished he'd have wished me luck with Mya also.

Chapter 14

Sunshine and Rain

The hospital had sent the wheelchair home with me telling me that I could come back on Monday and exchange it for one from the Red Cross. I could also pick up an array of other helpful devices like a walker and commode if I liked. Mitch lifted me into the chair and wheeled me to the back door. Bobbie met us and held the door open. Sadie ran straight to me and tried her hardest to climb up on my lap. I petted her and spoke to her like a mother would speak to a small child. Mitch did his best to settle her down as he let Bobbie wheel me into the kitchen where the rest of the family awaited us.

A huge Welcome Home MOM banner and dozens of balloons greeted me. The sweet aroma of home cooking woke up my appetite. My first meal home after my abdominal surgery Ivy had made Belgian waffles with all the trimmings for me. It was my favorite breakfast, and every time I came home from the hospital, or needed a boost, Ivy would see that I had waffles. I was not surprised to see that they along with sausages, bacon, hash brown, and scrambled eggs were on the menu.

After Ivy and I had a tearful reunion we all sat down to a late afternoon feast. It was 4 P.M. As usual the kids had bets on how many waffles smothered with strawberries and whipped cream I could eat. I pushed my plate away after one promising that I would be back for more later.

Mitch sent us girls into the "gathering room" as Jake had so named the living room. He settled me unto the sofa where a soft bed of comforters had been laid out. He propped a large pillow under my leg, kissed me, and went back to KP duty with the guys in the kitchen. Vali and the boys had not questioned me when they had visited me at the hospital. I had assured them that I had weathered the ordeal with only minor abrasions, and that I would give them a blow by blow narrative later. That time had arrived. I wanted to get it over with once and for all.

Mitch handed me a cup of coffee. I asked him to sit with me. I didn't mince words. They were all adults and would probably know if I was holding anything back. They laughed and clapped when I relayed how I had escaped from Brian. There were groans and grimaces when I related how I had injured my leg and my subsequent problems because of it. Vali and Ivy sniffled throughout my narrative. They all said how proud they were of me for being so brave and being able to deal with such harsh conditions. I told them it was because of them that I had fought so hard to defeat the elements. It was hard to say what would have happened if I hadn't fallen and injured my leg. Maybe I would have been successful in evading Brian. Maybe he would have given up…maybe, maybe, maybe.

"That's how it all went down, and you can all see for yourselves that I am perfectly well. The knee will heal in time. Some very bad people were set on my never returning to you all. On the other hand, they were outnumbered by the good people who helped me; Dr. Low, Sakuri, and Misaki. Of course the real heroes were the VPD, especially Rory and my hero… this man here."

More tears and hurrahs. "I am going to call it a day. I have to use the lavatory and get out of these damn silk pajamas. Are you up to it Mitch?"

"If I want to live up to the hero stature, I guess I had better be brave enough to take on the role as caregiver. Shall we give it a go?"

I said I was ready. He lifted me back into the wheelchair. "I love you all." I said as one by one my family, which included Ivy and Jake, hugged me and sent me on my way with kisses and love. I patted Mitch's hand and hoped he'd understand what I was about to tell him.

I was glad the elevator was still working. Mitch wheeled me into the bathroom and sat me on the toilet. I always hated that word as it sounded so uncultured. He pulled my bottoms off while I undid the top. He left to find me a nightie and give me some privacy. I didn't feel exposed at all sitting there in the nude because it wasn't as if Mitch hadn't seen me naked before. I cringed a little as a picture of me standing naked in the ocean at Brian's mercy came into my mind's view. I tried to stand, but my knee wouldn't cooperate. Mitch caught me as I let out a little whimper.

"What the hell are you doing Mayria?"

"I wanted to wheel myself to the sink so I could wash. I really want to have a bath, but Dr. Low told me not to get the dressings wet."

"What do you think I'm here for?"

"I don't want to be a burden Mitch." I was trying hard not to blubber. "Brian said that I was nothing but a thorn in his side because he was always waiting on me through all my self-inflicted injuries. He said he was beginning to doubt my worth."

"I'm not Brian."

"I am very thank-full of that, but this is only the first day. Ivy or Vali can help me…"

"If you would rather have them just say the word."

"I wouldn't. I'm sorry if I hurt your feelings."

He wheeled me over to the sink, filled it with warm water and handed me a facecloth. He washed my back while I washed the rest of my body. He passed me the lotion, put a dollop in his hands and gently massaged my back. He slipped my nightie over my head and said he'd see what he could rig up for me so that I could have a real bath tomorrow.

He pulled the covers back on the bed, picked me up and laid me down in the middle. I remarked that I didn't know how one little piece of wood could rack such havoc.

"It would have been a lot worse if the poison had of entered your blood stream. I guess we owe the mysterious Dr. Low a debt of gratitude don't we?"

"Yes, but it's unlikely that we will ever see him again."

"Probably; I'm going to have a quick shower and then I will get you a pain pill okay?"

I told him I didn't think I would need one. He smiled and said we'd talk about that. Perhaps I wouldn't burden him with my fears.

I heard the shower door and then the other bedroom door open. I supposed that he was getting dressed as he still had clothes in there. He emerged dressed in his usual white shirt and blue jeans. He had the electric shaver in his hand as he rejoined me. He sat on the edge of the bed, asked me how I was, and finished shaving. He ran his hand over his face and said that would have to do. I knew he wasn't a fan of the electric shaver, but probably hadn't wanted to take the time with a hand razor.

"Do you want to tell me what is bothering you or do you just want to go to sleep? I thought I'd sleep in the other room so I won't disturb you as I can't promise you I won't snore."

"You don't snore Mitch. Is that just an excuse because you don't want to sleep with me?"

"Of course I want to sleep with you, but I'm thinking that you might be more comfortable without me Hon."

"Are you sure that's the reason, or are you dreading touching me because Brian's hands may have been all over me?"

"Why would you say such a thing?"

"Because it is all that I am thinking about. I was drugged so many times, and have no idea what he may have done to me while I was blacked out."

"Oh Baby, why didn't you say something earlier? I had no idea that was what was causing your apprehension. I mean you have been through so much, but for you to think that he may have taken advantage of you has to be nerve wracking. Let's figure this out together all right?'

He climbed unto the bed resting his back on the headboard. I inched my way up until I could lay my head on his chest. I asked him to take his shirt off as I wanted to hear his heart beating.

"Sure you do." He said laughing. "I know you have an ulterior motive."

"I do as I like to run my hands through your furry chest. I've missed your warm body so much Mitch. I never thought I'd ever see you or the kids again." I said trying not to cry.

"I missed you every minute we were apart too Mya, and frankly, I don't know if I could have lasted another day without going crazy worrying about you."

We kissed for a very long time. I never wanted to let him go, but I needed some assurance that Brian hadn't taken advantage of me while I was drugged. I had no idea what Mitch had in mind to curb my fears, so I asked him.

"I am an investigator remember, so I believe with your help, we can reason things out."

"Okay, but I don't see how."

"By forming a time-line. Let's start with the time you received the first phone call from Brian. Can you estimate what time it was?"

"It was 10:50. I know as Ivy and I had just sat down to a cup of tea. I knew you hadn't eaten before you left for the office, so we were planning an early lunch for when you got back. Brian called a few minutes later, and then five minutes after that. I had called Jake in between those two calls who confirmed that Vali was gone. I didn't waste any time, just grabbed my bag and the car keys to the old blue. It would have been 11:05 or 11:10

"That's a good start Hon. How long did it take you to get to the Quik Mart?"

"Brian didn't give me precise directions, only to take a right in the round-about after Stuart Way, and continue to Division until I saw Jimmy's Mart or whatever it was called. I missed the turn the first time around, so it probably took me almost twenty minutes to get there."

"Let's go with 11:30. How much time elapsed before he injected you?"

"Not long; five minutes maybe."

"It would have taken him at least forty minutes to drive to any marine way, and ten minutes or more to get an unconscious person, that being you, in the car and then again unto the boat without attracting attention. Of course, he may have had help with the same men who helped with the abduction of Vali."

"Do you know who they are?"

"They are awaiting trial in the PCD lockup. I think Brian had you in the boat and was on the way to Suppression Island at approximately 12:45 not counting for heavy traffic, or if he had another stop along the way. We have no idea regarding that so let's just move the time up to 1 P.M. We know the distance to the island from the RCMP docks, and it has been documented that it takes one hour and forty-five minutes by speed boat to travel that distance. I don't suppose you know what kind of a craft it was?"

"I don't know Mitch, and I have no idea how long it took us to get there as I didn't wake up until we were just a few feet from docking."

"That's okay Hon; we'll figure it out. What happened after you docked?"

"I wouldn't get up so he dragged me to the front of the boat and threw me overboard."

"What?" He said angrily.

"I wasn't going to make things easy for him, so I sat down and refused to move. He picked me up roughly and dropped me over the bow. Luckily, we had landed in the sand."

"The bastard; I wish I had of shot him when I had the chance!"

"I abhor him, but am glad you aren't facing a murder charge."

"It wouldn't have been murder, but he is going to suffer in prison for eternity. So, according to our calculations you arrived at the island at approximately 3 P.M. Does that sound about right?"

"What would it matter? He had time on the way over to do whatever he wanted to me."

"In all probability, sex was the last thing on his mind. He had to know that the waters would be flooded with vessels searching for you. He would have had only one objective, and that was to get you out of sight. I'm not saying that he didn't have malicious plans for you that night, but you foiled him didn't you?"

I smiled. "I did, and I am fine with the next two days, but then I was drugged again before we reached Dr. Low's house. This Mug guy gave me some sweet tea. I had a feeling that it might contain some sort of sedative, but I was parched so drank it all. What did it matter anyhow…I was never going to see you again so maybe it was time to quit fighting."

"I'm glad you didn't Hon. Where did this Mug person come from?"

"Brian ditched the boat on some little island that we had been circling for some time. That's when I hit my forehead on the dash. Chris was waiting there for us, and then this other covered boat pulled in. Brian yelled at Mug who was the pilot to help him with me. Brian ordered Chris to do it, whatever it was. A few minutes after we left the island there was a loud explosion. I think now that Chris had set a charge to blow up Brian's boat as they all cheered after the explosion. The last thing I remember after the tea was Brian hollering for someone to open the gates. When I woke up Sakuri and Misaki were comforting me telling me that I'd had a bad dream. That's it, I can't account for what happened between the tea and waking up in the bed."

"We're not done yet Mya. Do you have any idea what time you left the island?"

"It was daylight, that's all I know. Just a minute; Brian was yelling at me because I had made him late. He had to be somewhere at eleven and we were already running an hour behind time. Do you know what time it was when I called you?"

"It was 6:30 a.m."

"I stalled him as long as I could by making him take me to the biffy outside, and then I told him that I needed to wash. He carried me to the boat and set me down in the water. I lost my balance and went under. I had no intention of resurfacing, but of course he pulled me up."

Mitch stiffened. "You don't mean that?"

"I did at the time."

"In my wildest dreams I never thought I'd be thanking him for anything, but thank God, he didn't let you drown."

"We are still no further ahead in quelling my fears are we?" I asked doubtfully.

"Maybe; can you estimate how long it was before you met up with Chris and Mug? Did anyone mention the time, or did you see a clock on either of the boats?"

"I wasn't thinking about time Mitch. Give me a minute." I closed my eyes trying to visualise the instrument panel on the boats. I sat up too quickly. My leg began throbbing. I clenched my teeth. Mitch asked me if I was all right.

I said that I would be and that I had just visualized a clock on the boat's dash and it said 3:15.

He said it was time for me to take something for the pain. He wouldn't take no for an answer and passed me a pill and a glass of water from off the nightstand, and asked when that was.

I swallowed it, and thanked him. "Do you remember when I told you that Brian had dragged me off the boat that first day? I think it was then, so I should have noticed the clock again shouldn't I have?"

"Not necessarily; like you say, you weren't thinking about the time."

"No, I can do this, it might be important. We've kind of decided that we left the island about sevenish, right? Brian had stopped the boat or maybe it was just idling. He had thrown a bag of clothing at me. I tried to get dressed by myself, but I couldn't manage as the pain was too much. I guess he couldn't stand listening to me sobbing because he came to help me put the pants on. I was so cold. I couldn't stop shivering. He took his coat off and put it on me, wrapped a blanket around me, and sat me down beside him at the helm. That was the one and only time that I felt he still had some decency left. I pulled the blanket over my head and huddled down in the captain's chair to protect myself from the wind. I remember now that I had caught a glimpse of the clock. It was 7:40. I do not know how much time passed because I think I fell asleep. Next thing I know he is yelling at me to hold on. That's when I hit the dash. It was 10:10."

"Good girl." He rubbed my head then said he was sorry. "We were out an hour at the departure time. Two hours travelling time makes more sense. I'm certain that we have the first two days covered, and chances that he would have assaulted you in front of Chris and Mug is highly doubtful. He needed to meet that deadline for some reason, and I'm sure that is all he had on his mind. He needed to keep you subdued for some reason also. Once you were in Dr. Low's care, you were safe, right?"

"I was sedated when he worked on my knee. When I woke up from that Brian was standing over me so I can't say for sure. I'll know for sure in three to four days."

"You'll know what?"

"I'll know whether I am pregnant or not." I said flatly.

"Pregnant…what the hell are you talking about?"

"Well, I have always been regular so…"

"How could you possibly think you might be pregnant? You had a hysterectomy didn't you?"

"No, where did you get that from?"

"From Vali I guess when she told me about your surgery."

"Well, I didn't require a complete hysterectomy as I still had one good ovary. It's highly possible that I can still conceive."

"So, all the times you and me…"

"Yes, but I wouldn't have minded if you and me had another child Mitch."

"Really? It doesn't really matter anyhow because chances of that ever happening are pretty slim wouldn't you say?"

"It happened once."

He laughed. "Yeah, thirty years ago, and that might have been a fluke. Let's just concentrate on finding the daughter we know exists. We'll discuss what to do about you and me when you are up to resuming our love life, okay?"

"Who said that I am not ready right now? I can't take the chance that I might already be pregnant, and that you might very well be the father, so we are going to have to use protection. You may choose not to be with me again because there would always be the doubt in your mind that I had betrayed you with Brian."

"Are you just assuming that something may have happened when you were unconscious, or did you willingly submit to him?"

"How could you think such a thing?" I was repelled by his suggestion. I turned away from him.

He pulled me back. "I don't think anything of the sort, and you know it. I just want to point out the absurdity of your remark by asking you an outrageously stupid question. I love you, and I will always want to be with you. I can't make that any clearer. If I can, tell me how?"

"I know you love me Mitch, but suppose, just suppose…"

"Suppose nothing, as nothing happened."

"I asked Dr. Nelson her opinion, and she said the same thing. She did a routine examination and said that I had no bruising inside or out, and that there was no evidence of me having sexual interaction within the last twenty-four hours."

"Why didn't you tell me that to begin with? You're worrying for nothing so put it out of your head for the night and get some rest."

"There are still those unaccounted hours on the boat…"

"Life with you is like a merry-go-round. We seem to get one thing settled, and then out of the blue comes a new twist, and round and round we go again."

"Do you want off the merry-go-round Mitch? Do you want to go back to your uncomplicated life with Irene?"

He snickered. "And, be bored out of my mind? No thanks; I'm quite happy right where I am."

"Do you ever think about her? I mean really think about her like what it was to be with her. You know what I mean…"

He lifted his arm off my shoulder. "I beg your pardon."

"I asked if you ever…"

"I heard what you said. I meant that I would pardon you for your silliness."

He clambered out of bed, put his shirt back on and headed for the door saying he needed some fresh air.

"Mitch!" I yelled, but he didn't turn around. "Damn, me and my insecurities!"

I waited twenty minutes for him to come back. He hadn't brought my chair out of the bathroom. Somehow I was going to have to get it on my own and go after him. Okay, I told myself, you can use the night table as a crutch. Once you're around it you can push yourself along the wall until you reach the closet. There is an umbrella in there which you can use as a walking stick. Come on girl, you are in much better shape now then you were on the island. If you fall down you'll just have to crawl. I let out a little yelp as my feet hit the floor. I kept the weight off my left leg as much as I could. It probably took me ten minutes to reach the closet, but I was still standing. I found the umbrella, made sure it was snapped closed, and made my way to the bathroom door. I stopped to take a deep breath just before I made the final pitch.

"Exercising our independence are we?"

"I didn't know if you were coming back and I needed to find you and apologise. Are you annoyed with me Mitch?"

"Yup." He said sharply. He had come in with a tray covered with a tea towel. He put it down on the chest of drawers and retrieved the wheel chair for me. He sat me in it and said he had brought dessert if I was interested. I said I was. He left me and laid the tray on the bed.

"Come on then before all the whipped cream melts."

"Aren't you going to help me?"

"Nope; I won't stand in the way of your self-determination. Oh here, I brought you a present."

He pulled some packets out of his pockets and tossed them to me. They were condoms.

I didn't know if I was amused or angry. "Where did these come from?"

"We made a quick trip to the pharmacy as I didn't think you could keep your hands off me for five days…you know; the pregnancy thing." He winked at me.

"Whose *we*?"

"The dog and me."

I threw the boxes back at him. He said he loved me too.

I awoke the next morning to find Mitch sneaking out of bed. I asked him where he was going.

"You're not the only mistress I have you know. I have to go and tend to her needs."

"Will you be taking her to breakfast?"

"Probably." He said kissing me. "Go back to sleep."

"Say hi to her for me. Are you coming back?"

"Yup; I'll be back in an hour or so to help you get up."

"I can manage myself."

"Do you want to go to Saanich tomorrow or not?"

"Where is Saanich, and why would I want to go there?"

"Oh, I just thought that you might like to go and see our daughter, that's all."

I sat up so fast my head was spinning. Mitch asked me if I was all right.

"Yes, yes…you've found her then? When are we going? Have you talked to her?"

He laughed. "One question at a time. No, I have not talked to her, and we do not know exactly where she is. Her mother is in a care facility in Saanich, and that is where we will start. That's all I know for sure. I found a message from Mel on my phone last night when I was up. He contacted Mrs. Robinson yesterday and she is anxious to see us. We have an appointment with her for ten a.m. tomorrow."

"Tomorrow, why not today and why am I just hearing about this now if you knew last night?"

"I didn't tell you because we were a little busy, and you wouldn't have slept all night. You need your rest so I am glad that you have today to get a little stronger. But, it might be a good idea if we take a late afternoon ferry and check into a hotel so we will be ahead of the game tomorrow. What do you think?"

"I want to go right now!"

"It's only six thirty, and there are a few things we need to discuss with Mel, so what I suggested stands. Now give me half an hour to deal with Sadie, and then I'll be back to get you into the shower."

"Are you bossing me again?"

"Yup."

"Mitch, you promised you wouldn't do that anymore, or keep anything from me, and you said I could have a bath?"

He ran two fingers over my lips. "There's my pouty baby. I knew she was in there somewhere."

I tried to bite him. "I'm not pouting, and I'm not a baby!"

He pulled his hand away grinning. "You wouldn't bite me now would you? I beg to differ with you on the pouting thing, and you will always be my baby. Now the reason I thought twice about the bathtub was because we'd have one hell of a time getting you in and out, and you would probably end up hurting a lot more than you are already. I'll set a lawn chair in the shower and you can sit and relax to the calming sounds of the rain forest. I'll wrap your leg up in plastic so the stitches don't get wet. What do you think?"

"It sounds good. You could get me in the shower first and then go and tend to Sadie you know, and then I'll be all done when you get back?"

"I'm not leaving you alone in the shower, so no."

"What do you think is going to happen to me in such a short time?"

"You could fall off the chair which I haven't even found yet, the water might reach the boiling point, or the drain could clog up and you could drown, or a dragon..."

"Okay, okay," I moaned holding up my hand to stifle him. "I get the picture. Go, and see to your serf duties so you can don your armor and save your queen again."

Three hours later we were sitting at the kitchen table with the family, and Mel and Shannon. I was very impatient to hear about Mel's conversation with Mrs. Robinson.

He had thought at first that she was almost hesitant to be talking to him. He had taped their conversation. She had agreed to it saying it didn't matter anymore. Mel was trained in voice analysis. He said that he could feel her apprehension radiating over the phone.

The conversation started off with Mel introducing himself to her explaining to her that he was a private investigator and was a liaison for Mitch and me. She asked who we were.

"The first question I have for you Mrs. Robinson is, do you have a daughter?"

"Has something happened to her, he hurt her didn't he?"

"What does she mean Mel, what does she mean?" I interrupted petrified.

Mitch took hold of me. "Quit panicking Mya. Let's hear the rest. Don't you think that Mel would have already told us if something was wrong?"

Mel reached across the table and squeezed my hands. "He's right Mayria. I'm not saying that there isn't a problem, but if I was to comment on that, it would just be conjecture, understand?"

I said I did "sort of", and to continue with the tape.

"I do not know your daughter Mrs. Robinson so have no idea of her welfare. I can look into it for you though if you think she is in harm's way. Who is the *he* in question?"

"Her rotten husband. He is keeping Alma and my grandchildren away from me. I can't even get her on the phone anymore. "

Mitch's grasp on me increased at the word "grandchildren."

"Is Alma your daughter Mrs. Robinson?" Mel prompted.

"Call me Thelma. Yes, my only child. She is all I have left; her, and Carter and Dahlia. My husband passed away three years ago. Alma and Larry moved me over here shortly after...that was before Larry turned mean."

I was so tense I could feel my muscles tighten up right down to my toes.

"Thelma, is your daughter thirty years old? Was she born on August 29th 1988 in Vancouver?"

"Yes, how do you know that?"

"It will all be clear to you shortly. Alma's adopted isn't she?"

"What does that have to do with anything?"

"Her biological parents are my clients."

Mel shut the tape off and grinned. "Didn't know what else to call you guys."

"Clients sounds good." Mitch assured him.

There was silence when Mel started the recording again. He prompted her asking if she had heard him.

"I heard you Mr. Dixon."

"Do you recall their names?"

"I never met the father. To be truthful, I don't think she knew who the father was. I only met her and her aunt." Thelma answered tersely. "The adoption was all legal if that's what you're wondering."

"I'm sure it was. Am I to understand that you don't recall the woman's name who is Alma's biological mother?"

"She was not a woman; she was but a child. She couldn't have been more than sixteen years old, a little waif of a girl. Her name was Mayria Joseph. It's not someone I have ever forgotten. She was our last chance of having a child, so I have been ever grateful to her. Why has she come forward now, thirty years later? What does she want?"

Mitch had winched when Thelma described what I had looked like. He wasn't the only one at the table who was holding back tears. I smiled patting Mitch's hand and asked Mel to continue.

"I can assure you that Mayria did not forget her daughter. She has been looking for her for a very long time, but up until a few weeks ago she couldn't even remember your name, and was denied any information regarding her daughter. Being reunited with Alma's biological father, Adam Mitchell, brought everything full circle and my firm tracked you here. I admit, it was no easy task finding you."

Thelma laughed a little edgily. "But, here you are. Mayria couldn't get access to Alma because it was a private adoption. So, she wants to see Alma does she? Have they spoken?"

"No; we do not have her number. Are you against Mayria and Mitch contacting her?"

"On the contrary Mr. Dixon, I'm hoping they will be able to do what I can't."

"Which is what Thelma?"

"Get her away from her husband! I am seventy nine and my health is failing rapidly, and besides Jim Mackie, no one takes me seriously when I say that Alma's life is in jeopardy."

I gasped. "Mitch; your dreams, they were tangible!"

"What dreams?" Vali asked.

"I'll tell you later. Right now we need to hear the remainder of the interview. Carry on Mel."

"Right you are Boss."

We heard Thelma's voice again. She was pleading with Mel. He asked her why she thought that Alma was in danger, and who was Jim Mackie.

"Larry got fired from his job and suffered a nervous breakdown a year ago. It appeared as if he won that battle until three months ago. He has a new job that enables him to work his own hours. He came home one day and found Alma with Jim who happens to be his best friend, and blew up. They were only having coffee, but he banished Jim, made Alma quit her job, took

Carson out of school, cut off the land line, took her cell away from her, and forbid her to have any contact with me. She managed one phone call six weeks ago on his phone while he was in the shower. She told me that Larry had relapsed and she was caring for him full time and couldn't see me for a while. She said the ringing of the phones irritated Larry so she had shut them off. She said. "Don't worry Mom; he'll be back to normal soon. I love you. We just have to be patient. I have to go now." I have talked with Jim, and he thinks that Alma and the kids are being held prisoners. Larry has put bars on the windows. Apparently, the blinds are never open. He has taken his fears to the police. They were granted entrance and found nothing that warranted further investigation. They were just a family dealing with a health crisis. Larry was receiving help, and his wife was on board with the change in their lifestyle. They were going to send a social worker to the house. I have no way of knowing if that ever took place. I am very worried as you can imagine, and have no idea what to do next. Should I call the police?"

"That may not be necessary Thelma because Mayria and Mitch will see to her safety. One last question, does Alma know that she is adopted?"

"I told her when she was a teenager. She wasn't interested in finding her birth mother so we never spoke of it again. Who is Mitch?"

"Sorry, his given name is Adam Mitchum, but he goes by Mitch. Incidentally, he is also my boss. Believe me when I say he has a lot of clout. Is ten tomorrow morning convenient for you to meet up with them?"

"Yes, yes; the sooner the better."

"Thank-you for your candor Thelma. Hopefully, this will all be resolved tomorrow."

That was the end of the session. Mitch thanked Mel and Shannon for all the hours they had logged in looking for our daughter. He nudged me wanting me to acknowledge their dedication.

"I'd hug you both if I wasn't in this cumbersome chair. Thelma has only added to my fears though. To think that Lylah and the children are being held captive by a deranged man…" I shuttered as visions of my own ordeal passed before me.

"Oh Honey, I know what you're thinking, but Lylah's situation is no way similar to yours. We don't know anything for sure. It may just be misinterpretation from a mother's point of view. " Mitch tried reassuring me.

"I'm a mother, and I know something is wrong. You do too or else why would you have been dreaming about her asking you for help? To think that we have come this far and it may all be for naught. We have to go, we have to go now!"

Bobbie and Vali were at my side. Bobbie bent down and kissed me. "It's okay Mom. Come on, take a breath. There, that's better. We have a 4 p.m. reservation for the ferry. That's only a few hours from now, and then we will call the nursing home and see if we can visit Thelma. Are you on board with that Mitch?"

He said that he was.

Chapter 15

Rory's Summary

They weren't going to quit pestering me about the dreams, so I may just as well get it over with. "The dreams started about three years ago. They were disturbing because I don't usually remember my dreams, and if I do, they don't make any sense. I have no idea if Lylah was even the young woman who was asking for my help as I don't know what she looks like. At times I thought that she looked like Mya when she was seventeen. I guess I probably just chalked it up to regret for leaving her the way I did. I told Mya about my dreams a while back. We pinpointed my dreams to the day she came to tell me about Lylah, but of course she had that episode in the tea house, and so never told me."

Vali asked how we had come up with that particular day.

"It was the same day that Bob hung the dragon sign up. I had a dream about dragons that night. I laughed when I woke up and recalled it, but then the vision of the woman came into view. I didn't think that the two could be connected so I blamed the dreams on too much indulgence in celebrating at Shannon and Mel's tenth anniversary party. I only remembered that date when Mya was abducted. I guess I believed that she was the one in my dreams who was asking me to help her. I was helpless in the dreams just like I was powerless to save Mya from Brian. I should have paid more attention to the little voice in my head, but both my feet have always been planted firmly on the ground, so the idea of the dream being a prediction never occurred to me. I should have been more perceptive."

"So what do you call the hunches you have Mitch? Don't you think that they may be a form of divination? Jake and I can attest to your determination that what you feel in your gut is authentic. You're like a bull dog with a bone. By the way, the actual date for that party was March 2ⁿᵈ." Mel said trying to appease me.

"I guess that sounds about right. Does it correspond with your visit to the tea house Mya?"

"I had been to your offices before but had never noticed the dragon sign before so I guess it makes sense."

"It doesn't answer the question though. Are you the woman in my nightmares, and why couldn't I picture where you were?"

"Hey, you're not Kreskin, but you knew that the dragon yacht was a clue didn't you? I was there with you when you discovered that it was gone. For an instant I saw the look of defeat on your face, but it was only short lived before you took up the search again. You found Mom and brought her home to us, relatively unscathed, and we'll be eternally grateful for that."

"It wasn't all me Bobbie; in fact anyone on the team, especially Rory, could have saved her."

Mya smiled at me with her hypnotic green eyes. "No one had as much invested in the rescue as you did, and no one could have done it with as much pizazz as you. You did find me, and now we know where Lylah is. It is all because of your diligence, so quit beating yourself up."

I promised I would tomorrow just as soon as we found our daughter. My cell rang. "Speaking of the devil...How's it hangin Rory?" I flashed a know it all look around the table. "Get any sleep last night?"

"Probably about as much as you got Pal. Wondering if you have time for an update on the saga before you head off to the island?"

"We'll be waiting with baited breath." I hung up, and announced that Rory was on his way.

"Good; I like him." Mya stated.

"You like him? You only met the man for fifteen minutes."

"He's your friend, so what's not to like?"

"She's got you there Mitch. We're all a lovable bunch aren't we Mayria?" Mel quipped.

"It's getting a little thick in here. I think I'll take Sadie out for a run and wait for the man of the hour." I stopped at the fridge and grabbed two cigarettes. "You coming Vali?"

"You know she's trying to quit don't you Boss?" Jake asked.

"Don't worry", Vali answered, "I've learned to puff without the fire."

She asked me if I was worried about her mom as she threw the Frisbee for Sadie. I wanted to confide in her, but if Mya wanted her to know about her fears she would tell her. I'd keep Mya's excessive doubts about my feelings for Irene to myself. I wondered if Rory's update would have an adverse effect on her. I guess I'd just wait and see, and if it did, I would deal with the consequences.

He arrived fifteen minutes later. We embraced as only comrades who have shared similar or the same battles could. I told him that a receptive audience awaited him inside. He greeted everyone and then went straight to Mya. He pulled up a chair and squeezed in between Frankie and her. Ivy passed him a cup of java and asked him if he would like a sandwich. He said he was good, but would take a piece of that decadent looking chocolate cake that everyone else was enjoying.

He took her hand. "You're looking extremely lovely and content this morning Mayria. I don't suppose that big bloke sitting next to you had anything to do with it?"

"You clean up pretty good yourself Rory. I'm afraid Mitch didn't do as good a job on removing four days of stubble as you did, but it was adequate. I hope you had a pleasant reunion with Bernice." She said provocatively.

He laughed. "As you did with Mitch I'm sure."

"I suppose that sometimes one has to experience the loss of everything that is dear to them before they can truly appreciate what really matters, and that is love. The love of my family and Mitch is something I will never take for granted again. I don't think that we can express our thanks to you and your department for coming to my rescue ever enough."

"Amen!" The voices at the table echoed.

"If you were a little steadier on your feet Mayria, I'd suggest that we'd have a dance to celebrate your homecoming."

"You do know that she is already spoken for don't you Buddy?" I asked jokingly.

"I seem to recall hearing those very same words from you before, am I right friend?"

"Were you two in competition for the same fair lady at one time? Oh my God, was it Irene?"

Rory and I broke out in raucous laughter. "No, my Dear, it was not Irene." I assured her.

"When I first met your man he was already shackled to Irene, and believe me, even then I knew he had made a mistake. He can be the one to tell you about hers and my hostile relationship. No, our mutual affection was for a dame much pleasanter and adorable than her. I found the two of them together. Her eyes were begging him to take her home with him. I had visited her several times before as my marriage was on the rocks. I needed a new companion, but I couldn't make up my mind so Mitch beat me to her, but he lets me visit her, so it's all good."

I shook my head in amusement as Rory pushed his chair back and called Sadie to his side.

"See, she still loves me."

"Have you ever thought of taking your twisted sense of humor on the road?" Jake asked.

Mya looked at me, eyes sparkling with affection. "Its official then, the two of you are twins from another mother. Not only do you share the same attributes in stature and professions of a sort, but you both have the same ability to charm with mischievous story telling. Are you bossy too Rory? That is one trait I do not like of Mitch's."

"I know you don't Honey, but sometimes it's necessary for your own good." I quipped.

"Mitch is right Mayria, but that is between the two of you to come to terms with. Now, if you really want to hear a fascinating story, boy do I have one for you." Rory promised.

I told him that the floor was all his.

"You all know about Dr. Low and Regina, right? The house where Mayria was found was registered in her name which was Regina Lord. An anonymous phone tip was left at the VPD for Mitch stating that Mayria Tessa Fulton could be found at that address. We now believe that the informant was Dr. Low. I'm sure Mitch has told you that we could not find the address and were ready to call it quits thinking that it was a bogus call until the helicopter appeared seemingly out of nowhere. This property is a very elaborate set-up. There is a subterranean garage that houses the helicopter and every other type of vehicle including an old rebuilt bus. The banks of the channel that run alongside of the house are solid concrete. The only way to describe the entrance into it is to liken it to a drawbridge. Its mechanism allows the span to be opened and closed. Marty Allen, a structural analyst, says the water can be completely drained from this waterway just like a dry dock can be filled or emptied of water for a ship's repairs by large pumps. He believes that this passage's water is diverted underground via a drainpipe of sorts. The trench will have to be emptied before there is a satisfactory answer. It is not a priority at this time, but will be explored in days to come. We have canvassed anyone living in the vicinity as to their knowledge of the stronghold. We are referring to it as such for lack of a better word. The closet neighbour is to the north of the field we set our heli down in, and have never met the Lows. In fact, they had no idea who occupied the establishment. The construction started around five or six years ago. They and other neighbours further up the coastline believed that it was a government run factory of some sort that built and housed marine vessels, perhaps even submarines. That theory has been debunked. I do agree that the building does look more like a fortress than a house. These people also say that they have heard and seen helicopters coming and going many times over the past four years. They are long-time residents of the area and recall that the construction was completed in less than a year. No one had ever seen the drawbridge open and close, but there was usually a vessel of some sort in the bay. The consensus was that they were surveillance vessels. No one ever saw the Jeudanzee though, but she's there sitting pretty inside the channel. She's a fine looking boat Mayria."

"The Jeudanzee again…what is it doing there? Is this woman who bought it somehow mixed up in all of this?" Mya was outraged.

"Mitch?" Rory gave me a puzzled look.

I put my hand over Mya's. "Sorry Honey, we never did finish our conversation yesterday about your yacht. I should have told you last night, but I figured we had enough on our plates as it was. I did not see it at the compound, but Rory told me it was there. I had come across it at the Keg Marina a few days ago. Of course I did not know that it had once belonged to you until much later. Actually, it still does as the sale was null and void because Carmen used a fictitious name to buy it."

"Carmen... Carmen Santos, Brian's secretary, what does she have to do with anything?"

"Actually, it was she who purchased it from Black and Black Marina under the bogus identity of Lorena Diaz. Did you receive a cheque from a woman with that name or did you have her deposit it directly into your account?" Rory asked.

Mya's response was of a defensive nature. "I am a lot of things Detective Adams, but one of them is not a gullible business woman. Frankie, will you be a dear and run upstairs and retrieve the bank draft from Ms. Diaz from my safe? You remember the combination don't you?"

Frankie said he did. I didn't know that Mya had a safe as I had seen no signs of one. I did wonder why she hadn't mentioned it to me during our investigation into Brian's dealings as perhaps he shared it with her. I dismissed that notion almost immediately.

"Honey, I don't think that Rory meant that you were naïve."

"I certainly didn't. Sorry Mayria; I did not assume any such thing, but I can understand how you interpreted it. I thought I had left my constabulary hat back at the precinct, but am afraid it goes everywhere with me. This case has so many twists and turns, and I forget that you were not privy to all our findings. We have questioned Carmen Santos a number of times, but so far we have not been able to connect her to your kidnapping. This bank note you kept may be the icing on the cake as it will definitely incriminate her on the charge of forgery."

Frankie opened the envelope with "Dragon Sale" written on it and passed it to Mya. She gave it to Rory. "You'll be needing this then."

I asked her why she hadn't cashed it.

"It arrived in the mail on Monday afternoon. Ivy does most of the banking, but it was for a paltry amount so I didn't even give it to her. After that I was too busy being kidnapped."

Mya had answered so calmly that she scared me, and when was tow hundred thousand dollars a paltry amount. Something was up with her. Rory passed me the cheque.

"It's dated September 11ᵗʰ. That's the same day we filed your divorce papers Hon. I guess when he said he'd see you around he was already planning his next move. Whisking you away on your own yacht would be his retaliation. He was a hell of a lot more cunning then I gave him credit for. I still don't know how he expected to flee the country on a yacht that the whole world was looking for."

Mya laughed. "Oh, he was that, and a hell of a lot more. It wouldn't surprise me one little bit to find out that he was also planning on bringing his mistresses with us to Shangri-La."

"What do you mean Mom; are there more than one?" Vali asked hesitantly.

"I only know of two, but that doesn't mean there aren't more."

"Who else besides Carmen, Mom?"

"Her Royal Highness, Regina Lord." Mya took the brakes off her chair. "I need some air. I will leave you all to your discuss my husband's adulterous affairs." She started to back up.

Vali asked her why she thought Regina was having an affair with Brian.

"Because she told me so. I think her actual words were; "Who do you think has been keeping your husband warm at night when you were bed-ridden with one of your fictitious diseases?" That was after she said that she couldn't see what Brian saw in me, and that I would only be a burden to him, and that I was sexless. As she had entered the room she had said she had come to see what a threat I was so I guess Dr. Low was also an adulterer. I was running in that pack so thought nothing of it. Do you mind helping me to the patio door Bobbie?"

He was at her side before I could volunteer. She asked him to stop at the freezer and grab her a cigarette and that matches were in the overhead cupboard.

As soon as she was out of ear shot I asked the table if I should go after her.

"Don't look at me Mitch. I'm on my third marriage remember?" Rory self-proclaimed.

Ivy just closed her eyes and shook her head. Frankie and Jake both thought I should give her a few minutes. Mel said he would defer to Vali and Shannon. They both agreed that I had better go. I agreed, grabbed the package of cigarettes and a coat for her, asked them to wish me luck, and went to find out if I would be welcomed.

I asked her if I was intruding. "No, as a matter of fact we were just talking about you Dear."

I put the coat over her shoulders, asked her for the matches, and said that my ears were afire.

"Not to worry Mitch, Mother is singing your praises." Bobbie said. "You two talk while Sadie and I go for a little walk."

"You're not going to light that cancer stick are you?" Mya queried "Well, you lit yours, so what the hell." I answered defensively.

"Yes, but I am not addicted like you are, and I don't inhale."

I felt the nicotine hit my lungs. It was almost sensual. Mya grabbed the cigarette out of my hand and ground it, along with hers, to a pulp in the ashtray.

"Hey...why'd you do that?" I moaned.

"I saw that look when you inhaled; the look that is supposed to be reserved for me, and I will not be the reason you take up the addictive habit again."

"It is reserved for only you Honey and you're the only addiction I need. Sorry if Rory and I have upset you. I should have told you everything I knew last night. I can't imagine what a shock it was for you to hear about Carmen and the yacht you thought you had sold."

"I guess I am a little shocked, not to hear that Carmen was also at Dr. Low's, but that the yacht, my yacht, somehow figures into all of this."

"Did Rory say that Carmen was at the house because he never told me that she was? To tell you the truth, I thought she was still in custody."

"Maybe I just assumed it. Soon as Bobbie gets back we'll go in and see what else Rory has to tell us. What else could there be?"

"I have no idea, but it will all be news to me too."

We found everyone walking around stretching their legs. Mya said she needed somewhere soft to sit so suggested that we follow her into the "gathering room." I wanted her to lie down but she refused and asked me to sit with her in the loveseat. I pulled up the hassock and rested her leg on it. Her ankle was swollen so I asked Vali to get her one of the water pills the doctor had sent home with her and a cold pack. She patted my head like I was a good boy. I smiled and sat down beside her. She asked Rory if he had time to continue with his findings at *the* house, or was Bernice waiting for him.

Rory pulled up a chair next to Mya. "I have no plans until six this evening when I'll be taking Bernice and her granddaughter out for a night on the town. They will be busy shopping and doing girl things all day. After I leave here I'll drop by headquarters and see what is happening there. I'm quite enjoying my time with your family as my own is strewn across the country. You are very lucky to have everyone under one roof. I thank you for inviting me to join you all."

"You are more than welcome. Do you have any grandchildren of your own?"

"No, I have one daughter from my first marriage. She's in Germany somewhere working in some school tutoring. Charlotte is Bernice's only grandchild. Her mother is the only offspring from Bernie's first marriage. She has recently split with her husband and moved down here from up north to be close to us. A sign of the times I guess. It's sad, but at least we have some family now. Dotty is six and has stolen my heart. I'm a big ole softie where she is concerned."

"I'm sure you are as it is written all over your face. You are always welcome here Rory, and maybe you will bring your whole family over to visit when we get our daughter and grandchildren home here with us. Now I suppose it is time for you to don your other hat again, and get on with the story. I will apologize for any further outbreaks ahead of time. You and Mitch are not to blame for anything that my ex did; I'm sorry for my insolence."

"Honey, no one thinks your reactions were disrespectful at all." I don't why she had thought that she had to apologise, and I also wondered why she thought that Lylah and her children would be coming home with us. I'd discuss it with her later.

"No need for any apologies Mayria. Now I think that you and everyone else will be surprised at what we have uncovered. Ready to play a little guessing game?" Rory teased. "What's everyone's opinion regarding the Lows' or Lu's...jury is still out on them, and Fulton's connection? What do you think the house was used for?"

Smuggling drugs was the consensus. Rory asked Frankie why he thought that.

"What else could it be? Unless it is as the neighbors thought...?"

Jake agreed or that maybe they could be in the illegal arms business.

"What's your take Mitch?"

"Taking into consideration that Low is a doctor, I kind of go along with the drug thing. Brian had to get the anaesthetics he used on Mya and Vali somewhere, so why not from his buddy Low who would have everything he needed rather they were legal or not. Has the toxin in the dental office been identified yet? Even after assembling all of this I still feel there was something else."

"I think you are all wrong." Mya interjected. "Dr. Low is a kind and caring man. He was not at all happy with what Brian had done to me. He called him a nincompoop. I can see him bringing in cancer medications, drugs as you call them, from Mexico as some aren't available here yet. Nothing that Brian did would surprise me. Maybe he was blackmailing Dr. Low, and using his and Regina's residence for his own use, whatever that was. That doesn't make sense though if he and Regina are lovers, does it, or maybe it's her and him behind everything. Perhaps the drug used on Vali and me was choral hydrate. Dr. Low administered it to me before my surgery. I told him I did not want to be sedated. He said it was to keep me calm, but may make me sleepy, and it did. He gave me a small dose, according to him, with a glass of water. I guess it worked because I didn't wake up until much later. I have no idea what else it could be used for so don't know why I even mentioned it."

"Everything you remember is important Mayria. I will look into its uses. So thanks for that. Now why do you think the Lows had the Geisha girls working for them?"

"Why not? Sakuri was Dr. Low's assistant. She may very well be a nurse. She and Misaki were very kind." Mya answered.

"They led me to you so I am in their debt." I said giving her a hug.

Rory wasn't through with Mya yet. "Did you think that there may have been more girls there?"

"I was only there for the one day and night before Mitch came, and most of that time I was under some anesthetic and bed-ridden so have no idea. Just a minute…are you suggesting that the house was used for some sinister purpose with the girls?" Mya was horror-struck.

That was one theory I had not explored, but it was perfectly feasible.

Rory leaned forward, amusement twinkling in his eyes. "How I love your virtue Mayria."

I think she was trying to shock him. "Believe me Detective, I am not virtuous. Do you not think that I may have thought that myself for a few minutes? I dismissed it almost immediately because that beautiful house did not resemble any of the brothels I had ever encountered."

Well, she shocked me and everyone else. Rory didn't appear to be surprised.

"Yes children, I have visited many houses that cater to men's fancies. Do you boys remember Christine and Margo Rule that I brought to the farmhouse in Wye to live with us? Margo had been forced into the wayward life to support herself and her daughter Christine. You were all so young at the time that you wouldn't have understood what was really going on. I had been approached by Dame Arlene Stanhope, a very rich and respected woman of London society to help in the liberation of young girls from the sex trade. So yes children; I have been in many harsh working houses. I had taken up the challenge once before when I was at the Legend helm before we went to Spain, but had not got as involved as I did in Wye. I'm sorry Mitch."

"What for? It's just another reason why I love you and am so proud of you. The list just keeps growing and growing." I hugged her.

"How come you have never told us Mom? I'd love to hear more about your endeavours. Do you boys remember them?" Vali asked.

Frankie said he sort of did. Bobbie said he had forgotten their names, but did remember them. He never thought anything of it because Mya was always helping someone.

"So my dear Mayria," Rory said, "you are not only the rescued, but the rescuer. You are going to be very interested in what I am going to reveal. You were all right in a way because the Low house was used for smuggling purposes...people smuggling... young ladies to be exact."

Mya stiffened. "I so didn't want to hear that Rory. It makes me very sad."

Rory took her hand. "Then, this should make you happy. These girls, and many others have not been brought into the country for the sex trade. They have been rescued by the Lows from such lives elsewhere."

"Rescued...what the hell does that even mean?" I interjected.

"I was just as surprised as you, but believe me, it's true. Let's go back to Tuesday. While you and Jerry were rushing Mayria to the hospital, Phelps and the rest of us were busy apprehending Fulton's cronies. Besides him, we have two of his accomplices, Mug and Chris in custody. Mayria confirmed that they were the names of the men who had joined her and Brian. We also arrested a Clive Martin, and Les O'Halloran. I believe you know Les, don't you Mitch?"

"Yeah, I have had dealings with him before and was not at all surprised that he turned up as an employee of Brian's. So, what's his story?"

Rory laughed. "No one's talking yet, no one in custody that is, but the girls pointed us in the right direction. First of all, there were no other girls in the house. They took Phelps and me downstairs to the quarters of an older Japanese woman. They called her Mama Sann. Apparently, she was their teacher. They had been rescued two years ago from a massage parlor in San Francisco by Regina who in turn handed them to Mama Sann for schooling and guidance."

"To what end?" Mya cajoled anxiously.

"It's all good, I promise. The girls who attended to you were only two of thirty or so that the Lows have rescued from various unscrupulous businesses. So far we have only been able to locate three of these young women. Mama Sann provided us with names and addresses for all of them and assured us that the list was legitimate. We've discontinued the search for the weekend, but will resume the mission again come Monday. So far..."

"You still haven't answered my question have you Rory?" Mya interrupted.

"Sorry; I guess you want to know what these ladies were trained for. First of all, I want to make it clear that they are all here illegally, even the two from right here in Vancouver, so lawful citizenship is an issue. We have no jurisdiction in that department so I am hesitant as to offer an opinion as to what their future holds for them. I understand your concern Mayria, but let me put your fears to rest. Most of these girls are all gainfully employed as au pairs or care givers. Others, according to the documents that we were presented with from Mama Sann are enrolled in secondary schools, or working in the hospitality field, and by that I mean restaurants or the like. It appears as though Regina took a liking to Sakuri and Misaki and kept them in her employ. They are well paid, according to them, and are free to do whatever on their days off. By the way, the girls are of various nationalities including Russian and Vietnamese."

"Thank-you for clearing that up. I am somewhat comforted, but I can't believe that Regina Lord is in the business of liberating girls from the sex trade. I only met her that once, but she did not come off as a person with any moral code...oh, look whose calling the kettle black."

"Mom!" Vali scolded.

"Well, it's the truth; I'm no saint. I was a married woman who stole a married man from his wife. I am not ashamed because after all, he was mine to begin with." She cuddled up to me and smiled. A single teardrop escaped from her eyes. "I love you with all my heart Mitch and can't imagine my life without you ever again."

I kissed her. "You never have to Babe. I love you more and more every day, but if we are calling a spade a spade then I had better make it clear to everyone that I was the one who did the pursuing. For a while I wasn't sure that I would ever be able to convince her that I loved her and that we belonged together, but here we are. Love won out, I'm happy to say." I kissed her again.

"Anyone with half a brain can see that the two of you belong together. Even though I just met you a day ago Mayria, I know you are the right match for Mitch. The eyes don't lie. However, on the other hand, there is a lot we do not know about Regina Lord. I never met the woman, but one thing for certain is that she has an agenda, and it isn't just about saving young girls. She was in full disguise when she confronted you. According to Sakuri and Misaki that mode of dress was what she adopted before she went off on a mission. They did not elaborate. This may come as a shock, but she was not Caucasian, but Chinese. Apparently, she herself was rescued from some brothel by a kind man whom I am assuming was Dr. Low. My shackles were up at that revelation, and again I felt that he was really Lu despite the difference in stature. I suggested that to the girls and Mama Sann that Dr. Low was really Zang Lu in disguise. I was met by laughter. Then I was truly perplexed by what was revealed next. As close as I can recall these are Mama Sann's words.

"Mansour Detectives, you are how they say, jokers? You think that Dr. Low can transform himself into Mr. Lu? He would have to put on much weight and walk as a hunchback to be as puny as Mr. Lu, and Dr. Low is not Chinese. See how misguided you are?"

"Jesus Rory, there's two of them; Lu and Low? This sounds like a confirmation. How are they connected…and Fulton, how does he fit into all of this? Who's working for whom?" I was more than a little confused.

"Low, Lu, and Regina are all in the wind. Fulton isn't talking and awaiting some big shot lawyer, so what I know, you all know for the time being."

"Would that be the wild, wild, wind?" I asked winking at Mya. It put a smile on her face.

"There you go again Mitchum with the wild, wind thing. You know that he compares you to the wind don't you Mayria?" Rory stated as if she didn't know.

"Yes; you haven't seen his boat have you?"

"No, but if explains his obsession I guess I had better."

Mya agreed that he should. "May I ask you a question?"

"Of course; what is it?"

"You said that the Jeudanzee was in the canal; did you go inside?"

"I did, and if you are wondering what shape she is in, the answer is that she was sparkling clean inside and out. Those dragons were as real as I would ever want one to be. By the way Mayria, Carmen DeSoto was not on the yacht, or in the compound."

"Thank-you, but I could care less about her. I suppose the yacht is in police custody?"

Rory grinned. "So to speak, yes."

"I just wanted to know if it was sea worthy, you know for when Brian was planning on taking me to Shangri -La"

"Oh Mayria, I don't know if this is going to give you relief or not, but the yacht wasn't purchased for you and him, but for the Lows. They were going to use it to smuggle more girls into Canada. I can't say that I know that for a fact, but Mama Sann said that Regina had shown her the yacht, and was very pleased that it could transport many bodies."

"I guess I am wondering if I am responsible for its illegal sale and any criminal actions that may have arisen because of it."

"Why would you think that Hon? Actually, the yacht has answered a lot of questions for us, isn't that right Rory?"

"You are right about that Mitch. Carmen DeSoto is responsible for its illegal sale and delivery into Canada. We know what it was intended for thanks to Mama Sann. You are not responsible for any of this Mayria, and you should quit worrying your pretty little head over anything else. Now, if there are no more questions, I will take my leave and let you get on with your day as I know you will all be leaving for Nanaimo soon."

"Actually, we are spending the night in Saanich as that is where Lylah Jayne's adoptive mother, Thelma Robinson, is. We believe that Lylah lives in Sidney, but will know for sure tomorrow when we meet with Thelma."

Rory asked me for one of my business cards. I did not have one but Jake did. Rory wrote a name on the back of it. He said that if we ran into any trouble of any sort to get in touch with Chief Constable Jeff Caulfield of the Saanich P.D. They had shared barracks at the police academy boot camp and had kept in touch throughout the years.

"He's your man Mitch if anything unexpected arises."

I thanked him. He bent down and kissed Mya on her forehead, and told her to look after me.

I laughed. The guys came over and shook his hand thanking him also. Vali hugged him, tearful as usual. I walked him to the door.

"I'm forever in your debt Rory. I can't thank you enough for keeping Phelps off my back. I'm pretty sure you broke a few rules in the search, but hope bringing a noted criminal to justice will exonerate you. As soon as we know where we stand with our daughter I'll be back in full force on the hunt for the Lu-Lows so get lots of rest." I patted him on the back.

"Can't wait; see you soon Buddy. Good luck on the island." He saluted me.

The house phone was ringing as I shut the door. I picked it up. It was Bebe. She asked for her mother in a rather distressed voice. I picked up the handset and walked into the living room and passed the phone to Ivy.

Her face and voice said it all. "Oh no; are you sure you're all right? Of course I'll get Mellie and bring her here, but first I want to see you with my own eyes. What hospital are you in? Don't worry; Frankie will drive. He's already on his feet. We're on our way."

"What's happened Ivy?" I asked concerned.

"She's been in some sort of accident. She says she is all right, but may have whiplash. Thank God Mellie was at the neighbours. I'll call you from the hospital."

Bobbie said he was going with them. Jake and Vali said they would go and pick Mellie up and meet them at the hospital. Mya said that she wanted to go too. I talked her out of it saying that we had to be at the ferry terminal in an hour, and the kids had everything under control.

I scooped her up and into the wheelchair. "What's up with you thinking that we will be bringing Lylah and the kids home with us?"

"Maybe it is just wishful thinking. Thelma doesn't think they are safe so if they're not, what else could we do but bring them here with us?"

"We'll cross that bridge when we come to it as there is no use in speculating. Let's go pack an overnight bag and extra dressings in case you spring a leak."

Chapter 16
The Last Dragon

Just as I was thinking about calling Vali and asking her what was going on Mitch's cell rang. He put it on speaker. It was Frankie. "Sorry Mom, but I am going to have cancel going to the island with you. I need to stay with Bebe as Ivy will have her hands full with Mellie."

"Of course you do Dear. There is no need to apologize for I think the five of us can handle whatever we encounter. How is Bebe? What happened to land her in the hospital?"

"Didn't Vali phone you? No matter; she was running an errand for her neighbour, the one she left Mellie with when she was rear-ended by a new driver. She doesn't have a scratch on her, but has pain in her neck and shoulders. The doctor thinks she may have whiplash so has put her in a neck brace and shoulder support. She can go home, but needs to stay immobile as much as possible so that is where I come in. Bobbie left me the car and he, Jake and Vali are bringing Ivy and Mellie to the house. They said they will try their best to make the four o'clock ferry."

"If they don't they can come over tomorrow. Take good care of Bebe and give her our love and best wishes for a speedy recovery. Why don't the two of you come here? I'm sure she will want to be with Mellie."

"Thanks Mom; I think we might just do that. I love you guys. Good luck with finding Lylah."

"Love you too…oh, Mitch found Vali's phone. It's on the counter charging. See you on Monday. We'll call as soon as we know anything."

Mitch was grinning. "I think we are going to have to put those bedrooms to use in the basement don't you?"

"If we need to then we will. Is this crowded house becoming overwhelming for you?"

"Hell no; I have gone from living a dull, solitary life to one of exciting activity and love in a matter of weeks. I am very happy. A man couldn't ask for more. I do feel like I am sponging though;

guess I'd better come up with some way to earn my keep. Any ideas fair lady?"

"Umm; I'm sure I will think of something."

"I don't take kindly with being known as your boy toy." He teased.

"You are so much more than that Adam Mitchum. I do plan on taking full advantage of being your first mate though, and you'll only have to pay me in kind."

He laughed. "Yeah, and I know just what kind you have in mind."

"Good; let's get going then. I hope Sadie will be okay by herself."

He patted her and told her to watch the house and told me she'd be fine.

We were third in line at the ferry terminal, but still had a forty-five minute wait. Vali called me a few minutes before we boarded and said they were at the back of the queue. She told us they'd meet us at the front of the boat.

I told Mitch not to bother getting the wheelchair out of the trunk as there was an elevator and I could walk that far. He completely ignored me, and told me to sit pretty. I told him that he must be tired of catering to me when he picked me up and transferred me to the chair.

"If this is what you call catering then I am pleased to say I could do it for the rest of my life."

He asked me if I wanted to sit in one of the seats up front while we waited for the rest to arrive. I said I'd stay in the wheelchair as it was probably more comfortable.

"Okay, whatever you want. On second thought, I think not." He said spinning me around.

"Is that Adam Mitchell? I'd know that voice anywhere." A woman screeched.

Mitch had a very distinctive sensual voice when he spoke to me privately. I hoped this woman wasn't one that he had spoken to in that manner. I told myself not to worry because the tone in his voice was one of annoyance. I put my hand on Mitch's to stop him from turning me as I wanted to see who she was. I looked over my shoulder. I was about to ask him who the woman was when the woman sitting next to her turned and smiled sardonically.

"That's why." Mitch sneered.

I was glad that I had Vali do my hair that morning, and I knew I looked particularly becoming in the outfit I had chosen because Mitch had told me so. "Wheel me over Darling." I said sweetly, but loudly. "Let's say hello to the ladies."

I could just picture the face he was making. He stopped me to the side of them. I said hello to Irene while smiling at her stunning companion who demanded an introduction. Irene chose to ignore the request and asked Mitch what he was doing here. The other woman stood and introduced herself.

"Just ignore her. I'm afraid she is off her oats these days." She winked at Mitch. "I am Daizie Wall, a friend of these two feuding characters. Are you by any chance the object of Adam's affection at the moment? That would make you Mayria wouldn't it? I do hope that the wheelchair is only temporary and not a permanent consequence of your ordeal."

Irene was smiling triumphantly. Before I could speak Mitch did.

"Yes, this is *my* Mayria. You can stop calling me Ms. Wall or Wallace, whatever name you are going by today, as I am not taking any new cases. And, not that it is any of your business Irene, but we are going to see our daughter and grandchildren. Shall we go Darling?"

"Yes, thank-you for your concern for my health Ms. Wall, but this chair is only short term. Have a nice day ladies. Do you not have any gentlemen friends to share it with?" I asked cattily.

Mitch turned me quickly. I'm sure he thought our little exchange would escalate into something nastily if we stayed any longer. The kids were walking towards us. I had reinforcements if needed. Vali asked who I was talking to. I told her that it was Mitch's soon to be ex in the tan coat, and her friend whom I assumed was an acquaintance of Mitch's.

"Really? I think I will just have a little walk-by. Want to join me Jake?"

"I'll pass; thank-you. Make it quick, and don't start anything." Jake cautioned her.

We watched as she strolled leisurely up to the front and positioned herself at the window pretending to be absorbed with the view. A few minutes later she turned and glanced directly at Irene and Ms. Wall, smiled, and made her way back to us. She had mischief written all over her face. Mitch shook his head before she could utter an opinion. He said we were going to grab a brew at the cafeteria if anyone wanted to join us. Vali waited until Jake and Bobbie joined us at the table with our drinks of choice before she teased Mitch. She looked directly at him, eyes twinkling. "Well, you do go for the lookers don't you Dad?"

He answered her bluntly. "You know that beauty is only skin deep Vali. I will say that it beats looking at an ugly mug over the morning newspaper. However, a man needs more than that to sustain him. He needs a partner that understands his every need. Irene did not fit that bill, but I was too naïve on what constituted a good partnership to know any different. I may have never come to that realization if your mother hadn't come back into my life. Her beauty expands deep inside her heart and soul. She comes with a ready- made family who I am pretty fond of. She loves me more than I ever imagined being loved, and I love her more and more every day. Life without her would not be worth living. I'll get off my soapbox now...oh, one more thing; she's rich, so that doesn't hurt."

I hit him lovingly. "Thanks for the testament Dear, but a question remains. Who is that woman who calls you Adam, and what is she to you, and why did she want to hire you, and why does she have two names?

"Umm, sounds rather dubious to me." Vali said raising her eyebrows.

"Is that right Boss; she wanted to hire you?" Jake asked curiously.

"Hey, one question at a time people!" Bobbie interjected.

Mitch sighed. "There is nothing to tell. I can't say for sure if she wanted our services. She phoned the office and demanded to talk to me. She was very rude when Shannon refused to give her my private number. Sorry folks; that's all I know. To answer your other questions Mya, she isn't even a friend. She is some half-assed one of Irene's. She came over to the house a couple of times. I didn't hang around to engage in their gossip. Irene dragged me, along with Mel and Shannon to one of her plays once. She insisted we all join her for drinks afterwards in her dressing room. Contrary to what Shannon thinks, that's all there is."

"Maybe she wanted you for some other *service?*" Vali suggested.

"Are you trying to get me into trouble with your mother young lady?" Mitch asked her.

"Of course not, but Shannon seems to think differently."

"Shannon has an overactive imagination. She thinks that Dazie was flirting with me at the theatre. If she was, I took no notice. Irene was there and she never said anything. If Shannon interpreted her friendliness as flirting, so be it. I'm not saying that I am against a little harmless flirtation among consenting adults. How do you think your mother got my attention?" Mitch put his arm around me and winked. "Believe me; she's the queen of the art."

"Thanks for the title Dear. You're not so bad at it yourself, but you're not off the hook just yet. Is this Dazie an actress, and why does she have two names?" I questioned.

"She is some kind of actress. I believe her theatrical moniker is Wallace Davis, but off the stage she goes by Dazie Wall. Don't quote me on that as I'm not entirely sure. Maybe it's the other way around. Anyhow, I'm no critic, but after the one performance I was coerced into attending, I would not give her acting a thumb's up. Are we all done with the questions now?"

I answered for everyone. "Yes, we are. How about you take me for a little stroll around the sundeck Mitch?"

He said there was no sun, but would be delighted to take me for a spin. He made arrangements with Jake to meet up at the motel as we would most assuredly get separated, and we did. Bobbie chose to ride with us in case Mitch needed help with me. I wish everyone would quit worrying about me. We decided to have dinner before checking in, and luckily there was a nice family restaurant attached to the motel. I had a large garden salad and veal cutlets with French fries. I counted 13 fries out and placed them on a small plate and passed it to Mitch to go along with his steak and baked potato. Bobbie asked what was up with that. Vali groaned and said, "Don't ask."

Mitch answered him. "It's just a little exchange your mother and I have. It started when we first started dating thirty years ago. If you noticed Vali, I did not get 12 fries, but 13. That's because your mother always said that she loved me one chip more than I loved her."

"You let her get away with that?" Vali asked laughing.

"Oh, he did and still does, but he outdoes me in many other ways." I answered for him.

"I try." He answered with his usual wink.

Mitch placed a call to Meadows, Thelma's retirement home, and inquired if it was possible to visit her. The nurse he talked to said that Thelma wasn't feeling well, and that she had been given her sleeping pill earlier than usual and was already asleep, so tomorrow would be better.

There was a Jacuzzi in our room. I so wanted to climb in and soak. Mitch vetoed that idea right away citing that it wasn't sanitary as other people had probably used it, and my knee didn't need another infection. I wheeled myself to the bed, undressed and waited for him to find my nightie. Instead he kneeled and undid the binding covering my stitches leaving the dressing on. He wrapped a huge towel around my leg and secured it with the sash from my housecoat. He picked me up and carried me to the tub. I didn't say a word. I hope my smile said it all. He undressed and climbed in beside me. A few minutes later I asked him why he had changed his mind.

"I didn't want to see you pout all night, and after what you have been through I thought what the hell, let's give her what she wants, germs be damned."

"I was pouting wasn't I?"

"Yeah, and you are really good at it."

Twenty minutes later Mitch wrapped me in my robe after undoing the wet towel and sat me on the bed. He gently removed the four by four covering my stitches and put one of the new bandages on. He said I didn't need the big wrap. I patted his head and told him he was a good boy. He said that I shouldn't let it go to my head. He climbed into bed with me and snuggled me into his chest and said we needed to talk. I asked him if he was breaking up with me.

"Yup; I want to ditch you as my girlfriend and my mistress. I want you to be my wife."

I looked up at him. "I know you do Darling, but that can't happen for a year or more. Irene hasn't even agreed to give you a divorce."

"As soon as we see that Lylah Jayne is safe I'm petitioning for one. I've been dragging my feet on this, sorry, but a little kidnapping got in my way. I'm pretty sure she is going to make it as hard on me as she can, so this is the only way out."

He reached over to the nightstand and handed me a little box. "It's not the ring I want to give you, but I want you to have this until we go shopping for the proper one."

I opened it. "Oh Mitch, is this your class ring? I never knew you had one."

"It never fit properly so I stored it away and forgot about it. I never returned to Sommerset before mom and dad moved, so they cleared out my room. They sent me the ring plus a few other things they thought I might like. I kept the ring. I placed it in the safe at my office where it has sat for ten years. I rescued it last Tuesday and planned on giving it to you that night, but something unforeseen foiled my plans. Anyhow, here it is and I'm asking you to wear it."

I sat up, tears flooding my eyes and extended my left hand to him. He placed it on my finger and laughed saying that we'd need to have it resized. I told him I would wear it on a chain around my neck until then. He said that it was official then... we were engaged to be engaged. I told him I didn't deserve him.

"Probably not, but with a few minor adjustments I think you'll make the grade." He teased.

The five of us walked into Meadows at nine a.m. the next morning. Mitch and I introduced ourselves to the woman at the reception counter. She welcomed us and called for Sharon, the supervising nurse, informing her that Thelma's family had arrived. She directed all of us to a private waiting room. Sharon arrived before we had even sat down. She was glad that we had arrived earlier than was expected as Thelma had been moved to the palliative care unit. She had taken a turn for the worse during the night. They still hadn't been able to reach her daughter and were on the verge of calling the police in hopes that they could track her down. They had no contact information other than the one phone number for Alma, and it was not in service. Sharon said that the night staff had found Thelma incoherent and barely breathing at nine last evening. They called the doctor who had her transferred to palliative care where she was put on oxygen, and was being closely monitored. She had not been expected to last the night, but had rallied and in her ramblings had asked for Alma and us.

This was not the same woman whose strong voice we had heard yesterday. She lay motionless in the bed. Her coloring was very ashen. Her sad eyes darted back and forth between Mitch and me. I took her cold hands in mine and told her who I was and asked her if she remembered me. She nodded ever so slightly. I called Mitch over and explained to her that he was Alma's biological father. She blinked and attempted to raise a trembling finger towards him. Her lips were moving, but no words were audible. Mitch bent down so that he was only inches from her face. He spoke in a soft, calming tone telling her that we were going to bring Alma to see her, but she had to help us as we knew not where to find her. She whispered something to him. A single tear slid down her face as she closed her eyes and slipped into a deep sleep. Sharon assured us that she was still breathing. She asked Mitch if Thelma had managed to give him a clue as to where he could find Alma. Neither she nor I had heard her say anything, but he had. She had whispered to him "Silver Street."

Mitch called Jake and told him to find the directions for Silver Street in Sydney, and that we'd meet him and the rest outside. I told him to go as I was only going to slow him down, so I would stay with Thelma.

He laughed lightly. "You really think I am going to meet our daughter for the first time without you? I'll get your chair from the car so sit pretty and wait."

Sharon had tuned in that I had some sort of a problem with my leg and offered the use of a wheelchair. Mitch thanked her and said he hoped Thelma could hold on until we found Alma.

Jake led the way to Sydney. We did not have a house number, so Jake turned right at the intersection to Silver Street; Mitch turned left. It was somewhat of an isolated area. Halfway down the street he stopped in front of a house with an unkempt yard. We could see the bars on the dark windows through the overgrown hedge. There was a semblance of a fence with a padlock on its rickety gate. He asked Bobbie and me what we thought. We agreed that it could be the one. Mitch asked me to stay in the car while he and Bobbie checked it out. I watched as they pushed their way through the gate and started towards the door. I opened my window and called out for them to stop. I didn't even notice that Jake had pulled in behind our vehicle.

"What's wrong Mom?" Vali asked opening my door.

"It's yellow." I said bluntly. "The door... it's yellow. Dragons live behind yellow doors."

"There aren't any dragons here Mom." Vali said soothingly.

Jake popped the trunk and brought me the walker. I said that I'd better just stay put.

"Okay; I'll see what Mitch has discovered."

Vali said she would stay with me.

A few minutes later Jake and Bobbie rounded the corner of the house and disappeared. Mitch joined us and said that there was no way to gain entrance to the front door as there was a heavy padlock and rod securing the front door. He said he was going to have to try to get Alma's attention by banging on the door. He thought I should be with him so if she opened the curtains she would see me.

"She doesn't know me Mitch; I think I'll just wait here okay?"

"Did your pain pill not kick in yet? Are you hurting too much to move?"

"I'm afraid of what is beyond the yellow door."

"Oh Baby," He crooned. "the door, sorry, I didn't even notice. I swear that there is nothing ominous behind it. If you remember, sometimes there are nice surprises on the other side, aren't there? Our daughter and grandchildren are waiting inside for us."

"You don't think that it's ominous?"

"No Darling, I don't. Here's Jake; how's it looking back there?"

"Nothing that an axe can't fix."

I asked him what color the door was. He said it was brown. I told Mitch to go and tell Lylah that we were here. The walkway was very uneven so I proceeded carefully with Vali's guidance. Mitch knocked heavily on the door. There was no answer from within. He kept at it. Still there was no answer. He beckoned me to come closer. He raised his voice assertively.

"Alma, My name is Mitch, and I am here with Mayria. You know who she is don't you? If you look out the window you can see her. She very much wants to see you. Can you open the door for us please? We just want to make sure you and the children are okay. Thelma is very worried about you. Can you hear me?"

We could hear a faint "You should go away."

"We can't Alma, and we are not leaving until we see you."

The curtain parted slightly. "I can't open the door; they are all locked. You have to go before he gets back. If he finds you here he'll hurt my mother."

"Thelma is safe Alma, but you're not. Go to the back door, and stand back from it. Don't ask questions, just do what I ask."

I couldn't help but smile as Mitch was giving orders to someone other than me. Vali and I arrived in the back yard just as Jake took one last swing at the door. It shattered into a hundred pieces. Mitch stepped over the debris, reached out for me, and together we gazed in awe at our daughter and grandchildren. Carter and Dahlia were clutching onto Lylah. She was trembling. It was as if we were all frozen in time; no one spoke, no one moved. Carter broke the ice.

"Look Mom, she looks just like you and we can go out now. Can I Mom, can I?"

Mitch squeezed my hand. I stepped forward with arms open and tears streaming down my face. Lylah was hesitant, not knowing what to do. I'm sure she was wondering who all these strangers were who had just broken into her home. I told her who I was.

She stuttered shaking her head. "No, no, it can't be. You can't be *her*."

"I am. I'm Mayria, and you are my daughter. I have been looking for you for a very, very long time. I am so sorry, so very sorry that I couldn't find you and that I had to give you up. I was young, and Mitch had left, and I didn't know what else to do. I have regretted that decision all my life. I only got to hold you once, but you were with me for nine months...I so need to hold you again." I sobbed.

I heard Mitch's sudden intake of breath behind me.

Alma took a step towards me, and finally my long lost baby was in my arms again. She was weeping. "I've been looking for you too, but he took away my computer and my phone. I was so close, so close, and then he told me you were dead. He said your husband killed you..."

I tightened my hold on her and kissed her forehead. "He got it wrong didn't he because I am here. We will talk about that later, but right now I want to meet my grandchildren."

I knew I was going to regret it, but I lowered myself with Mitch's help until I was face to face with them. "You must be Carter and Dahlia. I am so pleased to meet you. Do you think you can give your grandmother a hug?"

Carter looked up at his mother. "I already have a grandmother don't I Mom? Her name is Granny. How come those men broke our door?"

"Because we didn't have a key and we wanted to see you. Is it all right if you have two grandmothers because I really want to be yours and your sisters'?"

"I guess it would be okay. This is my sister; we call her Dahl."

I got my hugs. Alma was smiling through tears. It was time to introduce her to her father.

I felt his hands on my shoulders again. "I think we had better help your grandmother up Carter as she has a sore knee. Do you think you can help me?"

Carter and Dahlia said they could, and they both put their little tiny hands on my arms just as Vali and Bobbie arrived to help. Bobbie asked if he and Vali could meet their sister.

Alma clasped her hand over her mouth. "I have a brother, and a sister?"

"You do. I am Bobbie, one of two brothers, and this is your sister Vali." Bobbie announced.

Mitch and I stood back as the three of them embraced. Bobbie was fighting to keep control, but the two sisters wept openly. Before I could intervene and present Mitch to his new family he took the perfect opportunity away from me again.

"Sorry to break up the party kids, but we need to get Alma to see Thelma. Help them pack up a few belongings will you Vali?"

"My Mother; you've seen her? Is she all right?"

I put my arm around her. "She's taken a turn for the worse so we need to hurry." I said gently.

Bobbie picked Dahlia up and Vali took Alma and me by the hand and told her sister to lead the way. Carter trailed after Bobbie. Mitch told Bobbie that I needed to sit down and to shut the bedroom door before company arrived.

"Right you are Boss." Bobbie waved.

"Why do we have to pack? Are we going somewhere?" Alma questioned.

"You don't want to stay here do you?" I asked.

"As long as he is in jail and can never get out!" She stated emphatically.

"Until then, we want you to come and live with us. We can sort everything else out later. Just pack a few things like a change of clothes, pyjamas and a few special toys."

I felt a tugging on my sweater. It was Carter and he was holding a giant red and grey mechanical dragon and asking if he could bring Magic with him. I broke out in childish laughter.

My three children looked at me. Vali and Bobbie just shook their heads.

Vali offered Lylah an explanation. "Mother has had a thing with dragons since she was a young girl. Sometimes they befriend her, and other times she sees them as ill-omened. She also has a thing about yellow doors believing that dragons live behind them, and your front door is yellow, so...Mitch bought her a plush dragon and placed it outside the yellow door on his boat to show her that all dragons aren't menacing, and then there is her boat..."

"I think that is enough for now Vali." I turned my attention back to Carter. "You certainly may bring Magic with you. Maybe he can be a big brother to mine."

"Does yours have a name Grandmother?"

"Yes, his name is Snap. I think grandmother is such a long word, so how about if you just call me gramma, or Mya?"

"Okay. Do you want to see Magic do magic."

"I would love to, but right now you need to show Vali what to pack. I promise that we'll have lots of dragon time later okay?"

Lylah walked over to where I was sitting by the door and opened it a crack. We could hear loud angry voices coming from the kitchen. I guessed that Larry had arrived.

"Who is that man who seems to be in charge? He's the one who called himself Mitch when he talked to me through the door. Bobbie called him boss; does he work for him, or is just because he's bossy? You said that Mitch left you...he's not the same Mitch is he? Of course he's not because if he was then he would be my father wouldn't he, but he isn't is he? I guess Mitch is just a common name. He seems to be concerned for you. Are you two involved...or married? No, of course you're not because you are married to someone else aren't you, the man who kidnapped you?"

The unabridged story of Mitch and me was going to take a lot more time than we had right now, so it would have to be put on hold. We needed to get my daughter to the mother who had raised her before it was too late. Mitch had not stepped forward announcing that he was her father. He wanted the spotlight to remain on me, but she needed to know.

"You're right Alma. We are both married, but not to each other. We are taking steps to rectify that. He is worried about me because he loves me, and I love him. It's a long, long story, and I promise that you will know everything that there is to know about us. I should not have said that he left me the way that I did. I was so emotional that it just came out. I have always known that I had a daughter somewhere and hoped that I would find her one day. Mitch only found out a few weeks ago about you as we too have been separated for thirty years. It's important that you know that he did not know that I was pregnant with you when he left. Without him, I may never have found you. The important thing is that we are all together now. I'm very proud and happy to tell you that he *is* your father Lylah…sorry Alma; Lylah is what I named you. Please excuse us if we still call you Lylah now and then. Mitch has no other children, but has come to love mine. He has been very anxious waiting to meet you. I know you will come to love him just as we all do because he is a wonderful man. Yes, he is a little bossy, but as he says, it's always for our own good."

"He's not Vali and Bobbie's father?"

"Unfortunately, he is not, but it makes no difference to them or me."

The yelling and cursing seemed to have reached a crescendo. Alma had her hand on the doorknob. She opened it slightly. I peeked out with her. Mitch had her husband Larry in a choke hold. Jake pushed a chair under him and together they pinned Larry to the table. Two cops burst in with guns raised just as Mitch's cell rang.

"Thank God you're here Lyle. These two goons broke into my house and nearly killed me There holding Alma and the kids in the bedroom. Get me out of here!" Larry begged.

"Put your guns away boys. I have Chief Constable Jeff Caulfield on the phone. He wants to know who is in charge here." Mitch said in a calm voice.

One of the officers said that he was. Lylah whispered that he was a friend of Larry's.

"Right, passing the phone to Sergeant Lyle McClean Sir. I appreciate the quick response. I'll be sure to pass that on to Rory."

Lyle said he understood; yes, he would take Mr. Scott into custody, yes, he would secure the house, and yes, he would wait for the forensic team. No, it did not interfere with his other duties. He would look forward to the chiefs' visit. He passed the phone back to Mitch. They exchanged words which I could not hear. Lylah asked if Mitch would protect her. I said he would with his life. She opened the door and scurried out before I could stop her.

Chapter 17

Mitch's Girls

I heard the bedroom door open. I turned; she was walking towards me. She stood at my side and asked me if she could talk to me. I said, "Certainly." I took her arm and moved her away from Larry and the cops.

"Mayria says you're my father; is she right?"

I smiled into the green eyes of my daughter. "You will come to see that Mayria is usually right, and she is definitely right in saying that I am your father. I like the moniker Dad better though."

Larry was begging for her to help him. Jake told him to shut up. She asked me if I had her back. I said I did.

She walked over to Larry. "Don't you dare ask for my help after what you have done to us!"

"I was just protecting you from them Alma. I couldn't let them take you away from me."

"You call threatening my mother if I didn't adhere to your demands protecting me? No one was taking me anywhere, but now I am going and taking the kids with me! You will never see us ever again!"

"You can't do that Alma. I'll die without you, and there are laws…"

She didn't let him finish. She slapped him so hard that his head snapped back.

"Then I guess you are going to have to die."

"Why did you hit me?" He cried rubbing his cheek.

"You think that hurt…" She took her sweater off.

Ugly bruises covered her arms from her wrists to her shoulders. She pulled her hair aside revealing what appeared to be choke marks on her neck. I wanted to kill the little bugger right there and then. Jake saw the anger in my eyes and told Officer McClean to get him out of here. Larry tried pushing himself away from the table uttering threats and calling Lylah a tramp. Jake pushed his face into the table.

"One more time little man and you're going to be picking your teeth up off the floor!"

McClean took his cuffs out and he and his partner roughly escorted Larry out through the broken-down door promising to put a sock in his mouth if he didn't shut up.

I put my arm around Lylah. "Feel better now?"

She nodded and said she did.

"That's my girl. Now, let's collect the kids and the rest of the family and vacate this hell hole."

"I've had a father, but never a dad. I'm not sure how this is supposed to work."

I laughed. "Well, I have never had a daughter before, so I guess we will find out together won't we, and with Mya's guidance, we'll be just fine. I kind of feel like I know you already though as you have been walking through my dreams for some time now."

"For how long?"

"Three years I guess."

"How can that be, Mayria says you just found out about me two weeks ago?"

"She put you there. Don't ask, it's too hard to explain, but all will come clear to you over the next few days. Are you good with that?"

"I guess I will have to be. You need to help Mayria as I am pretty sure that she is in a lot of pain as she can barely stand up. Why do you call her Mya?"

"You know what, I really don't know. I think it just slipped out all those years ago. Some call her Mayria, or Tess or Tessa, and even Tessie, but she's Mya to me."

I asked Jake to get the wheelchair. Big tears were running down Mya's face.

"Are you hurting Sweetheart?" I asked concerned.

"Not too much." She answered.

"What's with all the waterworks then?"

"I can cry if I want to."

"Of course you can, and you're very good at it. Jake's gone for your chair. Let's sit you down as you shouldn't be standing on those feet."

"Well, they are the only ones I have, so what else do you suggest?" She asked huffily.

I wanted to laugh, but didn't dare. "Honey, your feet haven't healed yet, and between them and your knee, it's painful for you to stand or walk, so will you please just sit, and relax? I hate to see you in so much pain."

"I can handle the pain; you know I am a champion at that. The tears are not pain tears, but emotional ones you big boob! I have just witnessed my daughter and her father make first contact..." She burst into uncontrollable sobbing again.

Dahlia put her little hand in Mya's. "Don't cry Mama."

Yeah, that really helped. Now all the women were crying. I bent down. "And, just who are you young lady?"

"She's your granddaughter Mitch. Her name is Dahlia, and this is your grandson Carter. Say hello to your grandfather kids." Alma said proudly.

"Is a grandfather like a grandmother?" Carter asked.

I shook his hand. "Yeah, I think so."

"Are you with Mya? She's my new grandmother."

"You bet I'm with her. She's my lady, and I'm her fella." I scooped Dahlia up, sat her on Mya's lap, and picked Carter up. "Come here girls." I beckoned Vali and Alma to join us around Mya. "You too Bobbie; get over here. Can you believe this? Three weeks ago, I was basically alone, and now I have two daughters, two grandchildren, two sons, and here's Jake who's the brother I never had, and my best friend. Now, this is what I call a family, and it's all because of this beautiful woman whose love has brought us all together." I bent down and kissed the love of my life who reminded me that I had forgotten to add Frankie, Ivy, Bebe and Mellie to our family.

"I guess I did, but it certainly wasn't intentional. Carter, you and I are going to have to stick together because we are greatly outnumbered by the women folk. What do you say Son?"

"Is that okay Mom, can I go with him?"

"We are all going with him Carter. We are going to be going to their house and stay with them for a few days. First I have to go and see Granny as she is sick, okay?"

"What about Daddy?"

"You know he is sick too Honey, so he needs to go to the hospital and be looked after."

"I'm glad he isn't coming with us because he yells all the time. He wouldn't let us go outside, and he hurts you." Carter said sadly.

I swallowed hard. "Hey, do you like dogs because we have this dog who likes to run fast, and we can't keep up to her. Do you think you might be able to?"

"I can run pretty fast can't I Mom? How fast can she run?"

"Pretty fast, fast like the wind, the wild, wild, wind."

Mya smiled and said that we should get Alma to her mother.

Jake and Bobbie left to see if they could find Alma's car as the kids' booster seats were supposedly in it. She gave three addresses where he might have stored her car; his work place, his step mother's, or at Jim Mackie's, Larry's supposedly best friend. Vali and Alma strapped the kids in beside them. I promised to drive slowly. Next stop was McDonalds because Carter was starving. I was soon to learn that children are always hungry. Alma knew Carter would be okay with Vali, but she was worried about Dahlia.

"Don't worry Mom, me and Auntie Vali will look after her." Carter assured her.

"You bet we will. Oh look, there's a playground inside! This should be fun." Vali said as she closed the door.

I told her to call Jake and tell him where she was. She nodded her head as her hands were busy holding onto her new niece and nephew.

I let Alma out at the front door of Meadows telling her that I would park and we'd meet her inside. Mya was trying to get out before I even had my own door open.

"Hold on Sweetie; I want to have a look at your leg." I scooted around the car not trusting that she would wait for me to get there.

"Do you want me to take my pants down out here?" She asked smart-alecky-like.

"I don't think anyone will see you, so no harm, no foul." I joked.

"Sure, because it wouldn't be your hinny being bared to the wind. Don't you dare say it!"

"Say what?" I knew perfectly well what she meant, but pretended I didn't."

"It's impossible for you to just say 'wind' without all the adjectives isn't it?"

"Sure I can; wind, wind, wind." I kissed her and rotated her so that I could roll her pant leg up.

"I don't like the looks of it Mya. It's all red and angry looking. Wait; I think some of your stitches have snapped. It looks like one is digging into your knee. I need to get you to a hospital."

"You're being over dramatic Mitch. It's not that bad. I need to be with Lylah right now. There's no time to be running around searching for a hospital."

"Well, that's exactly what we are going to do. You are not getting blood, or any other kind of poisoning on my watch. I'll take you in to see Alma for a few minutes while I get directions. I guess I could call Jake and get him to find the nearest clinic or hospital."

"Why don't you get your own GPS? You can also find things out on your phone you know."

"I'm usually with Jake, so I don't think about it. I suppose I could have made good use of one though the day I was trying to find your house, and you were pretending that you didn't know where we were."

"I didn't."

I laughed, transferred her into the wheelchair that we had borrowed from the Meadows, raised the leg rest, and place her leg gently in it. She held her breath, closed her eyes, and grimaced. She asked me if I was all right. I told her I had never been better. I now had two more girls to add to my harem, so everything was honkey-dory. She smiled saying she hadn't heard that saying for a very long time.

We went directly to Thelma's room. Sharon was sitting with Alma. She got up as we entered. I told her not to leave on our account and relayed the reason why. I asked her advice on where we should go. She asked if she could have a look at Mya's knee.

"I think you are right Mr. Mitchum. It does appear as if a couple of stitches have burst. I can remove them if you like, but first I have to get the doctor's approval. Is that all right with you?"

We both agreed that it was.

"Good; then I will go and hunt Dr. Low down."

Mya gasped. I put my hand on her shoulder. "I hardly doubt that he is *your* Dr. Low Hon."

"Suppose if he is…he'd be in trouble wouldn't he? I don't like this."

"Let's just wait and see Mya. Low is a very common name, and I cannot visualize that Zane Low would be working here. This isn't exactly what I would call hiding out."

Alma looked puzzled. I told her that it was nothing to worry about, and that we'd explain it later, and that she shouldn't concern herself with anything except her mother.

Sharon returned and said Dr. Low was in his office and would take a look at Mya's knee. I told Alma that I would be right back. I didn't dare let Mya meet the doctor on her own…just in case. I laughed to myself asking who was paranoid now.

I knew immediately that he was not Zane Low as I'm sure Mya did. I believed him to be much older than her Dr. Low. He rose to greet us. I estimated him to be about five feet, five inches tall; much shorter than Zane. He was very pleasant. Sharon had explained to us that he had taken up residence here at the Meadows after his wife's passing. He was here most of the time anyhow, so he may just as well live here. I could see the relief in Mya's eyes that it wasn't Zane. She told me to go back and sit with Lylah, so I did.

It was the first time that I was totally alone with my daughter. I thought it might be awkward, but it wasn't. She smiled at me when I walked in, and asked if Mya was okay. I said that she was, and sat down beside her. I put my hands over hers that were covering her mother's. She said tearfully that she didn't know what she would have done if we hadn't shown up when we did.

"I knew Mom's days were numbered because the last time I had spoken to her I could hear it in her voice. Larry's suspicions and temperament were completely out of control. It was just a matter of time before he started in on the kids. Carson was so brave and tried to keep him from hurting me, but Larry just tossed him aside. I was so scared. I knew I had to do something…I was going to have to kill him somehow while he slept…"

I pulled her into my arms. "Come here; I'm here now, and no one is ever going to hurt you again Lylah, no one, no one."

She let three months of abuse wash away as I comforted her. Tears weren't very far from my eyes. I was her dad, so I was going to have to suck it up and pass my strength unto her. After a few minutes her body relaxed against mine. I told her I was so very proud of her.

"I should have gotten to you sooner." I whispered woefully.

"How could you have; you didn't even know about me."

"The dreams; I didn't know who you were, but it was obvious that you were in danger. I should have made the connection as soon as Mya told me about you. I'm sorry I didn't."

She was so like Mayria. "None of this is your fault. We didn't know either existed. I was fifteen and going through the rebellious stage when Thelma told me that I was adopted. I told her that I knew. She asked me how. I told her I didn't resemble her or Art in anyway, and that he didn't like me. I had thought that maybe she'd had an affair and someone else was my father, and that was why he resented me. I always had the feeling that we were running away from something because we moved so much. Sometimes I thought that he might be a fugitive because he was so suspicious about everyone and everything. I left home when I was sixteen because the tension seemed to have reached a climax between the two of them. They were arguing all the time. I was pretty sure that I was the reason. As it turns out, I wasn't. Mom discovered that he was having an affair and kicked him out and sued for divorce. Somehow they worked out their problems, but I couldn't go back. I worked as a waitress here and there, and had a few unsuccessful relationships. I stayed in touch with Mom, but never saw Art again. When I was nineteen, I met Larry. He talked me into going back to school, and he supported me while I did. I graduated, so was very thankful to him for that. We married shortly after. I had a job as assistant manager at a hotel. We bought a house, and then the children were born, and three years ago, Larry had the breakdown, and life as I knew it, went to pieces. It was then I started to fantasize about my real mother and father, and wondered if I could find them. Mother had said that she only met Mayria. She said she didn't think that Mayria knew who the father was. Is she right, are you just standing in as my father because you love her?"

It was uncanny how much she and parts of her life mirrored Mya's. I sat her down. "You are right about one thing Alma; I do love Mya. I loved her the day I walked out on her. I have regretted it ever since. I'd like to say that if I had of known she was pregnant, I wouldn't have left, but who's to say. I may have run away even faster with my tail tucked between my legs. I don't want to elaborate anymore for my reasons why I left her at this time. But, one thing is evidently clear, and that is that I *am* your father, so get any other notions out of your head. I will have a paternity test if it will convince you."

She was trying hard not to cry. "I want you to be my dad Mitch. I wanted you to be the moment I saw you through the window. This may sound crazy, but you are exactly how I pictured you in my fantasies."

"Well Sweetie, you'll fit right into our little family because there is a lot of craziness going on in it. I too fantasized about you. I pictured you as looking exactly like your mother, and guess what...I was right. I loved you before I even met you. When Mya told me that I had a daughter, I was beside myself. It's important that you know that I never once questioned that I was your father. Mya and I hadn't seen each other for thirty years, and yet it was just as if it was yesterday. She amazes me every single day, and I already know that you are going to also. That you come with two beautiful children is an added bonus."

"I feel guilty Mitch. I am sitting here knowing that the woman who has been my mother all my life is dying, and all I can think about is that maybe Carter and Dahlia and I have another chance at life with a new family."

"You have nothing to feel guilty about Alma. We are your family. It was heart- warming to see the way you reacted to Mya, and to

Vali and Bobbie, and then you came over to me…" I had to clear my throat. "I'm sorry that you didn't have a great upbringing, and I'm sorry I wasn't there for Mya. We could lament over and over about what could have been, but in the end, the results would always be the same. If things had of been different, chances are that you wouldn't have Carter and Dahlia, and Mya wouldn't have her kids, and maybe Barb and Donna wouldn't be alive."

"Who are they?"

"Two young ladies that I rescued from a pedophile."

"You rescued them? How?"

"I'm a private investigator, so part of the job is finding, and rescuing people."

"You're a PI?"

"Yup, have been for fourteen, or so years now."

"Is it dangerous? Have you ever been injured?"

"Not really; the job can be very tedious at times as there is a lot of surveillance involved. None of my team has ever been seriously hurt as we steer away from cases that require a lot of muscle. Headaches, sleepless nights, and aches and pains are all par for the course. Jake is my number one man, and you've seen how he handles things, so I don't worry about safety, or getting beat up. However, we have had our share of unreasonable clientele. Most of our cases revolve around finding people who have disappeared. Unfortunately, we are not always successful."

"But, you found me, and you rescued Mayria, didn't you? You're a hero."

"I'm no hero Alma. Shannon and Mel Dixon, two of my invaluable staff, did all the leg work in finding you. They had nothing to go by except your mother's name, which incidentally, Mayria couldn't even remember until I came into the picture. Luckily for all of us, you were found relatively easy. I worked closely with the VPD in finding Mya. I may never have found her if it wasn't for their diligence, especially Detective Rory Adams."

She squeezed my hand without saying anything. For thirty years I had assumed the role as a thick-skinned, macho, somewhat domineering bloke. Now twice I had been dismissed to an emotional and doting ordinary man. First, Mya had brought me to my knees, and now my daughter had. It was love, pure and simple. I knew where and when it had begun, and it now lived inside of me. I hoped that I would never have to live without it again.

Alma spoke hesitantly. "I've been Lylah to you and Mayria for a long time haven't I?"

"Lylah Jayne was my grandmother's name. Mya named you after her."

"Then I should like to be her. I want to be Lylah Jayne Mitchum. I want to be named after someone important to you and Mayria."

Her hand was on mine. I looked at her wondering how she had managed to slide in next to me without making a sound. She saved me from making a complete fool of myself.

"You were named after someone Alma. Thelma named you after her, and she was your mother for thirty years, and she will always be your mother. She raised you and loved you. Yes, you have been Lylah Jayne to me all these years, but you are Alma now, and we have no aspirations that you change your name. You are our daughter, by any name."

She always knew the right thing to say. Alma acknowledged her new mother with a smile, said thank-you, and asked her how she was.

"Dr. Low and Sharon fixed me up. I have to see Dr. Nelson tomorrow, or the next day in Vancouver. Has Thelma opened her eyes yet? Mitch, you should go and find Vali and the kids."

"All taken care of Hon. Jake found Alma's car and the seats. They have reregistered at the motel, so all is well. Dahlia is having a nap, and Bobbie and Carter have gone to the store for snacks and whatever. How about I call Jake to come and pick you up?"

"I'm staying here, but you should go and rest."

"I don't need a rest Dear, but you do. You should be lying down and elevating your leg."

"I'm taking care of that." Sharon announced as she entered the room. She placed a pillow under Mya's knee on the leg rest. Then she wrapped it in a cold pack. "Okay, for now. The kitchen is sending lunch up for three."

I thanked her and said that I wouldn't be staying for lunch. I was about to take my leave when Mya told me that I might want to call Rory. I asked her why.

"Oh, just thought that he might like to know that Zane Low has a brother." She said casually.

"And, how would you know that?"

"How do you think? I asked this Dr. Low; his name is Lane, if he had a brother. He said he did. I relayed that a Dr. Low had did my little surgery, and wasn't it a coincidence that the two of them shared a last name. He replied, just as you had, that Low is a very common name. I told him that Zane was his name, and wasn't it funny that their first names rhymed. He said it wasn't so funny because Zane *was* his brother."

"This is most unusual. The odds are astronomical that we would run into a relative of Zane's here, or anywhere. Your curious nature might just have given us the break we need. Rory will be most interested. I think I will stop by the good doctor's office and do a little more digging." I kissed her on the lips. "Good work Hon." I winked at Alma. She winked back.

"All righty then; be off with you now. I need some alone time with my daughter."

"Call me if you need me. I mean it, the second you start to waver. Can I trust you to keep an eye on her Alma?"

"You can count on me Mitch. Where's your phone Mayria?"

She said she didn't have one. I gave her mine and asked her if she left hers at home.

She looked uneasy. "I think I lost it on the island. It didn't work anymore anyhow."

I apologised for forgetting. She told me she loved me anyhow.

Just as I got to the door Mya laughed and said that she just had a wild thought. "Suppose if Dr. Lane Low is really Dr. Zang Lu?"

I replied that it was probably the wildest idea that she had ever had, and then I wondered what would made her say such a ridiculous thing. Had she found out something about the good doctor that would have led her to that assumption? I hadn't expected to be doing any sleuthing on this trip, but damn it, I'd have to now, if only to appease her.

Epilogue

Thelma Robinson passed away at eleven pm that September night. Her father was by her side. Alma had insisted that I go and rest at four that afternoon. Mitch dropped Vali off for her shift, and then retuned at seven to spend the rest of the evening with her. I was glad that he was the one who was there to comfort her. Thelma had prearranged her own funeral procedures, so there was nothing to do but call the funeral home. She did not want a service of any kind. Her only wish was that she be cremated and placed in the plot next to her husband. Mitch had tried to give Alma some privacy with her mother before she was taken away, but she said she didn't want to be alone, so he stayed.

Jake had rented us a two bedroom suite. I had put Carter and Dahlia to sleep in one of the bedrooms. They asked me to tell them a bedtime story. I had no problem making a fairy tale up for them. It involved two golden hair children who travelled to mysterious places on the wings of a red and yellow friendly dragon. I fully intended on going to my own bed once they fell asleep, but I couldn't talk myself into leaving them.

I was awakened from my own sweet dream by Mitch and Alma. I knew instantly that Thelma was gone. I comforted Alma as much as I could. She didn't cry. She just wanted to be with her kids. I shut the door quietly and went to console Mitch who was more upset than Alma had been.

He was worried that she was so unemotional. I coaxed him into getting into bed. I told him to move over because he was on my side. He moved over to the far side.

"Well, not so far!" I scolded.

He asked me how I always knew the right thing to say. I said I had a good teacher. I held him close to me. He laid his head on my breast and cried silently. The tears weren't for Thelma; they were for the daughter he had rescued, and all the years that he had missed with her.

December 19th

It was three in the afternoon. Mitch and the children sent me upstairs so they could put the finishing touches on my forty-eighth birthday celebrations. It wasn't a surprise, so I didn't understand why I couldn't stay and help, but I went anyway. I was getting good at taking orders.

Two months ago, we had found Lylah, Carter and Dahlia. A lot had transpired since then. Our daughter and grandchildren fit into our lives like a glove. The house was now a home, and was overflowing with all the people we loved. One member was missing; my eldest son.

Bobbie had phoned me last night to wish me a happy birthday. He had some amazing news for us. He would be returning to Canada in four months. He would be stationed at CFB Esquimalt, Canada's Pacific Naval base. That was just a hop, skip and jump away. I was ecstatic.

Unknown to us, Rory had given Bobbie his daughter Allison's address in Germany. As it turned out, she was only ninety kilometers from the airport that he was stationed at. He contacted her in October. They met, and apparently hit it off, and had been seeing each other ever since. She was lonesome for home, and was going to return as soon as her contract was up. All was good. I was happy that he may have found the "someone" that made his heart sing.

Frankie had a month left with his job in Seattle. He was too principled to quit outright. Luckily, his replacement could take up the reins two weeks early, so he arrived home in late September. Bebe and Mellie had remained living with us. Bebe was on medical leave until October. She had been unable to return to her apartment as mold had been found in some apartments and the whole complex was being assessed. She was without a home to go back to. We liked having her and Mellie with us, so it was no problem. She was stressed to say the least which did not help with her recovery. However Frankie come home with an engagement ring, and put the smiles back on her face

My children had always paid their own way. For reasons I never understood, they didn't like to dip into their Legend Hotel Dividends. Frankie had relented and put himself through college on his "father's legacy" he had said. Now was the time to make another withdrawal. He and Bebe went house hunting, and bought a three bedroom house a few miles away. They did a bit of remodeling and moved in last month. They have set a wedding date for February 14th.

Vali and Jake had moved into the basement and relinquished the upstairs suite to Lylah, and the children. They were looking for an apartment that they could afford. Vali had only relied on Legend funds a few times in her life. She was not a Jones, so had no right to them she thought. Of course, the boys and I had set her straight on that, but she was still reluctant. Anyhow, she and Jake were moving out. I was desolate. Mitch said he couldn't have me moping about all the time, so he had better do something to remedy that. It was a quick fix. Vali and Jake hadn't wanted to leave us, but were just trying to give us more room. They took readily to Mitch's plans to renovate the "games room" into a proper and private suite. The renos are almost complete, and we are all happy. Someday Jake will be my son-in-law I am sure.

Lylah fit into our lives as though she had always been here. She may never call us Mom and Dad, but it's only been a few months, so one never knows. Mitch and her went back to

Sydney where she packed up a few more belongings. Mitch had called Jim Mackie the night everything happened, and asked him to board up and secure the house until he was able to get return. He then hired Jim and the company he worked for, to repair the house and spruce up the property, and make them suitable for resale. Lylah inherited a paltry sum of money from her mother, so she wanted to find a job and earn her keep. The only job she had ever had was in hotel management, so she was going to update her resume and submit it to a few hotels. I remember that day as if it was yesterday.

It was shortly after she and Mitch had returned from the island. We were all sitting around the kitchen table. Mitch had given me the probing eye when she had announced her intentions. I guess he wanted me to jump in and talk her out of it, or he wanted me to hire her as a Legend employee. I wasn't sure exactly what he wanted, so I didn't say anything. I just smiled at him.

He smiled back shaking his head. "You do know that Mayria has a foothold in a large hotel chain don't you Alma?"

"Yes, sort of, but she doesn't have much to do with it anymore. I'm not too proud to ask her for help, but she's retiring, and there are no Legend operations here anyhow. I don't want to leave town anyway. I am sure I can find employment somewhere, and it doesn't necessarily have to me in the hospitality field. I really need to find something to do."

Vali said she knew exactly how she felt. "How would you like to be my partner in a new venture? I too am tired of loafing around, and need to get out there in the business world again. No hotel business for me, thank-you very much. I'm kind of into flowers."

Two weeks later the girls had bought a florist shop close to Mitch's office. It was on a large property, and also had two greenhouses. Vali asked me if I could give them instructions on the seeding and growing of vegetables and plants. I said I would be delighted.

"Are you sure it won't interfere with Mitch's retirement plans?" Vali had asked.

"What are you talking about? Mitch is not retiring!" I had answered vehemently.

"I may have given them that idea." Mitch said sheepishly.

I asked him if he wanted to retire. He said "Sort of", and that he'd have more time for me then, and we could spend more time up at the cabin and on the houseboat.

"Well, we have been together twenty-four- seven for weeks now, and frankly, I am getting tired of you following me around..." I didn't finish the sentence because I broke out laughing.

"I'm tired of you too, so I guess I'll go back to work next week."

That brought on a round of laughter from everyone.

"Good. I would never ask you to quit your job Mitch. You love it, and there are probably many more children for you to rescue. We'll still have lots of time for our excursions."

I was very happy staying at home with the grandchildren and Mellie. She and Dahlia were inseparable. I moved all of my junk out of my little room, and Mitch and Jake turned it into a playroom for the children. Carter was back at school and loving it. He and Dahlia had adopted Mellie's name for me. I was now Tessie again. I kind of liked it better than gramma. Mitch was grampa or Mitchy.

I had a visit with a gynecologist. I was not pregnant, and the odds that I could ever conceive another child were astronomical. What would be would be. My headaches completely vanished. My knee healed, but still gives me a little trouble now and then. I probably won't be running too many three-legged races with the grandchildren.

I was summoned downstairs at four in the afternoon. My birthday celebration was overly excessive. I shed a lot of tears, not at the gifts, but at the sentiments. The cake was four layers high. I have no idea when Ivy had made it, or where she had stored it. Lylah presented me with the last gift. It was in my and Mitch's name. We opened the envelope together. Inside was another envelope that read: "To My Mom and Dad". I burst out crying. Mitch was not far behind me, but at least he could read the words on the legal document. Our daughter had legally changed her name. She was now LYLAH JAYNE ALMA

MITCHUM. Between tears I managed to wail that my daughter was a Mitchum before I was. Mitch told me that I was already Mrs. Mitchell in his eyes so I should stop pouting. I said I wasn't pouting and smiled lovingly.

He said, "That's my girl."

Rory and his wife Bernice were surprise guests. He had filled us in as he had been doing for months on "the case." Brian was still not talking. His and his cronies court dates were on the January docket. Rory figured the trial would go on for months if not years. Dr. Lane Low was exactly who he said he was. Mitch had come to that conclusion after he had his little answer and question chat with him that September day. Rory had followed up on it, and too was positive that Lane Low was indeed Lane Low, and not Dr. Lu. Oh well, my hunches weren't always right. Unfortunately, Dr. Low and his brother were estranged. He had not seen or heard from Zane for four years; not since Zane had come home with "that woman." He was no help as he did not know where Regina was from. Rory had received a memo from Agent Phelps. It had read: Hey Rory; thought I'd pass this little tid-bit on to you. There has been a siting of Dr. Zane Low in the Shikoku District. Keep me informed of any developments that come your way. See you when I'm called to testify in the Fulton trial."

"So," Rory said looking at Mitch and me, "Bernice and I are due for a little holiday. We thought Japan might be a good place to see at this time of year. What say the two of you join us for a little R and R, and anything else that floats our boats?"

"I can't speak for my better half, but I'm game." I said enthusiastically.

Mitch laughed. "She can, and she just did speak for me. What do you say kids…should we break the Jeudanzee out of the compound, and get this show on the road?"

I said I'd had enough dragons for a life time, so how about we take the "Mayria" instead.

Rory and Mitch both said, "Hell, yes!"

ππππ

www.ingramcontent.com/pod-product-compliance
Lightning Source LLC
Chambersburg PA
CBHW071213210726
48293CB00002B/407